# The Last Lap

*Other books by*

**WILLIAM CAMPBELL GAULT**

# The Last Lap

WILLIAM CAMPBELL GAULT

E. P. DUTTON & CO., INC. NEW YORK

*2-74  G.fh  4.82*

Published simultaneously in Canada by Clarke, Irwin & Company Limited, Toronto and Vancouver

SBN: 0-525-33390-8   LCC: 72-78085

Designed by Dorothea von Elbe
Printed in the U.S.A.
First Edition

*For Elliott Graham*

# 1

~~~~~~~~~~~~~~~~~~~~~~~~~~~~~~~~~~~~~~~~~~~~~~~~~~~~~~~~

The winners drove Hudsons in those hungry days when my Uncle Luke first went out to try his luck on the fairground circuit. That was the winningest stock car in America at the time. My Uncle Luke drove a Packard.

It was five years old and badly damaged when he bought it, but he was a handy man around machines and so was my dad. And they both had plenty of time to work on it; the mine had closed down that week.

In Shale, Kentucky, where I grew up, there were three kinds of citizens: the people who ran the mine, the people who dug in it, and the people who made a living off the first two. Every time the mine closed down, that town suffered.

My Uncle Luke was single, so an interruption in his income wasn't exactly a catastrophe. But there were four in our family: Dad, Mom, my sister Judy, and I. I was seven at the time, and Judy only five.

If my dad was worried about the future, he didn't show it. He and my uncle worked to get that Packard ready for some stock car sprint races due to be run over the Independence Day weekend at the county fairgrounds.

The fairgrounds were at Calhoun Corners, only twelve miles away, and we planned the trip as a family picnic. I don't know if that was my dad's strategy or my uncle's, but it was a smart way to make sure that Dad got to the race, where he could be the one-man pit crew. My mother loved picnics.

I was seven, I repeat, so that was a long time ago, but I clearly remember that day. We went over in the Packard, the only transportation we had. Most of the upholstery had been taken out. My mother sat in the front seat; Dad, Judy, and I sat on the uncarpeted floor in the back.

There was a grove of Spanish oaks next to the dairy building at the fairgrounds, with picnic tables and stone cooking pits and a small refreshment stand. We drove in there.

And before any door of the car was open, Mom said, "John, you may think you are going over to watch your uncle practice, but you're not. You will stay here and play with your sister."

"Play what?" I asked. "What can girls play?"

"You will stay here," she said.

I stayed in the picnic area and played with my sister. I listened to the growl and whine of those unmuffled engines working out on the track and played hide and seek among the oak trees with my sister. It was the only game she knew. I did it without complaint; I was a saint!

When Dad and Uncle Luke came back for lunch, they were optimistic. "The hottest thing out there is a Hudson," my uncle explained. "And when was there a day that a Hudson could beat a Packard?"

To answer his question, that was the first of many. He was not only beaten by the Hudson that day; he was beaten by Fords, Chevrolets, Plymouths, and two Studebakers. He still accomplished what less than half of the starters accomplished; he finished every race. But he didn't finish in the money in any of them.

He wasn't discouraged. "There's a lot to learn in this trade," he admitted. "But I intend to learn." He was a stubborn man.

I didn't see another race for three years. In those three years, the mine shut down and reopened at least half a dozen times and Uncle Luke raced at tracks in four states, all southern, with what a reasonable person would have to call limited success. He won third place in a twenty-five-mile race in Georgia and fourth place at the same track a year later.

But he had learned some things, as he had said he would after that first race. One thing he had learned was that the Packard was too high and too heavy to compete with the cars he was meeting. He put the upholstery back into it and drove to Louisville one Saturday to see if he could trade for something more suited to the track. He took me along with him.

My uncle loved to work on cars, and he loved to drive them. And on this trip, I saw another side of him—he loved to dicker for them. That was a feeling he shared with just about every other male in America. I suppose it's an extension of the old horse-trading. Most men will pay the advertised price for everything but an automobile.

We went from lot to lot in Louisville. I knew he was going to buy the car we liked on the first lot we visited. It was a three-year-old Hudson, clean and solid, and the dealer put a fair appraisal on the Packard.

But we went from lot to lot, just the same, looking and arguing, no longer offering. The dealer, himself, would finally make the offer. My uncle would put it all down in a notebook, the car and the price, the trade-in allowance and the address, and we'd head for another lot.

We had a late lunch at a hamburger stand. I said, "Uncle Luke, when are we going back for that Hudson?"

He smiled. "You noticed, huh? Did I look too interested?"

"It's what you wanted. It's the kind of car you've been talking about."

"I've been talking about them because they're winning. And because the factory helps out."

"How does it help?"

"It's too complicated to explain to a ten-year-old kid," he said. "Take my word for it—they help."

It was a couple years later before I learned and could understand how they helped. What the Hudson people did was to include in their parts catalogue as "stock" or "factory option" any modification that a Hudson driver or mechanic installed to improve the car's performance.

**4**

The publicity they were getting from racing was about all that was keeping the Hudson Motor Company in business.

The sun was almost down before we went back to the lot that held the car my uncle had decided to buy that morning.

"It's still here, I see," he said to the saleman.

The man smiled. "So are you. Let's not argue anymore. You dicker once every three years. I do it every day, all day. It's getting late and I'm getting hungry. I'll add twenty-five dollars to my allowance on that Packard and I'll put an extra five gallons of gas in the Hudson. Are you going to drive it home?"

"You've made a sale," my uncle said.

We stopped at a truckers' stop about halfway home and had supper. There were a lot of truckers there, joking and laughing, weathered men, healthy men, happy men.

"They're different from miners, aren't they?" I said.

"Everybody's different from miners, except maybe gravediggers," my uncle said. "What kind of a man would spend his life burrowing like a mole?"

"You're a miner," I said.

"Because your grandfather was," he explained, "and your pop and I didn't have enough sense and gumption to refuse the jobs he arranged for us. But once I get that Hudson ready and start winning with it, it's good-bye, coal mine!"

"Is there much money in stock car racing?"

"There's more every year."

"It's dangerous, though, isn't it?"

"Not as dangerous as a mine," he said. "Johnny, you're not planning to be a miner, are you?"

I shrugged. I had ideas at the time about being a famous western movie star, but it wasn't something I was ready to admit.

It was late when we got home and only Mom had waited up for me. So Dad didn't see the Hudson until next morning. That was the day I gave up the dream of being a western movie star.

Because my father said, "Why don't you come along and help us work on that car?"

From that day until the day I graduated from high school, I went through a double education. The after-school education was the most interesting to me. I learned by helping my superiors work on the Hudson and, later, by doing my own work on the ancient Ford I bought during my junior year in high school.

That first car of mine was the last of Mr. Ford's V-8 flatheads. I guess just about every speed shop in America made equipment for that engine. It was the hot-rodder's primer.

The part-time wages I made at the filling station were needed at home, so all the improvements in the flathead came from my labor and not from the glossy catalogues. I planed the heads, enlarged the jets, reground the cams, polished the ports.

That much souping didn't make it competitive for any of the tracks my uncle visited. There were other tracks. They were short and dusty, and their owners were not so strict about the age of a driver or the safety of his equipment. Rheem Haskell kept talking the

The Haskells owned the mine, but Rheem
the poor branch of the family. His father ran the
station where I worked. Rheem worked in the
office after school; his uncle planned to put him throu
college and train him for management.

Rheem had other ideas. They varied from week to
week. After I bought the flathead, Rheem decided he
would become a racing mechanic.

If the car had been Rheem's, I suppose, I would have
been his choice for mechanic. But like the neighborhood
kid who owns the bat and ball, property rights give a
man the choice of positions. I would be the driver. I
would win the money that would allow us to buy a
faster car and make even more money, to buy a still
faster car, and so on. . . .

It was all based on a lot of facts not in evidence, as
the lawyers say, but Rheem was never discouraged by
reality.

The filling station wasn't open on Sunday and neither
was anything else in town. When my Uncle Luke raced
at nearby tracks, I went along as half of his pit crew.
But when he traveled out of state, to tracks beyond
a day's driving, I was doomed to a dull Sunday in Shale.
That all helped to make Rheem's arguments stronger.

At Deverest, about fifty miles away, a former carnival
operator was putting on some kind of auto show every
week from April to November. He ran demolition derbies, thrill and stunt shows, and stock car racing.
Neither the United States Auto Club nor the National

**7**

ar Auto Racing thought enough
to consider it worthy of a sanc-
Rheem.

at's why we can race there.
t a sanctioned track."

," I said. "I've heard that's
"

here?"

rs and mechanics, friends of my uncle's."
d folks!"

I shook my head. "Nobody racing for a living can be
called old folks. Let's call them—mature?"

"Call 'em what you want," he said. "I call 'em old.
Look, Johnny, would it hurt if we went down there just
to watch, some Sunday?"

"I suppose it wouldn't hurt."

"Okay," he said. "Pick me up around ten in the morning. I'll be ready."

I stared at him. "What are you talking about?"

"You said we could go to Deverest some Sunday. Tomorrow's Sunday."

"Okay," I said. "But we're only going there to watch,
aren't we?"

He shrugged. "Whatever you say. It's your car."

# 2

Rheem Haskell wasn't being devious, exactly. He was working by indirection. Some people might call that devious. The way he probably figured, if he could get me to Deverest as a spectator, my natural competitive urge would take over and I would wind up out on that dusty, unbanked third-of-a-mile track, rubbing hubs with the rest of those wild men.

He turned out to be right, but for the wrong reason. It wasn't the competition that lured me; it was the money.

The purses weren't much, judged by the pay at the sanctioned tracks where my uncle raced. I was too young to race where my uncle raced. The pay here looked big to a man working in a small-town filling station.

Every sprint paid a minimum of fifty dollars for first place and twenty-five dollars for second place. The feature this Sunday was worth one hundred and fifty dollars to the winner.

The watering truck was just leaving the track when we arrived, and there were only two cars in the pits, both Chevs. The Hudson was no longer the favorite on the major-league tracks; Pontiac was the new king. On these smaller tracks, it was all Ford, Chevrolet, and Plymouth.

"May as well drive into the infield," Rheem said. "It's not as dusty there as it is in the stands."

There was no tunnel under the track, but there were plenty of gaps in both fences. We bumped through the high grass of the infield and parked next to the white-washed judges' stand. One of the Chevs left the pit and went growling into the first turn. The man who had been standing next to the other Chev came over our way.

He was a tall man, in his thirties, with the pale complexion of a miner. "You boys here to watch or run?" he asked.

"Watch," I said. "We paid our way in."

He frowned. "Haven't I seen you somewhere?"

"You might have seen me in Luke Pilgrim's pit. He's my uncle."

"That was it," he said. "My name is Joe Quade. I used to work Fireman Flynn's pit but I've gone into driving now."

"Glad to meet you," I said. "My name is John Pilgrim and this is Rheem Haskell."

"The mining Haskells," he asked, "from Shale?"

Rheem shook his head. "Same family. My branch eats

lower on the hog. What's under the hood of that Chev?"

"Nothing special. Loving care, mostly. You see, Duke runs all kinds of special races. One of them is limited to flathead Fords and cast iron Chevs. He's even got a volunteer technical committee to see that nobody cheats on specs."

Rheem laughed. "You're kidding—! Who wants to see that?"

Quade shrugged. "He's been drawing good crowds and meeting all purses. I figure Duke knows his business."

"Who's this Duke?" I asked.

"Duke Whitney," he explained. "You'll have to meet him. I'll introduce you when he gets here."

The weather-bleached stands across the way held only a few kids when we got there; the adults started to arrive a little before noon. The pits were filled with cars by then, and the track was full of dust and noise. Most of the drivers were younger than Joe Quade; only the cars were old.

We were eating lunch in the infield with Quade and some other drivers when the man who ran it all, that former carnival operator, Duke Whitney, arrived in his spring-green Aston Martin.

I had never known any carnival operators, but I had assumed they were big, burly men with cheap clothes and loud voices. Duke Whitney wasn't anything like that. He was tall, but not heavy, and he wore fine threads.

Joe Quade introduced me to him as Luke Pilgrim's nephew. Whitney looked interested. "I hope you inherited some of his stubbornness," he said. "We can use some drivers like Luke around here."

"He's not a driver," Quade explained. "He's just here to watch. And he's got the cleanest flathead flivver you ever saw."

"Almost strictly stock," Rheem added. "Probably a lot more show than go."

Whitney, Quade, and Rheem smiled, but I didn't. I said, "My friend talked me into coming here and now he's trying to insult me into the competition."

"You mean the money isn't attraction enough?" Whitney asked.

"I'd have to *win* the money," I said. "I could wreck the car without winning a nickel."

"You wouldn't be racing against the hot stuff," he pointed out. "You'd be competing against cars as old and as slow as yours. Where is this gem?"

I pointed toward where it still stood, next to the judges' stand. He went over to get a closer look.

"He wants you," Joe Quade said. "He wants the Pilgrim name."

Uncle Luke was not exactly a national figure, but he was well known to racing fans in this section of the country.

When Whitney came back, he said, "I can see why you'd be nervous about risking it. That's a beautifully reconditioned car." He paused a second. "How much do you have invested in it?"

"In cash, less than two hundred dollars. In labor—I couldn't even guess."

He lowered his voice, so the others couldn't hear.

"Okay, you total it, I'll pay you two hundred dollars. Any serious damage you have, I'll pay for it—unless you win that much. Fair enough?"

"I'll think it over," I told him. "I'm not really prepared. I didn't come here to race."

"The offer's good for an hour," he said. "No entries accepted after one o'clock." He nodded good-bye and went down the track to talk to some of the drivers and mechs in the pits.

Out on the track, a Plymouth and a Ford were stirring up dust in a mild little crowd-pleasing dogfight. Both of them had badly dented bodies and creased fenders; both had the doors bolted shut.

Rheem was right; my car was more show than go. But not dented and not creased.

Quade asked, "Did Duke's silver tongue sell you?"

"Not yet," I said. "Not quite."

He took a deep breath and expelled it. "This place doesn't look like much, I'll admit. But—well, a man has to start somewhere!"

"Start—?"

"Start getting out of the mine," he explained. "Digging in a mine or running a still, that's where most of us ridge runners seem to wind up. They can both lead to a pauper's grave."

"So can racing."

"It can also lead to the money. I've been underground for twelve years. That's long enough."

In my unqualified opinion, Joe Quade was starting too late with too little to hope for the big money. We were a few light years from Daytona. At his age, he needed to be beyond this level of competition if he hoped to make it his profession.

He went back to his pit and Rheem asked me, "What's the great secret?"

I didn't answer.

"Why did Whitney lower his voice? Did he make you an offer he didn't want the other drivers to hear?"

"I suppose. He offered to pay for any damage I might have—unless I won enough prize money to make it up."

"That ought to cinch it. What can you lose now?"

"Only my life," I said.

"Oh, man!" Rheem shook his head. "You turned him down, huh?"

"Not yet. I have an hour to decide."

"Why don't we look over the competition while you're thinking? I haven't seen anything that scares me."

The dented bodies and crumpled fenders were what scared me the most. I had put in a lot of hours painting and waxing my sweet chariot; it seemed criminal to take her out where she would have to mix with all those battered roughnecks.

There were only three Chevs and two other Fords that would run in our category; even on a track as short as this one, it should be possible to stay clear of the competition in a six-car race. This is what I told myself, but I knew that *possible* was not *probable*. In the heat of competition, among cars of roughly equal speed, we would be bunched. The possibility of damaging contact was high.

Joe Quade's remark came back to me: *"Digging in*

*a mine or running a still, that's where most of us ridge runners seem to wind up."*

"We'll need some wire," I said to Rheem. "We'll have to wire those doors shut."

"I'll find some wire," he answered. "What made you change your mind, Johnny?"

"I can't say it any better than Joe Quade did. A man has to start somewhere."

I had driven Uncle Luke's car on the tracks we visited, but never in competition. They were longer tracks than this one, but dirt is dirt, I told myself. A few practice spins should give me the feel of these turns.

The plural might have been the wrong choice of words; it was really just one long turn, with my deck in a constant skid and the front wheels plowing a furrow. I covered three laps at a speed slightly below that of a trotting horse, and then tried for a fast one.

Nobody had a watch on me, but I felt sure that last lap felt faster to me than it actually was.

Rheem was frowning when I pulled in.

"Was I that bad?" I asked.

"You'll get it," he said cheerfully. "If not this time, next time. You have a lot of low-end torque. You won't be outclassed, not in equipment."

"But my driving—?"

"It's all new to you," he explained. "You're just not used to a short track—yet."

"Don't evade the issue!"

He took a breath. "Okay, okay! You didn't look so good."

Well, neither had Uncle Luke, the first time I'd watched him. And now his name was earning me special attention here.

Mine had been the last entry in the field for the ten-lap special race. There were no time trials for this sprint; it was first come, first served. That meant I would start in the last row on the outside. There were three two-car rows.

All five of my battle-torn, growling competitors were on the track when I brought the polished lady out. There were some jeers from the stands and some laughs.

I had borrowed a helmet from a friend of Joe Quade's; I stared straight ahead, ignoring the jeers, trying to look as professional as possible.

There was some delay in the front row, and Rheem came over to stand next to the car. "Don't do anything foolish. I feel responsible."

"That must be a new feeling for you."

"Don't be sarcastic."

I laughed. "Rheem, I make my own decisions. This might be a bad one, but it was mine. Go back to the pits and hold your thumbs. I'll see you ten laps from now— or sooner."

"Sooner—?"

"If it gets too nasty out there, I may come in. I haven't anything to prove."

"Okay," he said. "Luck." He went back to the pit.

Ahead, the starter was waving us forward for the flying start. Five cars growled, my lady purred—and twenty yards later all of us were just barely visible shapes in a cloud of dust.

I shifted to second gear, keeping even with my flanking car, watching the car directly ahead for my line.

I never saw the green flag in all that dust; I knew the start was official because the car in front of me took off. I stayed in second gear, went wide, and bottomed.

Luck was riding with me. The driver ahead had moved in toward the rail, hoping he had enough power to give him clearance past the third-place car. He didn't get it. Both drivers had to hit the brakes.

That put a three-car jam behind me. I had gone from sixth place to third place in a quarter of a lap and could see the cars in the lighter dust ahead as we came plowing into the backstretch.

The cars behind were still recovering from their tangle. The cars in front were fighting it out nose to nose into the grandstand lane. Nobody was near my undented car. Perhaps with a lot of luck and a little skill. . . .

I was dreaming the improbable. At this level, stock car racing could be called a contact sport. There was no point in lagging; we would all be closer before the ten laps were run.

Three laps later, I was up with the leaders. They were both Chevs. One of them was piloted by Joe Quade. He had the rail, a big advantage on a track as heavy as this one, and Joe was a hungry man. I rode in his wake, making no challenge. With almost seven laps to go, there would be plenty of time to challenge.

There was another thing that could happen with almost seven laps to go and it happened; the three cars from behind began to move up on the leaders. Two-thirds of a mile from the checkered flag, five of us were bunched closely enough to make me fender-conscious and the last-place car was less than fifty feet behind.

The dust was like a wall. But it wasn't thick enough to hide Rheem, waving me on with a victory sign every time I passed the pit. He had a lot of confidence in me, more than the situation warranted.

I had come here to watch, not to race. The track was rough and dusty, and my chance of winning a purse was less than even. These facts should have made me unhappy, but they didn't. I was glad to be where I was. It was exciting, it was competitive, it was my natural world.

Joe was the man to beat, I decided. The Chev flanking him was beginning to smoke. It was beginning to lose ground in the short stretches.

I still had a fifteen-foot lead on the fourth-place car. Only first and second place paid off in this six-car sprint. If I wanted to finish in the money, I would need to make my move soon.

I made it about fifty feet short of the waving white flag, moving well to the right, almost to the guard rail of the grandstand, before shooting toward the growing gap between Joe and the smoking car that was dogging him.

The smoking car turned out to be no problem. It was the car behind that I had overlooked. It had been fifteen feet behind me just before I'd made my move. But the driver must have made his move at the same time. And he had taken a more direct route.

He cut inside the ailing Chev as I came charging past

on the outside. He had the groove and the right of way —and a blind trust that I would honor that tradition.

His instincts were sound. I was forced high, into the loose dirt of the outer track. The front end dug in, the rear end came around, and the engine almost died. I downshifted into first gear for control and traction— but it was too late.

Every car on the track, including the crippled one, paraded past below. I would finish last in my first race.

# 3

I finished the lap and took the checkered flag. There were some jeers from the stands, but some cheers, too. There are as many kinds of fans as there are people, and there had to be some knowing ones in the crowd who realized how close I had come to finishing in the money.

Rheem knew. His face was as sour as my mood when I idled in. He looked at me and I looked at him—and then we both had to smile, just for the change of face.

"No dents," he said. "That's something."

"No dents," I agreed. "No dents and no money. I looked pretty good there for a while, though, didn't I?"

"You surprised me," he admitted. "You looked good for nine-tenths of the race. I was counting our winnings. What happened?"

"I looked good but forgot to look behind. Let's talk about next week."

"Demolition derby next week," he said. "Two weeks

from today is the earliest you can get your revenge."

"It's not *revenge!* What made you say that?"

"The grim look on your face when you came in. You looked as if you were angry at somebody."

"At myself. At dumb me. I beat myself. Just because I didn't look behind."

Rheem shrugged. "The whole field was moving up on you. All these short races are last-lap races."

I had known that. I had learned it watching Uncle Luke through the years. I hadn't profited from what I had learned.

Two pits away, Joe Quade was laughing it up with his crew.

"Let's be sports," Rheem said. "Let's congratulate Joe."

We did that and then I went to the judges' stand to find out from Duke Whitney who was the man in charge of his unofficial technical committee.

"Art Parent," he told me. "Plan to make some changes?"

"If they don't cost too much. I understand you're having another sprint in this category in two weeks."

"We are. Will you be here?"

"I'll be here. Where do I find Art Parent?"

Whitney smiled. "He's the man who moved inside you on that last lap. He's the man who forced you out of the money."

Art Parent's car was a Ford a year older than mine. In answer to my question, he lifted his hood and showed me the obvious changes: a four-barrel Kayden carburetor and a pair of Kayden high-turbulence heads. Kayden was a former Ward engineer, new to the accessory field.

"How about the camshaft?" I asked.

"Any grind you want." He paused. "You don't really need any more car. You had enough car to beat me *and* Joe today."

I said nothing.

"No offense," he went on. "The way I heard it, this was your first race. You did very well until you wandered into the heavy part of the track."

This was the man who had forced me into the heavy part of the track. I continued to say nothing.

He grinned. "Okay. You asked for information, not advice. I've made some Xerox copies of the specs. I'll mail you one."

"Thanks," I said. "You may be right about the car. But I guess it won't hurt to add a horse or two."

There were still some more events to be run that afternoon. Rheem and I stayed to watch them, hoping to learn. We didn't learn much; most of the drivers were almost as unskilled as I was.

"We could buy a junker," Rheem said, on the ride home. "We could pool our money and buy a junker and soup it and run in what they call the Open Division."

"Why should we do that?"

"So your shiny car doesn't get all mashed up."

"I'll have to take that chance," I said. "I don't have any extra money and I don't want to sell this car to get the money."

Rheem was silent for about five miles. And then he said, "If you race to win—" He paused.

"This lady's going to get bent out of shape," I finished for him. "I know that—and I want to win. We're going to have to install some brackets to bolt those doors shut."

"We—? Are you making me your official mechanic?"

I nodded. "And authorized pit crew."

"I accept. We'll need some hood pins, too. Or *something* that will keep that hood from popping open."

The sour remembrance of defeat was dimming into history; there was another race to be run in two weeks. Another race meant another chance.

Looking forward to the race wasn't our only pleasure. We were still young enough to enjoy working on a car. Even repairing it was fun. Improving it ranked second only to driving it.

We didn't do much to the engine. We tuned it and changed to a hotter coil. Then we stiffened the rear suspension, installed the brackets for bolting the doors, removed the side glass, taped the headlights, and removed the wheel covers.

The work was done at the station in our spare time, under the not completely approving eye of Mr. Haskell. Mr. Haskell was no more in favor of Rheem working into the mine management than Rheem was. But, in his judgment, stock car racing was not the most sensible alternative.

Rheem explained that it was only a sport, so far, not a trade. If it became obvious that he had no future in racing, he would still have his mechanic's skill to sell. Both his father and I had to admit one thing: if a thing was saleable, Rheem could sell it, including that explanation.

We left for Deverest early enough to give me a chance to get in some practice. We were the first to arrive, except for the man who drove the water truck.

During the half hour it took him to fill his tank, I had the track all to myself. It was loose and treacherous, the way it would be toward the middle of the afternoon, when my class was due to run. That stiffer suspension in the rear improved the traction. The hotter spark from the changed coil kept the low-speed torque constant, without choke-up.

"Better?" Rheem asked, when I pulled in.

I nodded.

"Much better?"

"Enough," I said. "I don't need much. I had almost enough two weeks ago."

"You finished last," Rheem said. "Dead last!"

"Don't be nervous," I said. "In a big money race like this I can't afford a nervous pit crew and senior mechanic."

"Funny, funny, funny!"

His conscience was still bothering him. He had seen all the fender banging and sideswiping last week; he knew it was a simple question of time before our car began to look like the others. But the decision had been mine, not his; there was no need for him to feel guilty.

I showed Art Parent the new coil when he arrived and he okayed it as being within specifications. The track had been dragged, rolled, and watered by this time. I went out for more practice.

I had been lucky two weeks ago. Everything had worked right for me in the first hundred feet of that race. I had gone through nine lucky laps and lost because of my own carelessness. I couldn't expect the same lucky start today.

There were other tracks as rough and as short as this one, where drivers who couldn't afford better cars hoped to make enough money or build enough reputation to work up to the higher paying tracks.

Most of the boys who had made the jump had made it on reputation rather than money, building an audience, and finally attracting a sponsor. Racing at the Grand National level cost more than a man was likely to save out of his winnings on these short tracks.

We ate lunch in the infield again, in the shade of the water truck. It was another hot Sunday but nobody seemed dispirited. They were all men (and boys) who were doing what they wanted to do, and weather was only one of the expected hazards of their trade. Though stock car racing had spread to all the states, by now, it was still most popular in the South. And the South is hot in the summer.

The talk was car talk, generally about the longer tracks and richer races. That was where all the young drivers and too many of the older ones intended to wind up. There wouldn't be room for all of them, and certainly not for many of the older men who hadn't achieved it by now.

Art Parent was an exception. He ran a successful garage and service station near Lexington; racing was to him what playing golf or tennis was to other businessmen, something to do on his day off.

Art had known Duke Whitney before he had run

away from home to join the carnival; he had known him in high school. "He's supposed to be a hustler," Art said, "but he paid back every dime he ever borrowed from me and he kept every promise. I've had good friends do less."

Joe Quade winked at us and said to Art, "That money he borrowed could be the money that went into this track."

Art nodded. "It could be. Think of that next time you're planning to pass me."

"I'll think of it when I need a backer," Joe said, "when I make my move to the big time."

The big time. . . . The profession where that phrase had been born no longer existed; it was a phrase out of American vaudeville. It was still an entertainer's term and had carried over into sports as the role of the amateur in all sports grew smaller and smaller.

Today, sports were designed to please the spectator, not the player. We were all actors in a sense, all in the entertainment field.

The first act opened at one o'clock. It was not an easy show to grade. If the Hobby Division of NASCAR would add one more category and call it the Junker Class, these heaps would have qualified.

It was not a question of the fastest car having the best chance; the winner would be the survivor. The fenders made more noise than the engines, as these young kids in ancient, ponderous, careening sedans tried to crash their way to the head of the parade.

Art Parent said, "Every once in a while, at times like this, I remember what Duke's enemies say about him."

I gestured toward the cheering fans. "He has an excuse. The public seems to like it."

"It's possible the Roman public enjoyed seeing Christians eaten by lions," Art said. "I don't think a businessman is unreasonable if he doesn't give the public *everything* it likes."

Joe Quade said, "I'm behind you, Art, if you want to complain to Whitney. We're entitled to some kind of standards."

"I'll talk to him," Parent promised. "I'll sound out the other boys and we'll figure out some minimum standards and present them to Whitney."

The class that Art, Joe, and I drove in already had both safety and equipment specifications and I could see why that had happened. Art and Joe were not only older than most of the other drivers, they were first-class mechanics. The boys had good reason to follow their advice.

They were also seasoned competitors, and they had the row in front of me when we lined up for the flathead Ford versus cast iron Chev Duke Whitney deluxe ten-lap sprint superspecial of the afternoon.

"Hard men to get around," Rheem said.

"Don't tell me the obvious. Say something encouraging."

"The new coil should make the difference."

"That's better."

He grinned. "Same field. You finished sixth last time. How about trying for fifth?"

"No money. It has to be first or second."

"Don't force it. Nothing *has* to be!"

"You're making me nervous, Rheem."

He nodded, sighed, and went back to the pit as the starter began to wave us forward. The same cars, the same drivers, the smallest field on the day's card. The dust seemed to be lighter and I knew every driver in the field; these were the changes from two weeks ago. And there would be another change—I would keep a sharp eye to the rear. If necessary.

Art and Joe maintained a straight front line and an easy pace through the flying lap. I was on the rail in the second row, a starting position determined by lot. Junior Jessup (two hundred pounds and still growing) flanked me in a barn-red Chev, flanked me and crowded me, even on this pre-flag lap. I hoped I would get the jump on him. He was a good man to steer clear of, heavy in hand and foot.

The lines stayed even, the green flag dropped. Junior's flaming chariot came crowding closer. My right foot found the floor and the response saved us. His front fender missed my rear fender by less than an inch, as he jammed toward the rail.

Directly ahead, Art had moved out in front of Quade and there semed to be a lot of daylight to the left of Joe. I shot for the gap, and this time it was Joe who should have looked behind. I had the groove—and second place.

I held it for almost three laps without any challenge from the rear or much hope of catching Art Parent in the Ford ahead. That car of his was geared and sprung for this one race on this track. He held his lead easily.

The first threat from behind came in the fourth lap. Quade had been riding about five feet to the right and behind my deck since I'd passed him, and suddenly he was no longer there. He had dropped back about ten more feet and was hugging the inner fence.

It wouldn't be kind to say Joe had run for cover. It would be accurate to say he wanted to give the man coming up plenty of room. Junior Jessup's red Chev was storming to the front along the heavy upper track. Only a man of great strength could keep a car straight in that wheel-twisting surface. Junior was such a man.

Art saw the threat and stepped up his pace. I was already moving at my rookie's limit. I didn't follow Art. I held my speed and hoped that churned upper track would eventually slow down the charging Junior.

It was one of my luckier guesses. In the sixth lap, on the second turn, a pile of dirt that had been growing larger through every event almost tore the front wheels from his mount. The rear end swung wide and bounced off the fence, sending timber flying.

Any lesser man would have been out of the competition right then. But somehow Jessup muscled the front end around again and started downtrack toward the solid footing.

The roar of approval from the stands was loud enough to be heard above the blast of six unmuffled engines. Junior was a crowd pleaser.

But no threat to me any longer. With only four laps to go, and the Chev still slowly plowing its way to a tractionable surface, my lead on junior Jessup was safe.

The nearest challenger was again Joe Quade. I didn't have what I needed to take Parent today; I still had a hope for second.

It was the same idea Joe Quade had. He moved up in the seventh lap and pulled wide in the eighth, waiting for his chance.

It never came. He made his first and final challenge about half a lap short of the checkered flag. But I had groove and the horses and the luck that day.

I finished in second place in my second race.

# 4

"You were great," Rheem said. "You were like a pro! Did you ever earn an easier twenty-five dollars?"

"Never. Half of it's yours. You helped get the car ready, and it was your idea to come here."

"Why don't we salt it away?" Rheem asked. "Why don't we start a fund?"

I climbed out the window and went over to the water jug. I drank three aluminum cups full of water and asked, "What kind of fund?"

"A *money* fund. What other kind is there?"

I said patiently, "Your mouth is getting ahead of my brain. Start at the beginning. A fund for what?"

"For us. For our career in racing. Maybe we'll need money for a different car or maybe we'll need eating money on the road."

"On the road—?"

"The road between the tracks," he explained. "That's

how drivers and mechs get to different tracks. Don't you use roads when you travel with your uncle?"

"Quite often," I admitted. "All right, we'll start a fund. But if it doesn't get any bigger, remember that twelve and a half dollars of it is yours."

He shook his head. "You think too small!"

And he—? A fund for our *career* in racing? It was possible he didn't think small enough. Career was a big word to a boy working in a filling station.

Joe Quade came over to congratulate me and added, "There's going to be a drivers' and mechs' meeting after the windup. I hope you boys can stick around for it."

We told him we could and would. I had won twenty-five of Duke Whitney's dollars and might have felt guilty about joining a complaint committee so soon after. But a glance across the track at the crowded stands eased my conscience. Those people hadn't paid to see Duke Whitney. We were contributors to his affluence.

There were two meetings after that last race. Almost all of the drivers and mechs were at the first, held in the infield. Art Parent explained how he felt about the lack of standards and asked how many in the crowd agreed.

Most of them raised their hands, and Joe Quade suggested, "Why don't you pick one man to represent the young drivers and the two of you talk to Whitney?"

So yours truly attended both meetings. It was the second time I had come under the persuasive power of Duke Whitney. This time I watched it work on a man who knew him well.

Art explained how unhappy he and the other boys were about the dangerous clunkers that had made up the opening race.

And in his heartiest promoter's voice, Whitney said, "I'm glad you came in. I've been worried about the same thing, myself."

Art looked at him suspiciously.

"We're starting a circuit," Whitney went on. "And we're going to need rules and specifications."

"Who do you mean by *we*?" Art asked.

"About half a dozen operators of small tracks. We had a meeting Wedneday night and organized the Southeast Racing Association. How do you like the sound of that?"

"Sounds impressive. It might work. And you're going to have standards, are you? You're actually planning to have some minimum safety specifications?"

"Absolutely! And that's where you can help. If you would pick a committee that could come up with a tentative set of standards, it could be worked out with the track owners."

Art smiled. "I'll bet. What power do we have?"

"Power—? You're *it*, man! You're the show! What do I have without you boys?"

These were the sentiments I had brought into the meeting. I was glad to see management agreed.

Art asked, "Sort of a bush-league NASCAR, is that what you have in mind?"

Whitney's face stiffened. "I had in mind a circuit of short tracks. I have never thought of myself as bush league."

Art smiled. "You're not. But we are—and that's our

biggest disadvantage. Okay, Duke, I'll talk it over with the boys."

Art was chuckling when we went out. "I hit a nerve," he said quietly.

"You mean the bush-league remark?"

He nodded. "He's very sensitive about being thought small time. He is an extremely ambitious man."

"You make it sound like a vice," I said.

"Ambition is no vice, but any extreme can be. Duke's going to be rich. It's his lack of patience that bothers me."

"He looks rich to me, already," I said. "Our family could live for three years on what that Aston Martin cost him."

Most of the boys were still waiting in the infield. Art told them about the new Southeast Racing Association and Mr. Whitney's suggestion that we form a technical committee to work with the track owners.

This was my first experience with a committee and I learned how they were formed. They were automatically composed of the man who first opened his mouth and the people he picked to help him. Art picked Ned Allis and me.

Ned had never done any competitive driving; he had been a racing mechanic all his adult life. He had worked in pit crews at every level and in every kind of racing from the county fair to Indianapolis, Darlington, and Le Mans. He was at this sad little track only to keep an eye on his nephew, Junior Jessup.

They were a contrast. Ned was old, small, and quiet. Junior was young, large, and loud.

"But they make a good team," Rheem said, on the drive home. "Junior isn't *all* foot."

"No. He has strong hands."

"And guts," Rheem added.

"He has room for them," I explained, "in that size forty-eight stomach."

Rheem laughed. "I have a feeling Junior Jessup isn't on your list of favorite people."

"It's not personal," I said. "His type makes me nervous on the track and on the highway. I don't like to be crowded either place."

"His uncle will keep him in line," Rheem said. There was a silence for a few seconds before he added, "I hope!"

"Maybe we can come up with some rules at the meeting," I said, "that will keep everybody in line."

The meeting was at Ned Allis' house on Tuesday night. He lived in Calhoun Corners, where Uncle Luke had made his first racing appearance. This was going to be one of the tracks in the new Association.

Safety specifications and categories were all we talked about at that first meeting, not any rules of track behavior that would keep the leadfoots under control. Steering, brakes, glass, suspension—these were what we talked about mostly. There wasn't much talk about categories; the track owners would want the right to set these up according to what was popular with the fans.

That word *career*, that had seemed to remote when Rheem had used it, seemed closer now, within reach. This new Association could be what the minor leagues were to baseball players, a place to learn and to earn while learning.

My sweet custom flathead hummed happily through the night on the trip home from Calhoun Corners, never suspecting that she and I were soon to part.

In the few minutes we had spent talking about categories at the meeting, I had learned that Whitney was the only promotor who presented the cast iron Chev versus flathead Ford event. One ten-lap race a month could not support a career. I would need a car that was eligible for more than one race at each meet.

Rheem and I talked about it at the station next day. He was kind enough not to remind me that only two weeks ago I had scorned his suggestion along the same lines.

He favored buying a Chev. "There are more to choose from," he pointed out, "and more speed shops make equipment for them."

I couldn't argue with that; he was right. But for some reason I had this partiality to Ford. Maybe it was because all the famous names in NASCAR were Ford men that year and about 70 percent of the engines in the Indianapolis 500 were Ford-built.

Uncle Luke had gone over to Chrysler that season, and he thought I should go shopping for a used Plymouth. "Either way," he said, "I want to go along. You need a champion bargainer with you."

"I'd like to go on a Saturday," I said, "so Pop can go, too."

My dad still worked at the mine. Uncle Luke was living off a combination of his track winnings and part-time garage work.

Rheem wouldn't be going along because he was substituting for me at the station. But when Mom and Judy heard we were planning a trip to Louisville, they declared themselves as nonpaying passengers. While we were shopping for a car, they could be shopping for the things that interested them. And later we could all meet at the Blue Grass Inn for a big chicken dinner.

So Mom and Judy rode down in the family car and Dad, Uncle Luke, and I rode down in mine. What I had decided to look for was a two-door Ford sedan with the 260-cubic-inch engine.

"You'll have to find a dealer who appreciates this car," Uncle Luke explained. "Somebody who appreciates the hours you've worked on it."

"Do you know a dealer like that?"

"I know a man who might know one," he said. "When we get to town, I'll phone him."

The man he knew was home when Uncle Luke called. The man knew a dealer who could appreciate a car like mine. He was a dealer who dealt in classics, customs, and rods and he knew the value of my car. But there was a hitch; he had no car on the lot that I could use.

I looked at Uncle Luke, who looked at my father, who looked at me. Nobody had a solution to *this*.

The dealer said, "You boys are missing the obvious."

"Spell it out for us," my father said. "We're small-town people."

"What's the best way to buy a car?" the dealer asked.

My father shrugged. "Not for cash. Most dealers would rather have the customer buy on time."

"Correct. Guess again."

"Without a trade?"

The dealer nodded. "So, if I buy your car you'll be able to bargain better at the next lot."

That made sense—except that we would need transportation to get to the next lot. I mentioned this.

"First let's decide if I'm going to buy your car," the dealer suggested. "Did you have a price in mind?"

I said nothing, waiting for a signal from my father or from Uncle Luke.

"Well—?" the dealer said, finally.

I took a deep breath. "Three hundred dollars."

"I'll give you two hundred and seventy-five dollars," he said, "and let you use the car the rest of the day."

Luke nodded. My father said, "It sounds fair to me."

"I'll take it," I said.

"Bring it back before five o'clock," the man said. "I'll have your check waiting. Unless you need the cash for the car you're planning to buy—?"

I shook my head. "I have enough to bind any deal."

What I had was a hundred and fifty dollars. This gave me the impressive total of four hundred and twenty-five dollars to invest in a sound and reworkable 260-cubic-inch, two-door sedan. If I could find one.

There were plenty of them in town, two on the next lot we visited. But I must have looked at a dozen of them on eight or ten lots before I found one that seemed worth four hundred and twenty-five dollars.

The dealer thought it was worth more. The card on

the windshield read: A CREAM PUFF! STEAL IT FROM ME FOR $475.00!

While I was looking it over, I noticed that the salesman was glancing doubtfully at our transportation, parked at the curb.

Uncle Luke noticed his interest, too. "That's a classic," he explained. "That's a vintage model."

The salesman nodded. "But this isn't a museum. What did you expect to get for it?"

"I have a buyer for it," I said. I told him the dealer's name.

"I know him. He has customers for those oldies. Did he make you a firm offer?"

I nodded.

"How much?"

"Not enough," I said, "to bring my bankroll up to four hundred and seventy-five dollars."

"Well," he said slowly, "of course, without a trade, I might be able to shade that price a little."

I won't bore you with the details; fifteen minutes later that 260-cubic-inch cream puff was mine. We had spent most of the day in making the rounds. It was time to meet Mom and Judy at the Blue Grass Inn.

Most mothers, I suppose, wouldn't be happy about a son buying a car he intended to convert to track racing. But my mother had lost a grandfather and an uncle in the mine, had seen her father develop black lung disease, and had spent her married life trying to budget the erratic income of a miner husband. Any trade that could keep a man above the ground probably looked better to her.

# 5

▰▰▰▰▰▰▰▰▰▰▰▰▰▰▰▰▰▰▰▰▰▰▰▰▰▰▰▰▰▰▰▰▰▰▰▰▰▰▰▰

At his house on Sunday morning, Rheem walked around and around the new car like an awards judge at a horse show.

"How do you like it?" I asked him.

"I wish you'd bought a Chev. But we can make this one go, I guess, if there's any money left for equipment."

"Not in my bank account," I said. "It's a good thing we're partners. How much do you have?"

"Two hundred and twelve dollars and change." He lifted the hood. "She's really clean, isn't she, inside and out?"

"Yup. Let's take her over to the station and put her on the lift. I want to check the frame."

He nodded. "I'll get the key." A pause. "Two hundred and twelve dollars wouldn't make me a partner. You spent more than that for this car."

"Money didn't make you a partner," I said. "I did. Hurry; get the key to the station!"

We stayed at the closed station all day, working on the car. Until the new Association set up specifications for its classes, we wouldn't know how much or what kind of equipment we could install for power. But we ran compression tests on each cylinder and checked the timing and balanced all the wheels.

Then Rheem said, "We can be sure of one thing; the doors will have to be bolted. We could work on that."

We followed the USAC specs, two ⅜-inch bolts on each door. It wasn't likely that the Association would demand more. And, not knowing or caring whether the Association would demand it, we installed a bracket below the drive shaft, forward of the center line, to prevent it from dropping on the track. That could be a lethal spear if it broke.

On Friday of that same week, Association headquarters sent mimeographed copies of the classes and specifications they had planned for the new circuit.

Rheem and I looked them over that night and decided that we would just about be able to afford the Southeast Racing Association's version of the Hobby Class. There were so many options legal in the Modified Class, it seemed certain that the boys who could really afford to soup their engines would be running away from the field. We didn't have that much money.

The class we planned to compete in limited engine size to 280 cubic inches, carburetion to one four-barrel carburetor. We could use any grind on the cams but no roller tappet. No supercharging, fuel injection, or special intake manifolds were permitted. Suspension could be reinforced.

It's designed for us," Rheem said. "It's tailored for us."

"How?" I asked. "There are a lot of good engines under 280 inches."

"It's tailored for us," Rheem repeated. "We can make all the changes for two hundred and twelve dollars!"

He was only about ten dollars wrong. We had the cams ground to a semirace contour. We wedged the suspension and installed a four-barrel Kayden carburetor and polished the passages, both intake and exhaust. We built a roll-bar cage and put in seat belts.

The new valve action didn't make it a very enjoyable road car but we wouldn't be towing it to the races; it was our only transportation. This was an inconvenience we would probably share with the other competitors in the league. Poverty kept us equals.

The first Association race for points was scheduled to be run at Elm Grove the Sunday after we had finished working on the car. Our timing had been right.

The Elm Grove track was the best and most successful of the tracks that had combined to form the SRA. It was one kilometer long (roughly five-eighths of a mile), well banked and well packed. As a matter of fact, after the dry spell we had been going through, that clay was baked hard enough to pass for pavement.

In the Hobby Class, our tire selection was limited. But the other classes that ran at Elm Grove had a wider choice, and the drivers who switched to asphalt tires that hot Sunday had a big advantage.

There were some good looking cars in the pits when Rheem and I arrived. Not any of them were cars we had seen at Deverest.

"We're among strangers," Rheem said.

"We're early. The familiar faces will be here before the first race."

A lot of the familiar faces showed up in the next hour. But not all of them brought the cars they had raced at Deverest.

Junior Jessup had a new mount. It had too many cubes for the Hobby Class; I would not be competing against him. Art Parent had switched to a small-block Chev; I would be racing against him.

Joe Quade was running the same car. He was permitted the maximum in changes because of the age of his engine, and he figured the changes he'd made would keep him a competitor. It was an optimistic opinion.

The short tracks I'd visited with my uncle the last few years had all been NASCAR tracks. Most of them had been aggressively promoted and successful. Very few of them had attracted a bigger crowd or a bigger field than we saw at Elm Grove for the initial race of the Southeast Racing Association.

The sight of all those fans warmed our greedy hearts. Because the purses in the Association would be determined by a standard formula—a minimum guarantee plus a percentage of the gate.

Junior had changed to the asphalt tires and it showed in his qualifying round. He won himself a spot on the outside of the first row for the opener.

**43**

"He's in fast company," Rheem said. "He's the only rookie in the field, I'll bet."

"And the only driver with a car prepared by Ned Allis," I said. "That's *his* edge."

It was a twenty-mile race, thirty-two laps on a clay track so hard it was almost dust-free, despite the heat. It was an exciting opening show. There wasn't a single clunker in the twenty-three-car field. No car was lapped in the entire race.

Junior Jessup carried his old habits over into his new car. He was outfoxed at the green flag. Both rows behind him anticipated the start better, and both rows went sliding past him below as he reacted too heavily from his slow start and went broadsiding high into the first turn.

That put eight cars in front of him. He had gone from third place at the flag to ninth place in the backstretch. It was not the kind of situation that sat lightly on his temperament. He began to bull his way through traffic to the front of the pack.

They were cars about equal in power. The other drivers were more experienced and just as determined. But Junior Jessup steadily improved his position.

"You were right," I told Rheem. "Junior isn't *all* foot."

Rheem nodded, watching him. "He doesn't look as wild today."

Twenty-three cars in five-eighths of a mile didn't leave much room for showboating. Jessup was simply adjusting to his environment. There was more muscle than finesse in his strategy, but there was enough finesse to bring him up to fourth place with seven laps still to be run.

The three men in front of him, however, were not there by chance. Mark Ryer, in third place, was a driver I had watched many times in traveling with my uncle. He had left the NASCAR trail last fall to devote himself to his tire business. Although he had never won a major race, he had picked up quite a few checks in the big league.

He knew the track and the best lines into its turns, and he knew his rights. Twice, in those last seven laps, Junior came diving down the bank under full bore, aiming for a spot in front of Mark's Plymouth. It was a move that might intimdate a novice, but Mark never backed off, holding his legal groove and his pace.

The three in front stayed in front. Junior had to fight off a threat from behind through the last lap to finish fourth. Though he looked unhappy as he pulled into the pits, he had finished high for a beginner. He was an impatient man.

There were two races to be run in our class that afternoon. The first was an eight-lap sprint that would act as a qualifier for the forty-lap second race.

Starting position in the qualifier was decided by lot and we were lucky, drawing the inside slot in the second row. The field was only slightly smaller than we'd had in the curtain-raiser; there were twenty-one entries.

Art Parent was buried back in the ruck. Joe Quade was in the row ahead of me. There were some other respected competitors I had met at Deverest and some strangers wheeling fine sounding cars. But we were sounding pretty mellow, ourselves, and I was no more nervous than I knew I would be.

"We picked a lucky number," Rheem said. "Good omen."

"Sure."

"You finished second last time out."

"You have a marvelous memory."

He smiled. "Everybody else is nervous, too. Don't do anything foolish. Good luck." He went back to the pit.

All the engines were running. The starter's green flag was furled as he waited for his two assistants to check each car against the entry list.

This was a smoother operation than Duke Whitney ran; perhaps the example set here would upgrade the other tracks in the new circuit. Duke was here, standing behind Art Parent's pit.

Maybe everybody else was nervous, too. If a man had any imagination, he would almost have to be nervous before a race. The assistants signaled the starter and he waved us forward with the green flag still furled. We would see it unfurled and waving a lap from now if the start was clean.

A blond kid in a 265-inch Chev was flanking me, crowding me like a middleweight Junior Jessup. I ignored him, holding my line, keeping my distance from the car in front. Even on the NASCAR tracks, there were drivers, *winners*, who couldn't seem to get through a lap without scraping somebody.

In the middle row ahead, blue smoke puffed from the tail pipe of Joe Quade's ancient chariot as she coughed and wavered. The lines slowed for a few seconds but then his engine regained its tempo and we went briskly through the backstretch.

There was a possibility she would cough again when Joe bottomed at the flag. The blond kid was directly behind him and undoubtedly he was also considering that possibility and planning his escape route.

It had better be to the outside, because I planned to claim the track directly in front of me. The car on the pole was driven by a man I had watched at Deverest. He was a man who anticipated the flag well. He would give me room to move.

As we came around the south turn, the pacemaker row ahead was setting a strong pace and holding a clean line. I decided the flag would drop; I didn't hesitate with my right foot.

All the labor Rheem and I had put into the engine paid off in that first surge. The man ahead moved even quicker; there was room to get past his flanking car, to be free and clear, running second in a field of twenty-one cars.

For the first half of the race, the two of us were undisturbed. I was the tail to the leader's comet. There was no other close contender. And then the blond kid in the 265-inch Chev began to move up on us.

He had enough to take me, I think. I was at my traction limit and he was shortening the gap between us. But the same car that had stymied him at the jumpoff now came back to haunt him. Joe Quade's Chev, trailing blue smoke, was holding down last place and the center of the track ahead.

There was room below, and I was still in front. The car chasing me was higher on the track; the blond had two alternatives and only a few seconds to make his choice. He could jam his brakes and follow me through the gap below, or he could slide past Joe above and hope to hold his car on the track through the turn coming up.

He took the high road. His traction seemed sound as he entered the turn. But before he was out of my view behind, I saw his rear deck start to climb and the scream from the stands told me he was in trouble. He saved himself short of the fence, I learned later, despite blowing his right rear tire.

I now had two second-place finishes in three races, better than any rookie had a right to expect. Both times I had been challenged in the later laps. A rough track had saved me from Junior's threat, a blocked track from today's.

I mentioned this to Rheem, who was doing a victory dance in the pit.

"So what?" he said. "*So what!* We just won a hundred dollars plus a percentage, man!"

I said, "I wanted to point out how lucky I've been, that's all."

"Luck, luck, luck—! You don't know if either one of those cars would have caught you."

"They would have. Both of them."

He took a breath and looked at me thoughtfully for a few seconds. "Okay, we'll say both of them had caught you. You still would have finished third in both races. And that's pretty good for a greenie, isn't it?"

I nodded.

"So what's bothering you?"

"I was thinking of how we time an engine to the exact degree, how we fit parts to ten-thousandths of an inch. I'd call that—scientific, wouldn't you?"

"I suppose. Go on."

"Well, luck isn't science, that's all. I mean, depending on luck is—dumb!"

"We didn't *depend* on it," Rheem said. "We *prepared* for it. Just like a sailor prepares for a favorable wind. We were ready."

"You're right," I said. "You're bright, too. That's a sharp simile!"

He shrugged and smiled.

"How does a sailor prepare for a favorable wind?" I asked him.

"Johnny," he said patiently, "nobody knows every-thing!"

"Then get the smug look off your face," I said "and let us prepare for our favorable starting position in the feature."

We had earned the right to start in the middle slot of the first row. In a forty-lap race, that might seem like a trivial advantage. But with the size of the fields we were drawing here, traffic was a problem as important as traction and torque. The blond in the Chev had been a victim of it.

Rheem had been the nervous partner in the first two races, probably because he had felt responsible for risking *my* flathead in competition. But why was I nervous, now?

All but one of the same cars I had run against would be in the forty-lapper. Joe Quade's Chev was too sick to run. Joe came over to help us get ready.

"Back to the wrench," he said bitterly, "where I wasted my best years with Fireman Flynn."

"Then you were a pit monkey," Rheem said. "Now you're a driver helping a friend. There's a difference."

"It doesn't seem different. The work's the same."

"It's a two-way deal," Rheem explained. "You bring that Chev over to Shale next week and Johnny and I will help you put it in shape."

"I figured you might," Joe said. "That's why I'm here."

It was only Joe's little cynical joke. In most of the pits, drivers and mechs were helping each other. They were all friends—until the green flag dropped.

Twenty cars for forty laps. Yours truly, second-place finisher in two consecutive races in two separate cars on two different tracks, would line up in the second-place starting spot.

"Too many twos," I said.

My partner stared at me. "What—?"

"Two times twenty is forty," I said. "Twenty cars for forty laps and I'll be in second place. Did you ever study numerology, Rheem?"

"It's the sun," he guessed. "Or those hot dogs you had for lunch. Maybe Joe could drive this race for us."

I shook my head. "It was just a silly combination of numbers I thought of—and I think I know what triggered it."

"Im waiting to hear."

**50**

"Two twos," I said. "Two seconds. I did better than we had any right to expect. I'm a rookie. I have more to learn before I should expect to finish second."

"Half an hour ago you were worrying about luck and now you're bugged by numbers. When did you start being a worrier, Johnny?"

"When I saw all those cars here," I confessed, "all those cars that cost more than ours and all those drivers with more experience than I've had."

Joe Quade had been listening to all this and smiling. Now, he said, "One race at a time, Johnny. Don't look back in this business and don't guess about the future. One race at a time, one turn at a time. Each one's a new problem."

I agreed with a nod. "I should have known that from watching my uncle."

"It's different in the driver's seat," Joe said. "I felt it, too. Everybody on the team contributes, but the burden's on the driver. The others contribute—but the driver has to *deliver!*"

"Man, you make it sound grim!" Rheem said. "Johnny doesn't *have* to do anything. Aren't we here for the fun?"

"Partly," Joe agreed. "But mostly for the money."

That appraisal fit me. I had gone to Deverest for the fun and competed for the money. But why had I traveled with my Uncle Luke? I guess it would be fair to say that even if I had been a millionaire, I would have enjoyed racing. It was nice to get paid for doing what I enjoyed.

That's speaking in a general way, of course. There

are different degrees of enjoyment in this game. At the top would be winning. Grading down from there to the less and less enjoyable would be taking second place, third place and so on, down to where I had finished in my first race, down to last place.

The most enjoyable period in that forty-lap, small-engine final was lining up for the start. Because there we were, right smack in the middle of the first row, heading a seven-row parade. There was a Plymouth on the pole and a Chev to my right; 90 percent of the fans had a favorite in the first row.

The Ford fans were the happiest forty laps later, but not because of yours truly. Mark Ryer, who had driven a big Plymouth to third place in the opening race, piloted a Ford to victory in this one.

He passed me in the backstretch of the third lap. He was the first to pass me but there were quite a few others. Seven more went by me before I finally saw that checkered flag. That put us out of the money.

I wasn't being bothered by too many numbers or troubled by any hard luck. So far as I could judge, I was driving as well as I ever had. But cars kept going past.

Rheem said nothing to me when I came in and I said nothing to Rheem. Joe Quade was still there and he said only, "Tough luck, Johnny," before he went back to his own pit.

We were picking up, getting ready to go home, before Rheem said, "What happened?"

"I don't know," I said. "I can't explain it."

# 6

The silence of the pit lasted for about a third of the trip back to Shale. Then, as we were going through Borton, Rheem said, "The winning time in that forty-lapper was slower than the speed in the race where you took second place."

"So—?"

"So what happened? You finished *ninth!*"

"I'm as puzzled as you are. I don't know what happened. And I don't want to talk about it."

A sigh from him and more silence. This silence lasted from Borton to Alda, which is sixty miles. This time I broke it, saying, "Maybe it was that remark Joe Quade made, about the burden being on the driver. Maybe I was thinking about that and it made me too careful."

"That could be." he paused. "Most of the cars that passed you did it in the last half of the race, in the last twenty laps. You were still riding fourth, halfway through the race."

"Did you have a watch on me?"

"No. And the total time is the only time the board showed. Well, it's over, it's history. Let's not dwell on it."

His advice was sound but my memory was not a faucet. I couldn't turn it off. All the laps in the race were run over again in my mind on the drive home.

It was dark when I pulled into our yard after dropping Rheem off. My Uncle Luke had just come back from a race in Lexington. He was having a late supper in the kitchen, and Mom had set a place for me.

"Long face," he commented, as I sat down. "Long face, bad day?"

"I took a second in the qualifier," I said, "but I was a sad case in the category final."

"How long was the final?"

"Forty laps. Twenty-five miles."

"You're too green to expect to do well at that distance. Luck can win a sprint but experience wins the long ones. I mean experience *and* luck!"

"And skill," I added. "How did you do today?"

"I made a hundred and nine dollars more than my expenses."

"You owe me sixty for board," Mom said. "I'll take it now, rich brother-in-law."

"I can give you forty," he said. "I have to save the rest for expenses."

Here he was, an experienced NASCAR driver and part-time garage mechanic and he could just about pay for his board and room. What chance did I have of making a living in the Association?

My mother's thoughts must have been running a parallel track. Because she said, "If you intend to make racing your career, Johnny, don't plan to get married."

"I can name you four NASCAR drivers," my uncle said, "who earned over a hundred thousand dollars last year, Liz."

"Four out of how many?" she asked. "Don't give the boy a false picture."

"He never has, Mom," I said. "He's taken me where I can see the picture for myself. And I like it."

She looked at both of us in turn and sighed. "Two against one. I surrender." She smiled at my uncle. "Luke, I'm sure you know I didn't mean to downgrade you."

It was still several hours short of bedtime so Uncle Luke went out to the garage to be with his only love, his car.

My mother said, "I shouldn't talk that way to him. He's a fine man. But ever since we were all children together, it's been *cars, cars, cars* with him!"

"And with Dad," I said. "And now with me. What else is there? The mine? The still?"

"Your father settled for the mine so that he could have a family and a home. Aren't you glad he did?"

"I'm glad to be here so I'm glad for me. I'm not glad for him. I love my father."

"And you think he's unhappy?"

"I think he could have found happier work. But I guess that's true about most working people, isn't it?"

Mom shrugged. "I don't know. It's true for working people who don't like to work." She began to pick up the dishes. "That wouldn't be you. You've been bringing money into this house since you were nine."

"Wonderful me!" I said.

She winked. "I've seen worse."

I'd always enjoyed my work for two reasons; the money it earned had not only helped at home, it had bought my wheels. The paper route had paid for my bicycle, the filling station for my cars. And now the wheels would pay for the wheels.

And perhaps a few things more, such as board and room?

Rheem agreed with my Uncle Luke. "Experience," he said Monday, "of course! Pacing over the long route, it takes time to learn that. We expected too much. We've been lucky. We'll get plenty of experience before the summer's over."

A new day and a new Rheem. I agreed with a nod.

"We'll need the experience," he went on, "if we decide to make our move next year."

He was on another flight. Taking off from the home base of reality—but heading where?

"Move?" I asked. "Next year? Make sense!"

"I said 'if,'" he reminded me. "*If* we decide."

"I heard that. I didn't get the sense of any of it. What move could we decide to make next year?"

"Up," he said. "We wouldn't move down, would we? Up to the big league."

"Do you mean NASCAR?"

"Or USAC. Why not? You'll be old enough next year."

"And good enough?"

He shrugged. "Who can say now? We'll know by the end of the summer."

The burden, as Joe Quade had said, is on the driver.

We would have another man in our pit crew next Sunday. Uncle Luke had an open date and he had decided to come with us to Calhoun Corners for the Association's second event.

Except for that nighttime meeting at Ned Allis' house, I hadn't been to Calhoun Corners since my uncle had last raced there, four year ago. A new promoter had taken over since then and talked the county supervisors into improving both the stands and the track. He had been slowly building up his attendance.

As we drove past the picnic area Sunday morning, the place where I had played with Judy that Fourth of July, Uncle Luke asked, "How long has it been since I brought that Packard here, Johnny?"

"Thirteen years," I said.

"I haven't exactly set the world on fire since, have I?"

"You're doing what you want to do," I said.

He nodded slowly. "Yup. But I should be better at it."

He had been well over thirty then; he was well over forty-three now. He had started too old, with equipment too cheap, and he must have known it. I didn't know his exact age.

But he was a well liked man, and his spirits perked up once he got to talking engines with Joe Quade and Art Parent and a few of the other veterans sprinkled through the field of youngsters. He was with his own comfortable people, professionals who respected each other.

Duke Whitney was in Junior Jessup's pit, talking earnestly with Junior and Ned Allis. There was a rumor circulating that Whitney planned to back Junior with a new sedan for the NASCAR tracks next season.

It didn't make sense to me. There were men with more skill and a lot more experience than Junior Jessup here today, men as hungry to move up. And would Whitney desert this new Association so soon after he had helped to found it? Well, probably. . . .

Rheem suggested, "How about a few laps to find the feel of the track before it gets too crowded?"

That was a sound idea. It would not only get crowded later, it would get dusty and rutted. As I edged out from the pit, I noticed that Uncle Luke was watching me and I could guess that he might be here today because I had complained about my bad finish in the forty-lapper last week. He would be looking for weaknesses in the long one today.

There are horses for courses and cars for tracks. It can't be explained logically; it was something I felt instinctively. This car was not for this track. The turns came on too quickly and they were a chore to get through.

Remembering last week and knowing that Uncle Luke was watching added to my frustration. I tried too hard, played it too heavy—and almost crashed the fence in the grandstand turn. When I came back to the pit, there was still some tremble in my hands.

Uncle Luke's grin was knowing. "You didn't feel at home out there, did you?"

"Not for a second."

"It happens," he said. "Don't let it beat you. You can still do well enough to make your expenses."

I laughed. "That's about it. The expenses for the twelve-mile trip from Shale to here."

He didn't laugh. He asked, "Mind if I try it?"

"Be my guest."

He wore my helmet. He took three exploratory laps, high and low. He had driven here often enough to know where the speed groove had been before the track was resurfaced. But a change in the mixture of clay and loam can change the groove.

When he had finished his laps, he told me, "It's not the same track I drove. It's a lot softer. I'd stay away from the upper edge as much as possible. I think we ought to tighten the shocks."

We did that and I took her out again and it was a little better, but not enough to make me feel comfortable. Which I stated.

"So okay," Rheem said. "So today it's work instead of play. This is our trade. It's not supposed to be easy, right?"

"My trade," I said evenly, "is pumping gas. And yours is trying to outguess your rich uncle. When did this become our trade?"

He didn't answer. He just looked at me sadly—tolerant, long-suffering Rheem.

My uncle said softly, "Come on, I'll buy you both a hamburger. This is a *team*, remember!"

"That track's made me nervous," I apologized. "I'll be all right."

It wasn't only the track. It was the memory of last Sunday. I didn't want to look that bad again, and especially not in front of Uncle Luke.

Junior Jessup was at the snack shack, laughing it up with the boys. Win or lose, finish or not finish, Junior was a cheerful man. Was it his confidence that made him cheerful or did he pretend to be cheerful to mask a lack of confidence?

"Nice wheels you bought," he said to me, as he started on his third burger. "You should have bought the big engine, though."

"Why?"

"So you can play with the big boys. Compete with the best, I always say."

Uncle Luke asked, "How about learning the trade first?"

"I can't think of a quicker way to learn," Junior answered, "than competing with the best."

It sounded like simple arrogance but there was truth in it. When you compete with the best, you have more reason to watch their moves, to learn strategy from the winners.

Rheem said, "There's a rumor going around that Duke Whitney wants to back you on the money circuit next year."

Junior shook his head. "It's my Uncle Ned he wants as his chief mechanic. He wants a *name* behind the wheel."

"Don't be bitter," Rheem said. "You'll be a name one of these days."

"I'm not bitter," Junior assured him. "Just impatient."

He and Rheem had that in common. I suppose everybody at the track under the age of thirty might have been guilty of impatience. But it takes time to learn to be a winner at a level where winning has any meaning. It takes time and thought.

And confidence. My Uncle Luke said, "Keep a positive attitude. If you stay in this business, you're going to run into tracks where you won't feel comfortable. Rheem's right—it's not always going to be fun."

Despite my pessimism, it wasn't a bad day. In the qualifier, I started in the front row, because of my second-place finish in last week's qualifier. I didn't quite make the first row at the flag, but I finished fourth. To me, on a track where I didn't feel at home, that was a respectable finish.

Rheem looked pleased when I came in and my uncle nodded his approval. "Solid," he said. "Professional."

The final for our class would be forty laps long and twenty-three cars full. That refugee from NASCAR, Mark Ryer, would hold down the pole in his Ford. He had also qualified high in his friend's Plymouth for the big engine finale that would wind up the afternoon.

My uncle told me, "Watch Mark's line when you get a chance. He's a smart driver. Try to stay away from that upper edge. There's nothing to prove, so don't force anything. Just be ready to take advantage of any situations that might develop."

There was nothing to prove; he was right about that. I had raced in jalopies and drags, but I was still a raw beginner in the stock car field. I had brought home a couple of lucky seconds in short races and it had given me delusions of excellence.

Winning was the goal, but no race was a waste if a man learned. Pacing hadn't been important in those short races, and strategy had been confined to meeting the immediate challenge. Over the longer routes, a driver had to estimate the field better, judge who the front runners were, who were the men who did best in the stretch drive. He then had to relate that to the cars they were driving.

This kind of judgment wasn't picked up in a few short races. I had learned some of it from the pit where I had watched my uncle compete through the years, but the view from behind the wheel was a different perspective.

The sun had grown steadily hotter through the day and the dust heavier. The sharp odor from a dozen exhaust pipes drifted back to my starting position in the fifth row. The nervousness I had felt since that first trial lap was still with me, but diminished. I had nothing to prove and a lot to learn.

My view of Mark Ryer was limited to the wait before the cars went into their flying lap. After that, the dust was too heavy and Mark too far away. So I couldn't study his lines into and out of the turns, as Uncle Luke had suggested. I studied some other lines and tried to find a successful line of my own.

As I have stated earlier, I was not a stranger to the world of competitive wheels. I had grown up learning about traction, gravity and centrifugal force, acceleration and braking; I had grown up around wheels.

I don't think it's immodest to say there were men all around me driving cars that were not as well prepared as ours and showing skills inferior to mine. There weren't enough of them, I'll admit, but there were some and fourteen of them finished behind me.

I finished ninth in a field of twenty-three. "Solid," Uncle Luke said, once again. He didn't add "professional" this time.

The big-bore windup was a fifty-lap event and the most exciting show of the day—thanks to Junior Jessup. He only led for three laps but he dogged every man who forged to the front, keeping each moving at his personal limit. He finished in second place by less than ten feet.

Whitney was in his pit to congratulate him when he came in.

"Maybe," Uncle Luke said, "Duke's getting some second thoughts about hiring a name driver. That kid's got a lot to learn, but he's also got a lot of natural talent."

"I always thought so," Rheem agreed, "but I didn't like to say it in front of Johnny."

# 7

▰▰▰▰▰▰▰▰▰▰▰▰▰▰▰▰▰▰▰▰▰▰▰▰▰▰▰▰▰▰▰▰▰▰▰▰

I guess that summer would have to be written off as education, that first season I spent in the Southeast Racing Association. The season cost us almost twice as much money as we won, but it seemed reasonable to me that a man had to pay for his education.

I took one more second that year in a curtain-raiser at Deverest, and a third in a small-bore final at Elm Grove. Those were the high spots. I was encouraged, though, by my generally better finishes in the long races. I was getting beat by the competition, now, not by myself.

And the competition was better because the purses were, and the purses were better because attendance was better than any racing circuit had a right to expect in its first year.

With a solid start like that behind us, most of the Association members looked forward hopefully to the spring opener at Deverest. Around Christmas, Whitney announced that he would be backing a car on the NASCAR Grand National circuit next year. Ned Allis would head up his pit crew; Junior Jessup would be behind the wheel. All it meant at the time was that SRA would be losing the chairman of its Technical Committee and its most colorful young driver.

Joe Quade was elected to the committee vacancy and Art Parent elevated to chairman. We had a February meeting at Art's house—and heard more bad news. Whitney had applied for a NASCAR sanction for his track.

"Does that mean we won't open the season there?" I asked.

"We'll open there *this* year," Art told me. "I've already discussed that with Duke. He'll have to honor all existing contracts even if NASCAR accepts the track—and they probably won't do that until this fall."

Joe Quade said bitterly, "This whole Association was his idea and now he's getting ready to desert it. I'll *never* understand that man."

Art shrugged. "He's ambitious and self-centered. He's not unique. He hasn't hurt us—yet. There are other tracks in the league, most of them better than Deverest."

Art was taking an optimistic view of it. There were better tracks than Deverest in the Association but Duke Whitney had been the organizing force, the spark plug among the owners. Without him, the league would be weaker.

Rheem had made no more comments about moving

up. Although he didn't say so, it was possible he agreed with me that I needed more seasoning.

His dad was putting in fewer hours at the station now; Rheem and I worked at the station and on the car together that winter.

In March, there was an explosion at the mine. Twenty-one miners were buried alive. That ended any lingering doubts I may have had about earning my living underground. My future would be linked to the automobile, one way or another.

All the familiar faces except Junior Jessup's were at Deverest for the April opening of the SRA season. If anybody was gloomy about Duke Whitney's defection, it wasn't evident. It was spring and optimism was the spirit of the season.

"It's pollution, I know," Rheem said, "but I like it. It's my favorite perfume."

"What is?"

"The combination," he answered. "Dust and carbon monoxide and burning oil and hot rubber."

The smell was only part of it. There was the expectancy in the pits and in the stands, the promise of action to come. And there was tension, of course. In a trade this hazardous, there is always tension. There are critics who claim it is the hazard that attracts the fans. Statistics don't support this claim; the safest tracks have the best attendance records.

Joe Quade had a different car, a Plymouth he had bought from his former boss, Fireman Flynn.

"I'm glad to see you're running the big engine," I

told him. "It means I won't have to compete against you."

"Nor I against you," he said. "That should make us both happy. And Junior Jessup won't be around. I ought to pick up some purses this year."

He earned the first installment on his prophecy a couple hours later. He led a pack of hungry young tigers all the way to the checkered flag in the qualifying sprint for his class. Deverest was one of Joe's favorite tracks.

It had always served me well, too, but I didn't quite match Joe's success in my opener. The blond kid in the 265 Chev, Al Downing, almost ran me into the upper rail when he took the first turn too fast. By the time I had fought my way back to traction, the entire field was half a lap ahead.

Making up half a lap in a fifteen-lap race was not impossible. In a field as balanced as this one, though, on a track this crowded, any hope of finishing in the money seemed dim.

It looked a little brighter six laps later. There was a four-car tangle at the head of the parade. It didn't result in any major damage. It did allow a couple of the laggards to gain ground. One of the laggards was me.

The other was Al Downing, riding in the style of his hero, Junior Jessup. He came charging down the bank on the north turn, threading his way between the cars like a man on a ski slope weaves his way between the trees.

I stayed low and found an unoccupied alley next to the fence. I used all the 260 cubic inches under my foot to streak up to where I could play with the big boys.

Only three of them were too big for me. I finished fourth. With the crowd we had here today, fourth-place money should cover the expenses of the trip.

In the pit, Rheem muttered, "If that Downing hadn't gone into that first lap slide—"

"I might have done better," I admitted. "And if Quade's old Chev hadn't blocked the track, Al might have won at Elm Grove last season. It happens to all of us."

"I remember," Rheem said. "He took the high road that day, too, didn't he?"

I nodded.

"That's no place to travel on the dirt," Rheem said.

On the big tracks, on the hard surface tracks, some of the boys took the high road, up on the rim, driven out there by the centrifugal force of their great speed. When we moved up, *if* we moved up, that would be a new technique to learn. But Rheem was not mentioning "moving up" this spring.

So I did. "Maybe we'll never have to move up. Most of the Association tracks made money last year and look at this crowd here today!"

"Whitney always drew crowds," Rheem reminded me. "Even for demolition derbies. And next year this track won't be in the SRA."

"Okay, Rheem," I said. "I'll try to do better. I'm improving."

He stared at me. "What are you talking about?"

I laughed. "Nothing. I was talking nonsense, just voicing some private thoughts. You watch my dust in the windup."

"I admire a confident man," he said. "I'll be watching."

It was a strong start to a mixed year. I threw enough dust in the final to prevent Mark Ryer from loafing to his victory. He beat me to the flag by less than a dozen yards.

That season opener was both a financial and a spiritual tonic. The money we won gave us the base for a solvent season; the confidence I gained by taking second in the long race stayed with me through the whole campaign.

A driver point system had been set up that spring. I was never lower than fifth in the Small Engine Class, never lower than fourth after the middle of June. Among the younger drivers, only Al Downing gave me any serious competition.

The thought I had voiced in the spring looked more practical with each meet. We were not only making money on the circuit; the racing publicity we were getting was attracting repair and tune-up customers from all around the county. Who needed NASCAR?

In July, at Elm Grove, as we watched the overflow crowd pouring into the temporary infield stands, I asked Rheem, "Who needs NASCAR?"

"Big thinkers," he answered.

"Big dreamers," I corrected him.

He shrugged. "Big dreamers who can think."

"Explain. Think aloud for me, big dreamer."

"It's simple. In a race, you try to work your way to the front. In a trade, a profession, a business, you try to work your way to the top."

"That's simple, all right," I agreed. "Too simple."

"Why?"

"We're still making more money at the station than we are on the track. Maybe that's our trade. That NASCAR circuit is too widespread for weekend racing. We wouldn't be spending much time at home, where we're making our money."

"Shale," Rheem said, "has a couple of hungry men I can name who are as handy with a wrench as we are. We could hire them on a percentage arrangement."

"Well, maybe," I said. "We'll see—"

"Nobody ever got rich holding a wrench," he said.

"And not too many holding a wheel," I added. "One day at a time, Rheem."

That day was one of the bad ones, though not for us. In the big engine finale, Joe Quade and Mark Ryer kept trading the lead through sixty noisy laps. They were driving Plymouths with the same displacement and neither car seemed to have an edge in torque. Mark had a little more finesse, but the track was tire-torn and treacherous by now and Joe was the stronger man. His big wrists kept the car under firmer control.

They had already lapped a third of the field when they came charging into the heavy dust of the north turn. A rookie in a sputtering Ford was lost in that dust and Mark saw him too late. He jammed his brakes and tried to cut to the inside. That swung his rear end wide, right into the path of Joe's trailing sedan.

There was the clang of crumpling metal, the bang of an exploding tire—and Joe's car went sliding up the bank and through the fence!

All the drivers were getting the yellow flag. Rheem and I kept our eyes glued to that ragged hole in the fence. I don't know about Rheem, but I was holding my breath and my thumbs, hoping against hope that there would be no flash of flame or puff of smoke showing against that dusty sky.

The ambulance inched along the piled dirt of the upper track but couldn't find enough traction to work down to the car. The driver stayed behind the wheel; the other attendant stood for a few seconds on the rim of the track and then started down.

"No stretcher," Rheem said. "That's a good sign."

An even better sign appeared a few minutes later, the tall, thin silhouette of Joe Quade. He was walking slowly, supported by the attendant. He was conscious, he was mobile.

Applause rippled through the stands as the ambulance went past with Joe in the front seat. The green flag waved again and Mark Ryer went on to victory with a smashed rear end.

Joe Quade, we learned an hour later, was physically sound. Considering the condition of his car, that was a minor miracle. His recently purchased Plymouth was fit only for the junkyard.

Art Parent brought this information over to the hospital where we had waited to get the word on Joe. It affected Rheem; he was unusually quiet on the trip home.

"It could have been worse," I said. "Joe could have been damaged, instead of his car."

"That would have been worse," Rheem agreed. "But either way he's out of business."

"Hasn't he enough money to pick up another car?"

Rheem shook his head. "He still owes Flynn about four hundred on that Plymouth. Johnny, we could use him in the pit. We could pay him a few dollars. We could start to build a team."

I was still thinking about the wrecked car; the word "team" didn't register on me at the time. At any level of racing, you need one man in the pit. If you are lucky enough to have two, you can call them a *crew*. But a *team*—? That's big league. I was looking back at the accident. Rheem was looking ahead, as usual.

Rheem subscribed to the NASCAR *Newsletter* and we read about Junior Jessup from time to time. He was doing well for a rookie at that level of competition, though probably not well enough to keep him happy. With Whitney's money and Ned Allis' wrench to support his talent, Junior's future seemed to be bright.

I didn't envy him—much. I was earning more money than I ever had and enjoying myself. It's possible that I might have argued against making a move next year, but the choice was taken from me.

Calhoun Corners entered into the decision. Most of the other drivers had no serious problems with that surface, but it was still my least favorite track. I had raced there last season, and three meets had been scheduled for this season. I didn't do very well in the first two; it's possible that pressured me more than it should have.

We had gone through a dry fall and the track was as hard and fast as it had ever been. So it couldn't have been only the surface that had bothered us before; it was simply a track our Ford didn't like. I came in from a trial cruise feeling frustrated.

Joe Quade had been working with us for a month. He said, "If it makes you nervous, I'll drive today."

I shook my head. "The car likes it less than I do. Maybe I can figure out a new strategy."

"The corners are too short," Joe explained. "Your best bet, with the track this hard, is to ride the upper half. It's a longer road, but it could be faster."

That was exactly opposite to Uncle Luke's advice last year, but the track hadn't been hard then. I tried the high road in the qualifier and it stretched those tight corners, giving me a longer line, in and out. In a twenty-two-car field, I finished fifth.

That won me enough points to lock up third place in the driver point standings for the season. Even a win in the final wouldn't advance me to second place; I had nothing to gain in that race but the purse and the pride of competition.

But the strategy Joe suggested had worked so well, I decided to extend my luck in the final. I had a starting position to encourage it, the middle of the second row, and the track was harder than I would be likely to find it again.

Both Al Downing and Mark Ryer were in the row ahead, Ryer on the pole. Mark, I was sure, would set a fast pace for the flying lap and try to charge out to an early lead, avoiding the traffic. Al would try to stay with him. Both of them would lose traction if they tried too hard on that baked first corner.

Neither of my flanking cars had much low-rev torque. I felt confident that I could get the jump on them. And if Mark was forced high, he would sweep Al up with him. It might be time for a change in strategy, a temporary shift to the low road. I could go back to the upper route after I stole that first-lap lead.

This sounds optimistic and maybe even arrogant. But it worked. Al was nose and nose with Mark when he started to drift high; I pulled away from the other two in my row, and for a few seconds there was a stretch of unobstructed daylight in front of me. The Ford and I led the jammed and snarling pack into the backstretch.

Our lead held for ten laps before anyone came up to make a sustained challenge. It was Al. He had a chance to finish in the top five for the year and he was determined to pick up some points today.

For two nerve-stretching laps, we rubbed fenders, while the fans cheered and the dust began to cloud our vision ahead.

It would be wrong to blame the dust for what happened. It was my judgment that was to blame, not the dust. This small-bore final was the last race of the day. No matter how hard that Kentucky sun had baked the track, there were bound to be soft spots in it after all *that* traffic.

At the speed Al and I were traveling, it wouldn't take much of a jolt to spoil our traction. We were moving within a hair of our tractionable limits. These are dangers I realize now; I was too involved in the competition to think about them then.

In the third lap of our dogfight, the preparation of Rheem and Joe began to pay off: we began to spread the daylight between us and the Chev. It added some adrenalin to my bloodstream; I was in a good position to win the last race of the SRA season.

That kind of emotional thinking can impair a man's judgment. I plead guilty. The car was perking, the track was hard, I was winging.

Five or six laps short of the checkered flag, another contender moved past Al and came up to haunt me. He was a local driver in a short-block Chev, a first-year man.

He played it close, elbowing me on the turns, riding my rear fender on the stretches, making a big man of himself in front of his neighbors.

This was only twelve miles from Shale; some of those people in the stands were *my* neighbors. I stayed in front, knowing my pride had carried me too far beyond the calculated risk, knowing but not caring. Both the car and I were determined to win this last race of the year.

We almost made it. We went past the white flag with a twenty-foot lead and into the first turn of the final lap still under control and gaining ground.

We got through that turn and the second and came into the backstretch still holding our lead. Ahead, a gray sedan was limping along, at least one lap behind and maybe more.

It was in the middle of the track and there was room below, but I decided we couldn't make the turn if we took that route.

Why the driver in the gray car should move uptrack as we were trying to get past above, I never learned. His rear fender caught my front wheel as I swung violently toward the rim.

I heard the shriek of tires and saw the dusty top rail of the fence. It was right in line with my eyes—before the lights went out!

# 8

The dreams that I remember from that time were dreams about the mine. I had never worked in the mine; I had been down in it only once. But those are the dreams I still remember having during those hours I was unconscious.

When I opened my eyes, Rheem was sitting next to the bed.

"What's wrong with me?" I asked.

"Concussion," he said. "Broken leg. You're in the county hospital in Calhoun Corners."

"Have you phoned my folks?"

"They were here all night. Your mother's taking a nap in the waiting room right now."

A pain moved from behind my eyes to the back of my neck. I could feel my heart beating in my head. "All night—? How long have I been out?"

"Almost twenty-four hours." He took a breath. "Are you—I mean—how do you feel?"

"I ache. The car— How about the car?"

"You're lucky to be alive," he said. "Don't think about the car!"

"Tell me, Rheem."

"It's totaled," he said. "It's junk. The frame's a pretzel." He stood up. "I'll go wake your mother."

Her eyes were red when she came in. Her voice was shaky. "How do you feel?"

"I ache," I said. "My head aches and my whole right side from my shoulder to my toes. I'll be all right, Mom."

"Oh, yes!" she said. "You'll be perfect, ready to race again. We'll talk about that later."

There was a silence. Then she said, "I'm sorry. It's not the right time to scold, is it?"

"I don't know. I kept dreaming about the mine. I was only down there once. Why should I dream about it?"

"The mine or the track," she said. "You probably think of them as your only choices. You've had a limited view of the world, growing up in Shale."

"It's not just the track, Mom. I like everything about cars."

"So sell them," she said. "Get a lot, get an agency."

"That takes money."

She didn't have time to argue. An intern came in then. He took my temperature and felt my pulse and looked into my eyes with one of those pencil flashlights. He told Mom I had better get some rest.

I'd just had twenty-three and a half hours of rest, but

I was glad he had ordered more. It wasn't the strategic time to argue about racing with my mother.

When I woke up the second time, Dad and Uncle Luke were there. They weren't big talkers, either one of them, and I didn't press them for any answers. But I had the feeling that *they* didn't expect me to give up racing.

The leg wasn't fractured; it was only a hairline crack. I was walking with a cane by the end of the week and working at the station by the end of the month.

Nobody in our house mentioned racing through this time. There wasn't much reason to; my four-hundred-dollar sedan had been turned into forty dollars worth of salvage. I didn't even have a car for personal use. And I didn't have enough money to buy one; every dime I had saved had been used to pay my hospital bill.

It wasn't a happy time. I didn't like being a pedestrian, and I didn't enjoy looking forward to a future that *might* not include racing. The silence on that subject was not confined to home; Rheem avoided talking about it at the station.

He had invested money in the car but I was sure it wasn't losing his money that kept him silent. I opened the subject myself, finally, one slow morning at the station.

"Are we through with racing?" I asked him.

He shrugged. "You tell me. You're the one who had the accident."

"What does that mean?"

"I mean—if I had been unconscious for as long as you

**79**

were, I don't think *I'd* want to race again. And the way your mother was talking at the hospital—" He shook his head.

"My mother doesn't make my decisions anymore," I said. "I'm of age. I don't understand you, Rheem. All you ever talked about was racing, moving up, getting into the big time."

"I'm a great talker," he admitted. "I talked you into your first stock car race. And look what that led to!"

"I had an accident," I said evenly, "because of a mistake in strategy. I let my ego interfere with my judgment. It had nothing to do with you or the first race or any other race. I made a dumb move and I paid for it. That's past. Let's talk about the future."

"Let's talk about the present," he said. "What do we race—bicycles? What do we use for money?"

"We've got a whole long winter ahead. We can save enough money before spring to pay for some kind of heap. And we've got the tools to get it ready. And our great skill. Come on, Rheem, get back to normal!"

He grinned. "I didn't want to open the subject, Johnny, but I'm glad you did. I really thought we were a team without a driver."

"We have everything we need," I said, "except the car."

That was optimistic. I figured Rheem needed the encouragement. He hadn't talked about his favorite subject for three weeks; he had to be depressed about it.

Opening the subject with him had been easy enough. It wasn't as easy for me to open it with my mother, but I did it that afternoon.

She told me the same thing I had told Rheem. "You're of age. You don't need my permission."

"You're still my mother. Didn't we always talk these things over?"

"Always is the right word," she agreed. "I *always* took one side and the men in my family *always* took the other. I'm talked out on the subject, Son."

I said nothing.

"Don't sulk," she said. "You're not likely to get a 100 percent approval on anything in this life. Your world of wheels just happens to be a world I don't understand."

It was a world I hoped to survive in, to succeed in, but I was a jockey without a horse. And what kind of horse could I buy with just one winter's savings?

It wouldn't be as fast or new as the one I had wrecked, which meant I would be competing at a lower level. It might even be at a level below the SRA, the level of the unorganized, unregulated tracks. This was the thought I voiced to Rheem about a week after the previous conversation.

"That's going into reverse," he protested. "That's a retreat. This team moves only forward, man!"

"And how do we do this without a lot of money?"

"I'm not sure. I've a couple of ideas cooking, but they're not ready. They're still in the oven."

"You mean they're half baked?"

"I mean I've been putting some thoughts together this week with some things I heard and I might come up with something smarter than saving our pennies for a junker."

"Trusted partner," I asked him, "tell me what you heard."

"Owen Dean's Plymouth is for sale." He paused for the proper added effect. "And two extra engines!"

Owen Dean was a Louisville driver, in the top twenty among NASCAR Grand National drivers for three straight years.

"I read he was retiring," I said, "but he's bound to put a stiff price on that car and those engines."

Rheem nodded. "Probably. He's a good friend of your Uncle Luke's."

"So?"

"So we could get credit from him, couldn't we?"

"Uncle Luke might. I don't think we could."

"That," Rheem explained, "was one of the thoughts I was putting together. When I said 'we,' I was including your Uncle Luke."

We were out there again, out in space, and I didn't remember even leaving the launching pad.

"Could we go back and start over?" I asked humbly. "I've lost my coordinates."

"I was thinking of a team," he said. "Joe Quade, your Uncle Luke, you, and I." He paused. "And your father, when he's not working."

"And who'd be the driver?"

"You and your uncle. At that level, of course, he'd have to work you in gradually and—"

"Level?" I interrupted. "We're talking NASCAR again?"

"We're talking NASCAR Grand National," he said. "That car of Owen Dean's is too hot for anything less."

Grand National, the top NASCAR circuit. . . . While I was trying to figure out a way to buy a junker for the county fairground league, my spiritual leader had been thinking in Grand National terms.

I waited for my mind to reach his plateau. Then I said, "You are planning to desert the SRA?"

"That's another thing I heard. There may not be an SRA next year. Deverest and Elm Grove are going over to NASCAR."

"Where'd you hear that?"

"From Duke Whitney. He was in last night. That team of his made money this season, Johnny. And they didn't win any big ones."

Junior Jessup had just been named NASCAR Rookie of the Year. He'd had the Whitney money behind him and Ned Allis' preparation. I didn't voice it to Rheem, but that looked like a stronger combination than the one he was planning. And how far along were his plans?

"What makes you think Uncle Luke would be interested?" I asked him.

His smile was sheepish. "When neither of us was talking to you about racing, we were talking to each other about it. He likes the idea."

I don't know why, but a thought I'd had before came back to me—*the burden's on the driver*. On Uncle Luke, at first, and later it would be on me.

I said, "The five of us probably haven't enough money to buy that car of Dean's. And I doubt if he'd give us credit on property as easy to destroy as a racing stock car."

"We'll see," Rheem said. "We'll see."

Just for the record and not for gloating, I was right about the credit. Owen Dean needed more money than we could raise. But what would be the end of a road to most people was just the start of a detour to my partner. There were other things he'd heard and one was that Art Parent had sold his car. He didn't plan to race next season.

Art Parent had money and mechanical knowledge and organizing ability. And he had another attribute that helped Rheem talk him into joining our team. Art loved the sound of unmuffled engines. He might be getting too old to drive, but he would never get too old to listen.

We had the money now and we had the team and we had a big Plymouth Hemi with two extra engines. I should have been happier than I was.

But I had a sense of moving too soon into company that was too fast. Though my uncle would be our number one driver, all of us (including him) knew it wouldn't be for long. Uncle Luke was getting old; he was losing the reflexes that keep a man alive at NASCAR speeds.

The Ford Motor Company announced in November that it would no longer support or maintain factory racing teams in the stock car field. General Motors had made the same announcement years earlier. That should have brightened my mood. It meant the independent teams would have a much stronger chance for the big-money finishes.

Don't get the idea that I was going around with a long, sour face. Though I worked with every man on the team that winter, getting ready for our February debut, only my mother noticed that I was more serious than usual.

And one day when I came home for lunch, she asked me why.

"I don't know, Mom. I guess too much is happening."

"Too much work?"

"No. I like the work. Too much—responsibility."

She looked at me blankly.

"I mean—I'm going to be the driver, eventually, of this new team. All that money and all that work we invested is going to be in my hands. I'm not used to being the only breadwinner for other people."

"Neither was your father before he was married. Your problem isn't as important as his was. Nobody depending on you is a child. If you don't win, they'll still find a way to eat." She smiled. "Have as much confidence in yourself as they must have in you."

I hadn't thought of it that way. Art Parent had put up most of the money and, despite his love for racing, he was not a man to let sentiment cloud his business judgment. What I needed was a transfusion of Junior Jessup arrogance.

The mine had been working two shifts a day and probably would all summer, so my dad was not included as a regular in our plans for this year. We would confine our competition, we'd decided, to southern tracks. At the Grand National level, that meant most of them; only nine of the year's seventy-plus events would be run on northern or western tracks. We would open at Daytona Beach in February.

So far as NASCAR goes, Daytona is *it*, their national headquarters. The tradition of racing on the hazardous surface of the beach went back to the beginning of the century, when it was a one-way track of tide-packed sand.

It's a different layout today, two and a half miles of paved surface, no longer affected by the tides or the weather. It is D-shaped, with a long, straight back-stretch and a trioval front stretch, an unusual design that permits frightening speeds. Since 1959 it has been the stockers' Indianapolis.

There was a sports car road course in the infield almost four miles long. There was a fully staffed hospital, a cafeteria, and six huge grandstands. Coming from the county fairground league to this was more than a step, it was a long ride in an elevator.

I guess it's fair to say that I was awed. As Rheem and I stood on the high rim of the second turn, it seemed as though there was nothing but track in sight, all the way to the horizon.

"She's really banked, isn't she?" he said.

I nodded.

"Did you ever expect to see it?"

"Not this soon," I said. "Even for Uncle Luke, this is a first."

"Through no fault of his," Rheem said. "He might have had the stuff to win here; he just never had the car to make the trip worthwhile."

Maybe, maybe, maybe. . . . He was here now, and he would be our driver for the qualifying race and (if he qualified) for the 500. February was a busy month here.

There would be sports car and Modified Sportsman races before the pair of 125-mile qualifiers for the big one.

It was hot and this was a fast track; there would be some rubber burned. Running on our budget, we needed as little tire wear as possible, but running a slow race was even harder on the budget.

Though it was true that my Uncle Luke had never raced here, he had raced at Darlington and Atlanta and Charlotte. So the delicate art of staying in one piece on a NASCAR superspeedway was nothing new to him.

"The only difference," he told me, "is that I've never had a car or a crew this good before." He shook his head. "That's some partner you have. He doesn't stand still, does he?"

"He should have been an aviator," I said. "All he thinks of is up, up, up!"

My uncle smiled. "Up, up, up? What other way is there to get out of the mine?"

"He never would have gone down," I said. "He was being groomed for management."

"And how about you?" my uncle asked quietly.

I stared at him, not understanding.

"He's more than your partner," my uncle explained. "He's your friend. And I think he's determined to do something for you that very few people are lucky enough to have done for them."

"What's that?"

"He's going to force you up to a level where you will have to be better than you are."

# 9

Uncle Luke and I took our first shakedown cruises at Daytona early on Wednesday morning, while there was still a trace of the night's coolness in the air. Art timed both of us but I didn't ask him for the times. I didn't want it to be considered a contest.

It was plain enough that Uncle Luke cut the fastest laps. He must have had that humming Hemi doing 200 miles an hour down the long backstretch. When he came in, Art nodded and gave him the okay sign with thumb and forefinger.

Rheem said, "Your turn, Johnny. Easy does it, now!"

"Don't worry. I'm not out to prove anything. If I had my way, I'd be in Shale today, pumping gas."

"I know. I've been a bad influence. Go out and see if you're big enough for a track this size."

My laps weren't up to Uncle Luke's, as I mentioned. I still traveled faster on that paved, banked track than

I had ever traveled on the ground before. Both the car and the track were designed for the ultimate speed. I was well short of that—but close enough to make my heart pound and my mouth turn dry.

I was downing my second cup of water at the water jug when Uncle Luke came over. "Different, isn't it?" he asked.

"I'll say! I was—well—scared. But still—"

"You want to get right back out there," he finished for me. "I had the same feeling the first time I drove at Darlington. There's no connection between this and the dirt tracks. It's a different game."

On the dirt, there was a sense of pushing through the heavy turns, digging for traction after the early races had broken the crust of the track. On the superspeedways of the NASCAR circuit, it was a question of going *almost to* the edge of lost traction and not *through* it. The first loss of traction at big track speeds could be your last loss of traction.

In a way it was hard because it was too easy. The sense of feel that is developed on dirt is a coarse sense, not tuned finely enough to prepare a driver for the precarious slickness of the paved speedways.

Flyers claim there is the same degree of touch differential between piloting cars and planes, but they are not speaking of cars traveling 225 miles an hour.

The sun was high in the sky before we finished our morning practice runs. I was glad to be here. Rheem might never force me to be better than I was, but he had certainly helped to bring me to this place where I wanted to be.

We had lunch at the huge cafeteria. Some big names were there—Richard Petty, Bobby Allison, both Yarborough and his sound-alike, Yarbrough. Some small names with familiar faces were there, too—Mark Ryer and Al Downing.

They came over to sit with us. The SRA had gone out of business officially at a January meeting, and Mark had decided to bankroll Al in a car for the big time. It was a brand new Dodge they had worked together on all winter.

I thought it was a strange combination, Mark mostly finesse and Al mostly foot. Mark knew his business; he must have seen potential in Al. And my judgment was not exactly infallible. The knowledgeable NASCAR veterans who had voted Junior Jessup Rookie of the Year had also seen something I'd missed.

Who's perfect?

We had three mornings of practice before the first fifty-lap, one-hundred-and-twenty-five-mile qualifier. There was no groove I could find and there seemed to be none the stars favored. Petty drove it high, I noticed, and Johnson low. The low road should make sense; it would be the shorter route. But for some reason I felt more comfortable riding the rim. Uncle Luke liked the middle of the track, where he could move to either side for passing.

Junior Jessup must have been scheduled for afternoon practice; I never saw him until Saturday's qualifier. His pit was nearby and he came over with Ned Allis to visit us.

"Welcome to the majors," he greeted me. "I'm glad to see you're finally wheeling a hot one."

"My uncle will be driving today," I told him. "Congratulations on the award."

"Thanks." He grinned. "Did it surprise you?"

"A little," I admitted, returning his grin. "Is Duke in town?"

"Not yet. He'll be here for the big one—if I qualify. You know Duke; he's too fancy for anything less than the big one."

Some bitterness in his voice? I said, "Good luck. One race at a time."

"Sure," he said. "I hope when we tangle we'll be fighting for the lead." He waved genially at all of us and went back to his pit.

"Nice guy," Rheem said. "Why don't you like him?"

"I like him, I like him! It's his driving that makes me nervous, not his personality."

The view I had of his driving half an hour later showed very little change. He was a shade smoother, but still a charger, ramming his way from twenty-seventh place to eighth in the first fifty miles, a go-or-blow twenty laps of fender rubbing and dangerous drafting.

He was up with the names, then, with Petty and Bobby Isaac and the Baker brothers and his advance came to a natural halt. In the middle of the track, moving right up to the extreme that his middle-aged sanity would allow, my Uncle Luke moved from twenty-fourth to sixteenth in the same fifty miles.

The boys in front were really honking; it would be

poor strategy to make a bid this early. The heat was still with us. Attrition could improve our position as easily as challenging those leadfoots.

"Luke's got a sound sense of pace," Art said. "Today's a bad day for front runners."

Joe Quade nodded agreement.

Rheem said nothing. He seemed to be following Junior's car with the glasses almost as much as ours. I had a feeling he might have preferred something more spectacular than a man with a sound sense of pace. It was just a feeling; I'm not a mind reader.

In the twenty-third lap, Mel Callen, a charger out of Memphis, blew a clutch and our entry rode fifteenth. The sun and the pace continued to work for us. There were no challenges from behind; three more cars in front were victims of the heat. Uncle Luke brought our steed home in twelfth place, picking up nine hundred dollars in prize money and qualifying for the 500.

He came in looking like an old man, drawn and tired, his eyes red. He said, "I'll never be able to handle that 500 alone, Johnny. We're going to have to divide up the driving in that one."

"It's early in the season, Uncle Luke. Every year that first race has been the one that punishes you the most."

He smiled. "Right. And every year it gets worse. I'll start Sunday and go as far as I can. But I know my limits. So be ready to take over at any time."

From Calhoun Corners to Daytona Beach, from that custom flathead to a Grand National Hemi; that could read like a real American success story. But it wouldn't be, of course, if we weren't successful. The burden's on the driver. . . .

We were having a nine o'clock steak in a noisy restaurant, jammed with drivers and pit men, when Rheem said, "You're mighty quiet tonight. Worried about something?"

"Nothing important," I said. "Just not looking bad Sunday and staying alive and not smashing up a twelve-thousand-dollar car and a lot of little, trivial stuff like that."

Joe Quade suggested, "How about breaking me in as the relief driver? I'm overdue to get lucky."

"Nothing personal," Art said, "but *no*! Luke's our number one and Johnny's our ticket to tomorrow. Heck, you don't drive much better than I do, Joe!"

Joe laughed—and sighed. "I never really had a car that matched my skill."

He said it as a joke but it could have been true. And it probably could have been said about dozens of feisty young men through all the years auto racing has flourished in America. There were plenty of hot pilots who could never assemble the pit crews or afford the cars that matched their talents.

But here we were and we all knew why. His rich uncle hadn't tried to school Rheem for management purely out of nepotism.

Sunday was only a little cooler, with a breeze from the ocean. There would be forty-six cars revving at top speed for five hundred miles; Sunday wasn't going to stay cool where the action was. Our number one problem would be an overheated engine, and our second, excessive tire wear. We would be burning up tires. And though we had practiced high-speed changes all winter, we were still a green crew.

There were at least a dozen pit crews here who had worked together under the strain of racing conditions. Any experienced crew could fill a gas tank, change the outside tires, and clean a windshield in twenty-five-seconds. A winning team had to beat that time. In the pit as well as on the track, the old adage was confirmed: time was money.

Art Parent had come up with a handy gimmick. It was a template that matched the five lugs on the wheel, a template that held the lug nuts. The nuts we took off would be too hot to handle. This template, positioning all five fresh nuts for the pneumatic wrench, saved us precious seconds in a Friday dry run.

We would need about six pit stops for gas, and we hoped to make them while the yellow caution flag was showing. At that time, a stop would lose a driver about half a mile on the leader. When the field was going full bore, a pit stop could cost three times that distance. But who could anticipate a yellow flag?

There were ninety-four thousand fans in the stands and the infield when all those glistening late-model sedans growled down the bowed front stretch for the parade lap. The first of the year's big races was under way.

Our hopes rode in the fifteenth row. The car had been impounded for the last twenty-four hours, so we hadn't been able to get rid of our nervous energy by tinkering with an engine that didn't need it. Now, in the pit, we thought of other things to do. Keeping busy was our best pacifier.

Art Parent held the watch. I would keep a lap count to check against the board. Rheem and Joe were the equipment men. Though the pit looked like a junkyard, each tire, tool, and can was exactly where we could get to it quickest.

Uncle Luke had seemed rested this morning and he didn't act like a tired man when the green flag dropped. Our Hemi moved through that first chopping, fender-banging lap asking no quarter and giving none. The thunder was deafening, the haze of smoking rubber heavy enough to vulcanize. We lost no ground.

"Good man," Art muttered. "Good show! Hang in there, old timer!"

"He's probably the only man on the track who started in this business driving a Packard," I said.

Art smiled and nodded. "How old is he? He's kind of coy about mentioning his age."

"I don't know exactly," I said. "He's older than my dad. He's only been racing for fifteen years. A lot of those drivers have been racing that long."

"But most of them started as kids," Art said, "and the rest of them still are."

Ten miles into the 500, the famous names were already grouping at the head of the field, Petty, Isaac, and Allison. The lesser lights we knew were jamming up the middle, Downing, Fireman Flynn, and last year's new star, Junior Jessup. Uncle Luke was already saving gas, drafting behind another Kentucky entry, Graham

George's Ford. Actually, they were both saving not only gas, but engine strain, as they easily kept pace with the middle of the field.

"Good man," Art muttered again. "We'll make a dollar here today."

"I'm sure," a voice behind us said, "you wouldn't be here if you couldn't, Art."

It was Duke Whitney, tanned and smiling.

"I'd be here," Art said. "Speak for yourself. How's it going, Duke?"

"Couldn't be better." He looked at me. "Turned mechanic, have you?"

I shook my head. "Relief man. I'm a slow learner."

"Not like Junior, eh?"

"Not at all," I agreed. "You picked a winner there."

Art laughed. "You sure did, Duke. You tried to get Ned Allis and Junior was part of the package. Smartest decision you ever made—and you were forced into it."

Duke shrugged and grinned. He could take the needle. "I was lucky," he admitted. "We all need a little luck now and then. It goes with winning. It rides with success. But who am I to tell moneybags Art Parent about success?" He winked at me and went on to visit the next pit.

They were both successful; they had that in common. There was a difference, though. Art wouldn't be going from pit to pit, socializing, while his driver was competing on the track. Duke was a showman and one show was the same as another to him. There was only one show for Art, racing. I like a man who likes his trade.

Stubborn Luke Pilgrim had finessed his way into the

top twenty by the time he came in for his first gas stop. The tires looked sound, but we changed the right rear for insurance.

It had been a twenty-four-second stop under the green and would have lost us position except that almost every car on the track made a stop within the next five laps. The tanks were only standard size and those big, hungry engines were gulping a gallon of gas every four miles at these speeds.

As the Hemi snaked out into the traffic again, Rheem said, "He looked strong, didn't he? Maybe—?" He stared questioningly at Art.

Art shook his head. "Not the whole route, never!"

"Thanks for the vote of confidence, Rheem," I said.

"I didn't mean the *whole* route," he explained. "But I hoped he could handle at least half. Let's face it, Johnny, two hundred and fifty miles is about five times as far as you've ever raced."

"Don't remind me." I took a breath. "This is easier than ploughing through the dirt, Rheem. It doesn't take anywhere near the same strength. Don't you fret; I'll be all right."

"I know," he said hoarsely. "I know! It wasn't *personal*. I was thinking strategy. I was thinking of the team."

I was miffed at the time, but he was being practical. My uncle had taken years to develop a sense of pace that would keep a car in one piece and in contention over a long route. We needed him out there today as long as he could make it.

The first yellow flag didn't flash until the seventy-fifth

lap. Suddenly, there was more traffic on the pit road than there was on the track. Bobby Isaac, who'd had nearly a half-lap lead on the second-place car, came out again after his stop to find most of the field riding his rear bumper.

It didn't seem fair. There should be some way a man could keep a big lead under the yellow flag. The only thing that could be said in the rule's favor: it was equally unfair to everybody. In this case it helped us pick up nearly three-quarters of a lap.

Uncle Luke seemed no more tired to me when he came in than he had in the fifty-lapper, though he had again gone half as far. But he said, "The next yellow flag, be ready. If the flag doesn't show, I'll run twenty more laps."

"I'll be ready." I handed him the wet towel to bathe his face. "Anything I should know?"

"There's a slick spot high in the beginning of that grandstand turn. Watch out for it. Don't come into the turn much higher than the middle." He waved and gunned out again toward the action.

I knew the track and I knew the car by now. What I didn't know was how well I could perform in this kind of competition. They played it close and rough at frightening speeds. The winners at this level drove closer to Junior's strategy than to mine.

Twenty laps later, when Uncle Luke turned the car over to me, we were in sixteenth place. If I could hold that position, we would pick up about two thousand dollars. That, added to the nine hundred we'd won in the qualifier, would keep us solvent for the trip.

*Steady now,* I told myself. *This is the big wheel and these boys are the best in the world but you've raced against some of them before. There's not that much difference.*

There was a lot of difference. When you're going 3 miles a minute and the car that passes you ticks your bumper as he cuts back, you know for sure you are no longer at the county fairgrounds. Ahead, David Pearson was keeping his streaking Ford from bouncing into the fence by using Bobby Allison's Dodge as a buffer. They were in scraping contact all through the turn.

They were wild, woolly, and winning men, but a lap ahead of me and not my present problem. My present problem was closer to my level. Fireman Flynn had been running seventeenth, chasing Uncle Luke, when we'd changed drivers. He was now running sixteenth, and I was chasing him.

Joe Quade had worked his pit for years and Joe had once told me that Flynn hated to be crowded from the inside. It made him nervous and he would generally give ground. So I pressed a few more revs out of the Plymouth, and we closed in to get a better look at the Chev's left rear tire.

There was room to do it; Flynn's favorite groove seemed to be the center of the track. For two laps, I haunted him below. He kept looking back. He kept going wider on each turn.

And then, the third time he came into the grandstand turn, he moved too high. And as he started to slide I remembered my uncle's warning. Flynn had hit the slick spot Uncle Luke had told me about in the pit. He went pin-wheeling up the bank toward the rail.

I didn't have time to look back. There was traffic right in front of me that demanded my attention. There was a sickness in my stomach as I waited for the scream of the crowd above the roar of the engines that would tell me a car had gone over the rim.

The scream never came. Five laps later, I saw Flynn heading into the pit with a frayed tire. My nausea went away but not my memory of that Chev wheeling out of control at 170 miles an hour.

I was in the 187th lap when the winner got the checkered flag that afternoon, so Rheem's worry about the long route was over thirty miles shorter than he'd anticipated. I was in the 187th lap and in thirteenth place.

The ache in me was solid from the soles of my feet to the roots of my teeth. It took almost a full minute for me to unclench my hands from the steering wheel. I had improved our position by three places, I had helped to earn us twenty-seven hundred dollars—and I had made a decision.

# 10

■■■■■■■■■■■■■■■■■■■■■■■■■■■■■■■■■■■■■■■■■■

The low-bed trailer hauling the Hemi droned along behind our pickup. Art, Rheem, and Uncle Luke were
riding in the cab. Joe and I were lying on pads between
the tires and tools in the box, staring up at the fat Florida moon. We were on our way home with thirty-six
hundred dollars of NASCAR money.

"So you made a decision after Flynn's skid," Joe said.
"A decision about what?"

"About driving. And probably about winning—at this
level."

"Go on."

"There are things I can't do," I explained. "I can't take
advantage of a man's weakness. I can't use another
man's car as a guard rail to stay on the track. I don't
think I can drive like the winners drive and that could
lose us money, couldn't it?"

"I don't know. Let's take it piece by piece. What do

you mean, you can't take advantage of a man's weakness?"

"I used what I knew about Flynn to make him nervous. I could have killed him!"

"That thing of Flynn's, that's more than a weakness. That's a fear. And you shouldn't take advantage of a man's fears. What about a weakness in a man's strategy?"

"That's different," I admitted. "But that slam-bang driving, the way some of those hot dogs bounce off each other to get an advantage—I'll never be able to do that. But the big winners do."

"Some do, some don't," Joe said. "You finished ahead of a lot of slam-bang drivers today. You did a very nice job out there. Johnny, you drive the way you have to drive. I'm sure nobody on this team is going to complain."

"Well, maybe not— How did Junior finish?"

"Eighth." Joe chuckled. "But Al Downing finished thirty-seventh, and he drives the same way Junior does."

Not quite. Al was just as rough, but not as good. I said nothing.

Joe said, "Racing is dangerous enough. Making it personal makes it more dangerous."

"I know, Joe. Let's get some shut-eye."

We ate around two in the morning at a combination lunch room and filling station in Georgia. Then Joe and I took over the driving, while the others slept in the box. The money we saved on hotel bills would pay for all the gas we used at the race and on the road.

It was slow going between Nashville and Chattanooga, a steady light snow making the mountain roads treacherous. It was *some* change from the hot sands of Daytona Beach. Luckily, we had brought sleeping bags for the men in the box.

We wouldn't be going out to California for the February race at Ontario, so we had three weeks to get the drum of engines out of our aching ears. On March 7 we would be going to Virginia for a really hectic stock car scramble, the Richmond 500.

Richmond would be the first of the many short tracks we'd be visiting. Those short, paved ovals were the ones I feared the most and for the reasons I explained to Joe on the trip home from Daytona. There would be thirty powerful cars and thirty aggressive drivers on a track only a little more than half (.542) of a mile long. There just had to be, and there always was, a lot of grinding contact on a track that crowded.

Uncle Luke told us he didn't want to drive the entire five hundred laps; he would take the first two hundred. I had the feeling that it wasn't purely his decision. The rest of the team had probably talked it over with him after Joe had relayed my sentiments about rough driving. They wanted to condition me for situations we all knew would come up again and again this summer.

They picked the right race for it; it was bedlam on wheels, more like a demolition derby than a race. Mel Callen, the Memphis leadfoot, started it by scraping Al Downing in the first turn of the second lap.

It seemed accidental to me, but Al must have decided it was personal. On the third turn of the same lap, he cut downtrack without enough clearance and

**103**

took a piece of Mel's front fender with him. For the next five laps, they haunted each other, never more than two feet apart.

The big names were already in front, Petty, Dieringer, and Pearson. There was no contact there; there was no need for it—yet. But behind these three, the lesser lights were playing tag at 90 miles an hour.

Uncle Luke rode through it with the calm of a man who had gone through it often, which he had. While they were bumping, he was climbing. Both the speeds and our consumption of gas were lower than big track speeds, so our first stop was at two hundred laps. Uncle Luke turned the car over to me in twelfth place.

A track this size should have been closer to my experience than the broad curves of Daytona. I had improved our position there; I should do even better here.

That is what I kept telling myself as I picked my way between those clanging dogfights like a infantry scout edging his way through a mine field. Fighting cars take up more room than competing cars, and they are more likely to do the unexpected. On the track and on the highway, the unexpected can kill you.

Junior Jessup was running wheel to wheel with a heavily dented Ford from South Carolina, high on the rim of the third turn, as I barreled down the back-stretch. From that vantage point, I saw it all.

The Ford driver was not blameless. Though his car was above, almost scraping the rail, the moves he made were not intended simply to hold his groove. He was bumping; he was trying to intimidate Junior.

He had picked the wrong man. Junior had been leaning on the Ford all through the early half of the turn. Now, he put too much weight into it.

Half a dozen guard rail posts went flying through the air, and for one perilous second that battered Ford teetered on the brink of the high rim. It had lost most of its right side and both right tires. It was out of control.

It was the second the Ford paused on the rim that saved my skin. In the next second it had turned end for end and was rolling down the bank into the traffic behind me. I heard a crash and the crowd's scream and tasted the bitterness of gall in my throat.

For nine laps, we followed the pace car with the yellow flag at a steady 50 miles an hour. Most of the other drivers did as I did, they kept their eyes straight ahead as we moved wide to pass the three wrecked cars being removed from the beginning of the front stretch. We had seen the ambulance leave but I didn't know who was involved. Junior wasn't; he rode directly in front of me.

Actually, Junior was involved, but in a way I didn't know about at the time. And his involvement would involve me.

We had changed tires under the caution flag; I didn't come in again until after the four hundredth lap. I started to ask who and how many had been hurt, but Rheem shook his head and the others kept working, ignoring me. They were right. It wasn't the time to talk about it.

**105**

For ten laps after the green flag had sent us back into action, the field had seemed to take the lesson to heart. There was very little fender banging. Then some individual duels started up again and the clang of sheet metal was heard around the track.

Uncle Luke had turned the car over to me in twelfth place and I had hoped to improve on that. I didn't. Nor did I lose us any ground. We finished in twelfth place—but only thirteen cars were still running at the checkered flag.

"Good show," Rheem said. "Cool driving."

"I'll get hot," I said. "Patience!"

He shook his head. "Man, you sure hear things that aren't being said, lately!"

"Joke," I said. "A little sad joke. Who got hurt?"

"Only one seriously, believe it or not. The guy in the South Carolina Ford—Greg Halverson. He's still unconscious, last we heard."

I was at the water jug when a track attendant came to tell me I was wanted at the judges' stand.

"Who wants me?" I asked him on the way over. "Did I do something wrong?"

"I think you're wanted as a witness," he said. "I think it's about that Halverson-Jessup crash. Commissioner Woerner was watching the race and he's *unhappy!*"

There were administration offices below the stand, and Junior was sitting in the waiting room of one as we went through into the inner room. He winked at me.

John Sherman Woerner was one of NASCAR's most knowing commissioners and a man devoutly concerned about the future of the sport and the Association. He was a big man with a fierce face. He sat behind a desk too small for him and studied me. I felt like a bug on a pin.

"You saw it all, didn't you?" he opened.

"The Halverson-Jessup accident? Yes, sir."

"Jessup's a friend of yours, isn't he?"

"I know him."

"For some time," he added. "You were both in that league Duke Whitney organized, weren't you?"

"We were."

"Do you think you could judge him honestly?"

"I don't know what you mean, sir. I'm not a judge."

He inhaled heavily and held his breath for a second. "You saw it," he repeated. "Who was to blame?"

"I don't know," I said. "The track was full of cowboys, as you probably noticed. Jessup was crowding Halverson. Halverson was bumping Jessup. So far as I could see, they weren't doing anything a dozen other drivers weren't doing."

He frowned. "Halverson was bumping Jessup?"

"That's right. And not just to get clearance, either. They were both playing the same game a lot of the other drivers were. Only Jessup had the lower track. I guess that gave him the edge."

A silence. It grew.

Finally, I said, "How's Halverson now? Is he going to be all right?"

"We don't know yet. His condition is—fair. Are you Luke Pilgrim's son?"

"I'm his nephew."

"All right, Johnny, thank you. Will you tell Jessup to come in on your way out?"

I did as I was told. Junior didn't look worried. I tried to remember if I had ever seen Junior look worried. He winked at me again and went in to face the big man. I went back to the pit.

"What did the Commissioner want with you?" Rheem asked.

"A character reference for the Rookie of the Year. How much did we earn today?"

"Five hundred and seventy dollars. According to Art, if we don't eat on the way home, we'll break even on the trip."

"That's not much money," I said, "for a crowd this size."

"First place paid five thousand," he said. "Let's go. Everything's loaded."

My ears were still ringing. The smell of burned oil and burned rubber still hung in the air. The crowd was about half gone, filing out slowly. They'd had an exciting afternoon. Tomorrow, they'd go back to work as we would, away from the noise and the smell of competition. Away from the danger, too.

Rheem and I were riding in the box for the first part of the trip. As we snaked our way into the long line of cars leaving the infield, he said, "The Commissioner wanted your story on the accident, didn't he?"

"That's right. He halfway suggested that I might not give him the true story because I was a friend of Junior's. I told him both men were driving like the rest of those cowboys. I didn't rate Junior any worse than the others."

"He's not. That kind of driving bothers you, doesn't it?"

"Any mistreatment of an automobile bothers me. And it should bother you more. You're a better mechanic than I am."

Rheem smiled. "Driving a stock car 200 miles an hour in 103 degrees of heat—you don't call *that* mistreating it?"

"Not if it's necessary to win. But a man who has to bump to keep his traction or to scare off a challenger, well—I don't think he's learned his trade."

"So don't do it," Rheem said. "Run your own race, buddy. But could you smile once in a while? You never smile anymore."

"It's been a bad day. At today's speeds, I like a bigger track. I like enough room to let me steer clear of the cowboys. I'll smile next week."

We'd be traveling to the North Carolina Motor Speedway next week, to the sand hills near Rockingham where the track was banked and well paved and one full mile long.

Greg Halverson pulled through and Junior didn't lose his license. That was the good and the medium news that week. The bad news started as a sniffle on Monday and wound up with 101 degrees of fever on Wednesday. It happened to my Uncle Luke; he would not be going to Rockingham. My dad had two weeks of vacation due. He took four days of it to fill in our pit crew.

The burden was finally on *this* driver. I would be

responsible for the position of our car for a full five hundred miles, for more than four hours of constant competition.

I don't know why it didn't bother me. There must have been some inhalable optimism in that North Carolina air. I qualified the first day at a little better than 137 miles an hour. It would put us in one of the front rows, no lower than the third.

"You'd better wear blinders," Joe Quade suggested. "You'll be up at the head of the parade, surrounded by all those big names."

"They don't frighten me," I said. "I've got all their pictures—autographed."

Bobby Allison won the pole the same day with a lap at 26.329 seconds. That read out to 139.048 miles an hour. Tomorrow's qualifiers would start in the last half of the field, despite their lap times. There would be forty late-model sedans answering the green flag Sunday and most of them would start behind our proud Hemi.

In the pit Saturday morning, Rheem said, "Glad to see you're finally smiling."

"I feel good. I thought it would bother me, knowing Uncle Luke couldn't help out. But I feel good."

"Keep smiling," he said. "Here comes Junior."

Junior Jessup was coming over to our pit from his and he looked serious for a change. "I want to thank you," he said.

"For what?"

"For putting in a good word to the Commissioner for me. For saving my license."

"I didn't. All I said was that you were no worse than a lot of the others."

Now, he smiled. "You know what I like about you? You pretend to be the easygoer, Gentleman Johnny, but you're as competitive as the rest of us. Maybe more."

"If you say so, Junior. I wouldn't argue with a man your size. How are you getting along with Duke?"

"He's learned not to argue with me, too." A pause. "Let's be serious. I came here to thank you and I do."

"You're welcome," I said. "I only needle you to prove your point. I'm just as competitive as you are. But all men don't travel the same road, Junior."

"More or less," he said. "They all lead to the grave. Well, luck, Johnny."

"And to you."

Rheem chuckled as Junior walked away. "I think he won. He had the best tag line."

"Talking's his long suit," I explained. "I'm a driver."

So was Junior. I knew it now and he had always known it.

# 11

▰▰▰▰▰▰▰▰▰▰▰▰▰▰▰▰▰▰▰▰▰▰▰▰▰▰▰▰▰▰▰▰▰

Rockingham was a high point. It was the Sunday, I suppose, when the team built up hopes for the season that were dimmed in the Sundays that followed. I still don't know what the magic was. We all know days when everything goes right and days when nothing goes right. This was one of the lucky days.

I started in the second row, in the middle of six cars. In four of those cars were drivers who had each won over a hundred thousand dollars last year, Bobby Allison, Pete Hamilton, Richard Petty, and Bobby Isaac. Lee Roy Yarbrough, in the fifth car, had won twice that much.

For a yellow bumper pilot, this was heady company, but I didn't need the blinders. They were no closer now than they were in the pits, and I wasn't arrogant enough to think they would be this close after the first lap.

Actually, it was about a tenth of a lap. Three seconds

after I saw the green flag drop, I was practically alone in the first turn. I knew their cars were no faster. Either they had quicker vision or they knew how to anticipate the flag without fouling the start.

I wasn't alone for long. There were thirty-four hungry drivers behind us scrambling for more running room. I felt like a rabbit in front of a herd of stampeding buffalo. And I ran like one. Or rather, the Hemi did. She had never sounded happier.

At the head of the field, the big money stars gave their audience the show those people had traveled from all over the South to see. Behind them, I fought it out with my peers on a track I liked in cool weather behind an engine singing a sweet soprano.

Don't read me wrong; it wasn't all roses. Traveling 500 miles at 2 miles a minute takes all the energy a healthy man has. But the first hundred miles was a vacation and the last hundred was run in sparse traffic. It was a day too many drove too fast too soon. Yarbrough, Allison, and Petty all went out with mechanical breakdowns before half the race was run. Pete Hamilton and Bobby Isaac put on a duel for the top spot that is still being talked about.

I had most of my trouble with Al Downing. He hadn't done well at Daytona but he had come back to take a ninth at Richmond. Like the rest of us, he seemed to enjoy this track. He had that Dodge honking today. In the thirtieth lap or so, he moved up behind me to draft.

That was fine with me. Drafting saves gas for *both* cars and cuts down the strain on the engine. When the draft is broken, though, the change in wind resistance and rear turbulence will immediately affect the performance of both cars. Al knew that. He might have figured that if he broke the draft when I least suspected it, he'd have an edge.

It was only a guess but close enough to his general technique to keep me alerted. There we were, two yellow bumper rookies, traveling 120 miles an hour only inches apart. That was the way we rode for almost twenty laps.

Then, coming into the grandstand lane, sweeping out of the turn, something spooked me or I might have seen something too quick for the mind to record. Whatever the reason, I *knew* he was about to break the draft. I floored—and pulled high.

In my mirror I saw his Dodge react as though it had run into a wall of water. My own car shuddered at the sudden change in engine load, but Al got double that reaction. He had taken his foot off the accelerator in order to break the draft from behind. We must have gained twenty-five feet on him in the next fifty. He was still only halfway through the front stretch as we sailed into the bend.

Al is not a man who takes a defeat in strategy lightly. He was crowding us two laps later. And then he drifted below to lean on me, as I had on Fireman Flynn, as Junior had on Greg Halverson. He didn't bump, he didn't scrape. He just hung there, like a spider over a bed.

We weren't full out. It was too early in the race for that. I was setting a pace that seemed right at the time, barely fast enough to stay in contention. I had a better tuned engine than Al's so it was possible he was hanging there only because he didn't have enough torque to get past. But we had been traveling at the same speed when he had caught up to us from behind.

It wasn't a situation I enjoyed. We moved a few revs higher and the Dodge kept pace. Now I knew it wasn't any lack under the hood that was keeping him in our shadow. It had to be some strategy I didn't understand. I hated to change my own long-range strategy out of annoyance; I kept the pace.

In the sixtieth lap, oil was spilled on the third turn from a ruptured cooler and we got the yellow while the area was sanded. I went to the pit for a twenty-two-second stop and lost Al for about three laps after coming out again.

We were running hub and hub with a Chev from Evansville when I saw the Dodge again in my mirror. We had about a quarter-lap lead when I spotted them. They were again out of sight five laps later. Al was doing me a favor by haunting me. A third of the way through the race, I was running in seventh place.

It didn't even feel unnatural being this close to the front in such fast company, not today. It had to be the Carolina air. Though the early pressure of Al Downing helped. And luck played its part, as it must. There always seemed to be a yellow flag waving when I needed gas or a tire. That was some day, that March Sunday at Rockingham. We finished in fifth place and picked up twenty-three hundred dollars.

It was the longest stretch I had ever driven in competition, 475 miles, and I was a weary man at the finish, but no more tired than I had been after 230 miles on a much roomier track at Daytona. As the song says, it was just one of those days. I was glad my dad was there to see it.

He rode in the box with me on the first leg of our trip home. And the mysterious strategy of Al Downing was cleared up.

"I noticed he was camping in your hair," my dad told me, "and Mark Ryer was over at the refreshment stand when I went to get a hamburger. So I asked him about it. I guess this Downing thinks you've inherited your uncle's sense of pace. He's running the same cubes you are so he decided that today you would be his pacemaker."

"Why did he try to break the draft, then?"

"I don't think he did," my father said. "I think he backed off a little, coming out of that corner, just as you pulled wide. You really shook him up!"

"I was trying to."

My father smiled. "That's not your game. You were only guessing at his strategy. Maybe you misjudged him."

My father, like his brother, wanted to believe the best about everybody. My father, unlike his brother, had never seen Al drive before today. I didn't argue.

Rockingham was a bright spot. The first of the darker Sundays started in Bristol, Tennessee, another short but fast track. Uncle Luke wanted me to handle most of it. He was still weak from his fight with the flu. And furthermore, he explained half seriously, *he* had never finished as high as fifth at Rockingham.

We didn't even finish at Bristol, cracking a piston in the twenty-third lap. We figured to do better, easily, at Atlanta.

The Atlanta International Raceway is shorter than Daytona but, like Daytona, every inch of it is first class. The turns are banked 24 degrees and even the straight-aways have a slight bank. It's a mile and a half long, set in 502 acres, about twenty miles south of Georgia's proudest city. The cool weather we had picked up in Rockingham was still with us and the optimism I had felt at Rockingham came back.

"You're smiling again," Rheem said.

"We've got room to run, here. And room to hide, too, when the cowboys come gunning. We should get solvent again."

"We are solvent," Rheem informed me. "We've salted enough to carry us through four more races, even if we don't win a dime."

"Im glad to hear that," Joe Quade said. "Old Poor Mouth Parent has been complaining about my meal checks."

"With reason," Rheem said. "We can't believe you grew up eating steak three times a day."

"I didn't. But a man's entitled to a few extra comforts in his middle years. Ain't that right, Luke?"

"I guess," my uncle said. "I'll know better when I get to be your age."

We were cheerful, we were joking, we were optimistic. The cracked piston hadn't damaged the cylinder wall; the Hemi was as sound as ever. Young Uncle Luke had his strength back and we had money enough for four more trips.

Uncle Luke thought I should drive the qualifying lap, which I did, averaging a little better than 151 miles an hour. It didn't put us up with the stars, but it put us in the front half of the forty-car field. The pole sitter had missed 160 miles an hour by a whisper, clocking a hot 159.929.

I slept without dreams Saturday night. I had the same happy feeling about the Atlanta 500 as I'd had at Rockingham. Sunday, I was certain, was going to be a day to remember.

It was a day we remembered—for all the wrong reasons. It started at breakfast with cold and rancid leftover coffee. The restaurant had an electric kitchen and there had been a power failure in the area. Then the truck had a flat tire on the way to the track and a light rain began to fall. The rain stopped around eleven o'clock, but we were well soaked by then.

When the forty-car field lined up for the start that afternoon, I guess it would be accurate to say we weren't quite as cheerful as we had been yesterday—but I was almost as optimistic.

Two-thirds of the field started behind us; more than two-thirds were behind us when Uncle Luke made his first pit stop. It was a strong field and I thought he had driven a little faster than his sharp sense of pace approved of. I also thought he looked tighter than usual.

So did Joe. "He's pushing it. After your show at Rockingham, he probably thinks he's been letting us down. I don't like it, Johnny."

"Neither do I," Art said. "I warned him to let up a little."

"I guess he didn't hear you," Rheem said. "Look at those tires smoke!"

Puffs of smoke spurted from both right-side tires as our Hemi streaked through the first turn. This was not the Luke Pilgrim we were used to seeing out there. It made me nervous. Reaction time slows with age. If a tight situation should develop suddenly. . . .

Art had the watch on him. Two laps later, he announced: "If it was anyone else but your uncle, I'd have him flagged in for consultation."

There were two things that afternoon that combined for the calamity. But the worst thing, the thing I feared, didn't happen. So there was that silver lining to the cloud. My uncle did not run into a dangerous situation; that was the lining.

The sun came out about a quarter of the way through the race, bringing the seasonal Georgia heat with it. And Uncle Luke didn't cut his speed. Those were the two factors that combined for the calamity.

He burned up that sweet Hemi engine only two laps before he was due to turn the car over to me. He was running in second place at the time and crowding Bobby Allison for the lead.

There wasn't much dialogue in the pit. Nobody wanted to tell my uncle he had been driving too fast. I think we all must have realized that there comes a time when a man gets fed up with being thought of as a stubborn, steady performer with a sense of pace. I think every man who ever put on that fireproof jumper dreams of the day when he will be fighting Bobby Allison for the top spot in a big one.

My uncle had had his day. He looked unhappy but not ashamed.

The engine was a total loss, but we had two more. Joe and Uncle Luke spent the next week installing one of them. Rheem and I helped out when we weren't working at the station or the garage.

We had her all together in time but not in shape for Talladega. That's in Alabama, a superspeedway, and the posted awards exceeded a hundred and twenty thousand dollars. The dynamometer showed us the trip would be a waste of time. The engines were supposed to be identical. No two engines ever were.

Art Parent, the ignition genius, left his busy garage for a day and came down to find our trouble. Only a metallurgist would know why, but the brand new cables we'd installed weren't delivering the voltage they were supposed to be carrying. We changed them.

Back to the dynamometer. We had almost the same power curve the old engine had shown. This one peaked a few revs higher. On the Grand National circuit, no race is shorter than 250 miles. So we really didn't need any low-speed torque. This engine should do better than the original.

At North Wilkesboro, in that fine Carolina air once again, we had our first test of the substitute engine in the Gwyn Staley Memorial. Yours truly was now the official driver of the team. Uncle Luke had decided (almost) to retire. Unless, of course, there was an emergency call. . . .

North Wilkesboro is in the foothills of the Blue Ridge Mountains. The earliest (and shady) traditions of stock car racing came from these hills, as the bootleggers souped up their cars to run from the revenuers.

It's beautiful country and the speedway there is probably the fastest short track on the NASCAR circuit.

The track was fast, the car was right—but I wasn't. It was my Calhoun Corners of the big circuit; it was a track where I didn't feel at home. Because of television coverage, prize money was better than usual, paid all the way to the bottom. Nobody still running at the checkered flag finished *that* low. I was still running. I finished nineteenth, the last of the cars still running.

At Martinsville, Virginia, the distributor shaft snapped in the twelfth lap. By the time we were back in action, we were out of the important action.

Professionals try not to brood; I tried to think of this Sunday as only one of many. I tried not to think of it as the third bad Sunday in a row.

Darlington was next, the first long track since Atlanta, a track where a man had room to move. The pattern would change. The pattern would have to change. We were running out of money.

Darlington's in South Carolina, in the middle of the tobacco and cotton country. The track was built by men of vision, men who decided way back in 1949 that stock car racing had a future, men who were laughed at in 1950 when they staged the first Southern 500.

There were seventy-five cars in that first race. Thirty thousand fans filled every available inch of spectator space. It was the birth of big-time stock car racing in America.

A few decades later, yours truly, Johnny Pilgrim, didn't even get to start the race, blowing a clutch in his qualifying round.

# 12

Rheem and Art decided we should miss the race at Charlotte. It made sense to me. The next three after that would be out of the South, in Michigan, California, and Texas. That meant we'd have a rest we needed and a chance to get our attitudes reversed. We'd want to be thinking positively again before the big Firecracker 400 at Daytona on the Fourth of July.

What I didn't learn until late June was that Art didn't want to make the long trip to Daytona. After Darlington, Art had decided that it would be better to save what was left of the bankroll by making only the short trips for the rest of the season. Unless, of course, we began to show a profit again.

"Luke and I want to go to Daytona," Rheem explained. "Joe and Art favor the short trips only. How about you?"

"What is this, a vote?"

"More or less."

The burden's on the driver. . . . I said, "Art put up most of the money. Maybe we ought to—"

"Stop!" Rheem said sharply. "We don't owe Art or anybody else on this team any special treatment. We're all in this together. And anybody who wants to can drop out."

"Okay," I said. "I'll vote for Daytona. Our luck just has to get better, doesn't it?"

"We won't need much luck to finish in the top ten," Rheem said. "And that should win us enough to pay for the trip."

"You make it sound like an order," I said. "I'll do the best I can, boss."

It was a cold yardstick to measure our actions by, money, money, money. Racing was supposed to be a sport. We had our business in Shale. This wasn't the only sport where men were rated by their annual winnings. In golf it has overshadowed the traditional and honorable Vardon trophy list. In most spectator sports, the salaries at contract time get more sport-page publicity than the records of the athletes.

These are the thoughts I voiced to Joe in the box of the truck on the way to Daytona.

Joe grinned. "You trying to make me feel bad? You think Art and I don't love racing?"

I must have blushed. I felt like I should have. "I never thought of the—the vote, Joe, honestly— It was—"

"Don't get fussed," he said. "I know that Art's having money problems right now, with the market the way it's been and all. But the reason we wanted to stick with the nearby tracks was the same reason you wanted to go to Daytona; we like racing. We just wanted to make sure we'd be solvent enough to stay in it."

The burden's on the driver. . . . I said, "I almost hope we crack another piston. Then I won't be the one responsible for finishing off the bankroll."

"Nothing's going to crack at Daytona," Joe assured me. "Including you."

If you think Daytona is hot in January, you should visit it in July. There's always a breeze from the ocean, the natives will tell you, and they're right. It helps to keep the temperature under 100, at times.

Cale Yarborough didn't seem to be bothered by the heat. He won the pole in his Mercury with a 191.640 qualifying lap. All the first-day times were fast; the Hemi and I earned eighth place. If we could finish where we started, the trip would be considered a success in the ledger and could be entered in black ink. Why isn't that exciting?

Both Allison brothers were here, Bobby in a Dodge, Donnie in a Ford. They would be my nearest competitors at the green flag. Genial Junior Jessup had a better qualifying time than most of us, but he qualified the second day and that put him behind us—at the start. There were some other tigers behind us for the same reason, Buddy Baker and the Yarbrough without the extra *o*, Lee Roy.

And there was the man who had pushed me to the fifth-place finish at Rockingham, cowboy Al Downing.

He and Mark and another man from their team joined our table at the cafeteria for breakfast the morning of the race.

"I expected to see you at Charlotte," he said. "What happened?"

"We're running on a tight budget and we decided to skip it. Thanks for the assist at Rockingham. You were really haunting me."

"Mark explained that to your dad, didn't he?"

"Yup. I had no idea I was one of your models. I thought Junior Jessup was your hero."

"I admire your sense of pace," he said easily. "I admire his nerve."

"Today," I said, "you can admire the yellow color of my rear bumper."

"I probably won't see it unless I'm lapping you. I figured I'd use Bobby Isaac as my pacemaker today."

Later, when he got up to go, he said, "Well, luck, Johnny."

"To you, too," I said. "I hope we're both still running 160 laps from now."

He wasn't. In the twelfth lap he crashed the retaining wall in the backstretch—and spent the next two and a half weeks in a Daytona hospital.

The Allison brothers decided my area was not the proper neighborhood for stars. So at the green flag they zoomed up to where their friends were waiting for them.

The yellow flag in the twelfth lap let me join them again. We must have been moving faster than normal to stay in the same lap. It was hot, though, and the race was young. They could have been playing it cagier than usual.

They took off again when the green light went on. I didn't. Art had discovered a new radiator coolant that seemed to be keeping that engine cooler than usual, all factors considered. But the memory of Uncle Luke in the heat of Atlanta still colored my thinking.

*"I admire your sense of pace. I admire his nerve."* The man who'd said that was on his way to the hospital. By *nerve* had he meant *courage?* Nobody on this track lacked that or he wouldn't be on this track. That was a fact as clear as Kentucky spring water. But there are many roads to a goal. Junior had an answer to that one. This was not the time to think of *his* answer.

Our first stop was in the fortieth lap. "Fine, fine, fine," Rheem said. "Ninth place man! Solid!"

"She's perking," I told him. "This engine's finally right."

"Good. Easy does it, You know—*cool!*"

"You're the boss," I said. "Good-bye."

I hadn't been able to risk waiting for a yellow. We dropped to eleventh place in those twenty-one seconds. But both Neil Castles, riding tenth, and Wendell Scott, riding ninth, had also waited too long. When they went to the pits we were back to only one place slower than where we had started the race. There had been only three challenges from behind, one of them successful.

With the exception of Wendell Scott, all the names

were still in front of us, so far as I could judge. But Junior hadn't passed us on the track or while we were pitted. Maybe he had traded in his nerve for a sense of pace. Usually, he'd be heckling the big boys by now.

I had borrowed a trick from the basketball players, wearing sweat bands on my wrists to keep my hands dry. They were soaked and useless by the fiftieth lap and I tore them off. On a slightly cooler day, I would try them again.

According to the board, the leader in the seventy-fifth lap was Dodge Number 6, piloted by Buddy Baker. He had never passed me. That had to mean that almost halfway through the race we were still in the same lap as the leader! It didn't seem logical to me that a car in ninth place would be in the same lap as the leader almost halfway through the race.

It seemed more logical a lap later when I was streaking through the front stretch. Because in my mirror I saw a Dodge that looked like Buddy's and there were at least a half dozen cars chasing him, close enough to be covered by a midget's pup tent. And they were all getting bigger by the second.

What did it matter? If they all lapped me, I would still be in ninth place. If they all passed me and I kept this pace I found so comfortable, wouldn't I prove to Art Parent that the trip to Florida had been wise. What did it matter?

It mattered. Man cannot live by bread (money) alone. Even Joe would agree to that; he was a steak man. *Miss Hemi*, I said, *I don't mean to mistreat you in this heat but we are going to have to do better than this.*

I didn't actually voice it. I explained it with my right foot on the accelerator. This new engine was now better than the old one and I knew it. The man who had made it better, Art Parent, would have been content to see us finish ninth. I liked Art, but I had more important missions in my young life than making him happy. We had come a long way without strain; with only a little strain, we should be able to go much further.

I swung up to the rim, my favorite groove at Daytona, and set sail. The thundering herd behind was no smaller in the mirror. The thought came to me that the rim was the long way around. It was possible the cars behind weren't going any faster than I was but were on a shorter route. So I came down again to midtrack.

The same depressing situation prevailed; we didn't gain an inch. And then the lady took over again, Lady Luck. Harry Carter had an engine seizure and his locked rear wheels sent him bouncing up against the wall in the front stretch. The yellow came out and we went to the pits, one gallon shy of empty. So did the thundering herd.

Twenty-nine seconds later, when we came out, the yellow was still in command; the pace car led us all around at a sedate 70 miles an hour.

The leaders came out in a bunch, still in the same lap as we were. But now, instead of a two and three-eighths mile lead, they had only a hundred foot lead on us, due to a rule I thought unfair—until today.

And now they were not crowding us. We were crowding them.

The way I saw it, one more pit stop would carry us

through this race. The way I saw it, these stars I had always held in awe weren't much better than I was, today. Or maybe their cars weren't. We had a chance to do something more exciting than putting black ink in a ledger.

That was the way my mind was working, dreaming about the stars I might have a chance to catch. While from behind, some stars of the future were moving up, including one named Junior Jessup.

Buddy Baker was the man I was studying, trailing him by less than fifty feet, watching his lines, looking for flaws. He didn't have any flaws that I could notice. But I kept watching him.

I was watching him extra carefully when Junior charged up from behind and slid by me. I was still watching Buddy when Junior went by *him*. If I had come here to watch, I should have bought a ticket and sat in the stands. I forgot about Buddy and went after Junior.

He was logging. I didn't lose any ground. We went past some cars. Whether they were in the same lap or not was something I didn't know. I knew one of them was, Buddy Baker. That meant we had to be at least eighth.

At 116 laps, the yellow flashed again. There had been a two-car collision on the grandstand turn, and it looked like a two-lap yellow to me. I took a chance on this being our last pit stop.

"Aren't you crowding it a little?" Rheem asked.

"Yes."

He stared at me.

"Any complaints?" I asked.

He shook his head, speechless for a change.

I suppose it was arrogance. I suppose it was knot-headed. But I was sick of racing against a ledger.

"You're in sixth place," he told me.

I said nothing. The new tires were on, the car jolted to the ground and we were gunning back to the track, still under the yellow.

I moved up close to Junior, two feet back of him and below him. He waved and grinned. Junior loved this. He raced against people, not ledgers.

The green light flashed and the green flag waved and we were back at it, man to man. Racing shouldn't be personal, I'd been told. It *had* to be personal, man against man, car against car. There should be no animosity, but it had to be personal.

I knew Junior's strengths and I knew his weaknesses and I'm sure he knew mine. We moved hub to hub, wheel to wheel, and never once did he make contact. He might have figured he owed me that because of my good words to the Commissioner. But a better guess would be that Junior Jessup tailored his attack to match the competition and he knew I was no cowboy.

We passed some names in that drive, the Allisons and Bobby Isaac and young Jim Hylton and Richard Brooks. They were names to reckon with, but so were we, that hot Fourth of July at Daytona.

I watched the gas and I watched the engine temperature and I tried to figure out a way to get past Junior

Jessup. The accountant's goal of finishing high enough to break even was forgotten. Junior was my goal, not breaking even.

We were cutting 47-second laps and neither car showed one inch of advantage. We came down on the white flag so close no timer in the country could have clocked the difference. But there was no doubt that Junior had the edge.

And then, on the last turn, he pressed one degree beyond his best judgment and his rear end began to climb. He had the strength to pull it back in line but it had cost him half a car length.

That's what we beat him by, that Fourth of July at Daytona.

In our pit, they were all noisy, all but Rheem.

"First, first, first," Uncle Luke kept repeating.

"Who'd have thought it?" Joe said. "Twenty-three thousand dollars! That should keep us on the road. You won twenty-three thousand dollars, man!"

Rheem knew what I was thinking and he voiced it for both of us. "He won more than twenty-three thousand dollars," Rheem said. "He won a race."

WILLIAM CAMPBELL GAULT shares his keen interest in sports with teen-agers through his many books. He brings to life the competitive struggle, suspense, and realities of car racing, football, golf, horse racing, and baseball. At the same time he reveals characters and relationships that give each of his books a very special human appeal.

Among Mr. Gault's many and varied books for young people are: *Quarterback Gamble, The Oval Playground, Through the Line, Backfield Challenge, The Long Green, The Lonely Mound,* and *Stubborn Sam.*

Mr. Gault lives in Santa Barbara, California, where he devotes his working hours to writing and his leisure time to golf.

# FAERY TALES & NIGHTMARES

Also by
# MELISSA MARR

melissa marr

FAERY TALES
&
NIGHTMARES

**HARPER**

*An Imprint of HarperCollinsPublishers*

*To the Rathers*
*(aka the wonderful readers*
*on the WickedLovely.com fan site),*
*who've been such a joy to me*
*these past several years.*

*Thank you for conversations,*
*teas, and fab art.*

# Contents

# INTRODUCTION

*I*T'S NOT ALWAYS AS EASY TO SEE THE PATH when you're on it, but looking back is often much clearer. In 2004, I wrote a short story, "The Sleeping Girl," that turned into a novel (*Wicked Lovely*) that evolved into a series. At the time, I was homeschooling my kids, reading adventure with my son and YA books with my daughter, and still teaching university. A few years before that, I'd taught two defining courses. One was called "Girlhood Narratives." It started with fairy tales and worked forward into novels. The second was simply called "The Short Story." In retrospect, it's pretty easy to see that my children and my teaching were influential in writing the fairy tale that started my career.

Since then, I've continued to mix fairy tales and folklore together in novels and short stories. They're scattered in anthologies, ebook-only editions, and special editions of my novels, so I figured it might be nice to have some of them together in one book.

Well over half of these pages are taken up by Wicked Lovely world stories; the rest of the pages are reserved for other worlds. These are stories pulled from lore and nightmares, set in places I've visited and places I've imagined. In the tales, you'll find a selchie story influenced by Solana Beach, CA; a tale of vampires inspired by parties I once went to in a dead-end town I won't name; a goblin encounter set in the woods where I once picked berries; and a tale of dark contentment in a mountain town that owes a debt of gratitude to a Violent Femmes song I love. Of course, you'll also spend time with the Wicked Lovely faeries who have lived in my head and my novels since 2004. I hope you enjoy them.

# WHERE
# NIGHTMARES
# WALK

THE GREEN GLOW OF EYES AND SULFUROUS breath shimmer in the fog as the Nightmares come into range. The horses' steel-sharp hooves rip furrows in the field, trampling everything in their path.

"Over here!" my companion dog calls out to them, exposing me.

I didn't know he could speak, but there is no mistaking the source of the sound—or the fact that I am trapped in a field with Nightmares bearing down upon me.

The dog shakes, and his glamour falls away like water flung from his fur. Under his disguise, my helpmate is a skeletal beast with holes where its eyes should be.

"*Run*," it growls, "so we can chase."

I want to, but much like the rest of the things I want my legs to do, running is no longer an option. If

I could still run, I wouldn't be alone on the night when Nightmares walk free. If I could still run, I'd be out in costume trick-or-treating with my friends.

"I can't run."

I hobble toward an oak that stands like a shadow in the fog.

The monstrous dog doesn't stop me as I drop my crutches and pull myself onto the lowest branch. It doesn't stop me as I try to heave myself higher.

"Faster!" it calls out to the Nightmares, which are almost upon me.

The only question left to answer is whether their running or my climbing is quicker.

# WINTER'S KISS

ONCE—A LONG TIME AGO BEFORE CHANGE had come—there was a girl whose father was a king. Now, this was when there were a great many kings, so Nesha did not think it strange to be the daughter of a king. And though she had no brothers or sisters, Princess Nesha was happy—but for one thing. Nesha had within her the kiss of winter. When she sighed, her breath rolled out in an icy chill. When she blew a kiss to her father across their great hall, frost flowers formed on every dish.

In winter, Nesha could drape snows over every hill without fear, but in the summer, if she forgot herself and blew the white tops of dandelions gone to seed, if she laughed too freely and her cold breath spilled out, she would wither whole fields, blighting the crops her people needed to survive.

Her father built her a great tower with no windows

through which her cold breath could escape, but Nesha wept at being alone and enclosed.

So Nesha left her tower and sought out her father in the great hall. Gazing at the fields she could see through the tall window before her, she said, "I do not belong in this place with its long months of warmth and sun."

Though he knew she was right, the king wept, for he loved his daughter. "Nesha, stay. We can find a way."

She turned and rested her head against her father's shoulder, thinking of the windowless room and months indoors, of trying not to laugh for fear of the cold air that slipped through her lips. "No. I must go."

The king's warm tears fell onto her cheek, but he said nothing.

Nesha did not sigh or weep; she gazed out the window at the new plants in the fields, wondering why she had been cursed so cruelly.

The next morning the king walked his daughter to the edge of the wood. He held her only briefly. "Be safe."

After a few silent tears, Nesha clutched her staff and strode off into the dark wood.

She traveled for many days. One evening as she sat on a felled tree, she let her eyes drift closed. She imagined the icy rim that encircled the northernmost edge of the land, hoping she would soon reach it, and worrying she would not find welcome once she did.

When she opened her eyes, a great ice-bear stood before her. The bear lay down at her feet, his fur glistening as if he had been bathed in precious oils.

"What are *you* doing here?" she murmured, her voice trembling only a bit.

As Nesha looked into his eyes, she saw her own nervousness reflected there, and her fear disappeared like frost under a spring sun. "Are you lonely too?"

So she closed her eyes and exhaled gently—giving the bear thick snow upon which to rest.

The ice-bear stretched out in the snow and stared up at her until she climbed from the log and sat next to him.

She opened her pack and drew out a piece of thick meat. She broke off a small piece for herself, then offered the rest of the meat to the bear.

The ice-bear gently accepted the meat from her hand.

"Perhaps we can be lonely together." Nesha lay down to rest alongside the bear in their pile of snow.

When Nesha awoke the next morn, she found that the bear had curled around her, holding her body close to his furred limbs.

After a small meal, Nesha readied herself to travel.

The ice-bear lay flat in front of Nesha and glanced at her. He tossed his head toward his back.

Nesha ran her hand over his thick pelt. Then, she stepped past him. "Come. If you're to travel with me, we must be off."

The ice-bear bounded past Nesha, and once again lay prostrate before her.

She laughed and stepped past him once more. "We'll not get far if we stop to play."

For the third time the ice-bear leaped before her— this time, though, when he stretched his great length across the path, his body spanned the space between two boulders. She could not walk around him.

Grumbling, Nesha began to climb over him, but once she was atop his back, he stood.

"Oh," she murmured, awed that such a great beast would carry her. She was still tired from her days of walking, so she said, "For a short while, I suppose there's no harm in it."

So, atop the ice-bear, Nesha journeyed through the forest. The only sounds were the rippling of waters and the cries of creatures in the dense canopy overhead. A solitary owl called out from a hidden perch; squirrels chattered in their secret language. And despite her worries, Nesha felt joy as the bear ambled under pine boughs and outstretched branches.

Eventually, though, the ice-bear paused and lay flat.

Nesha slid to the ground. Beside her were thick berry brambles, heavy with fruit. With his muzzle, the ice-bear gently nudged her toward the fruit.

"I see." She smiled and began to pick the berries.

As she did so, the ice-bear clambered down the embankment to the swirling river. With his massive paws he pulled fish from the current.

Nesha glanced at the bear standing in the cold water, gathering food. "What a wise beast you are!"

After a while, the ice-bear had not returned up the hill, so Nesha put away the fruit she had collected and went to the top of the muddy embankment. Below her, she saw the bear looking first at the fish he'd caught and then gazing up the hill.

*He has no way to carry them,* she realized. Gingerly, she climbed down the slope, gripping tiny saplings for balance as she went.

"Let me," she said, peering into the bear's eyes.

Then she blew softly on the fish, freezing them so they were easier to grasp, and wrapped them into a cloth from her pack.

The ice-bear brushed her shoulder with his muzzle in what she now knew as a friendly gesture. Then, unable to stretch out on the briar-heavy riverside, the ice-bear bent so Nesha could scramble up again.

Once she was seated, the bear rapidly climbed up the hill and resumed their path, and Nesha absently stroked her fingers through his soft fur—thankful to have a companion on her journey.

And thus Nesha forgot the sorrow of carrying a curse. Together, she and the ice-bear found a rhythm to their travels, stopping to gather food when the chance presented itself and continuing on through the still forest.

Though she thought often of her home and her father, after traveling together for a full moon's passing, Nesha could scarcely imagine life without her ice-bear. In the evenings, they curled in a snowy nest she made for them. During the day, she traveled upon his soft fur and gazed at the increasingly cold land. Tall trees dotted the ground, and the river had a growing crust of ice upon it.

"I've never seen anything so lovely," she whispered.

The ice-bear glanced back at her, with a soft almost-growl, and continued on his way.

Nesha knew the ice-bear was unusual, but as they traveled onward she realized that the ice-bear followed a definite path. When Nesha thought to suggest another way, the ice-bear plopped down and refused to move.

One night after they neared the colder lands, the bear led her to a cave. Inside the cave, spires hung like ice from above; water trickled in rivulets down those stalactites. Nesha whispered, "Where do we go? Do you take me to your home?"

The bear simply gazed at her.

"Will there be others there? What if they aren't as kind as you?" She leaned against the ice-bear.

The bear moved closer; his muzzle pressed against her shoulder.

"I'm sorry," she murmured as she stroked his head. She closed her eyes. "You've been truly wonderful, but I miss human voices. I miss . . ."

Nesha paused. The thick pelt under her hand no longer felt right. Instead of coarse fur, her hand rested on silk-soft hair. She jerked her hand away and opened her eyes.

A boy stood beside her. His hair was as dark as the night sky; it was so long that it fell like a heavy blanket touching the earth, hiding a human form.

"Where? Who?" Nesha stepped backward, her words tangled as she stared at the boy. Frantically, she looked for her ice-bear.

"I knew no other way to show you," the boy was saying. He had not made any movement toward her. "Now that we've reached my village—"

"Village?" Nesha looked around her.

From the tunnels other ice-bears, including several cubs, approached.

The boy nodded. "My home . . ."

"Where is my ice-bear?" Nesha knew the answer, but she needed to hear him say the words.

"I'm here." The boy took a step toward her, hands outstretched. He was clad in clothes made of a heavy brown cloth, decorated with ivory beads. Over this he wore a fur cloak. "I caught the fish we eat." He gestured toward the still-glowing embers on the cave floor where she had cooked their meal. "I carried you through the rains and over the gorge."

"You are a boy."

"I am." He smiled tentatively. "And I am the beast who slept in the nests of ice and snow that you made.

My people are not bound to one form. . . . I am called Bjarn."

Nesha sat down. What he said was stranger than anything she'd ever heard, but as he moved, she knew it to be true. The boy-who-was-a-bear tilted his head a bit when she spoke to him, just as the ice-bear had. The startling black eyes that stared from the boy's face were the same eyes that had peered at her each morning when she woke. Bjarn spoke the truth.

Nesha wasn't sure what question to ask first. "Why travel with me? Why bring me here?"

For a moment, Bjarn stood silently. When he spoke, his voice was rough. "The lands grow warmer. My people struggle with the heat; the months when the cold seems to grow less cause such sickness." Bjarn sat down in front of her and took her hands. "Your gift . . . it would bring such peace to my people. The eldest suffer when the warmth grows too much. I am not skilled with words. I thought if I could bring you to my father, he would know what to say." Bjarn looked at the other bears and then back at her. "Will you stay awhile with us?"

Nesha imagined people cherishing her cursed breath, a life where she was not feared. "And if I wanted to return home in the coldest months?"

Bjarn looked solemn as he said, "I would carry you there if you wished. Or if you'd rather, there are others who could carry you."

As she considered what Bjarn had said, Nesha gazed at the waiting group of bears. Most sat nestled in the rocky crevices, but a couple wrestled with the cubs. She looked back at Bjarn. Though his form was different, Bjarn was the same kind creature he'd been as an ice-bear. "I would have *you* travel with me."

"I would like that very much." Smiling, Bjarn pulled her to her feet.

Clutching his hand in hers, she turned toward the mouth of the tunnels. "Can I meet them?"

He grinned and waved at the ice-bears. One of the largest ambled forward first.

"My grandmother stays in this form almost always since the snows are so brief." Bjarn rested his face on the great bear's head in a hug of sorts. "She had heard the stories whispered of you, of your gift, and so I traveled to find you. . . ."

"Thank you," Nesha murmured to the bear, joyous at hearing her icy breath called a gift, at finding a home where she would be welcome in the months away from her father's lands.

The bear rubbed her muzzle against Nesha's arm.

Bjarn pointed at several cubs who were rolling perilously close to a cluster of stalagmites. "The youngest, my sisters, stay furred as much as they can. They race through the cave tunnels"—he paused and shook his head as one of the cubs hurtled toward another, larger bear—"until my father takes them out to explore the ice dunes and give the elders a bit of quiet. . . ."

And so long into the night they sat and talked, the girl who carried winter's kiss and the boy who was a bear.

Thus began their new life. Bjarn still carried Nesha when they went out during the day, but now they were joined by Bjarn's family. Now, for the first time in her life, Nesha could laughed freely, setting snow squalls to dance over the ledges. Her new family-who-were-bears did not fear her; instead, they spun and laughed in the cold air. And when they returned to the caves, Bjarn walked hand in hand with her—listening as she told him of her life and dreams, and telling her of his life and dreams.

This was the way of their lives for many months.

Then, one winter afternoon, the sky heavy with

snow, Nesha said to Bjarn, "Come with me to see my father."

Bjarn asked, "To stay?"

"No. This is my home." She motioned toward the great white plain where the cubs were sliding in circles. "With them, with *you*. Now and always."

"Always," Bjarn repeated softly.

And so it was that Nesha shared the first of many kisses with Bjarn, the boy-who-had-become-her-beloved.

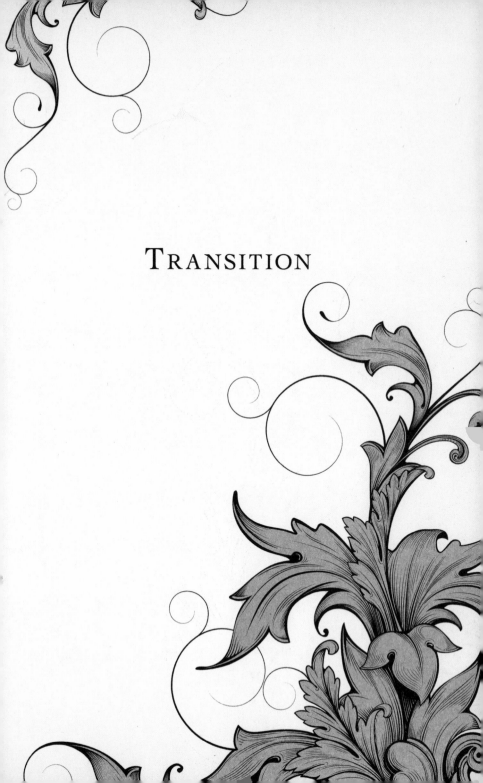

# TRANSITION

## TOMORROW

𝒮EBASTIAN LOWERED THE BODY TO THE ground in the middle of a dirt-and-gravel road in the far back of a graveyard. "Crossroads matter, Eliana."

He pulled a long, thin blade and slit open the stomach. He reached his whole forearm inside the body. His other hand, the one holding the knife, pressed down on her chest. "Until this moment, she could recover."

Eliana said nothing, did nothing.

"But hearts matter." He pulled his arm out, a red slippery thing in his grasp.

He tossed it to Eliana.

"That needs buried in sanctified ground, and she"— he stood, pulled off his shirt, and wiped the blood from his arm and hand—"needs to be left at crossroad."

Afraid that it would fall, Eliana clutched the heart in both hands. It didn't matter, not really, but she didn't want to drop it in the dirt. *Which is where we will put it.* But burying it seemed different from letting it fall on the dirt road.

Sebastian slipped something from his pocket, pried open the corpse's mouth, and inserted it between her lips. "Wafers, holy objects of any faith, put these in the mouth. Once we used to stitch the mouth shut, too, but these days that attracts too much attention."

"And dead bodies with missing hearts don't?"

"They do." He lifted one shoulder in a small shrug.

Eliana tore her gaze from the heart in her hands and asked, "But?"

"You need to know the ways to keep the dead from waking, and I'm feeling sentimental." He walked back toward the crypt where the rest of their clothes were, leaving her the choice to follow him or leave.

### TODAY

"Back later," Eliana called as she slipped out the kitchen door. The screen door slammed behind her, and the porch creaked as she walked over it. Sometimes

she thought her aunt and uncle let things fall into dis-
repair because it made it impossible to sneak in—*or
out*—of the house. Of course, that would imply that
they noticed if she was there.

*Why should they be any different from anyone else?*

She went over to a sagging lawn chair that sat
in front of a kiddie pool in their patchy grass. Her
cousin's kids had been there earlier in the week, and
no one had bothered to put the pool back inside the
shed yet. The air was sticky enough that filling it up
with the hose and lying out under the stars didn't
sound half bad.

*Except for the part where I have to move.*

Eliana closed her eyes and leaned her head back.
One of the headaches she'd been having almost every
day the past couple months played at the edge of her
eye. The doctor said they were migraines or stress
headaches or maybe a PMS thing. She didn't care what
they were, just that they stop, but the pills he gave her
didn't help that much—and were more money than
her aunt felt like paying for all the good they did.

*On to Plan B: self-medicate.*

She tucked up her skirt so it didn't drag in the mud,
propped her boots on the end of the kiddie pool, and
noticed another bruise on her calf. The bruises and

the headaches scared her, made her worry that there was something really wrong with her, but no one else seemed to think it was a big deal.

She closed her eyes and waited for her medicine to arrive.

"Why are you sleeping out here?" Gregory glanced back at her empty front porch. "Everything okay?"

"Yeah." She blinked a few times and looked at him. "Just another headache. What time is it?"

"I'm late, but"—he took her hands and pulled her to her feet—"I'll make it up to you. I have a surprise."

He'd slid a pill into her hand. She didn't bother asking what it was; it didn't matter. She popped it into her mouth and held out her hand. He offered her a soda bottle, and she washed the pill taste out of her mouth with whatever mix of liquor he'd had in with the cola. Unlike pills and other things, good liquor was more of a challenge to get.

They walked a few blocks in silence before he lit a joint. By the look of the darkened houses they'd passed, it was late enough that no one was going to be sitting on their stoop or out with kids. Even if they did look, they wouldn't know for sure if it was a cigarette—and since Gregory didn't often smoke, there was no telltale passing it back and forth to clue anyone in.

"Headaches that make a person miss hours can't be"—she inhaled, pulling the lovely numbing smoke into her throat and lungs—"normal. That doctor"—she exhaled—"is a joke."

Gregory slid his arm around her low back. "Hours?"

She nodded. Her doctor had given her a suspicious look and asked about drugs when she'd mentioned that she felt like she was missing time, but then she could honestly say that she hadn't taken drugs. The drugs came after the doctor couldn't figure out what was wrong. She tried the over-the-counter stuff, cutting out soda, eating different foods. The headaches and the bruises weren't changed at all. *Neither is the time thing.*

"Maybe you just need to, you know, de-stress." Gregory kissed her throat.

Eliana didn't roll her eyes. He wasn't a bad guy, but he wasn't looking for a soul mate. They didn't discuss it, but it was a pretty straightforward deal they had going. He had medicine that took away her headaches better than anything else had, and she did the girlfriend bit. She got the better part of the deal—meds and entry into every party. Headaches had taken her from stay-at-home book geek to party regular in a couple months.

"We're here," he murmured.

She took another hit at the gates of Saint Bartholomew's.

"Come on, El." Gregory let go of her long enough to push open the cemetery gate. It should've been locked, but the padlock was more decoration than anything. She was glad: crawling over the fence, especially in a skirt, sounded more daunting than she was up for tonight.

After he pushed the gate shut and adjusted the lock so it looked like it was closed, Gregory took her hand.

She imagined herself with a long cigarette holder in a smoky club. He'd be wearing something classy, and she'd have on a funky flapper dress. Maybe he'd rescued her from a lame job, and she was his moll. They partied like crazy because he'd just pulled a bank job and—

"Come on." He pulled her toward the slope of the hill near the older mausoleums.

The grass was slick with dewdrops that sparkled in the moonlight, but she forced herself to focus on her feet. The world spun just this side of too much as the combined headache cures blended. At the top, she stopped and pulled a long drag into her lungs.

There were times when she could swear she could feel the smoke curling over her tongue, could feel the whispery form of it caught in the force of her inhalation.

Gregory slipped a cold hand under her shirt, and she closed her eyes. The hard press of the gravestone behind her was all that held her up. *Stones to hold me down and smoke to lift me up.*

"Come on, Eliana," he mumbled against her throat. "I need you."

Eliana concentrated on the weight of the smoke in her lungs, the lingering taste of cheap liquor on her lips, the pleasant hum of everything in her skin. If Gregory stopped talking, stopped breathing, if . . . *If he was someone else,* she admitted. *Something else.*

His breath was warm on her throat.

She imagined that his breath was warm because he'd drained the life out of someone, because he'd just come from taking the final drops of life out of some horrible person. *A bad person who*—the thought of that was ruining her buzz, though, so she concentrated on the other parts of the fantasy: he only killed bad people, and he had just rescued her from something awful. Now, she was going to show him that she was grateful.

"Right here," she whispered. She lowered herself to the ground and looked up at him.

"Out in the open?"

"Yes." She leaned back against a stone, tilted her head, and pushed her hair over her shoulder so her throat was bared to him.

*Permission to sink your fangs into me. . . . He asked. He always asked first.*

Gregory knelt in front of her and kissed her throat. He had no fangs, though. He had a thudding pulse and a warm body. He was nothing like the stories, the characters she read about before she fell asleep at night, the vague face in her fantasies. Gregory was here; that was enough.

She moved to the side a little so she could lie back in the grass.

Gregory was still kissing her throat, her shoulder, the small bit of skin bared above her bra line. It wasn't what she wanted. *He* wasn't what she wanted.

"Bite me."

He pulled back and stared at her. "Elia—"

"*Bite* me," she repeated.

He bit her, gently, and she turned her head toward the gravestone. She traced the words: THERE IS NO DEATH, WHAT SEEMETH SO IS TRANSITION.

"Transition," she whispered. That was what she wanted, a transition to something new. Instead she was stretched out in the dew-wet grass staring at the wingless angel crouched on the crypt behind Gregory. It was centered over the lintel of a mausoleum door almost as if it was watching her.

She shivered and licked her lips.

Gregory was pulling up her shirt. Eliana sighed, and he took it for encouragement. It wasn't for him, though: it was for a fantasy that she'd been having every night.

*Eliana couldn't see the face of the monster. He'd found her again, though, offered her whispered promises and sharp pleasures, and she'd said yes. She couldn't remember the words to the questions, but she knew he'd asked. That detail was clear as nothing else was. Shouldn't fantasies be clear?* That was the point, really: fantasies were to be the detailed imaginings to make up for the bleak reality.

She opened her eyes, pushing the fantasies away as headache threatened again, and she saw a girl walking up the hill toward them. Tall glossy boots covered her legs almost to her short black skirt, but at the top—just below the hem of the sheer black skirt— pale white skin interrupted the darkness of the sleek vinyl and silk skirt. "Gory! You left the party before we got there. I *told* you I wanted to see you tonight."

Gregory looked over his shoulder. "Nikki. Kind of busy here."

Undeterred, Nikki hopped up onto the gravestone beside Eliana's head and peered down at them. "So what's *your* name?"

"El . . . Eliana."

"Sorry, El," Gregory murmured. He moved a little to the side, propped himself up on one arm, and smiled at Nikki. "Could we catch you later?"

"But I'm here now." Nikki kicked her feet and stared at Eliana.

Eliana blinked, trying to focus her eyes. It wasn't working: the wingless angel looked like it was on a different mausoleum now. She looked away from it to stare at Gregory. "My head hurts again, Gory."

"Shh, El. It's okay." He brushed a hand over her hair and then glared at Nikki. "You need to take a walk."

"But I had a question for *Elly.*" Nikki hopped down to stand beside them. "Are you and Gory in love, Elly dear? Is Gory that special someone you'd die for?"

Eliana wasn't sure who the girl was, but she was too out of it to lie. "No."

"El . . ." Gregory rolled back over so he was on top of her. His eyes were widened in what looked like genuine shock.

Nikki flung a leg over Gregory so she was straddling both Gregory and Eliana; she leaned down to look into Eliana's eyes. "Have you already met someone new then? Someone who you dream—"

"Nicole, stop it," another voice said.

For a strange moment, Eliana thought it was the wingless angel on the crypt. She wanted to look, but Nikki reached down and forced Eliana to look only at her.

"Do stone angels usually speak?" Eliana whispered.

"Poor Gory." Nikki shook her head—and then pressed herself against Gregory. "To die for a girl who doesn't even think you're special. It's sad, really."

He started to try to buck her off. "That's not funn—"

Nikki pushed herself tighter to his back. "You seem like a nice guy, and I wanted your last minutes to be special, Gory. Really, I did, but"—she reached down and slashed open Gregory's throat with a short blade—"you talk too much."

Blood sprayed over Eliana, over the grass, and over Nikki.

And then Nikki leaned down and sank her teeth into the already bleeding flesh of Gregory's neck.

Gregory arched and twisted, trying to get free, trying to escape, but Nikki was on his back, swallowing his blood and pressing him against Eliana.

Eliana started to scream, but Nikki covered her mouth and nose. "Shut up, Elly."

And Eliana couldn't move, couldn't turn her head, couldn't breathe. She stared up at Nikki, who licked Gregory's blood from her lips, as the pressure in her chest increased. She tried to move her legs, still pinned under Gregory's body; she grabbed Nikki's wrists ineffectually. She scratched and batted at Nikki as everything went dark, as Nikki suffocated her.

Graveyard soil filled Eliana's mouth, and a damp sensation was all over her. She opened her eyes, blinked a few times, and spit out the dirt. That was as much as she could manage for the moment. Her body felt different: her nerves sent messages too fast, her tongue and nose drawing more flavors in with each breath than she could identify, and breathing itself wasn't the same. She stopped breathing, waiting for tightness in her chest, gasping, *something*. It didn't come. Breathing was a function of tasting the air, not inflating her lungs. Carefully, she turned her head to the side.

She wasn't in the same spot, but the same wingless angel stood atop a gravestone watching her.

He was alive. He looked down at her with shadow-dark eyes, and she wondered how she'd mistaken him for a sculpture. *Because I couldn't see this clearly . . . or smell . . . or hear.* She swallowed audibly, as she realized what she didn't hear: the angel who had watched her die wasn't alive either.

She swiped a hand over her eyes, brushing something sticky from her eyelids. Not too many hours ago—*she thought*—she'd coated her lashes in heavy mascara and outlined her eyes in thick black liner. It wasn't eyeliner that she smeared over her temple. *No.* The memory of Gregory's blood all over her face came back in a rush.

Eliana could hear the sounds of people walking outside the graveyard, could smell the peculiar cologne the crypt angel wore, could taste the lingering mustiness of the soil that she'd had in her mouth. *And blood.* Gregory's blood was on her lips. Absently, she lifted her hand and licked the dirt-caked dried blood—and was neither disgusted nor upset by the flavor.

"Up." A boot connected with her side.

Without looking, Eliana caught the boot. She felt slick vinyl over a toned leg. Holding the boot, she looked away from the crypt angel and stared at the boot's owner.

"Nikki," Eliana said. "You're Nikki."

"Nice catch." Nikki crouched down. "Now get up."

Eliana was sober now—or perhaps completely mad.

Her face was wet with blood and dirt, and she was lying in a mound of fresh soil. It wasn't a hole. She hadn't been buried *in* the ground. Instead, she was on her back on top of the ground.

*Like I was when Nikki killed Gory . . . and me.*

But the moonlight falling on Eliana's soil-covered body felt like raw energy, pushing away all of her confusion, reforming her. It had saturated the soil in which she was lying, and the energy of the two pricked her skin like tiny teeth biting her all over. She wanted to stay there, soak in the moonlight and the soil, until everything made sense again.

"Get up." Nikki tangled her fingers in Eliana's hair and stood.

Eliana came to her feet, wishing she could stop or at least pause longer in the fresh-turned earth. *At least the moonlight is still falling.* It felt like a very light rain, tangible but too delicate to capture.

She stepped backward, and Nikki released her.

"You *killed* me," Eliana said. It was not a question or an accusation but something between the two. Things felt uncertain; memory and reality and logic weren't all coming together cohesively. "Suffocated me."

"I did." Nikki walked over and tugged open the door of the crypt where the angel had been perched. "Come, or you'll go hungry."

The angel from the crypt walked between Eliana and Nikki. "Kill her and be done with it, Nicole. These games grow tedious. You've made your point."

"Don't be difficult, or"—Nikki went up on her tiptoes and kissed him—"you'll go hungry, too."

He didn't move, even when she leaned her whole weight against him. The angel's expression remained unchanged. "Do you think she matters? She's just some girl."

"No. Here she is"—Nikki grabbed Eliana by the arm and shook her—"*proof* that you picked her. *Again.* How many of them has it been now? Twenty? Fifty?"

"I got careless." The angel shrugged. "Tormenting her is foolish, but if it amuses you . . ."

Nikki stared at him, her hand tightening on Eliana's arm. Then, still holding on to Eliana, she walked into the crypt.

"Wash. There's water over there"—Nikki pointed to the corner, where a cooler of melting ice sat—"and your outfit . . . hmm?"

As Eliana dropped to the floor in front of the melting ice, Nikki looked behind them at the angel, who'd come to stand just outside the door. She opened a wooden trunk on the floor. "What do you think?"

"Nothing you want to hear." Then the angel walked away.

Sebastian watched Eliana with growing doubt. He'd tried to pick a strong one this time. *Blood and moonlight.* That was the key. *Killed under the full moon with enough vampire blood already in them.* For two months, he'd kept her hidden, fed her, prepared her, yet here she was like a mindless sheep.

Nicole always waited to see if they woke; she knew how often he'd been unfaithful, but she always hoped. Sometimes, the newly dead girls hadn't had enough of his blood to wake back up. Nicole took those as victories, as if killing them before they'd had enough of his blood meant she was still special. She wasn't. If he could kill her himself, he would've done so decades ago, but her blood was why he was transformed, and vampires couldn't kill the one whose blood had remade them. *And mortals can't kill us.* It left him very few options.

"What are you doing?" Nicole had followed him. She shoved him face-first into the side of another mausoleum. "You don't just walk away when I have questions! How am I to get changed if I have to *guess* how I look? What if—"

"You look beautiful, Nicole." He wiped a trickle of blood from his forehead.

"Really?"

"Always." He held out the blood on his finger, and she kissed it away.

There wasn't any sense in arguing with her. It only prolonged the inevitable, and he wasn't in the mood to watch her take out her temper on the barely conscious vampire girl who watched them from the doorway of the crypt where Nicole had left her.

"She needs help." He kept his voice bland.

Nicole's gaze followed his to the shivering girl. "So dress her up. I want to go play before I kill her."

"Are you sure?"

With a vulnerability that he'd once thought

endearing, Nicole asked, "Does that bother you? Does she matter then?"

"No," Sebastian murmured. "Not at all."

The angel and Nicole returned. A dim voice inside whispered that Eliana shouldn't be standing here, that being in the dirty crypt was not good, but then Nicole smiled and Eliana's mind grew hazy.

"Sebastian will tell you what to wear, Elly." Nicole held out her hand, palm up. Obediently, Eliana extended her arm, and Nicole lifted Eliana's hand to her lips.

"Don't say a word," Nicole whispered before she kissed each of Eliana's fingertips. "Okay?"

"Okay," Eliana answered.

"I"—Nikki broke a finger—"said"—and another—"not"—and another—"to speak."

Eliana stumbled backward from the pain.

Sebastian caught her. He held her against him, keeping her from falling.

"Buttons." Nicole pointed at a wooden trunk. "There's pants that button all the way up on each leg. She can wear those."

Eliana watched her leave. Once Nikki was out of sight, some semblance of clarity returned again. "I remember you." Eliana stared at Sebastian. "You were *somewhere.* . . . I know you."

He didn't reply. Instead, he held out a pair of pants with tiny buttons from ankle to hip.

"Why is this happening?" she asked. "I don't understand."

When she didn't move, he dropped to the ground, tugged off her shoes. The motions, the sense of his proximity, felt familiar. "You just woke, Eliana. The confusion will fade."

"No," Eliana corrected. She held up her hand. "Why did she kill me? Why did she hurt me?"

"Because she can." He pulled off her muddy jeans and bloody shirt, leaving her shivering in nothing but her underwear. Silently, he ripped a T-shirt that was in the trunk, dipped it in the ice water, and started washing the blood from her.

"Can you do this?" he asked. "Like I am?"

Eliana grabbed the wet shirt. The pain in her hand should be bringing tears to her eyes. *A lot of things should.* She wanted to escape, to get away from Nikki. *And him . . . I think.* Her hand throbbed, but the hunger she felt was worse. "I'm a lot more capable than you think."

Sebastian changed into a black shirt and, oddly,

slipped a dark silk scarf into his pants pocket. His gaze was unwavering as he did so. "Let's not tell Nicole that."

"She killed me . . . and Gory, but"—Eliana shivered as she washed away Gregory's blood and felt guilty that the sight of it made her stomach growl—"I'm not . . . she's . . . you . . ."

"Just like you. Dead. Undead. Vampire. Pick your term." Sebastian took the wet shirt back and held out a pair of pants. "Step in."

"I see why you picked her." Nikki's voice drew Eliana's attention. "It'll almost be a shame when she dies."

Eliana's gaze fastened on Nikki. *When I die?* She looked at Sebastian. *He picked me? For what?* Neither vampire moved for a moment; neither spoke; and Eliana wasn't sure she wanted to speak her questions aloud—or if it would help.

"We're ready to go," she said.

*I'm not ready for any of this. Not really.* But it was here, and she felt pretty certain that getting out of the graveyard was a good first step to something. *Hopefully something that involves me not dying. Again.*


Sebastian swept Nicole into his arms. He'd watched Eliana assess both of them, seen her weigh and measure what she could glean of the situation, and he was excited. The new vampire was conscious and angry, and had no memory of him. After so many dead girls, he finally had the right one. *This must've been what Nicole felt when she found me.* It was almost enough to make him forgive her. *Almost.*

"Let's go to dinner, Nik." He couldn't keep the tremor out of his voice.

Nicole smiled and kissed him with the same passion they'd shared for decades—enough so that he debated one last tumble. But Eliana was hungry, and he was looking forward to a new future.

With Eliana trailing behind them, he carried Nicole through the graveyard and down the street. *Just as when we were first together.* On what he hoped would be the last night, he felt renewed tenderness for her. *And hope.*

No one spoke as they made their way through the streets to the party.

Sebastian lowered Nicole to the ground just outside the house, and she led them inside. She didn't doubt her superiority: *Why should she?* Eliana was no match for Nicole in a fight, and Sebastian was physically unable to strike her. Unless Eliana chose to take control of the situation, Nicole would be safe, and Eliana would die at the end of the night.

*And I'll have to start over . . . again.*

The humans weren't surprised to see any of them; if anything, a few of the assessing looks made Sebastian wish that he could keep both Nicole and Eliana for a while, but unless they were romantically involved, vampires of the same gender rarely had the ability to be around each other without territory issues.

The music thumped. Drunk humans danced and hooked up in shadowed corners. Finding a bite to eat was almost too easy. Sebastian missed proper hunting. Nicole insisted on staying in the graveyard, but she didn't like to hunt anymore.

*The precise opposite of the way traditions should be observed.*

He hated this, the tedium of plucking the humans like produce at a grocer. He hated living in the gloom and dank of graveyards. The soil was transportable. The humans were discardable, food on legs but with bank accounts. If his kind modernized, as he had begun to do, they could live in comfort: hunt food, gather funds, and relocate.

*If she'd changed, I wouldn't have to do this.* He cupped Nicole's face in his hands, kissed her, and manipulated her once more: "I can watch her while you—"

"Go find a snack"—Nicole caught Eliana's hand, though, not letting the new vampire free to find food— "since you wouldn't eat earlier. We'll *both* be here."

Eliana watched, studying him, obviously looking for the truth behind his words and actions. Lying to her would be harder. Winning her approval would be a true challenge. *Unlike Nicole.* Vampires had a peculiar protectiveness, an almost pathological adoration of the humans they turned. It was why Nicole had never killed him despite his perpetual unfaithfulness. *She's weak. I won't be.* He hadn't killed Eliana himself. It was his blood in her veins, but he hadn't murdered her.

He stared at them both. The music thrummed in the room, heartbeats beckoned, warm bodies surrounded them. Both Nicole and Eliana looked back at him, and he forced himself to look only at Nicole as he smiled. "My lady."

The hunger in Nikki's gaze as she watched Sebastian walk away was pitiful. For all of her cruelty, the vampire was desperate for Sebastian's attention.

"He's beautiful," Eliana murmured, "but he doesn't

really seem that into you."

Nikki's gaze snapped to Eliana. "He's been mine for longer than you've been alive."

The possessiveness that was creeping into Eliana was less about Sebastian than about taking him from Nikki. He *was* attractive, but attractive guys weren't worth fighting over. *Especially guys who stood by while someone murdered you.*

"He seems like the sort who would sleep with whatever's handy." Eliana paused at the words. He *was* that sort; she was sure of it. All the headaches, the fantasies, they made sense. Sebastian had come to her outside the library. He'd been charming; he'd paid attention to her. He'd asked to walk with her, to kiss her, to touch her, to bite her. *He gave me his blood.* For that, he hadn't asked permission. *He made me forget.*

"The fantasies . . . they were memories. When I wanted Gory to bite me . . . that was because of Sebastian."

"Yes," Nikki hissed. Her hold on Eliana's hand tightened. "But don't think you're special. He's strayed before. He—"

"Special?" Eliana laughed. "*I* don't want to be special to him. *You* do."

*He said I would be his if I was strong enough.*

Sebastian stood midway up the stairs. He really was gorgeous, and if the memories that were returning to her were true, he was even more so without the clothes. She licked her lips and was amused to see an answering smile from him.

*He didn't say I would be murdered.*

"Nik?" He called out to Nicole, but his gaze was on Eliana, not Nikki. "I changed my mind. Come with me?"

Eliana's stomach growled, but the music was too loud for anyone but Nikki to hear it. She remembered blood, the taste of it, the number of times she'd swallowed it. He'd assured her that when she remembered, she'd be strong.

*But you can't remember now, not until you wake, Elly,* he'd repeated. *Then you'll be strong and clever, and you'll know what to do.*

She did know what to do. Keeping hold of Nikki's hand, Eliana shimmied through the crowd.

At the top of the stairs, a girl leaned against the wall. Eliana had partied with her a few times, but not enough that she remembered the girl's name. Sebastian was nuzzling the girl's throat. He held a hand out behind him, and Nikki took it.

He pulled her close and hooked his arm around her waist. Beside them was an open door. With one arm around the girl whose throat he'd been kissing and one arm around Nikki, he took a step toward the unoccupied bedroom.

"Hey." The girl looked at Sebastian dazedly and stepped away. "What—"

"Shh." He released Nikki and led the girl inside. "Close the door, Eliana."

He shoved the girl toward Eliana, who caught hold of her with both hands and steadied her. Eliana felt a twinge of regret, but it was quashed by hunger.

"Do you really want her to eat?" Nikki asked. Desperate hope was plain in Nikki's expression. She reached up on her tiptoes and kissed Sebastian—who watched Eliana as he and Nikki kissed.

The drunk girl he'd found looked from Sebastian to Eliana. "I don't do the group thing. I mean . . . I'm not . . . I thought he was . . ." The girl looked over at Sebastian. "I don't know what's going on."

"Shh." Eliana stroked the girl's face comfortingly and pulled her closer. "There's no group thing. It's okay."

The girl nodded, and Eliana lowered her mouth to the girl's throat, covering the same spot where Sebastian had kissed. It was nature, not logic, that told Eliana where to bite. It was simple biology that made her canines extend and pierce skin.

Sebastian had his eyes open while he kissed Nikki, watching as Eliana bit the girl.

It wasn't disgusting. Well, it *was,* but not in a rather-die-than-eat way. It was instinct. Like any animal, Eliana hungered, and so she ate.

She didn't gorge, didn't kill the girl, but she swallowed the blood until she felt stronger. *If a bit tipsy.* The buzz that she got from drinking the girl's blood was somewhere between a good high and a delicious meal. *Familiar.* The taste wasn't new. *His blood was better.*

Eliana let the girl fall to the floor and looked at him.

Sebastian and Nikki were all over each other. Nikki had pushed him against the wall, leaving her back to Eliana, and he was cupping the back of Nikki's head with one hand. His other hand was on the small of her back.

"Nicole," he murmured. He kissed her collarbone. Without pausing in his affections, he lifted his gaze and looked at Eliana.

The temptation to rip Nikki out of his arms was sudden and violent. It was irrational and ugly and utterly exciting. All she wanted was to tear out the other vampire's throat, not to feed, not carefully. *Like she did to Gory.* Eliana couldn't: in a fair fight, Nikki would kill Eliana.

She felt her teeth cutting into her lip and opened her mouth on a snarl.

She stepped forward. Her hands were curled in fists.

*Fists aren't enough.*

"I need"—she looked at Sebastian—"help."

Sebastian spun so Nikki was now the one against the wall, with his body pressed against her. With one hand he caught her wrist and held it to the wall.

Nikki looked past him to Eliana. "For centuries he's been mine. A few weeks of being with you is *nothing.*"

"Two months," he murmured as he raised Nikki's other wrist, so he was holding them both in his grasp.

Then he kissed her, and she let her eyes close.

Sebastian reached back and lifted the bottom of his shirt. In a worn leather sheath against his spine, there was a knife.

Eliana walked toward him and wrapped her hands around the hilt of the knife.

She stood there, her knuckles against his skin.

*He made me this. He knew she'd murder me.* Eliana remembered the blood and the kisses. He'd picked her, changed her life. *But Nikki suffocated me.*

Eliana wanted to kill them both. She couldn't, though; even if he gave her access to his throat, she couldn't raise a hand to him. She wasn't sure why, but she couldn't do it.

*And with his help, I can kill Nikki.*

With a growl, Eliana stabbed the knife into Nikki's throat.

Sebastian held Nikki up, his body still pressed against her, and kissed her as she struggled. He swallowed her screams, so no one heard.

Then he pulled back. He held out his arm, and Eliana moved closer. She reached up and covered Nikki's mouth with her hand, just as Nikki had done to her.

"Go ahead," he whispered.

Eliana closed her mouth over the wound in Nikki's throat and swallowed. Her blood was different from the human girl's blood; it was richer.

*Like Sebastian's.*

Nikki struggled, but Sebastian held her still. He held them both in his embrace while Eliana drank from her murderer's throat. For more than a minute, they stayed like that. The sounds of drinking and soft struggles were covered by the noise downstairs.

Then Nikki stopped fighting, and Eliana pulled back.

Sebastian let her go, and he sat on the bed, cradling Nikki in his arms while he drank from the now motionless vampire. If not for the fact that she was staring glassy-eyed at nothing and her arm dangled limply, it would have seemed almost tender.

Sebastian wrapped the scarf that he'd brought with him around her throat to hide her wound. Then he and Eliana washed Nicole's blood from their faces and hands. They stood side by side in the adjoining bathroom.

Back in the bedroom, he slipped a few trinkets into his pockets and grabbed a messenger bag from the closet. Eliana said nothing. She hadn't spoken since before Nicole's death.

"There are clothes in the closet that would fit you," he suggested.

She changed in silence.

He took the bloodied clothes and shoved them into the bag, lifted Nicole into his arms, positioned her head, and carried her as he had done earlier. In silence, they walked downstairs and out the door. A few people watched drunkenly, but most everyone was too busy getting lost in either a body or a drink.

Eliana was more disturbed by murdering Nikki than she had been by being murdered *by* her—mostly because she'd enjoyed killing Nikki.

She closed the door to the house behind her. For a moment, she paused. *Can I run?* She didn't know where she'd go, didn't know anything about what she was—other than dead and monstrous. *Are there limitations?* There were two ways to find out if the television and book versions of vampire weaknesses were true: test them or ask.

Instead of following Sebastian, she sped up and walked beside him. "Will you answer questions?"

"Some." He smiled. "If you stay."

She nodded. It wasn't anything other than what she expected, not after tonight. She walked through the streets in the remaining dark, headed back to the graveyard where she'd been murdered, escorting the corpse that *she'd* murdered.

Inside the graveyard, they walked to the far bottom of the hill, in the back where the oldest graves were.

Sebastian lowered Nikki to the ground in the middle of a dirt-and-gravel road in the far back of the graveyard. "Crossroads matter, Eliana."

He pulled a long, thin blade from Nikki's boot and slit open her stomach. He reached his whole forearm inside the body. His other hand, the one holding the knife, pressed down on Nikki's chest, holding her still. "Until this moment, she could recover."

Eliana said nothing, did nothing.

"But hearts matter." He pulled his arm out, a red slippery thing in his grasp.

He tossed it to Eliana.

"That needs buried in sanctified ground, and she"—he stood, pulled off his shirt, and wiped Nicole's blood from his arm and hand—"needs to be left at crossroad."

Afraid that it would fall, Eliana clutched the heart in both hands. It didn't matter, not really, but she didn't want to drop it in the dirt. *Which is where we will put it.* But burying it seemed different than letting it fall on the dirt road.

Sebastian slipped something from his pocket, pried open Nikki's mouth, and inserted it between her lips. "Wafers, holy objects of any faith, put these in the mouth. Once we used to stitch the mouth shut, too, but these days that attracts too much attention."

"And dead bodies with missing hearts don't?"

"They do." He lifted one shoulder in a small shrug.

Eliana tore her gaze from the heart in her hands and asked, "But?"

"You need to know the ways to keep the dead from waking again, and I'm feeling sentimental." He walked back toward the crypt where the rest of their clothes were, leaving her the choice to follow him or leave.

She followed him, carrying Nikki's heart carefully.

"Killing on full or new moon matters," he added when she caught up with him.

She nodded. The things he was telling her mattered, and she wanted to be attentive to them, but she'd just killed a person.

*With his help . . . because of him . . . like an animal.*

And now he was standing there shirtless and bloodied.

*Is it because I slept with him?* She listened to the words he said now, trying to remember the words he'd said *then*. Those words mattered too. *He planned this. He knew she'd kill me. He watched.*

"She killed me under the full moon," Eliana said.

"Yes." He wrapped Nicole's heart in his shirt. "You were born again with blood and moonlight."

"Why?"

"Some animals are territorial, Eliana." He looked at her then, and it was like stepping into her own memories. That was the same look he'd given her when she'd first gone with him, when she'd been alive and bored: it was a look that said she mattered, that she was the most important thing in his world.

*And I am now.*

He was looking at her the way Nikki had watched him. He brushed her hair away from her face. "We are territorial, so when we touch another, our partners respond poorly."

"Why were you with me then? You knew that . . ." She couldn't finish the sentence.

"She'd kill you?" He shrugged again, but he didn't step away to give her more room. "Yes, when she found you, when I was ready."

"You *meant* for her to kill me?" Eliana put both hands on his chest as she stared up at him.

"It was preferable that she do it," he said. "I planned very carefully. I *picked* you."

"You picked me," she echoed. "You picked me to be murdered."

"To be changed." Sebastian cupped her chin in his hand and tilted her head up to meet his gaze. "I needed you, Eliana. Mortals aren't strong enough to kill us, and we can't strike the one whose blood made us. The one whose blood runs inside us is safe from our anger. You can't strike me. I couldn't strike her."

"You wanted her to find me and kill me, so I would kill her for you?" Eliana clarified. She felt like she was going to be sick. She'd been used. She *had* killed for him, been killed for him.

"I was tired of Nicole, but it was more than that." He wrapped his arms around her waist and held tight as she tried to pull away. "We still need the same nutrients that we needed as humans, but our bodies can no longer extract them from solid food. So we take the blood from those who can extract the nutrients."

"Humans."

He nodded once. "We don't need that much, and the shock and pain makes most people forget us. It hurts, you know, having holes ripped in your skin."

She dropped a hand to her leg in suddenly remembered pain. It *did* hurt. Her entire thigh had been bruised afterward. *And her chest.* At the time, she couldn't remember what the bruises were from. *And the bend of her arm.*

He kissed her throat, softly, the way she'd fantasized about afterward when she'd believed it was just a dream, when headaches kept her from remembering more.

"*Why?*" she asked again. "You needed a meal and a murderer. That didn't mean you needed to screw me."

"Oh, but I *did*. I needed you." His breath wasn't warm on her throat; it was a damp breeze that shouldn't be appealing. "The living are so warm . . . and you were perfect. There were others, but I didn't keep them. I was careful with you."

She remembered him looking at her and asking permission.

"Sometimes I can't help but want to be inside humans, but I won't keep them. We're together now." He kissed her throat, not at her pulse, but where her neck met her shoulder. "I chose you."

Eliana didn't move away.

"Nikki found out, though." He sighed the words.

"So she killed me." Eliana stepped backward, out of his embrace.

Sebastian had an unreadable expression as he caught and held her gaze. "Of course. Would you do any differently?"

"I . . ."

"If I left you tonight and sank into some girl—or

guy—would you forgive me?" He reached out and entwined his fingers with hers. "Would you mind if I kissed someone else the way I kiss you? If I knelt at their feet and asked permission to—"

"Yes." She squeezed his hand until she saw him wince. *"Yes."*

He nodded. "As I said, territorial."

Eliana shook her head. "So that's it? We kill, but not under full or new moon. We drink blood, but really not so much. If we *do* kill, it's some sort of territorial bullshit."

"An area can support only so many predators. I have you, and you have me."

"So I killed Nikki, and now you're my mate?" She wasn't sure whether she was excited or disgusted.

*Or both.*

Sebastian whispered, "Until one of us makes someone alert enough and strong enough to kill the other, yes."

She pulled her hand out of his. "Yeah? So how do I do that?"

Sebastian had her pinned against the crypt wall before she could blink.

"I'm not telling you that, Eliana. That's part of the game." He rested his forehead against hers in a mockery of tenderness.

She looked at the floor of the crypt, where Nikki's heart had fallen. The bloodied shirt lay in the thin layer of soil that covered the cracked cement floor. Moss decorated the sides where the dampness had seeped into the small building.

*Transition.* Eliana felt an echo of herself crying out, but the person she'd been was dead.

She looked at Sebastian and smiled. *A game?* She might not be able to kill him yet, but she'd figure it out. She'd find someone to help her—and unlike Sebastian, she wouldn't be arrogant enough to leave the vampire she made alive to plot her death.

*Until then . . .*

With a warm smile, she wrapped her arms around him. "I'm hungry again. Take me out to dinner? Or"—she tilted her head to look up at him—"let's find somewhere less depressing to live? Or both?"

"With pleasure." He looked at her with the same desperation Eliana had seen in Nikki's gaze when she watched Sebastian.

*Which is useful . . .*

Eliana pulled him down for a kiss—and almost wished she didn't need to kill him.

*Almost.*

# LOVE STRUCK

$\mathcal{D}$ESPITE IT BEING AT THE BEACH, THE party was lame. A few people were trying to turn noise into music: if Alana had been high or drunk, it might've been tolerable. But she was sober—and tense. Usually, the beach was where she found peace and pleasure; it was one of the only places where she felt like the world wasn't impossibly out of order. But tonight, she felt anxious.

A guy sat down beside her; he held out a cup. "You look thirsty."

"I'm not thirsty"—she glanced at him and tore her gaze away as quickly as she could—"*or* interested." *Eye candy.* She didn't date eye candy. She'd been watching her mother do that for years. It was so not the path Alana was taking. *Ever.* Instead, she stared at the singer. He was normal, not-tempting, not-exciting. He was cute and sweet, but not irresistible. That was the sort of guy Alana chose when she dated—safe, temporary, and easy to leave.

She smiled at the singer. The bad rendition of a Beatles song shifted into a worse attempt at poetry . . . or maybe a cover of something new and emo. It didn't really matter what it was: Alana was going to listen to it and not pay attention to the hot dreadlocked guy who was sitting too close beside her.

Dreadlocks, however, wasn't taking the hint.

"Are you cold? Here." He tossed a long brown leather coat onto the sand in front of her. It looked completely out of place for the crowd at the party.

"No, thanks." Alana scooted a bit away from him, closer to the fire. Burnt embers swirled and lifted like fireflies rising with the smoke.

"You'll get cold walking home and—"

"Go away. Please." Alana still didn't look back at him. Polite wasn't working. "I'm not interested, easy, or going to get drunk enough to be either of those. Seriously."

He laughed, seeming not insulted but genuinely amused. "Are you *sure*?"

"Leave."

"It'd be easier this way. . . ."

He moved closer, putting himself between her and

the fire, directly in her line of view.

And she had to look, not a quick glance, but a real look. Illuminated by the combined glow of firelight and moonlight, he was even more stunning than she'd feared: blond hair clumped in thick dreadlocks that stretched to his waist; a few of those thick strands were kelp-green; his tattered T-shirt had holes that allowed glimpses of the most defined abs she'd ever seen.

He was crouched down, balancing on his feet. "Even if it wouldn't upset Murrin, it'd be tempting to take you."

Dreadlocks reached out as if he was going to cup her face in his hand.

Alana crab-walked backward, scuttling over the sand until she was just out of his reach. She scrambled to her feet and slipped a hand into the depths of her bag, past her shoes and her jumble of keys. She gripped her pepper spray and flicked the safety switch off, but didn't pull it out of her bag yet. Logic said she was over-reacting: there were other people around; she was safe here. But something about him felt wrong.

"Back off," she said.

He didn't move. "Are you sure? Really, it'd be easier for you this way. . . ."

She pulled out the pepper spray.

"It's your choice, precious. It'll be worse once he finds you." Dreadlocks paused as if she'd say something or change her mind.

She'd couldn't reply to comments that made no sense, though—and she surely wasn't going to change her mind about getting closer to him.

He sighed. "I'll be back after he breaks you."

Then he walked away, heading toward the mostly empty parking lot.

She watched until she was sure he was gone. Grappling with drunk or high or whatever-he-was guys wasn't on her to-do list. She'd taken self-defense and street-defense classes, heard countless lectures on safety, and kept her pepper spray handy—her mother was very good about *that* part of parenting. None of that meant she wanted to have to use those lessons.

She looked around the beach. There were some strangers at the party, but mostly the people there were ones she'd seen around at school or out walking the reef. Right now, none of them was paying any attention to her. No one even looked her way. Some had watched when she was backing away from Dreadlocks, but they'd stopped watching when he left.

Alana couldn't decide if he was just messing with

her or if someone there really posed a threat . . . or if he was saying that to spook her into leaving the party so she'd be alone and vulnerable. Usually, when she walked home, she went in the same direction he'd gone, but just in case he was lurking in the parking lot, she decided to go farther down the beach and cut across Coast Highway. It was a couple blocks out of the way, but he'd creeped her out. *A lot*. He'd made her feel trapped, like prey.

When she'd walked far enough away that the bonfire was a glow in the distance and the roll of waves was all she could hear, the knot of tension in her neck loosened. She had gone the opposite direction of danger, and she stood in one of the spots where she felt safest, most at peace—the exposed reef. The ground under her feet shifted from sandy beach to rocky shelf. Tide pools were spread open to the moon. It was perfect, just her and the sea. She needed that, the peace she found there. She went toward a ledge of the reef where waves crashed and sprayed upward. Mussel shells jutted up like blunt black teeth. Slick sea lettuce and sea grasses hid crabs and unstable ground. She was barefoot, balancing on the edges of the reef, feeling that rush as the waves came ever closer, feeling herself fill up with the peace Dreadlocks had stolen.

Then she saw him standing in the surf in front of her, staring at her, oblivious to the waves that broke around him. "How did he get here first?"

She shivered, but then realized that it wasn't him. The guy was as defined as Dreadlocks, but he had long, loose, dark hair. *Just a surfer. Or Dreadlocks's friend.* The surfer wasn't wearing a wet suit. He looked like he might be . . . naked. It was difficult to tell with the waves crashing around him; at the very least, he was topless in the frigid water.

He lifted his hand to beckon her closer, and she thought she heard him say, "I'm safe enough. Come talk to me."

It was her imagination, though. It had to be. She was just freaked out by Dreadlocks. There was no way this guy could've heard her over the breaking of waves, no way she could've heard him.

But that didn't change her suspicion that somehow they had just spoken.

Primal fear uncoiled in her belly, and for the second time that night, she backed away without looking. Her heel sliced open on the edge of a mussel shell. The sting of salt water made her wince as she walked farther away, unable to ignore the panic, the urge to run. She glanced back and saw that he hadn't moved, hadn't stopped watching her with that unwavering gaze. And her fear turned to fury.

Then she saw the long black leather coat slung carelessly on the sand; it looked like a darker version of the coat Dreadlocks had offered her. She stepped on it and ground her blood-and-sand-caked foot on it. It wasn't smooth like leather should be. Instead, the material under her foot was silk-soft fur, an animal's pelt, a seal's skin.

It *was* a pelt.

She pulled her gaze away from that dark pelt and stared at him. He still stood in the surf. Waves curled around him like the sea had formed arms of itself, hiding him, holding him.

He smiled again and told her, "Take it. It's yours now."

And she knew she had heard his voice that time; she'd *felt* the words on her skin like the wind that stirred the water. She didn't want to reach down, didn't want to lift that pelt into her arms, but she had no choice. Her bleeding foot had broken his glamour, ended his manipulation of her senses, and she knew him for what he truly was: a selchie. He was a fey creature, a seal person, and he wasn't supposed to exist.

Maybe it was fun to believe in them when she was a little girl sharing her storybooks with Nonny, but Alana knew that her grandmother's insistence that selchies were real was just another type of make-believe. Seals didn't walk on land among humans; they didn't slip out of their Other-Skins. They were just beautiful myths. She knew that—except she was looking at a selchie who was telling her to take his Other-Skin.

*Just like the one at the bonfire.*

She stood motionless as she tried to process the enormity of what had happened, what was happening right now.

*Two selchies. I met* two *freaking selchies . . . who both tried to trap me.*

And in that instant, she understood: the fairy tales were all wrong. It wasn't the mortals' fault. Alana didn't want to stay there looking at him, but she was no longer acting of her own volition.

*I am trapped.*

The fishermen in the old stories who'd taken the selchies' pelts hadn't been entrapping innocent fey creatures: they'd been entrapped by selchie women. Perhaps it was too hard for the fishermen to admit that they were the ones who got trapped, but Alana

suddenly knew the truth that none of the stories had
shared. A mortal could no more resist the pull of that
pelt than the sea could refuse to obey the pull of the
moon. Once she took the pelt, lifted it into her mortal
arms, she was bound to him. She knew what he was,
knew the trap was sprung, but she was no different
from the mortals in the stories she'd grown up hearing.
She could not resist. She took the pelt and ran, hoping
she could foist it off on someone else before he found
her, before Murrin followed her home—because he
had to be Murrin, the one Dreadlocks was talking
about, the one that the creepy selchie had told her was
*worse.*

Murrin watched her run, felt the irresistible need to
follow her. She carried his skin with her: he had no
choice but to follow. It would have been better if she
hadn't run.

With murmured epithets over her flight, he stepped
out of the surf and made his way to the tiny caves the
water had carved into the sandstone. Inside, he had
his shore clothes: woven sandals, well-worn jeans, a
few shirts, and a timepiece. When his brother, Veikko,
had gone ashore earlier, he'd borrowed the soft shirt
Murrin had liked so. Instead, Murrin had to wear one

that required fastening many small buttons. He hated buttons. Most of his family didn't go shore walking often enough that they needed many clothes, but Murrin had been on land often enough that the lack of a decent shirt was displeasing. He barely fastened the shirt, slipping a couple of the tiny disks into the equally tiny holes, and went to find her—the girl he'd chosen over the sea.

He hadn't meant for her to find his Other-Skin like this, not yet, not now. He'd intended to talk to her, but as he was coming out of the water, he'd seen her—here and not at the party. He watched her, trying to figure how to walk out of the surf without startling her, but then he felt it: the touch of her skin on his pelt. His pelt wasn't to be there. It wasn't to happen like this. He'd had a plan.

A selchie couldn't have both a mate and the water, so Murrin had waited until he found a girl intriguing enough to hold his attention. After living with the moods of the sea, it wasn't an easy task to find a person worth losing the waves for.

*But I have.*

So he'd intended to ease her fears, to try to woo her instead of trapping her, but when she stepped on his Other-Skin, all of those choices had vanished.

This was it: they were bound. Now, he was left doing the same thing his father had once done, trying to convince a mortal to trust him after he'd trapped her. The fact that *he* hadn't put his pelt where she'd find it didn't change anything. He was left trying to wait out her fears, to find a way to convince her to trust him, to hope for a way to persuade her to forgive him: all of the very same things he'd wanted to avoid.

Mortals weren't strong enough of will to refuse the enchantment that bound him to her. It wouldn't make her love him, but selchies grew up knowing that love wasn't often theirs to have. Tradition mattered more. Finding a mate, making a family, those mattered more.

And Murrin's plan to buck tradition by getting to know his intended first had gone horribly off course.

*Thanks to Veikko.*

At the dirty bathrooms along the beach parking lot, Alana saw a girl clad only in a thin top and ragged shorts. The girl was shivering, not that it was cold, but from something she'd shot up—or hadn't been able to shoot. Usually, the junkies and vagrants clustered in small groups, but this one was alone.

The pelt tingled and resumed looking again like a beautiful leather jacket as soon as Alana saw the girl.

*Perfect*. Alana walked up and tried to hand it to the girl. "Here. You can use it to warm—"

But the girl backed away with something like horror on her face. She glanced from the coat to Alana's face, then out to the mostly empty lot. "I won't tell or anything. Please? Just—" She made a gagging noise and turned away.

Alana looked down. The pelt, still looking like a coat, was covered in blood. It was on her hands, her arms. Everywhere the seawater had been was now black-red in the glare of the streetlight. For a heartbeat, Alana thought she'd been wrong, that she'd hurt the selchie. She looked over her shoulder: a trail of almost perfectly tear-shaped droplets stretched behind her. Then, as she watched, those droplets shifted to a silvery-white, like someone had spilled mercury on the sand. They didn't sink. They balanced atop the sand, holding their shape. Alana glanced down and saw the blood on the coat shift to silver too.

"See? It's fine. Just take it. It'll—"

The shivering girl had already gone.

". . . be fine," Alana finished. She blinked back tears of frustration. "All I want is someone to hold out their arms so I can let go of it!"

With the same surety that told her what Murrin was, what Dreadlocks was, she realized that she couldn't cast the pelt away, but if someone was to reach for it, she could let go. It could fall to the ground, and then no one would be trapped. She just needed to find someone willing to reach out.

Twice more as she walked home she tried. Each time it was the same: people looked at her with terror or disgust as she held out what looked like a bloody coat. Only when they turned away did the dampness of the coat resume the appearance of thick, salty tears.

Whatever enchantment made her unable to resist taking the pelt was making it impossible to get rid of the thing too. Alana thought about what she knew about selchies; her grandmother had told her stories of the seal people when Alana was a little girl: selchies, seal women, came to the shore. They slipped out of their Other Skins, and sometimes, if they weren't careful, a fisherman or some random unmarried guy would find the skin and steal it. The new husbands hid the selchies' Other-Skins to keep their wives entrapped.

But Nonny hadn't said anything about male selchies; she also hadn't said that the seal women had entrapped the men. Nonny's stories made the selchies seem so sad, with their freedom to change to their seal shape stolen when their Other-Skins were hidden away. In the stories, the selchies were the victims; the humans were the villains—snatching helpless seal wives from the sea, tricking them, having power over them. The stories were all quite clear: the selchies were entrapped . . . but in the real world, Alana was the one feeling trapped.

By the time she reached her apartment, she was wishing—yet again—that Nonny was still around to ask. She felt like a little kid missing her grandmother so badly, but Nonny was the grown-up, the one who'd made everything better, while Mom was as clueless as Alana felt most days.

Outside her building, she paused. Their car was parked in the street alongside the building. Alana popped the trunk. Carefully, she folded the coat-pelt. After a furtive look around, she rubbed her face on the soft, dark fur. Then, with a level of care she couldn't control, she tucked it under the spare blanket her mother kept in the trunk—part of the emergency kit for when they broke down. It felt as if there wasn't any other choice: she had to keep it safe, keep it out of his reach—and keep him out of others' reach.

*Protect my mate.* The words came unbidden— and very unwelcome—to her mind. She slammed the trunk and went to the front of the car. And as she did so often when she needed to be outside at night, she stretched out on the hood. It was still warm from the drive home from whatever party her mother'd been out to tonight.

Alana stared up at the moon and whispered, "Oh, Nonny, I'm so screwed."

Then, Alana waited. He'd come. She knew he would. And having to face him with her mom lurking around, gleeful that Alana'd brought home a guy . . . it would only make a bad scene worse.

*Better to do this outside.*

Murrin saw her reclined on a car reminiscent of the ones he'd seen parked by the beach for days on end. It was unsightly—covered in rust spots, one door handle missing. She, however, was lovely, long limbs and curved body. Short pelt-brown hair framed her sharp-angled face. When he'd seen her on the beach several good tides ago, he'd known she was the one: a girl who loved the reef and the moon was a trea-sure. The waiting had been awful, but he'd watched her habits and planned how to approach her. Things weren't going according to his plans, of course, but he'd find a way to make it work.

"Wife?" His heart sped at saying it, naming her, finally saying the word to her. He stepped closer to the car, not close enough to touch her, but closer still. After so many years dreaming of finding a wife, it was a heady thing to be so near her. It might not be how he'd imagined it, but it still *was*.

She sat up, her feet scraping against the car's hood. "What did you call me?"

"Wife." He approached her slowly, hands held out to the sides. No matter how many mortals he'd watched, or how many he'd met, he was unsure still. Obviously, calling her "wife" was not the right tactic. He tried again. "I don't know your other name yet."

"Alana. My *only* name is Alana." She moved so she was sitting with her legs folded to the side, in a posture typical of a selchie girl.

It was endearing. Her words weren't, though.

"I'm not your wife," she said.

"I am Murrin. Would you—"

"I'm not your wife," she repeated, slightly louder.

"Would you walk with me, Alana?" He loved the feel of her name—*Alana, my rock, my harbor, my Alana*—on his tongue.

But when he stepped closer, she tensed and stared at him with the same cautious expression she'd had on the beach. He liked that, her hesitation. Some of the mortals he'd met on the beach when he'd been in this form had been willing to lie down with him after only the briefest of words exchanged. It had been fun, but that wasn't what he wanted in a wife. The lack of meaning saddened him: he wanted every touch, each caress and sigh, to matter.

"Would you walk with me, Alana?" He ducked his head, causing his hair to fall forward, offering her as meek a posture as he could, trying to show that he wasn't a threat to her. "I would talk to you about *us*, so we can understand each other."

"Lanie?" An older version of his mate, obviously Alana's mother, stood with the light behind her. "Who's your friend?" She smiled at him. "I'm Susanne."

Murrin stepped toward Alana's mother. "I'm Murrin. I—"

"We were on our way out," Alana said. She grabbed his hand and pulled. "For tea."

"Tea? At this hour?" Alana's mother smiled, laughter playing under her expression. "Sure, baby. Just come home after the sun rises. We'll all sleep late tomorrow."

As they walked, Alana tried to think of what to say, but she found no words to start the conversation.

She didn't want to ask him why she felt so drawn to him—or if it would get worse. She suspected that it was a result of whatever enchantment made her unable to give away his pelt. They were tied together. She got that part. She didn't want to know if he felt the same compulsion to reach out a hand and touch. But she knew resisting it took supreme effort.

*It's not real.* She glanced at him and her pulse sped. *It's not forever, either. I can get rid of him. I can. And I want to.*

She shoved her hands into her pockets and continued to walk silently beside him. Usually, the night felt too close when people—*well, just guys, actually*—were in her space. She didn't want to turn into her mom: believing in the next dreamer, chasing after the illusion that lust or neediness could evolve into something real. It didn't. *Ever.* Instead, the giddiness of the initial rush evolved into drama and tears every single time. It made more sense to end it before that inevitable and messy second stage. Short-term dating was cool, but Alana always abided by the Six-Week Rule: no one she couldn't ditch within or at six weeks. That meant she needed to find a way to extricate herself from Murrin within six weeks, and the only one who could help her figure out how was him.

At the old building that housed the coffee shop, he stopped.

Murrin glanced at her. "Is here good?"

"It's fine." Without meaning to, she pulled her hands out of her pockets and started to reach out. She scowled and crossed her arms over her chest. "It's not a date. I just didn't want you near my mother."

Silently, he reached out to open the door.

"What?" She knew she was surly, heard herself being mean. *And why shouldn't I? I didn't ask for this.*

He sighed. "I would sooner injure myself than harm your mother, Alana." He motioned for her to go inside. "Your happiness, your life, your family . . . these are what matter to me now."

"You don't know me."

He shrugged. "It is simply how things are."

"But . . ." She stared at him, trying to find words to argue, to make him . . . *what? Argue against trying to make me happy?* "This doesn't make sense."

"Come sit down. We'll talk." He walked to the far side of the shop, away from the well-lit central space. "There's a table open here."

There were other empty tables, but she didn't point them out. She wanted privacy for their conversation.

Asking him how to break some fairy-tale bond was weird enough; doing it with people listening was a bit too much.

Murrin stopped and pulled out her chair.

She sat down, trying not to be touched by his gentlemanly posture or seeming disregard for the girls—and a few guys—who were staring at him with blatant interest. He hadn't seemed to notice them, even when they stopped talking midsentence to smile up at him as he walked by their tables.

*And who could blame them for looking?* Alana might be unhappy being caught in this weird situation, but that didn't mean she wasn't just a little dazzled by how very luscious he was—not so much that she would want to stay with him, of course, but her heart sped every time she looked at him. *Pretty packages don't mean a thing. None of this matters. He* trapped *me.*

Murrin sat down in the chair across from her, watching her with an intensity that made her shiver.

"What do you want?" she asked.

He reached out and took her hand. "Do you not want to be here?"

"No. I don't want to be here *with you.*"

His voice was soothing as he asked, "So how can I

please you? How do I make you want to be around me?"

"You can't. I want you to go away."

A series of unreadable expressions played over his face, too fleeting to identify, but he didn't reply. Instead, he gestured at the giant chalkboard that served as a menu and read off choices. "Mocha? Americano? Macchiato? Tea? Milk?"

She thought about pressing him for the answers she needed, but didn't. Hostility wasn't going to work. *Not yet.* Fighting wasn't going to get her answers, so she decided to try a different approach: reason. She took a steadying breath.

"Sure. Mocha. Double shot." She stood to reach into her jeans pocket for money.

He jumped up, managing to look far more graceful than anyone she'd ever met. "Anything with it?"

"No." She unfolded a five from the bills in her pocket and held it out. Instead of taking it, he scowled and stepped away from the table.

"Hold on." She shook the bill and held her hand farther out. "Take this."

He gave her another small scowl and shook his head. "I cannot."

"Fine. I'll get my own." She stepped around him.

With a speed that. shouldn't have been possible,

he blocked her path; she stumbled briefly into him, steadying herself with a hand on his chest.

Sighing softly, he put a hand atop hers. "May I buy you a cup of coffee, Alana? Please? It doesn't indebt you to me or anything."

*Reason*, she reminded herself. *Refusing a cup of coffee is not reasonable.*

Mutely, she nodded and was rewarded with a warm look.

Once he walked away, she sat down and watched him wind through the crowd. He didn't seem fazed by the people jostling him or the crowded tables. He moved through the room easily, unnaturally so. Several times, he glanced at her and at the people seated around her—attentive without being possessive.

*Why does it matter?* She looked at him with an unfamiliar longing, knowing he wasn't really hers, knowing she didn't want to be tied to him but still feeling a strange wistfulness. *Is it a selchie thing?* She forced her gaze away and started thinking again of what to say, which questions to ask, how to undo the mess they were in.

A few minutes later, and again without any visible effort, Murrin moved through the crowd until he reached her, balancing two cups and a plate atop each one. The first plate had a thick sandwich; the second one was stacked high with brownies, cookies, and squares of chocolate. He handed her the mocha.

"Thank you," she murmured.

He nodded, sat down, and slid the plates to the center of the table between them. "I thought you might want to eat something."

She looked at the plate of desserts and the sandwich. "This is all for me?"

"I didn't know what you'd like best."

"You to leave," she said.

His expression was serious. "I can't do that. Please, Alana, you need to understand. This is how it's been for centuries. I didn't *intend* for you to be entrapped, but I can't walk away. I am not physically *able* to do so."

"Could you take it back? Your, um, skin?" She held her breath.

He looked at her sadly again; his eyes seemed as wet-black as the sea at night. "If I find it where you've hidden it without you intending me to do so. Pure coincidence. Or if I'm angry enough to search after you've struck me three times. Yes, there are ways, but it's not likely. You can't help hiding it, and I can't search for it without cause."

Alana had suspected—*known*—it wasn't something she could easily escape, but she still needed to ask, to hear him tell her. She felt tears sting her eyes. "So what do we do?"

"We get to know each other. I hope you discover you want me to be near you. You hope I say something that helps you find a way to get rid of me." He sounded so sad when he said it that she felt guilty. "That, too, is how it's been for centuries."

The next hour passed in fits and starts of conversation. Periodically, Alana relaxed. Murrin could see that she was enjoying herself, but each time she noticed she was doing so, he saw a shadow of irritation flit over her face, and she put her walls back up. She swayed toward him, but then darted away from him. Hers was a strong will, and as much as he respected it, he despaired that her strength was set against him.

He watched the tilt of her head when she was listening; he heard the rhythm of her words when she spoke of her life on shore. He knew that it was a conscious machination—that she was assessing the situation in order to get free of him. But he had learned patience and flexibility in the sea. Those were skills that every selchie needed in order to survive. Murrin's father had warned that they were equally essential in relationships, and though Murrin hadn't thought he'd follow his father's way, he'd listened. Tonight he was glad he had.

Finally, the shop was empty of everyone but them, and Alana was yawning.

"You need to rest, Alana." He stood and waited for her. Her eyes were fatigue-heavy. Perhaps a good night's sleep would help them both.

She didn't look at him, but her guard was low enough that she accepted his hand—and gasped softly when she did.

Murrin froze, waiting for her to determine their next action. He had no answer, no clue how to respond. No one had warned him that the mere touch of her hand would evoke such a feeling: he'd fight until his last breath to keep her near him, to keep her safe, to make her happy. It was akin to the sea, this feeling that pulled at him. He'd drown under the weight of it, the enormity of it, and he'd not object as he did so.

Alana tried not to react to the feel of his hand in hers, but there was something *right* in the sensation; it was like feeling the universe snap into order. Peace, an always elusive sensation, was filling her. She found that on the reef, under the full moon, but it wasn't a feeling she experienced around people. She let go of his hand briefly—he didn't resist—and the feeling ebbed. But it was like watching the sea run away from her, seeing the water escape somewhere she couldn't follow. The water would flee even if she tried to grasp it, but unlike the sea, this felt like something almost tangible. She grabbed his hand and stared at their entwined fingers. *He was tangible.*

*And of the sea . . .*

She wondered if that was why she felt this way—touching him was the same as touching the sea. She ran her thumb over his knuckles. His skin was no different from hers. *Now, at least.* The thought of him shifting into something else, something not-human, was almost enough to make her let go again. Almost.

"I won't hurt you, Alana." He was speaking then, murmuring words in a rhythmic way that was so very not-human.

She shivered. Her name had never sounded so beautiful. "People don't use names with every sentence."

He nodded, but his expression was guarded,

carefully empty. "Would you prefer that I don't? I like your name, but I could—"

"Never mind. Just . . . I don't know. . . . I don't like this." She gestured at their hands, at him, and back at herself, but she held on to him as they left the coffee shop. She was so tired, so confused, and the only moment of peace she'd felt was when she'd touched his skin.

Once they were outside, she shifted topics again. "Where will you stay?"

"With you?"

She laughed before she could help herself. "Um, I don't think so."

"I can't be too far from you now, Alana. Think of it as a leash. My reach only extends so far. I can sleep outside." He shrugged. "We don't exactly stay in houses most of the time. My mother does, but she's . . . like you. I stay with her some. It's softer, but it's not necessary."

Alana thought about it. She knew her mother wouldn't care: Susanne was utterly without what she liked to call "hang-ups," but it felt like admitting defeat to let him crash on her sofa. *So I tell him to sleep outside like an animal? He is an animal, though, isn't he?* She paused; he stopped walking too.

*What am I thinking to even consider letting him in my home?* He wasn't human, but an animal. Who knew what sort of rules he lived by—or if he even had rules or laws. She was no different from her mother: swayed by empty words, letting strange men into her haven. But he'd trapped her. And he wasn't the only one who'd tried. Something odd was happening, and she didn't like it. She let go of his hand and moved away from him.

"Who was the guy at the bonfire trying to give me his skin? Why were both of you . . . He said you were worse and . . ." She looked at him, at his face. "And why me?"

Murrin couldn't speak, couldn't process anything beyond the fact that his brother had tried to lure away his intended mate. He knew as soon as it happened that Veikko had taken Murrin's Other-Skin and laid it where Alana had found it, but he hadn't thought Veikko had approached her too. *Why did he?* Veikko still had rare bursts of pique over Zoë's leaving, but they'd talked about it. *He said he understood . . . so why was he speaking with my Alana?*

Murrin wondered if he ought to assure Veikko that Alana would be safe, that she was not like Zoë, that she would not be lost in a potentially fatal depression. *Perhaps he was trying to protect Alana? And me?* That would make more sense to Murrin, but for the almost certain fact that Veikko had been responsible for putting Murrin's Other-Skin in Alana's path. No other selchies had been on the shore.

*None of this makes sense . . . nor is it something to share now.*

It was far more complicated than Alana needed to deal with on top of everything else, so Murrin quashed his confusion and suspicions and said, "Veikko is my brother."

"Your brother?"

Murrin nodded.

"He scared me." She blushed when she said it, as if fear were something to be ashamed of, but the open admission was only a blink. Alana was still angry. Her posture was tense: hands clenched, spine straight, eyes narrowed. "He said you were worse, and that he'd be back. He—"

"Veikko—Vic—is a bit outdated in his interactions with . . . humans." Murrin hated having to use the word, but it was unavoidable. He was not what she was, would never be what she was. It was something they needed to acknowledge. Murrin stepped closer.

Despite her anger, she was in need of comfort.

"Why did he say you were worse?"

"Because I wanted to get to know you before I told you what I was. None of this was intentional. My Other-Skin was . . ." He paused, considered telling her that he suspected that Veikko had entrapped her, and decided against it. There were many years in which Alana and Veikko would be forced to be near each other: with a simple omission, the strife of her resenting him was avoidable. "It was not to be there. *You* were not to be there. I was coming to meet you, to try to date you as humans do."

"Oh." She crossed her arms over her chest. "But . . ."

"Vic thinks I am 'worse' than others in my family because I am going against tradition . . . or was hoping to." He gave her a sheepish smile. "He thinks it is worse that I would try to court you and then reveal myself. Not that it matters now. . . ."

"How is that worse?"

"I've been asking that question for years." He held out his hand. "It is not what I will teach my children . . . one day when I become a father. It is not what I wanted, but we are together now. We'll work it out."

She took his outstretched hand in hers. "We don't have to stay together."

He didn't answer, *couldn't* answer for a moment. Then he said, "I'm sorry."

"Me too. I don't do relationships, Murrin." Her fingertips stroked his hand absently.

"I didn't mean to trap you, but I'm not eager to let go, either." He expected her to argue, to grow angry, but like the sea, her moods weren't quite what he anticipated.

She smiled then, not like she was unhappy, but like she was dangerous. "So I guess I need to convince you then."

*She really is perfect for me.*

Over the next three weeks, little by little, Alana's doubts were replaced by a tentative friendship. *It doesn't hurt to be nice to him. It's not his fault.* She started telling herself that they could be friends. Even if she couldn't get rid of him, she didn't necessarily need to *date* him, and she definitely didn't need to *marry* him.

One night, she woke with a start in the middle of the night, shivering and thinking of Murrin. They were friends. Okay, he was crashing on her sofa, and he did share her meals, but that wasn't a commitment. It was practicality. He had nowhere to go. He couldn't sleep on the beach. And he bought the groceries, so he wasn't mooching. He was just . . . a good friend who was always there.

*And he makes me happy.*

She went into the living room. Murrin was standing in front of the window, eyes closed, face upturned. The expression on his face was one of pain. She was beside him before she'd thought twice about it.

"Murrin?"

He turned and looked at her. The longing in his eyes was heart-stoppingly awful, but he blinked and it was gone. "Are you ill?"

"No." She took his hand and led him away from the window. "Are *you?*"

"Of course not." He smiled, and it would've been reassuring if she hadn't seen the sadness still lingering in his eyes.

"So, what's up?"

"Nothing." He gestured toward her bedroom doorway. "Go ahead. I'm good."

She thought about it, about him being away from his family, his home, everything familiar. All they talked about was what she wanted, what made her happy, how she felt. *He* had just as much upheaval, more, even. "Talk to me. We're trying to be friends, right?"

"Friends," he repeated. "Is that what we are going to be?"

And she paused. Despite the weirdness, she wasn't feeling uncomfortable anymore. She touched his cheek and let her hand linger there. He was a good person.

She said, "I'm not trying to be difficult."

"Nor am I." He leaned his face into the palm of her hand. "But . . . I'm trying to be careful."

She put her hands on his shoulders and went up on her tiptoes. The touch of her hand against his skin was enough to make the world settle into that wondrous sense of completion that it always did. Over the last couple of days, she'd let her fingertips brush against his arm, bumped her shoulder into him—little touches to see if it was always so perfect. It was. Her heart was racing now, though.

He didn't move.

"No promises," she whispered, and then she kissed him—and that feeling of bliss that she'd brushed with every touch of his skin consumed her. She couldn't breathe, move, do anything but feel.

Murrin watched Alana warily the next day. He wasn't sure what had happened, if it meant anything or if she was just feeling sympathy. She'd been very clear in her insistences that they were friends, *just* friends, and that friends was all they ever could be. He waited, but she didn't mention the kiss—and she didn't repeat it.

*Perhaps it was a fluke.*

For two more days, she acted as she had before The Kiss: she was kind, friendly, and sometimes brushed against him as if it were an accident. It never was; he knew that. Still, she didn't do anything out of the ordinary.

On the third day, she flopped down next to him on the sofa. Susanne was out at a yoga class—not that it would've mattered. Susanne seemed inordinately pleased that Alana wanted him to stay with them; Murrin suspected Susanne wouldn't object to him sharing Alana's room. It was Alana who set the boundaries—the same Alana who was currently sitting very close, staring at him with a bemused smile.

"I thought you liked kissing me the other night," she said.

"I did."

"So . . ."

"I don't think I understand."

"We can *pretend* what we are is friends . . . but we're dating. Right?" She toyed with the edge of her shirt.

He waited for several breaths, but she didn't say anything else. So he asked, "What about your plan to convince me to leave?"

"I'm not sure anymore." She looked sheepish. "I can't promise forever or, truthfully, next month, but I think about you all the time. I'm happier around you than I've ever been in my life. There's something . . . magical when we touch. I know it's not real, but . . ."

"It's not real?" he repeated.

"It's a selchie thing, right? Like the urge to pick up the Other-Skin." She paused. Her next words came out in a rush. "Does it work both ways?"

She was close enough that it would be only natural to pull her into his arms. So he did. He lifted her onto his lap and threaded his fingers through her hair. He let the tendrils tangle around his fingers.

"It's not a selchie thing at all," he told her, "but it does flow both ways."

She started to pull back. "I thought it was just . . . you know . . . a magic thing."

He cradled her head in his hand, holding her close,

and said, "It *is* magic. Finding a mate, falling in love, seeing her love you back? That's real magic."

And his Alana, his mate, his perfect match didn't move away. She leaned close enough to kiss . . . not in sympathy or misplaced emotion, but in affection.

*Everything is perfect.* He wrapped his arms more securely around her and knew that, despite his inability to court her before they were bound, it was all going to be fine. She hadn't said the words, but she loved him.

*My Alana, my mate . . .*

The next evening, Murrin took the bag of pearls to the jeweler his family had always gone to see. Davis Jewels closed in a few minutes, but the jewel man and his wife never objected to Murrin's visits. Mr. Davis smiled when Murrin walked in. "Let me ring Madeline and tell her I'll be late."

Mr. Davis went to the door, locked it, and set the security system. If Murrin closed his eyes, he could watch the older man's steps in his memory, and they'd not vary from what was happening in front of him.

When Mr. Davis went to call his wife, Murrin waited at the counter. He unfolded the cloth he carried for such trips and tipped the bag's contents onto the smooth material.

Mr. Davis finished his call and opened his mouth to speak, but whatever he'd intended to say fled when he looked at the counter. He walked over, glancing only briefly at Murrin, attention fixed on the pearls. "You've never brought this many. . . ."

"I need to make a purchase as well this time." Murrin gestured at the glass cases in the store. "I am . . . marrying."

"That's why the necklace. I wondered." Mr. Davis smiled, his face crinkling into a maze of lines as thick as the fronds of kelp, beautiful in his aging skin. Here was a man who understood love: Mr. Davis and his wife still looked at each other with a glow in their eyes.

He went into the back of the store and brought out a case with the pearl necklace. It was strung with pearls Murrin had selected over many years.

*For Alana.*

Murrin opened it and ran his fingertip over them. "Perfect."

Mr. Davis smiled again, then he took the pearls from the cloth over to his table to examine them. After years of buying pearls from Murrin's family, the man's examination of the pearls—studying their size, shape, color, and luster—was cursory, but still a part of the process.

The order of the jeweler's steps was as familiar as the currents to Murrin. Usually, he waited motionless while the man went about his routine. This time, he stared into the display cases.

When Mr. Davis came over, Murrin gestured at the rows of solitary stones on plain bands. "Help me select one of those?"

The jeweler told Murrin how much he'd pay for the pearls and added, "I don't know how much of that you want to spend."

Murrin shrugged. "I want my wife to be pleased. That is all that matters."

Alana wasn't surprised to see Dreadlocks—*Vic*—leaning on a wall outside the coffee shop where she'd been waiting while Murrin was off on a secret errand. She'd thought she'd seen Vic several times lately. She didn't stop though. She wasn't sure she knew what to say to him. When she'd seen him watching, she thought to ask Murrin about him, but she wasn't sure what to say or ask.

Vic matched his pace to hers and walked alongside

her. "Would you hear what I have to say, Alana?"

"Why?"

"Because you are mated to my brother, and I am worried about him."

"Murrin doesn't seem like he's very close to you . . . and he's fine. Happy." She felt a tightness in her chest, a panic. It was so unlike what she felt when she was with Murrin.

"So you haven't seen him watching the sea? He doesn't ache for it?" Vic's expression was telling: he knew the answer already. "He can't admit it. It's part of the . . . enchantment. You trapped him here when you stole his Other-Skin. He can't tell you he's unhappy, but you'll see it in time. He'll grow miserable, hate you. One day you'll see him staring out to sea . . . maybe not yet, but we can't help it."

Alana thought about it. She *had* seen Murrin late at night when he thought she was asleep. He'd been staring into the distance, facing the direction of the water, even though he couldn't see it from the apartment. The look of longing on his face was heartrending.

"He's going to resent you in time. We always do." Vic's mouth curled in a sardonic smile. "Just as you resent us. . . ."

"I don't resent Murrin," she started.

"Not now, perhaps. You did, though." Vic toyed with one long green strand of his hair. "You resented him for trapping you. It's a cruel fate to be trapped. My mate resented me too. Zoë . . . that was her name. My Zoë . . ."

"Was?"

"I suspect it still is." He paused, a pensive look on his face. "But in time, we resent you. *You* keep us from what we deserve: our freedom. I didn't want to be angry with my Zoë. . . ."

Alana thought about Murrin being trapped, being angry at her, resenting her for keeping him landbound. The bitterness in Vic's eyes wasn't something she wanted to see in Murrin's gaze.

"So what should I do?" she whispered.

"A mortal can't be tied to two selchies . . . just lift up my skin. Murrin will be free then."

"Why would you do that? We'd be—" Alana tried not to shudder at the thought of being bound to Vic. "I don't want to be your . . . anything."

"Not your type?" He stepped closer, as predatory and beautiful as he had looked at the party when they first met. "Aaah, Alana, I feel badly that I bungled things when I met you. I want to help Murrin as my brother helped me. If not for him, Zoë and I would still be . . . trapped. I'd be kept from the sea. Murrin unbound us."

"It's cool that you want to help him, but *I don't want to be with you*." She repressed another shudder at that thought, but only barely.

Vic nodded. "We can work around that detail. I won't ask what Murrin has of you. . . . I don't seek a wife. I need to fix things, though. Maybe I didn't know the right words when we met. I can't say I have the kind of *experience* that Murrin has with mortal girls, but . . ."

Alana froze. "What do you mean?"

"Come now, Alana. We aren't exactly built for faithfulness. Look at us." Vic gestured at himself. That self-assured look was back. "Mortals don't exactly tell us *no*. The things you feel when you see us . . . hundreds of girls . . . not that he's been with every one of them . . . What you feel is instinct. It's not really *love*; it's just a reaction to pheromones."

Alana struggled between jealousy and acceptance. Vic wasn't telling her anything that she hadn't thought. In some ways it was just an extreme version of the logic behind the Six-Week Rule.

"I *owe* him this," Vic was saying. "And you don't really think you love him, do you?"

She didn't cry, but she wanted to. She hadn't said those words to Murrin, not yet, but she'd thought about it. She'd felt it. *Am I a fool? Is any of it real?*

She'd asked Murrin, but was he telling the truth? Did it even matter? If Murrin would hate her in time, she should let him go now. She didn't want that between them.

If Vic was telling the truth, there was no reason to keep Murrin with her, and plenty of reasons to let him go. *Soon.* He wasn't hers to keep. He wasn't really hers at all. *It's a trick.* He belonged to the sea, and with that came relationships, fleeting relationships, with other girls. *Is the way I feel a lie, or is Vic lying?* It made more sense that Vic was telling her the truth: people didn't fall in love this quickly; they didn't break all of their rules so easily. *It's just the selchie thing.* She forced her thoughts away from the roiling mix of emotions and took several calming breaths. "So how do we do it?"

Murrin found Alana sitting at the reef, but she wasn't happy. She looked like she'd been weeping.

"Hey." She glanced at him only briefly.

"Are you okay?" He didn't want to pry too much: her acceptance of him in her life still felt tenuous.

Instead of answering, she held out a hand to him.

He sat behind her, and she leaned back into his embrace. The waves rolled over the exposed reef and up to the rocky ledge where they were sitting. He sighed at the touch of the briny water. *Home.* He couldn't have imagined being this content: his Alana and his water both against his skin.

*Perfection . . . except that Alana seems sad.*

"I didn't expect . . . to care, especially so soon. I want you to be happy," she said. "Even if it's not real—"

"It *is* real." He took out the pearl necklace and draped it around Alana's throat. "And I am happy."

She gasped softly and ran her fingertips over the pearls. "I can't—" She shook her head. "Do you miss it?"

"The sea? It's right here."

"But do you miss . . . changing and going out there? Meeting other people?" She tensed in his arms.

"I'm not going to leave you," he consoled her. His mother had often looked at the sea as if it was an enemy who'd steal away her family if she wasn't careful. That wasn't what he wanted. He wrapped his arms around her again. "I am right where I need to be."

She nodded, but he could feel her tears falling on his hands.

Alana thought about it and decided that trusting Vic completely was foolish. He was right: she needed to let Murrin go before he resented her for keeping him from the sea. Murrin wasn't thinking clearly. Whatever enchantment made him need to stay close to her was keeping him from admitting that he longed for the sea. If he went back . . . there were selchies he could meet. None of that meant that she wanted to risk being tied to Vic—so she opted to try a plan she'd come up with before, but had rejected as too dangerous.

*And unnecessary because love took over.*

He was sleeping when she left the apartment. She thought about kissing him good-bye, but knew that would wake him.

She let the door close behind her; then she went silently to the street and popped the trunk of the car. It was in there, his pelt. It was a part of him as surely as the seemingly human skin she'd caressed when he sat beside her late at night watching old movies with the sound down low. Gently, she gathered the pelt to her, trying not to wonder at how warm it was, and then she ran.

There weren't tears in her eyes. *Yet.* She'd have time enough for that later. First she had to focus on getting to the beach before he realized what she was doing. She ran through the streets in the not-yet-light day. The sunrise wasn't too far off, but it was early enough that the surfers hadn't started arriving yet.

She knew he'd come soon. He had to follow the pull of his pelt when it was in her hands, but knowing didn't make it any easier to hurry. She felt an urgency to get done with it before he arrived, but she felt a simultaneous despair.

*It's for the best.*

She waded into the surf. Waves tugged at her, like strange creatures butting at her knees to pull her under the surface; kelp slid over her bare skin, slithering lengths that made her pulse race too fast.

*It's the right thing for both of us.*

He was there then. She heard Murrin calling her name. "Alana! Stop!"

*In the end, we'll both be miserable if I don't.*

The pelt was heavy in her arms; her fingers clutched at it.

He was beside her. "Don't—"

She didn't hear the rest. She let the waves take her legs out from under her. She closed her eyes and waited. The instinct to survive outweighed any enchantment, and her arms released the pelt so she could swim.

Beside her, she felt him, his silk-soft fur brushing against her as his selchie pelt transformed his human body into a sleek-skinned seal. She slid her hand over his skin, and then she swam away from him, away from the wide open sea where he was headed.

*Good-bye.*

She wasn't sure if it was the sea or her tears, but she could taste salt on her lips as she surfaced.

When she stood on the beach again, she could see him in the distance, too far away to hear her voice if she gave in and asked him to come back. She wouldn't. A relationship based on enchantment was ill-fated from the beginning. It wasn't what she wanted for either of them. She knew that, was certain of it, but it didn't ease the ache she felt at his absence.

*I don't really love him. It's just leftover magic.*

She saw Vic watching her from the shore. He said something she couldn't hear over the waves, and then he was gone too. They were both gone, and she was left reminding herself that it was better this way, that what she'd felt hadn't been real.

*So why does it hurt so bad?*

For several weeks, Murrin watched her, his Alana, his mate-no-more, on the shore that was his home-no-more. He didn't know what to do. She'd rejected him, cast him back to the sea, but she seemed to mourn it.

*If she didn't love me, why does she weep?*

Then one day, he saw that she was holding the pearls he'd given her. She sat on the sand, running the strand through her fingers, carefully, lovingly. All the while, she wept.

He came to shore there at the reef where he'd first chosen her, where he'd watched her habits to try to find the best way to woo her. It was more difficult this time, knowing that she knew so many of his secrets and found him lacking. At the edge of the reef, he slid out of his Other-Skin and tucked it in a hollow under an edge of the reef where it would be hidden from sight. Giant sea stars clung to the underside of the reef ledge, and he wondered if she'd seen them. His first thoughts were too often still of her, her interests, her laughter, her soft skin.

She didn't hear his approach. He walked up to stand beside her and asked the question that had been plaguing him. "Why are you sad?"

"Murrin?" She stuffed the necklace into her pocket and backed away, careful to look where she stepped, no doubt looking for his Other-Skin, then glancing back at him after each step. "I set you free. Go away. Go on."

"No." He had dreamed of being this close to her ever since he'd been forced away from her. He couldn't help it; he smiled.

"Where is it?" she asked, her gaze still darting frantically around the exposed tide pools.

"Do you want me to show—"

"*No.*" She crossed her arms over her chest and scowled. "I don't want to do that again."

"It's hidden. You won't touch it unless you let me lead you to it." He walked closer then, and she didn't back away this time—nor did she approach him as he'd hoped.

"You're, um, naked." She blushed and turned away. She picked up her backpack and pulled out one of the warm hoodies and jeans she'd found at the thrift store when they were shopping that first week. She shoved them at him. "Here."

Immeasurably pleased that she carried his clothes with her—surely that meant she hoped he'd return— he got dressed. "Walk with me?"

She nodded.

They walked for a few steps, and she said, "You have no reason to be here. I broke the spell or whatever. You don't need—"

"What spell?"

"The one that made you have to stay with me. Vic explained it to me. You can go get with a seal girl now. . . . It's what's best."

"Vic explained it?" he repeated. Veikko had convinced Alana to risk her life to get rid of Murrin. It made his pulse thud as it did when he rode the waves during a storm. "And you believed him *why?*"

Her cheeks reddened again.

"What did he tell you?"

"That you'd resent me because you lost the sea, and that you couldn't tell me, and that what I felt was just pheromones . . . like the hundreds of other girls you . . ." She blushed brighter still. "And I saw you at night, Murrin. You looked so sad."

"Now I am sad in the waves watching you." He pulled her closer, folding her into his arms, kissing her as they'd kissed only a few times before.

"I don't understand." She touched her lips with her fingertips, as if there were something odd about his kissing her. "Why?"

Even the thriving reefs weren't as breathtakingly beautiful as she was as she stood there with kiss-swollen lips and a wide-eyed gaze. He kept her in his arms, where she belonged, where he wanted her always to be, and told her, "Because I love you. That's how we express—"

"No. I mean, you don't *have* to love me now. I freed you." Her voice was soft, a whisper under the wind from the water.

"I never had to *love* you. I just had to stay with you unless I reclaimed my skin. If I wanted to leave, I'd have found it in time."

Alana watched him with a familiar wariness, but this time there was a new feeling—hope.

"Vic lied because I'd helped his mate leave him: she was sick. He was out with mortal girls constantly . . . and she was trapped and miserable." Murrin glanced away, looking embarrassed. "Our family doesn't know. Well, they might suspect, but Veikko never told them because he'd need to admit his cruelty too. I thought he'd forgiven me. He said . . ."

"What?"

"He is my brother. I trusted him. . . ."

"I did, too." She leaned closer and wrapped her arms around him. "I'm sorry."

"Sooner or later, we will need to deal with him." Murrin sounded both sad and reluctant. "But in the meantime, if he talks to you—"

"I'll tell you."

"No more secrets," he said. Then he kissed her.

His lips tasted like the sea. She closed her eyes and let herself enjoy the feel of his hands on her skin, gave in to the temptation to run her hands over his chest. It was the same heady feeling she dreamt about most every night since he'd gone. Her pulse thrummed like the crash of waves behind her as he moved to kiss her neck.

*He's mine. He loves me. We can—*

"My beautiful wife," he whispered against her skin.

With more than a little reluctance, she stepped away from him. "We could try things a little differently this time, you know. Go slower. I want you here, but being married at my age isn't good. I have plans. . . ."

"To see other people?"

"No. Not at all." She sat down on the sand. When he didn't move, she reached for his hand and tugged until he sat beside her. Then she said, "I don't want to see other people, but I'm not ready to be married. I'm not even done with high school." She glanced over at him. "I missed you all the time, but I don't want to lose me to have you. And I want you to be *you* too. . . . Did you miss changing?"

"I did, but it'll get easier. This is how things are."

Murrin sounded so calm, and while Alana knew that Vic had lied about a lot of things, she also knew this was something he hadn't needed to lie about. She hadn't imagined the sadness she'd seen on Murrin's face when she'd seen him staring toward the water.

She asked, "But what if you could still have the sea? We could . . . date. You could still be who you are. I could still go to school and, um, college."

"You'd be only mine? But I get to keep the sea?"

She laughed at his suspicious tone. "You do know that the sea isn't the same as being with another girl, right?"

"Where's the sacrifice?"

"There isn't one. There's patience, trust, and not giving up who we are." She leaned into his embrace, where she could find the same peace and pleasure the sea had always held for her.

*How could I have thought it was better to be apart?*

He smiled then. "We get each other. I get the sea, and you have to go to school? It sounds like I get everything, and you . . ."

"I do too. You *and* time to do the things I need to

so I can have a career someday."

She had broken her Six-Week Rule, but having a relationship didn't have to mean giving up on having a future. With Murrin, she could have both.

He reached over and pulled the pearls out of her pocket. With a solemn look, he fastened them around her throat. "I love you."

She kissed him, just a quick touch of lips, and said it back. "I love you too."

"No Other-Skin, no enchantments," he reminded her.

"Just us," she said

And that was the best sort of magic.

# OLD HABITS

# PROLOGUE

"YOU'RE GOING TO MAKE AN EXCELLENT king," Irial said.

And then, before Niall could react, Irial pressed his mouth to the long scar that he'd once allowed Gabriel to carve on Niall's face. Niall felt his knees give out under him, felt a disquieting new energy flood his body, felt the awareness of countless dark fey like threads in a great tapestry weaving his life to theirs.

"Take good care of the Dark Court. They deserve that. They deserve *you*." Irial bowed his head. "My King."

"No." Niall stumbled back, tottering on the sidewalk, nearly falling into the traffic. "I don't want this. I've told you—"

"The court needs new energy, Gancanagh. I got us through Beira's reign, found ways to strengthen us. I'm tired—more changed by Leslie than I'll admit, even to you. You may have broken our tie, seared me from her skin, but that doesn't undo what is. I am not fit to lead my court." Irial smiled sadly. "My court—*your court now*—needs a new king. You're the right choice. You have always been the next Dark King."

"Take it back." Niall felt the foolishness of his words, but he couldn't think of anything more intelligible to say.

"If you don't want it—"

"I don't."

"Pick someone worthy to pass it on to, then." Irial's eyes were lightening ever so slightly. The eerily tempting energy that had always clung to him like a haze was less overwhelming now. "In the meantime, I offer you what I've never offered another—my fealty, Gancanagh, my king."

He knelt then, head bowed, there on the busy sidewalk. Mortals craned their necks to stare.

And Niall gaped at him, the last Dark King, as the reality settled on him. He'd just grab the first dark fey he saw and . . . *turn over this kind of power to some random faery? A* dark *faery?* He thought of Bananach and the Ly Ergs circling, seeking war and violence. Irial was moderate in comparison to Bananach's violence. Niall couldn't turn the court over to just anyone, not in good conscience, and Irial knew it.

"The head of the Dark Court has always been chosen from the solitary fey. I waited a long time to find another after you said no. But then I realized I was waiting for you to leave Keenan. You didn't choose me over him, but you chose the harder path." Irial stood then and took Niall's face in his hands, gently but firmly, and kissed his forehead. "You'll do well. And when you are ready to talk, I'll still be here."

Then he disappeared into the throng of mortals winding down the sidewalk, leaving Niall speechless and bewildered.

# CHAPTER 1

*N*IALL WALKED THROUGH HUNTSDALE, trying to ignore the responses his presence elicited. He'd never walked unnoticed. Over the centuries, he'd been a Gancanagh and the companion to the Dark King; later, he'd been advisor to both the late Summer King and the current Summer King. None of those were roles associated with dismissal. He'd always had influence. When he was with Irial, he hadn't realized that his companion was the Dark King, but that hadn't meant that many of those he'd encountered were unaware. They knew the influence he'd wielded far before he did.

Dark Court faeries—*my faeries now*—scurried around him. They were always in reach, always in sight, always willing to do the least thing that he required. They sought his approval, and despite wishing he was impervious, he couldn't withhold his responses. Being their king meant feeling a connection to them that he'd only ever felt twice—to Irial and to Leslie. Perversely, perhaps, being the Dark King meant he felt even more connected to both the mortal girl and the faery. Leslie, although she'd severed her tie to Irial, was still protected by the Dark Court, and Irial, while no longer king, was the pulse of the court.

Worse, Niall could taste the emotions of every faery he passed. He knew the things they sought to hide with their implacable expressions. He knew their pains and their hungers. It made the world flex with sensory overloads.

Niall walked through the door of the Crow's Nest, the mortal club where his closest friend waited. Seth didn't stand when he saw Niall; he didn't bow or scurry. He merely nodded and said, "Hey."

The weight of the job Niall didn't want seemed to slip away. He sat down at the small table in the back of the dim building. The jukebox was turned on, but the volume was at a bearable level this early in the day. A few mortals threw darts; others watched a soccer match on the oversized television; and a couple silently drank their beers. It was peaceful.

Seth pushed an ashtray toward Niall. "What's up?"

Niall frowned. He'd unconsciously pulled out a cigarette when he sat. *The habit resumed the moment I was connected to him again.* Niall stared at the cigarette and refused to remember the first time he'd smoked. *Memories of Irial are never good to dwell on.*

"You look worse than usual today," Seth said.

Niall shrugged. "Some days . . . some days I hate Irial."

"And the other ones?"

That was the catch, the other days. Niall took a drag off the cigarette, enjoyed the feel of the smoke sliding into his lungs. He exhaled after a moment. "The other days, I know he was right. I *am* the Dark King and whining about it is futile."

"You could always give it away, right?" Seth leaned back, tilting his chair so it was balanced on the back two legs.

"Sure. If I want to be a fool." Niall signaled the waitress and ordered a drink.

Once the waitress walked away, Seth leaned forward. "So what *aren't* you saying?"

Niall exhaled a plume of smoke. "I called Leslie."

"Why?"

"I thought I could suggest that we could be friends.

Leslie and me." Niall paused, but Seth said nothing. The mortal simply stared at him, so Niall continued, "I wasn't calling to suggest we . . . date."

"Bullshit." Seth shook his head. "You don't want to be her friend. Listen to how carefully you had to phrase that lie."

"If it were a lie, I couldn't say it."

"Really?" Seth quirked one brow. "Try to tell me you just want to be her friend. Go ahead. Say it."

"I don't think that—"

"It would be a lie, wouldn't it?" Seth interrupted. "Telling me you want to be just her friend would be a lie. You can't say it."

"Why are we friends?" Niall muttered.

"Because I don't lie to you *or* pander to you." Seth grinned. "You don't like being adored or disobeyed . . . which makes you messed up enough to lead a bunch of crazy faeries, but makes you need a few friends who *aren't* crazy faeries."

They sat silently while Niall accepted the drink the waitress delivered. He'd never had much trouble attracting mortal attention, but he'd expected it to lessen now that the Gancanagh addictiveness was negated. Instead, he was able to touch mortals safely, but was no less appealing to them. In his life, the only one who seemed to want absolutely nothing from him was the mortal who watched him now. Unfortunately, Seth wasn't immune to the traits that made Niall interesting to most mortals. He was simply aware of them—and thus better able to know them for what they were. *Which is why he keeps his distance.* Seth was utterly nonjudgmental, but he was also utterly devoted to his beloved, Aislinn. *And completely hetero.*

The Summer King's ploy of encouraging Niall to watch over the mortal had had a few not entirely unexpected consequences. When Niall accepted that charge, he was still a Gancanagh—addictive to mortals. They hadn't discussed it, but Seth knew why he responded so strongly to Niall: Keenan had expected Seth to become addicted to Niall.

*Not that I objected then.*

The Dark King shook his head. It seemed perverse that the orders he'd carried out for another regent filled him with more guilt than the things he'd done as a king himself. He still spent time with Seth, and he considered the mortal a friend, but there was more than a little evidence that Seth had some degree of addiction to him.

*I was following orders. A few touches on his arm,*

*nothing more than an arm around his shoulders. It wasn't as if anything happened.*

Niall reassured himself with the lies he could whisper in his mind, but the truth was the truth. He'd injured Seth, and the fallout was that he was dangerous to Seth. He always would be, and it was difficult not to take advantage of the thread of addiction and the new allure that Niall wielded as Dark King.

Niall reached into his pocket and pulled out a nondescript stone. He slid it across the bar table. "Here."

"A rock. You shouldn't have." Seth lifted it between his thumb and index finger. A look of peace came over the mortal's face. "Damn."

"If you don't want it . . ." Niall stretched his hand out.

For the first time since Niall had become the Dark King, Seth didn't move out of reach. He also didn't release the stone. Instead, he curled his hand around it, so the stone was wrapped firmly in his palm.

Seth laid his other hand on Niall's forearm briefly. "I'd say no one's ever given me such a useful gift, but that seems too slight. It's . . . difficult being around the Summer Court, the Summer Girls especially. . . . They're good about trying not to manipulate me." Seth paused and looked up at Niall. "*Usually.*"

Niall smiled at the memory of the Summer Girls' lack of restraint. He missed them, some more than others, but he doubted that the Summer King would support the idea of Niall visiting them. "They aren't used to restraint. It speaks well of their regard for you that they even try."

"And you?" Seth prompted.

"I noticed your tendency to keep a table between us," Niall admitted.

"It's not personal, you know?" Seth flashed an amused smile then, one Niall hadn't seen in weeks. "If you were female, your . . . uhhh . . . *appeal* would be cool. Not that Ash would be good with me doing anything then, either, but I'm not into guys. No offense."

Niall laughed. "None taken."

As they talked, Seth had kept the stone clenched in his hand. He took a deep breath, laid it down in front of him, and reached back to unfasten the chain he wore around his throat. While he did so, he kept his gaze on the stone, and Niall realized then how difficult it must've been for the mortal to be surrounded by so many faeries. *And me.* Niall could write it off as merely a result of Seth's relationship with Aislinn, but it wasn't because of the Summer Queen that Seth sat here at the table with Niall. Aislinn would be happier if Seth severed ties with Niall; Keenan would be happier too—for entirely different reasons.

Seth slid the silver chain through a hole in the stone, and then he fastened the chain around his throat. When he was done, he tucked the stone under his shirt. "It's like the world got more in control all of a sudden. I owe you one." Seth poked at the ring in his lower lip. "Not that I have any idea how to repay *that* kind of gift, but I will."

"It wasn't given with a price attached," Niall pointed out. "It's a gift, freely given. No more, no less."

"Yeah, well, you don't look like . . . let's just say, it was a little weird looking at you and having thoughts that I *know* aren't what I think of you, and"—Seth bit his lip ring as he obviously weighed his words— "let's just say, not everyone has been as unaware of how they could affect me."

Niall felt his temper slip a little. "Will you tell me who?"

"Nope." Seth grinned. "I'm not offering you an excuse to start shit with anyone, and now that I have this, I think those head games will be entertaining for *me* for a change. It's all good."

For a moment, Niall debated pressing the matter,

but part of being a friend meant trusting that Seth would speak if he needed help. Niall tapped out another cigarette. "You'll let me know if you need intercession." He looked at Seth as he packed his cigarette. "I have a few faeries who might find it entertaining to assist you."

"Yeah, Ash would be thrilled if I sent the Dark Court knocking." Seth quirked a brow again. "If you want to pick a fight with him, you'll do it on your own. I'm not planning to give you an excuse."

Niall lit his cigarette. "Just don't forget."

"Not today, okay?"

Admitting defeat, Niall held up his hands.

"So how are you?" Seth prodded carefully. "Are you getting along any better with your . . . predecessor?"

The fact was that Niall did want to talk to Seth about that topic, but he didn't quite know what to say, not yet, at least. He took a drink; he smoked in silence.

And Seth drank his own drink and waited.

"He's gone missing regularly, and I don't know what he's doing." Niall shook his head. He was over a millennium old, and he was seeking advice from a mortal child. "Never mind."

"And you don't want to ask what he's doing, but you feel like you should."

Niall said nothing. He couldn't deny it, but he didn't want to admit it either. If Irial had handed all of the court's backroom bargains, illicit investments, and nefarious dealings over to him, he wasn't sure he'd be ready to be the Dark King, but he felt like he *should* know.

"Either let it ride or tell him he needs to report in more. There's not a whole lot else to say, is there?" Seth gestured at the now open dartboards. "Come on. Distraction time."

# CHAPTER 2

IT HAD BEEN HOURS THAT SORCHA SAT unmoving as Devlin brought forth the business that required her attention. One of the mortals that lived among them was mourning. It was a messy business.

"Should I send him back to their world or end his breathing?" Devlin asked her.

"He was a good mortal; he should be allowed to live a while longer." The High Queen moved one of the figures on her game board. "Remind him that if he's leaving us, he can't be allowed to see us. You will need to gouge his eyes."

"They do dislike that," Devlin remarked.

Sorcha tsked. "There are rules. Explain his options; perhaps it will inspire him to learn to temper his emotions so as to stay here."

Devlin made a note. "He's been weeping for days, but I'll explain it."

"What else?"

"Some of the discarded paintings were left in a warehouse for the mortals to 'discover.'" Devlin stepped closer and moved a figurine carved in a kneeling position.

She nodded.

"I've not heard any more of War's intentions." Devlin's expression didn't alter, but she saw the tension he was restraining. "The Dark Court seems unaware. The Summer Court remains clueless. . . ."

"And Winter?"

"The new Winter Queen is not receiving guests. I was refused entrance." Devlin paused as if the idea of being refused was perplexing to him. He had existed from the beginning of time, so it was somewhere between pleasing and befuddling for him when a faery managed to surprise him. "Her rowan said that I could leave a . . . note."

"So we wait." Sorcha nodded. The newer fey were peculiar; their methods seemed crude to her sometimes, but unlike her brother, she was not amused by it. It simply *was*. Emotional reaction to it was unnecessary. She lifted another figurine and dropped it to the marble floor, where it shattered into dust and pebbles. "That play hasn't worked for centuries, Brother."

Devlin lifted another piece and replaced it in the same square. "Will you take dinner or will you be in cloister?"

"I'll be cloistered."

He bowed and left the hall then, leaving Sorcha alone and free to meditate for the evening. She stood and stretched, and then she, too, left the stillness of the hall. Even the minutiae of business must be handled in the same way they always had been—in austere spaces with reasonable answers.

Only the swish of her skirt disturbed the quiet as Sorcha made her way to the small room where she intended to spend the remainder of the day. It was one of the indoor spaces where she meditated. The gardens were preferable, but tonight she'd opted to forego the openness of such places in favor of the intimacy of a tiny room.

Her slippers made no sound as she entered the empty chamber, nor did she verbalize the moment of discord she felt when she found the room occupied. "I did not summon you."

Irial stretched on one of the plush chairs she'd had brought in from a local shop. "Relax, love."

She leveled an unyielding look at the former Dark King. "Faeries of your court aren't welcome in my presence—"

"It's not my court. Not now. I've walked away." He stood as he said it, tense as if he had to restrain himself from approaching her. "Do you ever wish you could walk away, Sorch?"

Sorcha cringed at his bastardization of her name, at the familiarity in his tone. "I am the High Court. There is no walking away."

"Nothing lasts forever. Even you can change."

"I do not change, Irial."

"I have." He was barely a pace away from her then, not touching, but close enough that she felt his breath on her skin. It was all she could do not to shudder. He might not be the Dark King anymore, but he was still the embodiment of temptation.

*And well aware of it.*

He took the advantage. "Have you missed me? Do you think about the last time we—"

"No," she interrupted. "I believe I might've forgotten."

"Ah-ah-ah, fey don't lie, darling."

She backed away, out of reach. "Leave it alone. The details of the last mistake aren't even important enough to be clear anymore."

"I remember. A half-moon, autumn, the air was too cold to be so"—he followed, letting his gaze linger on her, as if her heavy skirts weren't in his way—"exposed, but you were. I'm surprised there wasn't oak imprinted on your skin."

"It wasn't an oak." She shoved him away. "It was a . . ."

"Willow," he murmured at the same time. He looked satisfied, sated, as he walked away.

"What difference does it make? Even queens make mistakes sometimes." Even though he wasn't looking at her, she hid her smile. She had always enjoyed watching him draw her emotions to the surface, enough so that she'd pretended not to know that the Dark Court fed on those emotions. "None of this explains why you are here, Irial."

He lit another of his cigarettes and stood at the open window inhaling the noxious stuff. If she did that, it would pollute her body. Irial—the whole Dark Court—was different in this as well. They took in toxins to no ill effect. For a moment she was envious. He made her feel so many untoward feelings—envy, lust, rage. It was not appropriate for the queen of the Court of Reason to be filled with such things. It was one of the reasons why she'd forbade members of the Dark Court from returning to Faerie. Only the Dark King had consent to approach her.

*But he's not the king anymore.*

She felt a twinge of regret. She couldn't justify giving in to his presence now, not logically.

*And logic is the only thing that should matter. Logic. Order.*

Irial kept his back to her while her emotions tumbled out of control. "I want to know why Bananach comes here."

"To bring me news." Sorcha began reasserting her self-control.

*Enough indulging.*

The former Dark King was kind enough to not look at her as she struggled with her emotions. He stared out the window as he asked, "I don't suppose you'll tell me what news?"

"No. I won't." She took her seat again, calm and in control of her emotions.

"Did it have to do with Niall?" Irial looked at her then. This odd honesty they had shared over the centuries was something she'd miss now that he was no longer the Dark King. No one save her brother and Irial saw this side of her.

"Not directly."

"She is not meant for ruling," Irial reminded her. "When she took the throne before . . . I wasn't there, but I heard the stories from Miach."

"She is a force of destruction that I would not unleash. I will never support her, Irial. I've no quarrel with Niall"—she frowned—"aside from the usual objections to the mere existence of the Dark Court."

And Irial smiled at her, as beautiful and deadly as he'd always been. King or not, he was still a force to fear. *Like Bananach. Like the Summer Queen's mortal.* Often it was the solitary ones who were the most trouble; the tendency toward independence was not something that sat well with the High Queen. It was un-orderly.

He was watching her, tasting the edges of her emotions and believing she was unaware of what he was doing. So she gave him the emotion he craved most from her, need. She couldn't say it, couldn't make the first move. She counted on him to do that. It absolved her of responsibility for the mistake she intended to make.

If he were to realize that she knew the Dark Court's secret, their ability to feed on emotions, she'd lose these rare moments of not being reasonable. That was the prize she purchased with her silence. She kept her faeries out of the Dark Court's reach, hid them away in seclusion—all for this.

The Queen of Reason closed her eyes, unable to look at the temptation in front of her, but unwilling to tell him to depart. She felt him remove the cord that bound her hair.

"You need to say something or give me some clear answer. You know that." His breath tickled her face, her throat. "You can still call it a horrible mistake later."

She opened her eyes to stare directly into his abyss-dark gaze and whispered, "Or now?"

"Or now," he agreed.

"Yes." The word was barely from her lips before she wrapped her arms around him and gave up on being reasonable for a few hours.

Afterward, Sorcha sat and replaited her hair while Irial reclined on the floor next to her. He never provoked her or pointed out the truth of their relationship during these quiet moments.

He smoked silently until she picked up her garments from the floor. When she held the pale cloth to her chest and turned her back to him, he extinguished his cigarette, moved her braid over her shoulder, and fastened the tight bindings.

"Bananach always presses for war . . . but things feel different this time," she admitted.

Part of politics for them had always been admissions that weren't public knowledge. During Beira's reign, Irial had come to her for solace; when he lost Niall, he had come to her for comfort; and when Beira murdered Miach, Irial had come to her—with all his unsettling presence—and together they had mourned the last Summer King. That was the first time she'd opted to indulge in the glorious mistakes they'd shared the past few centuries.

*Today is the last time.*

Sorcha finished dressing as she asked, "And Gabriel? Where does the Hunt stand?"

"With Niall."

"Good. There are factions enough already. With the trouble between Summer and Winter and between Dark and Summer . . ." Sorcha let the words fade away, not wanting to speak them into being.

"Niall strengthens the Dark Court. Had I stayed king . . . Keenan would've attacked in time. He's not going to forgive my binding him. Nine centuries is a long time for rage to fester." Irial's regret was obvious even if he didn't mention it.

They, and few others, knew the reluctance of his bargain with Beira. Binding Miach's son wasn't something the Dark King had wanted to do, but like any good ruler, he made hard choices. That choice had given his court strength. Sorcha, at the time, was grateful that Beira hadn't set her sights on Faerie. Eventually, she would've, but then . . . then, it was Summer's fall, Dark's entrapment, and her staying silent.

"So we wait." Sorcha reclaimed the calm reserve that was her daily mien. She gestured toward the door. "In the interim, I will send Devlin to greet the new king on my behalf."

Irial did not respond to her warning. Instead, he unlocked the door and left.

# CHAPTER 3

*A*FTER CENTURIES OF MAKING THE transition, Irial still found the journey from Faerie to the mortal world jarring. The differently colored landscape, the disconnection of time, and the hordes of mortals all thrilled and displeased him simultaneously. Faerie was unchanged for all of eternity, but the mortal world seemed to alter in a moment. He marveled at the ways it had evolved in the centuries that stretched behind him, and he wondered what would follow their already remarkable progress. Some faeries found mortals to be little more than vermin, but Irial was enthralled by them. *More so since I am no longer a king.* Of course, he was more fascinated by the faery he now approached.

The new Dark King stiffened as Irial came to stand beside him. It was a conscious effort, however: as Dark King, Niall knew where Irial was for several moments prior to this.

The king glanced at him. "Why are you here?"

Irial lowered his gaze respectfully. "I am seeking an audience with the Dark King."

"How did you know I was here?" Niall asked.

"I know you, Niall. I know your habits. This space"—Irial gestured at the small courtyard outside the mortals' library—"soothes you."

Irial smiled as he thought of the year it had been built. He'd been bored, and while he couldn't create, he could fill the architect's mind with visions.

*"Columns?" the man repeated.*

*"Strange, isn't it?" Irial murmured. "Utterly impractical. Who cares what a place looks like?"*

*"Right."*

*Irial continued, "And there were statues, towering nearly naked women; can you imagine?"*

Niall stood staring at the columns that stood on either side of the ornate wooden door to the library. "It always looks familiar."

"Indeed."

"The building . . . it's like somewhere I've seen before." Niall prodded, but he kept his attention on the building as he spoke. "Why is that?"

"It's hard to say," Irial demurred.

Niall glanced his way. "I can taste your emotions, Irial. It's not a coincidence that I find it familiar, is it?"

"You know, my King, it's much easier to get answers when you *order* people to obey you." Irial smiled at a young mother with a pair of energetic toddlers. There was something enchanting about the unrestrained enthusiasm of children of any species. He had a fleeting regret that he hadn't any young to indulge, but such regrets were followed by memories of half-mortal Dark Court offspring who were as easily contained as feral beasts. *Beautiful chaotic things, children.* He'd loved several of them as if they were his own.

"Irial." Niall's tone was testy now. "Why does the library look familiar?"

Irial stepped up to stand a bit closer than his king would find comfortable. "Because a very long time ago, you were happy in the courtyard of a building very like this one."

Niall tensed.

Irial continued as if neither of them noticed Niall's discomfort. "And I was feeling . . . a longing for such moments one day last century when a young architect was staring at his plans. I made a few suggestions to his designs."

The Dark King moved to the side. "Is that to impress me?"

Irial gave him a wry grin. "Well, as it took over a hundred years for you to notice, it obviously *didn't*."

Niall sighed. "I repeat, what are you doing here?"

"Looking for you." Irial walked over to a bench that faced the library and sat down.

As expected, Niall followed. "*Why* are you looking for me?"

"I went to Faerie . . . to see her." Irial stretched his legs out and watched a few mortals slide around on wheeled boards. It was a curious hobby, but he found their agility fascinating.

With a nervous bit of hope, Niall joined him on the bench—at as much of a distance as possible, of course. "You went to see Sorcha."

"I thought she should know that there was a change in the court's leadership."

"She *did* know," Niall snapped. "No one goes there without her consent."

"The Dark King can," Irial corrected.

"You are not the Dark King." Niall's temper flared. "You threw it away."

"Don't be absurd," Irial said. "I gave it to the rightful king."

The emotions coursing through Niall were a delicious treat. Irial had to force his eyes to stay open as the flood of worry, fear, anger, shock, outrage, and a tendril of sorrow washed over him. It was best to not mention that he could read all of this. In theory, only the Dark King could read other regents, but for reasons Irial didn't care to ponder, he had retained that particular trait. Most of his gifts of kingship had vanished: he was vulnerable to any faery who struck him, and he was once again fatally addictive to mortals. The connection to the whole of the court was severed, and the ability to write orders on Gabriel's flesh was erased. These and most every other kingly trait were solely Niall's, but the emotional interpretation was unchanged.

Even as his emotions flickered frantically, Niall spoke very calmly. "If she had wanted to, she could've killed you."

"True."

Several more moments of delicious emotional flux passed before Niall said, "You can't tell me you're going to be my advisor, and then get killed. A good advisor advises. He communicates. He doesn't do idiotic things that can result in infuriating the High Queen."

Innocently, Irial asked, "Does he do idiotic things to infuriate the Dark King?"

"You are far more trouble than you're wor—" Niall's words halted as he tried to speak that which was neither true *nor* his true opinion. He scowled and said, "Don't be an ass, Iri."

"Some things are impossible to order, my king." Irial grinned. "Would you like me to apologize?"

"No. I'd like you to do what you said you would— advise me. You can't do that if you piss off Sorcha enough to get killed or imprisoned or—"

"I'm here." Irial reached out, but didn't touch Niall. "I went to find out why Bananach visits her. The High Queen and I have had an . . . understanding these past centuries."

Niall opened his mouth, but no words came out.

Irial continued, "I needed to know that she wouldn't support her sister in any attempts on your throne. I know chaos is good for the court, but I will not sacrifice you for the court if it is ever in my power. Not again."

"A king's duty is to his court," Niall reminded him.

"And that, Gancanagh, is why I am not qualified to be a king," Irial said gently. "It is not a matter of being tired of my court, or throwing it away, or punishing you, or trapping you, or any of those very diabolical things you would like to believe of me. The court requires a regent who will put its needs first."

"And you think I would?" Niall asked.

"I know you would." Irial smiled to let Niall know that this was a *good* thing, but the taste of Niall's guilt was still heavy. Neither of them commented on what that meant about Niall's loyalties—or the choices Irial had made in the past. *Choices that put Niall second to the court.* There was nothing to say that would lessen the ugliness of those choices.

"If you are my advisor, I *will* know where you are. I will *not* need to worry that you are trapped in Faerie or dead by Devlin's hand because you angered Sorcha," Niall said with more of a snarl than Irial expected.

"Yes, my King." Irial knelt. "Do I take this to mean that my *understanding* with Sorcha is discontinued as well?"

Niall dragged his hand over his face. "Nothing's ever simple with you."

"I can ask her permission to visit her in the future . . . or simply remain here. I'm sure I can find other—"

"Until such time as I say otherwise, you will not enter Faerie," Niall interrupted. "What else did you learn?"

Irial remained kneeling, but he lifted his gaze. "Devlin will visit."

"For what purpose?" Niall made an impatient gesture. "And get up. You're far too amused by this posture, and it's not the least bit about re—" The words froze again.

Irial laughed, but he stood. "It is a *little* about showing respect, my king."

"Irial," Niall started.

"Devlin often seeks respite in the mortal world that he cannot find in Faerie. I have long offered him the court's hospitality; however"—Irial stared at his king then—"Sorcha knows of his visits. I am anxious over this first visit with there being a new king. Sorcha would not be remiss in making a statement. As your advisor, I'm strongly suggesting you keep the Hounds in-house. You should also have Bananach's staunchest supporters in your presence. Devlin tends to get bloody in his visits, and this could be a particularly . . . energetic visit. We can make use of that to rid ourselves of the disloyal. It serves several purposes—for us and for Sorcha."

"What aren't you telling me?"

"About this? Nothing." Irial shook his head. "I will stand at your side, as will Gabriel, and we will make quite clear that the Dark Court is not weak."

"We *are* weakened. If we weren't, you wouldn't have done the ink exchanges."

Irial stared at Niall. "The violence Devlin will bring will nourish them. It is part of why I make him welcome. This time, it will nourish *your* court, and therefore you."

"I require more than violence."

"Call some of the Summer Girls, summon the Vilas, a Hound"—Irial paused as he weighed the words—"*anyone* you desire is yours. Human or faery or halfling. Gabriel's daughter is strong enough to relax with you."

"No."

Irial repressed a sigh. "You weren't celibate in the Summer Court."

"I'm not ready to—"

"Leslie is gone, Niall." Irial crouched down and looked at his king. "She left. She needs a life in the mortal world, for now at least. You, my *Gancanagh*, require the pleasures you're denying. If I thought you'd forgive me, I'd arrange them delivered to you as they once were. You weren't so reticent then *or* when you were in the Summer Court. You are the king of the Dark Court. They are all yours to command."

"Now that I'm their king, they might not feel free to say no." The fear in Niall's expression was only a tiny portion of the overwhelming fear Irial could taste. Niall lowered his voice. "I don't want them to feel trapped."

"Don't be foolish." Irial caught Niall's gaze. "I would offer you anything you need. They would too. It's not a trap to offer happiness to one's regent." Irial's affection for Niall was not the least bit hidden. "If you worry, I will collect solitaries for you, or perhaps you ought to go see Sorcha yourself. . . . There are those who are not your subjects. Is that what you seek? Tell me, my King, and I will make it so."

"No. I simply don't want . . . emotionless sex." Niall looked away. "After Leslie—"

Irial growled. "She left."

"I *know*." Niall glared. "It's only been a moment, though, and . . . I can't."

"As your advisor, I am strongly suggesting that you listen to my advice. Don't weaken your court by being mawkish. You've never once been monogamous in your life, and if you think you could've been so with her, you're a fool. You were a Gancanagh. Now, you're the King of Temptation. You are what you are."

"You're a bastard. You know that?"

"I do." Irial stood. "By tomorrow Devlin will be here, and if you expect to be your best, I'd strongly recommend that you go get—"

"I hate that you made me their king," Niall said, and then he walked away.

After he was gone, Irial smiled.

*That went surprisingly well.*

# CHAPTER 4

*N*IALL STOOD AT ONE OF THE GATES to Faerie. Once he'd marveled that mortals didn't cross it more often, but unlike faeries and halflings, most mortals didn't see the gate. The mortals and halflings who ended up in Faerie were taken or stumbled there unawares. *Which isn't much different from Dark Court faeries.* The High Queen wasn't particularly tolerant of uninvited guests, especially those of his court. The Dark Court's exodus from Faerie had happened long enough ago that the whole of Faerie was her domain, while the mortal world was shared among the rest of the faeries.

*Not that I'd want to return the court* there.

If Irial could hear him, if Keenan could hear him, if most anyone he'd known these past several centuries could hear how easily he was slipping into the role of Dark King, he liked to think they would be shocked.

The truth, of course, was that more than a few of them had accepted his new role as easily as he had. *Because it was inevitable.* He understood that now. When Irial had first offered him the throne, Niall had thought it horrific, but time had a way of removing illusions.

The complications of Devlin visiting the Dark Court were unclear to Niall. There was obviously some element of the situation that Niall didn't know. Irial was a lot of things, but he wasn't prone to exaggeration. If he thought Devlin's visit was significant, it was.

Niall splayed his fingers over the veil that separated the worlds. The insubstantial fabric encased his hand as if it were a living thing. *I could go to her.* Once, Sorcha had been a friend of sorts. Once, Niall had imagined himself half in love with her. He hadn't been, but she was everything Irial wasn't. At the time, that was reason enough to try to call his friendship love.

"Help."

Fingers grabbed his hand and tugged. Someone on the other side clutched him, grabbed hold of his wrist, and clung to him. The voice that seemed to accompany the desperate gesture was thin.

"Please, I can't see."

A second hand grabbed Niall's arm as if to pull him through, and in the instant, any thought of entering Faerie fled. Niall tugged.

An old man came tumbling through the veil. He still held tightly to Niall's arm. "Please."

Niall steadied him and in doing so glanced down and saw the man's face: both of his eyes were missing. The eyelids drooped over empty sockets. "Who are you?"

"No one." The man wept. "I'm no one, and I saw nothing. . . . I promise."

"You're in Huntsdale," Niall said gently. "Do you know where that is?"

The relief on the man's wrinkled face was heartbreaking. He whispered, "I do. Home. This is where I should be. I was wrong before. I thought . . . I followed someone, but"—he shook his head—"she was an illusion. It was all an illusion."

There was no need to ask which faery he'd followed. It didn't matter. Mortals had been stolen away, misled, trapped, and tricked for as long as the two races coexisted.

"Let me help you." Niall had no obligation to the man, but he wasn't at ease with walking away. The Dark Court wasn't evil. It would've been easier if they were. A clear division between good and evil, right and wrong, would simplify everything, but life was rarely simple. His court was formed of passions, of shadows, of impulses. The Dark Court—and its king—were that which balanced the High Court. In this instant, balancing the High Court meant offering kindness.

"You're one of them." The man yanked his hand away from Niall. "I'm not going back. She had them take my eyes, said I'd be free. . . . You can't—"

"I have no intention of harming you. Unlike Sorcha, I am not cru—" Niall's words halted: he was capable of cruelty, but the difference was in the motivations. He'd never understood the High Court opposition to mortals knowing of the fey. He certainly never grasped the logic of breaking them for knowing. "You know we don't lie."

The man nodded.

"I offer you my protection. I cannot undo what she did to you, but I can offer you a haven." Niall waited for a moment, trying not to rush the man, but increasingly aware that someone would probably notice that a mortal had exited Faerie without permission. Keeping his voice calm, he added, "You are free to leave anytime you choose. There are no punishments for deciding to leave."

"She said this"—the man touched his face—"wasn't a punishment."

"I will not cause or allow injury done to you." Gently, Niall touched the man's wrist. "If you prefer, I will deliver you to a mortal physician. Either way, we should leave this place."

The man sighed. "I don't think mortals would be much use against your sort. I'll accept your offer—for the moment at least."

"I'm going to carry you," Niall warned, and then he lifted the old man, cradling him like a child. It was akin to lifting an empty sack, and Niall wondered how long the frail thing had been in Faerie. Once, Sorcha had explained that the blinding was for the mortals' good as well. *Seeing the changed world after so long is troubling to them," she'd said. "This is kinder." He'd disagreed, but Sorcha had merely smiled and added, "The fanciful ones, the artists, are fragile. Seeing us after they've left is far crueler."*

The walk through Huntsdale wasn't long, but it was long enough that solitaries and those of other courts saw him. None spoke to him, but more than a few faeries stared in blatant curiosity. The sensation wasn't displeasing: he was opposing the High Court and doing something that soothed his sense of guilt over past follies.

As he approached his new home, a thistle-fey scurried forward and opened the front door.

"Gabriel," Niall called.

The Hound—who had once been a friend, more recently an enemy, and was currently Niall's most trusted resource—entered the foyer with a silent grace that should've been impossible for such a bulky creature. "My King."

"King?" the man murmured.

"Her opposition," Niall soothed as he lowered the man's feet to the floor. "You are safe here."

Gabriel shook his head. "You trying to start trouble?"

"Perhaps," Niall admitted, "but I don't suppose that's a problem, is it?"

The grin on Gabriel's face was matched by his mellow tone as he said, "Nope, just making sure I understand."

"The High Queen blinded this man. I have offered him safety here." Niall made a beckoning gesture to one of the Vilas who always lingered wherever Gabriel walked. "You can go with this woman. She'll find you a chamber to rest in while you decide what you want."

The man reached out awkwardly, clearly not yet used to his lack of sight.

Niall took the man's hand and started to lead him to the Vila. "This is Natanya and—"

"What's *your* name, king?"

The belligerence in the man's voice made both Niall and Gabriel grin. This wasn't a mortal who would curl into himself and give up. His bravery made him even more worthy of protection.

"Niall."

"Am I safe from her here, Niall?" The man tilted his head. "They might be pretty, but they're monstrous. You know that, don't you?"

"We do," Niall said.

"Are you all pretty too?" the mortal asked.

It was an obvious curiosity, but it stilled everyone all the same. Natanya stared at Niall; Gabriel shrugged. Niall wasn't sure what answer was truth. *Pretty?* Gabriel was akin to a sort of menacing mortal who lingered in disreputable bars: slow to rile, but quick to strike if angered. He was lean, scarred, and silent. The gray-eyed, gray-skinned Vilas were all beautiful; even in violence, their movements were elegant; but they were as likely as not to dab blood on their lips for color. And Niall . . . being fey meant possessing an innate attractiveness to mortals, being a Gancanagh meant he'd been born to seduce. *Pretty?*

He'd thought so once, many centuries ago, but that was not a word he'd found fitting for a very long time. He'd been proud of it, though: he kept his hair shorn to emphasize the scar that he was certain made him anything but pretty. The trouble was that Niall didn't see the Dark Court denizens as ugly, either. Even while he hated things that happened in the court, even when he'd found a vast number of its faeries terrifying, he'd never thought them either pretty or ugly. They simply *were*.

"The High Court thinks we are monsters." Niall let his own emotions into the words. "I suspect that if you saw us, you'd think many of us are too. What we aren't, though, is calmly cruel. What we *aren't* is like them."

The man nodded.

Natanya and Gabriel were both smiling, and there was little doubt in Niall's mind that his own acceptance of his court was likely to be repeated throughout their number.

"Natanya?" Gabriel motioned toward the mortal. "Look after him for your king and for me."

"As if he were your own child, Gabriel." The Vila beamed at Gabriel. The silver chains that held her bone-hewn shoes to her feet clattered as she moved across the room to take the mortal's hand in hers. She led the man away, and for a moment Gabriel was silent.

He shot an assessing glance at Niall. "Salt in a wound when they learn that you brought one of Sorcha's discarded mortals here."

"That is true."

"There are only two faeries she could strike that would truly weaken your court—or make you look weaker," Gabriel pointed out. "Those are the logical choices. I'm not going over *there*, and if I'm not able to face Devlin, I need replaced as the Gabriel, so I'm not needing protection. The other one . . ."

"He was already over there. That's how I know Devlin's coming here."

"Huh." Gabriel snorted. "Didn't waste any time trying to protect you, did he? Threaten her, seduce her, or both?"

Niall didn't answer that, but he suspected that Gabriel knew the answer well enough. Irial might not have spoken to the Hound yet, but they'd been a team for as long as Niall had known Irial. Before the day was over, Irial would seek Gabriel out, tell him the things he thought necessary, try again to assure that Niall was safe.

*And not once think about the way he endangers himself now.*

A regent could prevent any of his or her subjects from seeing the gate, and a strong solitary could impose restrictions on weaker fey. A part of Niall thought stealing others' will was wrong, but he understood now that there were times that choices were a matter of opting for the lesser of several wrongs.

"It is my decree that none of the *subjects* of the Dark Court may enter Faerie without my consent." Niall looked at Gabriel's forearms as the command appeared there. "Until such time as I speak otherwise, the gates are unseen to my subjects."

The Hounds didn't offer fealty, so they could go to Faerie. Of course, they wouldn't do so unless Gabriel directed them. Irial, however, could no longer see the gates or enter Faerie.

# CHAPTER 5

ORCHA DIDN'T RESPOND WHEN DEVLIN walked into her gardens. She'd long since stopped acknowledging him when he did so. *As if it will make the future less difficult.* She hated that he was an anomalous creature—almost as much as she treasured it. He would be her undoing if she let him. Perhaps he would be even if she tried to stop him. In some matters the threads of possibility were seemingly determined.

"My queen?"

She didn't turn. Facing him as they lied in their omissions made the whole business even less palatable. "Brother."

"I have blinded the mortal as you commanded." His voice was as empty as it often was, but that too was a lie of sorts. Her brother might pretend to be High Court, but she was under no illusion that he was solely her creature. He was *hers*, though.

"I have business there that needs tending," she said.

He'd expected as much, but he'd hoped otherwise. She could see the resignation in the moment in which he frowned. The expression was gone too fast for most anyone to see, of course, but she saw much that no one else would. The pause before replying was infinitesimal, but it was still there.

"Whatever you command," he said.

She turned. "Indeed?"

Before she could catch his gaze, he dropped to his knees. "Have I failed you?"

Sorcha didn't speak. *Have you?* She knew he would, but had he? Her vision of the past was unclear. The present and future took her focus so fully, and eternity stretched longer than she could grasp. *Have you?* She waited, looking down at the first faery she'd made. Before he existed, there were only two, Discord and Order, twins who had once created one thing together. *You.* She reached down and ran her fingers through his multihued hair. It was unlike that which graced any other faery, and it was resistant to her will. He couldn't be altered by her touch, not now that he was real. Other faeries couldn't either, but they weren't her creations.

They'd stayed this way for hours before. Devlin had

the patience and willpower to kneel for as long as she required it. He didn't falter, didn't sleep, didn't wince. He simply waited. She wondered idly if he could out-wait her.

"Could we spend decades thus, Brother?" she murmured.

He lifted his gaze. "Sister?"

"If I demanded it, how long would you kneel thusly?" She traced up his cheekbones and down the outside of his jaw with her fingertips. "Would you falter from exhaustion first?"

"You are my queen."

"I am," she agreed. She cupped his face in her hands and held him still. "That's not an answer."

He didn't even try to resist. "Do you require me to falter or to succeed in waiting as long as you wait?"

She smiled then. "Such a wise answer. You will do whatever I require then? You will strive to not fail me? You will serve me forever?"

"As your servant, your Bloodied Hands, your brother, your advisor, I will do all that you demand." He bowed his head, and she loosened her grip to allow it. Then he added, "The last of those questions is unanswerable."

"It is." She turned her back, but she did not release

him. She fashioned a chair of flowering vines and sat down. In her hands, a book appeared. She hadn't created it. She had no such skill with art. She had, however, willed it to appear in her hands. Ignoring her brother, she began to read.

He stayed there kneeling for the next three hours as she read.

Sometime into the fourth hour, she lifted her gaze to look at him. "I need you to go to the new Dark King. Give him word of the High Court's acknowledgment of his new station. Stress to him that, while we are not at conflict, I will not hesitate to act as required to keep order."

Devlin stayed silent, awaiting the rest.

"It would be prudent to make clear your willingness to strike at the Dark Court should it be required," she continued. "Perhaps a fight with the former Dark King? The Gabriel? His mate? The action should be something that emphasizes your assets as the High Court's weapon."

"As you will," Devlin murmured.

The brief look of hurt on his face was reason enough for Sorcha to know that her actions were necessary. It would not do for Devlin to be coddled. Reminding him that he was a weapon to be utilized helped keep his tendency toward emotion in check.

*It is for the best.*

"Do you require death?" he inquired. "That will limit the choice of combatants."

Sorcha paused and sorted through the threads that had come into focus as Devlin spoke. The consequences of some deaths would be disastrous. *Unexpectedly so.* Later, she would mull the import of one such thread, but for now, she said only, "Not of that list. Injure one of them, or injure many. A lesser death is allowable, but not the new king's advisor or thug. A regent does tend to react poorly to such losses."

The moment was there, and she knew he would ask. In this, as in so many other things, her brother was predictable. He looked directly at her with those unnatural dark eyes and asked, "Would your *thug's* death elicit such a reaction?"

"My assassin is my advisor and my creation"—she pursed her lips in an expression that should convey the dislike she knew was an appropriate emotion—"so I would be sorely inconvenienced by your death. I dislike being inconvenienced."

He bowed his head again. "Of course."

"If I were emotional regarding any faery in my court, it would be you, Brother." She stood and walked over to him. "You have value to me."

The relief evinced in his slight relaxing of posture was noteworthy for him. This was what he required: reminders of his value, of his use, of his proper role. He never spoke of the fact that his choice of her court was a struggle, but she knew. *As does Bananach.* It was in his nature to crave both Discord and Order. In her court, at her hand, by her word, she could give him that. *And keep him from Bananach by doing so.*

"I expect there to be violence enough that the Dark Court will be suitably reminded of my strength," she added.

"As you require."

She expected that this was a moment in which she should offer him comfort. He evoked that in her, an urge to nurture, but it would hasten the seemingly inevitable future. *When he becomes my enemy.* Instead she said, "You will not allow yourself injured, Brother. The High Court is represented by your success in this. Do not fail me."

"I will not." He was still on his knees, still unflinching. "May I depart?"

She set a storm over his head and walked away. "When the next hour ends, you may rise."

As she left, she directed a small bolt of lightning to

strike him. There was no cry of pain. A tangle of wild roses grew around him as she opened the gate to exit the garden. The thorns didn't pull him off balance, but they would make his position increasingly unpleasant over the next hour. That pain would be predictable; the flowers' rate of growth would be precise. However, in deference to Devlin's discordant streak, she set the lightning strikes to a random order.

# CHAPTER 6

Aᴏғ ᴛᴇʀ ᴛᴇɴᴅɪɴɢ ᴛᴏ ᴀ ғᴇᴡ ʙᴜꜱɪɴᴇꜱꜱ matters that required negotiations that the Dark King didn't need to know about just yet, Irial finally approached what appeared to be a derelict warehouse to follow up on the last task of the day. The creatures that filled the building evoked fear and discomfort by their mere presence. When they ran, they were a beautiful nightmare—so much so that even the former King of Nightmares felt a flush of terror roll over him. It was a warning that even regents should heed: inside the stable, the Hunt ruled. No kingship, no law in either world, nothing other than Gabriel's word mattered once one entered their domain. Consequently, it was one of the few places in this world or in Faerie that Irial would approach with caution.

Irial stopped at one of the doors and waited for a moment.

One of the younger Hounds stepped forward and flashed a sulfurous green gaze at Irial. The sight of the green eyes in the dark was more comforting than menacing, but sharing that detail would elicit an undesired reaction from the Hound. Fighting was rarely one of Irial's preferred hobbies, so he kept his thoughts to himself.

"I would speak with the Gabriel." Irial didn't lower his gaze, but he didn't stare directly at the Hound.

A second Hound, who leaned against the building, crossed his arms. "Don't think Gabriel is expecting you."

"Do you deny me entrance?" Irial held his hand out, palm up, as one would for any number of feral beasts.

The first Hound sniffed Irial's hand. Then, he stepped closer and sniffed the air near Irial's face. "Smells like the other place."

"Faerie," Irial murmured.

The second Hound growled. "Can't run there. *She* says no visits. Wants us asking permissions first."

"I bring word of violence."

At that, both Hounds' attitudes shifted. One pushed off the building and pulled the door open. "Go ahead in. Gabriel's in the ring."

As always, the Hounds' steeds were in various forms. Cars, motorcycles, and beasts waited in wooden stalls. A few of the steeds sat in rafters in various guises. Here, they could adopt whatever form they preferred. Irial felt a twinge of longing for Faerie then. Once, forever ago now, these steeds could wear whatever form they wanted all of the time. At first, they continued to do so in the mortal world, but now, they were more cautious—for obvious reasons: the sight of the vibrant green dragon that slept in the center aisle would alarm most mortals.

The dragon stirred enough that a clear lens flickered over one of its massive eyes. It yawned, giving Irial a glimpse of teeth as big as his own arms. Then, scenting him, its nostrils flared. It had awakened.

Both of the creature's eyes were now focused on Irial.

"I'm here to speak with the Gabriel," Irial said. "I bring word of blood for the Hunt. A guest from Faerie will be coming here."

The dragon flicked a thin purple tongue out, not far enough to touch Irial, but close enough that for a moment, Irial thought he'd misremembered how close one could stand and still be at a safe distance. But then the tongue retracted, and the beast closed its eyes.

Irial resumed walking toward the ring at the far back of the building.

The scent of blood and the cacophony of snarls and rumbling voices were unaltered, but Irial had no doubt that they all knew he approached. The steeds shared nonverbal communication with their riders—and with the Hound who led them all. Everyone in the stable knew what Irial had said to the Hound at the door and to the steed that rested in the form of a dragon. That did not, however, mean that any of them saw reason to interrupt whatever fight was in progress. The Hunt had different priorities than the less feral faeries often understood.

Irial closed the distance, prepared to wait for the match to end. As he reached the edge of the crowd, the Hounds parted to let him walk to the front. At the side of the roped-off ring, Irial stopped and gaped.

There were few things that would be as unexpected as the sight before him: Niall stood in the center of the ring. Blood trickled from a set of teeth marks on his forearm and soaked the denim around a jagged tear on his leg. His opponent, an average-sized Hound, growled as Niall landed a punch that rocked the Hound's head backward. Before the Hound could respond, Niall followed through with a second punch to the throat, which had the Hound toppling to the straw-covered floor.

As Irial stared, Gabriel came up beside him. "Always was a ruthless bastard in a fight."

"Does he do this often?" Irial watched his king put one boot-clad foot on the fallen Hound's chest.

"Most every night since you made him king." Gabriel's emotions tangled between amused and content. "Seems to be taking to the job if you ask me."

"Perhaps I *should've* asked you," Irial murmured. He felt a curious wave of sadness that Gabriel had kept this from him. It wasn't wrong of Gabriel, but it was yet another loss.

Niall looked over his shoulder then to stare at Irial. While the Hounds couldn't taste emotions, the rest of the Dark Court could. Of course, that didn't mean they always *understood* the reason for the emotion— which was abundantly clear in the surge of fury that Niall felt.

The Dark King grabbed the Hound at his feet and hauled him upright. He shoved the injured Hound toward the rope and snarled, "Next."

If they had been any other two faeries, Irial would've pulled his king aside and explained that the sorrow was not over seeing Niall battering the fallen

Hound, but over Gabriel's secrecy. They weren't any other faeries though, so Irial did the next best thing: he stepped forward.

"Don't be absurd," Niall ground out.

Without taking his gaze from his king, Irial ducked under the rope. "If you would, Gabe?"

"Hear we're expecting blood. Who's visiting?" Gabriel asked.

"Devlin. Sorcha undoubtedly would like him to make a statement. It *is* traditional." Irial waited for a moment, listening to the receding footsteps and motors already coming to life. The Hunt was vacating the stable, undoubtedly at Gabriel's silent command.

Softly, Irial added, "The pups should stay close to home for a few days."

Gabriel's teeth snapped and a low snarl emanated from him. "My pups are—"

"Safe enough," Irial interrupted, "*if* they stay out of sight. Sorcha has issued orders to take halflings, so just tell them to stay low for a few days."

Niall took a step toward Irial and said in a low voice, "This is why I need you here. You have centuries of dealing with the nuances. The court needs that wisdom." He did not add that he needed Irial too, but the emotion was there for Irial to taste—as was the resentment. "I require your presence and your safety. The gates to Faerie are unseen to you now, Irial."

"Well, this evening is just full of surprises, isn't it?" Irial raised a fist. "You'd leash me then? I went there for—"

Gabriel cleared his throat loudly. "We'll stir up a little nourishment for the court tonight." He paused briefly and then said, "Niall?"

Niall glanced away from Irial.

"Your strength is the court's strength. Don't much matter whether you feed on fury or lust, or who you do that with, but you need to be strong." Gabriel put word to what they all knew. "I'll gather some of the solitaries or the Summer Girls if you'd rather—"

"The Summer Girls are *not* to be given to the court." Niall bared his teeth. "No one is permitted to be touched without their consent."

"We know that," Gabriel said. "The *old* king made that rule. The Hunt brings them, but they choose to stay or go."

Niall gave Irial a curious look, but Irial said nothing. If he'd told Niall, it wouldn't have changed a thing, but it would've started a conversation that neither of them had been ready for in the years that had passed. Knowing Irial regretted being unable to protect Niall didn't undo the past.

Finally, Niall looked away. "Do what you must to bring nourishment for the court."

"And you," Irial added. "A few fights aren't enough and you know it . . . although I'm glad you *are* fighting at least. Now if you were fu—"

"Stop." Niall's emotions were all over the spectrum. His gaze snapped back to Irial. "Don't think I'm going to be easy to beat just because there were a few Hounds trying to pummel me."

At this, Irial's flash of irritation vanished. He lowered his fist and laughed. "You've never been easy about anything, love."

The fist that slammed into Irial's face was faster than he remembered Niall's punches being, but it had been a very long time since Niall had hit him. Striking a king wasn't tolerated unless it was in an agreed-upon match, and for the past eleven centuries, Niall had known that Irial was a king.

*And that I withheld that little detail when we met.*

A second punch didn't come.

Niall stared at him. "We're in a ring, Irial. You can strike a king here."

Irial grinned as he heard Gabriel call, "We ride."

As the Hunt started to leave, the stable was a storm

of emotions that both he and Niall consumed. While those emotions were still flooding them, Irial said, "Should I have extended that offer to you a second time when you learned that I was a king?"

"Maybe." Niall smiled briefly. "I thought about this often enough."

"Hitting me?"

"No," Niall corrected as he swung at Irial. "Beating you half to death."

Then, they were too busy to argue. Irial wasn't as quick with his fists, but he let every emotion he felt free. Reading Irial's emotions and Niall's own rage-guilt-pleasure over the knowledge put Niall off-center enough that Irial was able to withstand the next hour better than either of them had anticipated.

Eventually, however, Irial was prone on the ground. He couldn't open his left eye, and he was fairly certain that at least one rib was cracked. "I'm done."

Instead of walking away as Irial expected, Niall plopped down on the floor. He was covered in blood and sweat, and he was content.

"It's easier than I thought," Niall said.

"I'm not *that* easy to beat." Irial smiled and then winced as the movement made his lip bleed more freely.

"It's easier being their king than I thought it would be," Niall corrected.

"I knew what you meant." Irial forced himself to sit upright, and immediately reassessed the number of broken ribs to at least three. "You were always their next king. You knew that. I knew it. Hell, Sorcha knew it."

Niall's eyes widened slightly. "She told you that?"

Irial had forgotten how much more open Niall had always been after a fight. "Not directly, but her emotions did."

Hesitantly, Niall asked, "What emotions? The High Queen doesn't . . . *does* she?"

"She does in the presence of the Dark King." Irial held Niall's gaze as best he could with one eye swollen mostly shut. "I asked if you were ever going to be the next king, and she felt both excited and sorrowful. I didn't know for sure then, but I hoped—and now, I think that she knew, that she looked forward to you being this."

They sat silently, but not without communicating. Over the centuries, Irial had read Niall's emotions without his knowledge. Tonight, for the first time, Niall consciously revealed his emotions for the purpose of sharing the things he couldn't verbalize. The years had changed them both, but those changes had only made Niall more suited to being the Dark King. Niall was both relieved and disappointed that this was so. He was also happier than he'd been since he'd left Irial's side more than nine centuries ago.

*As am I.*

Eventually, Niall stood. "Things will never be like they were before."

"I didn't think they would." Irial stared up at him.

Unexpectedly, Niall extended a hand—and then grinned as he tasted Irial's shock. "You fight better than I remember."

"You broke several ribs." Irial accepted Niall's hand and was pulled to his feet. "I can't see from one eye, and I think something in my knee ripped."

"Exactly." Niall released Irial's hand and grinned.

"Maybe next time I'll do better." Irial regretted the words as soon as they were out, but he wasn't going to admit that. He concealed his emotions and stilled his expression as best he could.

For a moment, Niall said nothing; his emotions were likewise locked down tightly enough that they were out of Irial's reach. Then Niall shrugged. "Maybe."

Irial lifted the rope for Niall to duck under.

They walked out together in silence. Niall did not tell Irial to depart as they walked to the house that had once been Irial's, nor did he invite Irial to stay. At the step, they paused, and for a foolish hopeful moment, Irial waited. Then, Niall reached out to the gargoyle that adorned the door, and Irial left for his current residence. It was a peaceful parting.

*Things might be all right after all.*

Irial knew they both were keeping secrets that could change the trust they were building, but it was progress. For now, that was enough.

*Once we get past the visit from the High Queen's emissary.*

What Irial had learned in his conversations with his spies had directed a course of action he'd intended to discuss with Gabriel tonight, but Irial had long since discovered the importance of improvising. A chance to mend his relationship with Niall outweighed the benefits of informing Gabriel of Irial's plans. He could handle matters quietly, and then apologize to Niall if he was found out.

# CHAPTER 7

*D*ESPITE THE THINGS LEFT UNSAID, NIALL knew that the house he lived in had not been intended to go to the new Dark King. If the last king had died, Niall would be entitled to all his predecessor's belongings. The last king, however, was far from dead. *He is very much here. Thankfully.* Niall smiled—and then paused. *Do I forgive everything?* He had set aside centuries of dislike for Irial in a few short weeks. *No.* Niall walked across the foyer, knowing that servants waited in hopes of his needing something, anything. There were those in the Dark Court that seemed to thrive on being given orders. It was perplexing to him. *Forgiving* everything *will never happen.* That didn't mean that Niall could cling to the illusions that he'd held to these past centuries: he couldn't forget the good things any more than the bad.

Ignoring the faeries that waited in every alcove and

around every corner, Niall made his way to his chambers. He opened the door and stopped.

"He said you needed me." She stared at him, not moving, not crossing the thick carpet to stand nearer him. Once, she would've. Now, she watched him and said, "The Hound. He brought me here because you needed me."

"No," he corrected. "I needed a *body* to be here. Not you. It's what I am now. I have need of a body."

She shrugged. "I am a body."

"No." He wasn't exactly *happy* to find one of the Summer Girls waiting there. He tried to think of her that way: one of the Summer Girls. He tried not to think of her as someone he'd once protected. It didn't work.

"You could be anyone." He slammed the door closed. "You—"

"You don't need to try to make me upset, Niall." She gave him a sorrowful smile. "Tell me."

"Tell . . ."

"What you need," she supplied. Even in this place, far different from her court, she swayed a little as if she heard music still. The long brown hair that she usually pinned into curls hung straight today. "The last Dark King invited us here often enough. Tonight, though . . . I hoped it was you I was here for when I saw the Hound. I would've come without that hope, but I'm glad to be brought to you."

Niall hadn't thought about it overly much. It made sense, though: the Summer Girls were without Keenan's hatred of the Dark Court. They were creatures of pleasure, the embodiment of only the joys of Summer. Later, he'd ask Gabriel how often the Summer Girls had visited the court—and how often they could visit safely. Even in his fury with Keenan, Niall still believed that the Summer King would not sit idly by if the Summer Girls were harmed. His former liege manipulated as freely as every other powerful faery did—*including me*—but often that was out of the protectiveness he felt for his faeries. The Summer Girls, former mortals who'd been cursed to be faeries dependent on Keenan for their very sustenance, were particularly important to the Summer King.

"He always asked about you. The last king"—she unfastened her sundress—"I thought of telling you sometimes. More than once, he asked me to come to him right after I'd lain in your arms."

Niall stilled. *Did you? Why? How often?* There was nothing he could think to say that didn't sound bizarre—not that she would be fazed by a bizarre statement. The Summer Girls were unflappable. He stared at her as she dropped the dress.

"We knew that one day"—she stepped from the dress that now puddled around her feet—"you'd return to this court."

If she had been any of the other Summer Girls, her words would've surprised him, but Siobhan had always told Niall things he hadn't thought anyone noticed. *She is my friend.* He remembered the years after she'd first joined the Summer Court, when she realized that Keenan's love was as fleeting as his attention had been.

As she watched him, she pulled her hair over her bare shoulder. "I remember when you taught me about this world, Niall. You spoke of them, of *his* court, with a difference in your voice. Your eyes grew dark when you spoke of him. Did you know that?"

The way she watched him was exciting. When he'd been in the Summer Court, he had always favored her, but the Summer Girls never seemed to care whose arms they were in. *Do they, and I just didn't know?* He turned away from her, dismissing her with effort, and walked to the low chest at the foot of his oversized bed. He propped one foot up and began unlacing his boots.

Without looking back at her, he said, "You could go. There are others—"

She laughed. "I *miss* you. I'm here by choice. My

king wouldn't like it, but we are not disloyal to him. We did not speak of our court here . . . except to Irial, and he only asked after you."

"Keenan would not approve," Niall pointed out rather foolishly. What the Summer King approved of wasn't Niall's concern. Even now, the Dark Court was strong enough to withstand any threat the Summer Court offered them. *Unlike the High Court or the Winter Court.* He unlaced his other boot and dropped both boots on the floor. The black of the leather almost blended in with the deep burgundy carpet. *I will not look at her.* He sat on the chest.

"Niall?"

He lifted his gaze.

In an instant, Siobhan had crossed the room and stood in front of him. Carefully, she reached out to touch his face. Gone was the impulsivity he'd known with her as one of the Summer Girls. Instead, she approached him much the way one would approach a wild animal. "You've been fighting."

Until that moment, the fact that he was blood-covered had slipped his mind. He flinched and pulled away from her touch. "You should g—" The untrue words halted. He tried again: "You *could* g—"

"No." Her hand was outstretched, but she did not

touch him this time. Her sorrow and her longing and her love flooded him. "I want to be right here."

*Love?*

He stared at her in wonder.

She stilled. "What?"

Silently, he shook his head. The ability of his court to taste emotions was secret. As carefully as she had, he reached out, and despite the number of times that he'd been with Siobhan, it felt new. He slid his fingers through her hair, brushing it back, letting it slip from his grasp to slide over her skin. "I do want you to stay."

As he touched her, she closed her eyes, and he tried not to notice that the vines that were on her skin wilted as he slid his hand down her bare arm. She was a part of the Summer Court; he was not. Like everyone else outside of the Summer Court, his touch was not nourishing for her now.

"Niall?"

He traced the wilting vines that trailed across her bare stomach. "You know you can walk away from here."

"I'm here by choice," she repeated softly. "I want to be here."

Her emotions were as clear in her voice as they were in the air around him. Her fear of rejection tangled with need. Even though he was bruised and bloodied, even though he was offering her nothing, she wanted him—and was terrified that he would send her away. He drank down both her terror and her lust as he pulled her onto his lap.

And in doing so, all of her hesitation vanished. She drew his lips to hers and wrapped her legs around him. *This* was the Siobhan he'd taken into his arms so often over the past century. She didn't apologize as she shredded what remained of his bloodied shirt or when she caused him pain by being too impatient with his bruised body.

Unlike every other relationship he'd known, Siobhan was uncomplicated. She didn't think about the future; she didn't ask about the past. *Or cause me to think of those things.* She was here, in this moment, in this place. She was a Summer Girl, demanding the pleasure that she considered her right. She took what she needed, and she shared herself because she wanted to do so. She was who she was, and she didn't try to hide that truth.

And in this, Niall admitted to himself, perhaps the Summer Court and the Dark Court were not so far apart.

# CHAPTER 8

*T*HE FOLLOWING DAY, FAR EARLIER THAN the court would gather, Irial was waiting in the alley outside the warehouse Niall had been favoring of late. Much like the changes Niall had made in what used to be Irial's home, this change was both comforting and disconcerting. The court owned plenty of clubs, both mortal and faery focused, but for reasons Niall didn't specify, he'd chosen to have meetings here in a vast warehouse. They'd hired mortals to refit it, removing the excessive steel so that it was bearable and adding wood and stone fixtures. The presence of steel weakened the faeries, but it also meant that only the strongest among them could act out. That, Irial had to admit, was clever. His own solution when he'd ascended the throne had been bloodier, but Niall was a different sort of ruler.

Irial had waited there since the sun rose, but it was

not until afternoon that he saw the faery he'd been expecting.

"Irial." Devlin moved with the same ease that shadows did, but rather than take advantage of that, he tried to announce his presence when he arrived—unless he was sent to assassinate someone Sorcha had declared troubling.

"I have made you welcome among us for centuries, but I understand that Her Unchanging Difficultness has sent you to make trouble," Irial murmured.

"My queen is wise in all things." Devlin stiffened. "She seeks to keep order, not promote conflict."

"By striking those in my—*the* Dark Court?" Irial grinned. "The High Court is a twisted place."

"You are no longer king. Nothing should prevent me from striking you." Devlin's voice had no inflection. In most cases, evoking obvious emotion in Sorcha's brother was a challenge.

"If necessary, I would offer myself up for you to take your pound of flesh." Irial gestured to the street. "We can deal with this out here before or after you say what you will to my king."

The expression on Devlin's face seemed to grow even more unreadable, and his already hidden emotions became absent enough that he was as a vacant body. "Regrettably, I think I will decline that offer."

The sound of Hounds approaching didn't evoke so much as a flicker from Devlin. Their steeds' engines growled and snarled; the exhalations—which mortals would see as vehicle exhaust—were tinted the same green as their eyes. While the Hunt did not ride in pursuit of anyone, they made their entrance with the same ferocity as they'd pursue an enemy with. Gabriel's steed was, uncharacteristically, a massive motorcycle with dual exhaust and a growl loud enough that the street shuddered. Gabriel himself snarled as fiercely as the steed, the act of which made his words almost unintelligible. "Irial . . . What. Are. You. Doing."

Irial widened his eyes in faux innocence. "Greeting a guest to the Dark Court. We were both in the street, and—" Irial's words were lost under another growl.

Utterly implacable as always, Devlin merely looked at the assembled Hunt as if they were nothing more than a group of mortal schoolchildren. "On behalf of the Queen of Faerie, I seek audience with the Dark King."

"Irial?" Gabriel said in a slightly clearer voice. "Go inside. Now."

Something in him rankled at being ordered so, but Gabriel had always been prone to treating Irial as an equal instead of as a king. *And now I am not a king.* Irial shrugged, glanced at Devlin, and said, "My offer stands."

The resounding snarls that greeted his words brought a look of true amusement—and matching burst of emotion—to Devlin. "I believe there is some opposition to your suggestion."

Gabriel extended his left arm; on it, the Dark King's commands spiraled out and made quite clear that Irial was to be kept safe. "Inside."

Devlin smiled broadly now. He glanced from the ink on Gabriel's arm to Irial's face. "Your king seems to disapprove of your propensity for protecting him."

At that, Irial shook his head. "Understand this: if you so much as lift a hand to my king, I will bring such destruction into Faerie as would make War in all her fury seem like an infant in a snit. There are more than a few who owe me debts I will not hesitate to call due." Irial lowered his voice, not to hide his words from those standing near him, but in hopes of keeping it from any hidden watchers. "I've spoken to those who carry word of the High Queen's orders. Whether it is now or for the rest of eternity, any who strike at him will answer to me."

"You unman him with such a threat," Devlin remarked.

"No," Irial corrected. "I *protect* him. It is no different from what you would do for your queen."

Devlin paused a heartbeat too long before murmuring, "Perhaps."

"Inside on your own, or they'll move you." Gabriel clamped a hand on Irial's shoulder. "I will not disobey my king—nor will you."

Several of the Hounds shifted restlessly. They would obey their Gabriel, but after centuries of protecting Irial, they were uneasy at the idea of manhandling him.

"Your words are noted and will be relayed to my queen." Devlin bowed his head, either to hide his expression or out of respect. Irial wasn't sure which.

Niall was fuming when Irial entered the building. A barricade of solid shadow snapped into place around the two of them, sealing out everyone but them. "What were you thinking? Did you ignore *everything* I said yesterday?"

"No." Irial was unabashed. He put his hand against the shadow-formed wall. "You are able to do things that I struggled with as easily as if you'd been king for several years."

"At least one of us is adjusting well."

At that, Irial paused. "What do you mean?"

"Instead of hiding the fact that you were informed that Devlin was to strike you or Gabriel, you should have told me," Niall said as calmly as he could. "You offered me the court, your fealty, your advice, yet you hide things that, *as your king,* I should be told."

For a moment, Irial stood in silence. "If Gabriel were to be injured, the Hounds could replace him, and we cannot be certain that another Hound would support you as Gabriel will."

"I know."

"So of the two, I am more expendable." Irial shrugged.

"You are not expendable. . . . And I couldn't speak it if it were untrue"—Niall held up his hand before Irial could interrupt—"neither could you, so we both believe we speak truths. You told me of this visit, advised me how to proceed, and then undermined me. You should have told me what you learned."

"I'm not very good at serving."

Niall put one hand on Irial's shoulder and pushed him to his knees. "I noticed."

The truth was that even as he was apologizing, Irial was not subservient. Kings weren't meant to become subjects, and after centuries of being a king, Irial wasn't likely to change overnight. *Or at all.* The consequence of that truth, however, was that the one faery in the Dark Court best able to advise Niall was also the one least suited to being anyone's subject.

"We need a solution or you need to go," Niall started.

Irial lifted his gaze. "You would exile me?"

"If you work against me, yes, I will." Niall frowned. "Tell me what you know. Maybe we need to do so every day. A meeting . . . or a memo . . . or I don't know."

Irial started to rise to his feet.

"No," Niall whispered. "You will kneel until I say otherwise."

A slow smile came over Irial's face. "As you will."

"I'm not joking, Irial. Either I'm your king or you are gone. If I am to rule this court, I need you"—Niall paused to let the weight of that sentence settle on both of them—"more than I think I've needed anyone since you failed me so many centuries ago. So tell me right now, do you want the court back, do you want to leave, or do you intend to be my advisor in truth?"

"I want to keep you *and* the court safe." Irial looked only at Niall despite the growing number of faeries outside the shadowed barrier. "That means I cannot be their king."

"Then stop trying to make all of the decisions." Niall ignored the fighting outside the wall as well. A fair number of Ly Ergs stood in front of Devlin, who was steadily throwing them across the room as if they were weightless. "You learned that the High Queen wanted a strike that would be a noticeable display of her assassin's strength."

"Yes."

"Gabe has arranged that—up to allowing you to act the fool," Niall said.

Irial startled. "I see."

"I sent Gabe to find out which of your spies you'd visited." Niall let his pleasure in the situation be obvious in his voice. "I manipulated you, Irial."

Irial turned away to watch another faery go sailing by the barrier. "May I rise?"

"No." Niall hid a grin. "You will give me your vow."

"On what?"

"I will have your vow that you will tell me when there are threats that you consider protecting me from, threats to me or to the court or to you that you consider withholding, and you will tell me what they are as soon as you are reasonably able to do so."

Niall had weighed the words in his mind as he'd sat stewing over Irial's deceit. "You will vow to trust me with ruling this court or you will become solitary, exiled from the court, and from my presence until I decide otherwise."

The flash of fear that Irial felt almost made Niall waver. Instead, he continued, "You will spend as much time as I require in my presence, teaching me the secrets that you are even now thinking I can't handle yet."

"There are centuries of secrets," Irial hedged.

"Either you kneel there and give me your vow to all that I just said"—Niall reached out, gripped the underside of Irial's jaw in his hand, and forced his once-friend, once-more, once-enemy to look at him— "or you may stand and walk out the door."

"If I tell you everything, neither of us will sleep or do anything else for months."

Niall squeezed Irial's throat, not hard enough to bruise—*much*—and asked, "If I directed you to tell me what you hide, would you be able to give me a full answer?"

"In time? Yes. Today? No. Centuries, Niall, I've been dealing in secrets for centuries." Irial stayed motionless in Niall's grasp. "I told you about my understanding with Sorcha. I had Gabe bring you one of—"

"Yes," Niall interrupted, squeezing harder now. "Did they spy for you?"

"Only on you."

With a snarl, Niall shoved him away. "You vow or go."

Even as he struggled to remain kneeling, Irial didn't hesitate in his words. "My vow . . . and full truth within the decade."

"Within the year."

Irial shook his head. "That is impossible."

"Two years."

"No more than three years," Irial offered. "You have eternity to rule them, three years is but a blink."

For a moment, Niall considered forcing the matter, but if it had taken him centuries to change, it was far from unreasonable for Irial to ask for less than a decade. Niall nodded. "Done."

"May I rise now?" Irial asked.

"Actually, no. You can stay like that. In fact, maybe you should always stay like that when you bring me news." Niall dropped the barrier and launched himself into the fracas.

*This, at least, I understand.*

# CHAPTER 9

*J*RIAL FELT UNCONSCIONABLY PROUD OF his king as Niall waded into the fight that was now more than a conflict between Devlin and the Ly Ergs. Niall had always fought with unrestrained passion. The Dark King was in the thick of the fight, swinging at Hounds and Ly Ergs and Vilas.

Glass shattered over Irial and rained down on him. With it came the remains of a bottle of merlot. The dark wine dripped on Irial, but he stayed exactly where his king had told him to stay: kneeling in the midst of the chaos of a beautiful bloody battle.

For several minutes, Irial remained kneeling in the midst of the fight, which now included a full three score of faeries. More than a few faeries took advantage of the melee to pelt things at him or at the walls and ceiling. Debris rained on him. At least three blows struck him. He didn't ignore them, but fighting while kneeling was a new challenge.

Finally Niall came over and grabbed him by the upper arm. "Get up."

Irial obeyed—which was the point of the exercise. He brushed bits of glass from his arms and shook splinters of wood from his hair.

"Stay next to me or next to Gabe," Niall demanded as he swung at an exuberant thistlefey. "Clear?"

"Yes." Irial grabbed a length of what appeared to be a chair and sent it like a spear toward Devlin.

The High Court assassin knocked it from the air with a nod. He wasn't injured in any visible way, but he was blood-covered and smiling. Devlin might choose to ignore the fact that he was brother to both Order and Chaos, but here in the midst of the Dark Court's violence, it was abundantly clear that he was not truly a creature of the High Court.

Another faery went sailing through the air, knocking into Devlin as if a running leap would make a difference. It didn't. The High Court's Bloodied Hands swatted the faery from the air and moved on to the next opponent.

"They lack structure," a Hound grumbled as she stomped on a fallen Vila's hand. "No plan in the attack."

"Was there supposed to be a plan?" Irial asked.

The Hound looked past him to Niall, who nodded. Then she answered, "No. Gabe thought a bit of sport would be good for everyone. The king agreed." She lowered her voice a touch and added, "*He* fights well enough that I'd follow him."

"He is remarkable." Irial glanced at Niall. The Dark King was enjoying himself as the fight began to evolve into a contest of sorts. In one corner, Devlin stood atop a pile of tables and wood; in another, Gabriel stood with his back to the wall; and beside Irial, Niall stood on a small raised platform. All around the room the Dark Court faeries scrabbled toward one of the three victors. Without speaking, the fight began to resemble nothing so much as a bloodier version of King of the Hill. Everyone wanted to topple one of the three strongest fighters, if even for a moment, and all of them were still having fun.

Devlin had more than held his own against the Dark Court's fighters, reminding them that he was not to be ignored. All of the faeries in the room had more nourishment than could have been hoped for as a result of the flare of violence and blood sport.

*And Niall had made his point.*

The new Dark King had played them all like pawns.

Irial started to back away, and the Hound next to

him clamped a hand on his arm. Irial glanced from her to Niall, who grinned, dodged a punch from a glaistig, and said, "I don't think you were dismissed."

The Hound and the glaistig both laughed.

*I love my court.*

"As you wish." Irial stepped around the Hound to lean against a wall out of the fight. He had more than his fill of fighting. If he could fight Niall, it'd be different, but fighting for random sport wasn't his preferred entertainment.

Almost an hour later, Devlin bowed to Gabriel and then to Niall.

The faeries dispersed, limping, bleeding, stumbling—and chortling with glee.

"The High Queen sends her greetings," Devlin said as he approached Niall. "She reminds the new Dark King that he is no different than any other faery and that she expects him to abide by the same restraints the last"—Devlin looked at Irial then—"Dark King observed."

None of them spoke the unspoken truths about the numerous visits that Irial had paid to the High Queen in Faerie, but they all knew of those visits. *Such is the way of it.* Irial kept his gaze on his king rather than reply to Devlin. It was the *king* who needed to answer the invitation implicit in those words.

Niall didn't disappoint.

"Please let Sorcha know that her greeting was received, that her assassin has made her willingness to strike at me and mine abundantly clear, and"—Niall jumped down so he was standing face-to-face with Devlin—"if she ever touches those under my protection without just cause, I will be at her step."

Devlin nodded. "Will you be requesting an audience with her?"

"No," Niall said. "There is nothing and no one in Faerie right now that interests me enough to visit."

For a breath, Irial thought Devlin was going to strike Niall, but the moment passed.

Then, Niall smiled. He gestured behind him, and a Vila escorted a sightless mortal man into the room.

"This"—Niall didn't turn to look at the mortal— "is unacceptable. My court has offered this man protection. He will not be taken to Faerie or otherwise accosted." He kept his gaze on Devlin.

The ghost of a smile flickered on Devlin's face, but all he said was, "I shall relay the message to my queen."

"And any discussion she has on Dark Court matters"—Niall stepped forward—"will be handled between regents or via official emissaries."

Devlin did smile this time. "My queen has only one emissary. Do you have a chosen proxy?"

"As of this moment, no, but"—Niall glanced at Irial—"perhaps that will change *in time.*" The Dark King turned his back on all of them then and said only, "Gabriel."

The Hound inclined his head, and Devlin preceded Gabriel toward the door. The two faeries walked out of the building, and then only Irial and Niall were left in the destruction.

Irial waited for the words that went with the frustrated anger that he could taste. He counted a dozen heartbeats before his king turned to face him.

"Don't push me again, Iri," Niall whispered. "I rule this damnable court now, and I'll do it with you on my side—*as you promised*—or with you under my boot."

Irial opened his mouth, but Niall growled.

"You tell me you care about them, and about me, so you better prove it." Niall blinked against a trickle of blood that ran into his eye. "I don't expect you to change today, but you need to trust me more than you have."

"I trust you with my life." Irial ripped the edge of his shirt off and held it out.

"I know that," Niall muttered. "Now, try trusting me with *my* life."

And to that, Irial had no reply. He kept his mouth closed as Niall stomped through the destruction and left. The Dark King was here, truly and fully, and Irial would do what he could to serve his king.

*As truthfully as I can.*

There was no way to tell Niall everything, but he had three years before he had to be fully honest. An otherwise unoccupied faery could get a lot accomplished in three years, and the sort of king Niall was could get their court in order in far less time than that. All told, the Dark Court was better off than it had been in quite some time.

*And so is Niall.*

# EPILOGUE

"IT IS INEVITABLE, BROTHER," SORCHA SAID by way of greeting when he finished his report.

"What is?"

"Her ascending to strength." Sorcha could not see her twin's future, but she knew well the results of Chaos' growing stronger. The world was not as it should be. Deaths that Sorcha would mourn, in her way, were coming.

As Sorcha reached into the seemingly empty space in front of her, she plucked at threads of possibilities. She let them slip through her fingers, each one as unsatisfactory as the next: her former lover dead, her brother dead, a pierced mortal dead, her once-friend dead, Faerie blackened. They were only possibilities, but none were pleasing.

"She is not going to be stilled easily," Sorcha whispered.

"You are stronger, Sister." Devlin smelled of blood. It wasn't visible on him, but the lingering scent of violence clung to him.

*A weapon to be used to keep Chaos at bay.*

"Will you help me?"

"I serve the High Court, my Queen. I cannot fathom any reason that I would do otherwise." He stared at her as he spoke. "Do you know of a reason I would do otherwise?"

There was no pleasing answer to that question. She knew many reasons that he would do otherwise: he was Bananach's creature too; he wanted things not found in Faerie in centuries; he resented her; he enjoyed violence. None of those were new facts. Logically, none were worth speaking.

"There is a mortal I see."

"An artist? A Sighted one? A halfling?"

Curiously, as Sorcha tried to look at him, the mortal. with the metal decorating his face, she saw only blackness. There was nothing. It was akin to attempting to see Devlin's or Bananach's future. *Or my own future.* In the moment between seeing the mortal and speaking of him, he had become part of one of the three of their lives. *He matters.*

"I don't know," she admitted. "Watch for him. He

is young but not a child. He will matter to one of us."

Devlin bowed.

Sorcha closed her eyes trying to recall other details, but her glimpse of him had been too brief. "He wears an assortment of metal in his skin."

"Steel?"

"I do not know. I cannot See him now." She opened her eyes. "He was a glimpse, and in that glimpse, he was still and bleeding, lying on the soil here in Faerie."

"Did that please you?"

She shook her head, but did not admit the curious sense she'd had that this mortal's pain *hurt* her. The Queen of Order did not mourn. It was illogical. "I do not believe it did."

Devlin approached her. Silently, he reached out and swiped a tear from her cheek. He lifted it and held it up.

They both looked at it, a silver droplet on the tip of his outstretched finger.

"The body does odd things at times," she whispered.

"It's a tear."

Sorcha lifted her gaze from the oddity to stare at her brother's face. "I do not weep."

"Yes, my Queen." He pulled his hand behind him, and she knew without looking that the tear was still held there.

She nodded and brushed past him. At the doorway, she paused for a servant to appear. She did not speak to him; in order to be worthy of being allowed in her private rooms, those most trusted sacrificed their hearing. At set locations, they waited with eyes downcast so as not to lip-read the words she spoke. The servant saw the hem of her dress on the floor before him, and so stepped forward to pull the tapestry away from the doorway.

"I will find him," Devlin said from behind her. "The mortal."

Her heart felt oddly constricted. "Not all threads are truths, Brother. What is truth is that Chaos grows. Every possibility I See shows me the results of her strength. I need you to be mine."

"My word that I will not fail you if ever it is in my power." Devlin's words were small comfort. He did not say he was hers, that he would stand with her against Bananach—*because he cannot.*

"When you visit their world, watch for a mortal of significance." Then she stepped through the doorway, trying not to ponder the odd reaction she'd had to the thought of one unknown mortal lying motionless in her presence.

# STOPPING TIME

NLIKE SOME FAERIES, *HE* DIDN'T BOTHER with a glamour. He sat on a bench across from the tables outside the coffee shop. Their silent late-afternoon meetings had become a routine of sorts the last few months, and each week, the temptation to speak to him grew greater—which was why she'd invited a study group to meet with her this week. Their presence was to be incentive to keep her from talking to him.

It didn't help. These together-but-not times were the closest thing she'd had to a date in months. She looked forward to seeing him, thought about it throughout the week, wondering what he'd be wearing, what he'd be reading, if this week he'd approach her.

He wouldn't. He'd promised her choices, and he wouldn't take them from her. If she spoke to him, it would be because she approached him. If she went to him, it would be of her own volition. If she wanted to stop seeing him, she could stop arriving here every week. That, too, was her choice. So far, she resisted approaching him and speaking to him. She did not, however, stop coming to the precise spot each week at the same time. They had a routine: he read whatever his book of the week was, and she studied.

*And tried not to stare . . . or go to him . . . or speak to him.*

She couldn't see the cover of his current book at first. His taste was eclectic in genre, but consistent in quality. She glanced at the book several times, trying for subtle, but he noticed.

*He still notices everything.*

With a grin, he lifted the book—one called *American Gods* this time—higher, hiding his face as a result. The extra benefit of that move was that she could look at him unabashedly while they both pretended he didn't realize she was admiring him. He appeared happier of late, far more so than when she'd left Huntsdale. Ruling the Dark Court had suited him, but advising the new Dark King seemed to suit him better. He hadn't lost his taste for indulgent clothes, though. A silk tee and tailored linen trousers flattered him without being ostentatious. The silver razor blade he'd worn before was accompanied by a small black glass vial. Without asking, she knew it was the same ink that she had in her tattoo.

*Maudlin or romantic?* She wasn't sure. *Both, maybe.*

He lowered the book, taking away her unobserved access, and stared at her for several heartbeats. Often, he stayed invisible when he came to sit near her. This week he was very visible, though. She saw him either way, but when he was visible to others, it was extra difficult to keep her gaze off him. His visibility was an invitation of sorts, an extra temptation to approach him.

*It means I could walk over and start talking to him.*

"He's got it bad," one of her study partners commented.

Beside her, Michael was silent.

Leslie tore her gaze from Irial and looked at her companions. "He's an old friend."

The curiosity on their faces was obvious. She shouldn't have met them here.

"A friend you don't talk to?" Jill's voice held the doubt that the others were too polite to voice. "What kind of friend is that?"

"One who'd move the earth for me, but"—Leslie

glanced back at Irial—"not one who brings out my better side."

His mouth quirked in a just-restrained laugh.

*Got to love faery hearing.* Leslie watched the girls check him out—as he preened for them. It wasn't overt, but she knew him. His tendency to arrange himself to his best advantage was reflex more than choice.

"Well if you don't want him . . . maybe I should go say hello." Jill flashed her teeth in what passed for a smile.

Leslie shrugged.

*Of course I want him. Everyone who looks at him wants him.*

Anger rose up inside of her as Jill stood and started across the grassy lawn that separated the coffee shop and the bench where Irial waited. Worse still, it embarrassed her to admit that she felt a familiar possessive pang. Irial was *hers.* That hadn't changed, wouldn't change.

*Except that it did.*

When she left his world—*their world*—she'd made it change. He still watched her, not in a predatory way, or even in an intrusive way, but she'd see him around campus. While Irial watched, Niall respected her requests not to visit; instead, he sent Hounds to guard her. Occasionally Aislinn's rowan-people or the Winter Queen's lupine fey looked in on her too. Leslie was safer than she'd ever been, guarded by the denizens of three faery courts, and pretending not to notice any of them.

That was an implicit understanding: she mostly pretended they weren't there, and they pretended she wasn't ignoring their presence. Sometimes ignoring the fey made her feel a kinship with Aislinn. When Aislinn was mortal, she'd had to pretend not to see them. They hadn't known she had the Sight. Leslie, however, didn't need to pretend.

*Except for myself . . . and for him.*

She smiled at Irial, letting the illusion slip for a moment—and immediately regretted it. He lowered his book and leaned forward. The question in his expression made her heart ache. She didn't belong in his world, not even now that he was no longer the Dark King. Talking to him was dangerous. Being alone with him was dangerous. It was a line she couldn't cross—not and still retain her distance. If she were to be honest with herself, it was the other reason she'd invited her study group this week. She could speak to them, say things she wanted him to know without admitting she was speaking to him.

*Faery logic.*

He stood.

She shook her head and turned away. There were moments when she failed, when she talked to the fey, but not to Irial.

*Never to him.*

Jill was beside him now, and he spoke to her. No doubt he said something charming but dismissive.

Leslie stared at the page, her notes blurring as she tried to look anywhere but at Irial. Resolutely, she read over the words in her notebook. School was the one thing that helped her focus; it was how she had kept it together when she lived in Huntsdale, and it was how she had continued to hold on the past few months. She'd rather hurt and keep trying than hide from her feelings. Irial had helped her see that.

Seeing anyone else near him hurt. Seeing him hurt. *Not seeing him hurts more.* That was the challenge, the dilemma she couldn't resolve: his nearness made her feel safe, made her feel loved and valued, but it reminded her of what she couldn't have. Two faeries, arguably the two most tempting faeries in the world, loved her, and she couldn't be with either of them— not without sacrificing too much. She couldn't be a good person and be in their world. Maybe if they were part of any other faery court or if she were a different sort of person, she could build a life with them, but the future she'd have in the Dark Court wasn't a future that she could accept. Monsters don't become house pets, and she didn't want to become a monster.

"Well"—Jill plopped down in her seat again—"that was interesting."

"What?" Leslie's heart sped. She might have the Sight, but that didn't give her faery hearing or reflexes.

"He said—and I quote—'Tell Leslie that I send my love or anything else she might need.'" Jill folded her arms over her chest, leaned back, and studied Leslie's expression. "Gorgeous guy, apparently loves you, and you—"

"Drop it." Leslie's calm faltered then. Her hand started shaking as she gathered up her notes. "Seriously. He's . . . a part of my past. He's why I moved here. To be away from him."

Michael put a hand on Leslie's arm. "Is he threatening—"

"No. He isn't here to hurt me. He . . . he'd protect me at his own risk. Our situation is just"—she looked in Irial's direction and caught his gaze—"complicated. I needed space."

She didn't look back at her study group. No one

spoke, and she couldn't think of anything else to say. The awkwardness of the situation was more than she wanted to deal with. *How do I say that I love and am loved by . . . Dark Kings? Faeries? Monsters?* There weren't words to explain—and the only one there who deserved her explanation already knew it.

She stood. "I'll catch you in class."

She slung her bag over her shoulder and walked away. She paused after she passed him and whispered, "Good night, Irial."

"Be safe, love. I'll be here if you need me," he promised her. There was no censure in his words; he gave her the reassurances he knew she needed: that he loved her, that he protected her, and that he did so from a distance.

*Faeries don't lie,* he'd once told her, *so listen carefully to what we* actually *say.*

By every mortal standard, the worst faeries in the world were those in the Dark Court. They fed on the baser emotions; they engaged in activities that the other—also amoral—faery courts repudiated. They were also the only ones she truly trusted or understood.

Irial watched her walk away until he was sure that she was within sight of her guards. She grew stronger every week. If any mortal could've survived the Dark Court, it was his Leslie. Her strength awed him, even as it manifested in choosing to continue loving two faeries but to be with neither of them. Few mortals had the mettle that she did.

But being strong didn't mean that she should hurt. If he had his way, she'd spend the rest of her life cosseted. *And that life would be as long as Niall's.* Irial had learned centuries ago that the world didn't always bend to his will. *Unfortunately.*

After he was sure Leslie was far enough away that she wouldn't think he was stalking her, he walked away from the coffee shop. There were always guards near enough to hear her if she cried out for help. He'd prefer that there were guards walking alongside her, but she would suffer more for that. Their visible presence saddened her, so the guards had been ordered not to crowd her. *At least not all of the time.* It was a delicate dance, watching her but not being too present. In this, as in so many other things, Leslie was an anomaly. She accepted their guardianship, but not their omnipresence. She accepted their love, but not their companionship.

*Everything on her terms or not at all. Just like Niall.*

He walked only a block before he saw Gabriel

leaning against his steed, which was currently in the form of a deep-green classic Mustang. If Irial asked, Gabriel could spout off the year, engine, and modifications his steed was currently adopting, and for a moment, Irial considered doing just that. It would be more entertaining than a lecture.

Gabriel pushed away from the car. "What are you doing?"

Irial shrugged. "Checking on her."

"And if Niall finds out . . . your *king* who told you to stay away from her? What do you think he'll say?" Gabriel joined him, walking in the direction Irial had already been going. The car didn't follow.

"I suppose he'd be angry." Irial smiled to himself. Angry Niall was far more fun than sulking Niall. If it wasn't so counterproductive, Irial'd spend more time actively trying to provoke his new king. *My only king.* Sometimes the fact that he had a king amused Irial to perverse degrees. After centuries of leading the Dark Court, he was monarch no more. He'd returned to what he was before, a Gancanagh, fatally addictive to mortals, solitary by nature—except that Irial had never really been one to follow anyone's conventions but his own. Rather than resume solitary status, as was typical of former Dark Kings or Queens, he swore fealty and stayed in his court as advisor to his new king.

Gabriel scowled at him. "Seriously, Iri, you can't see her if you want to stay in the court . . . and you know he needs you. You don't expect him to put up with this, do you?"

"I wasn't planning to tell him. Are *you* planning on spilling my secrets?" Irial stopped and stepped in front of his friend and former advisor. "Tell him the things I do when I'm not dutifully awaiting his attention?"

"Don't be an ass." Gabriel punched Irial. The force of it knocked Irial backward. Blood trickled from Irial's lip. The Hound had always hit with enough force to draw blood. Several garish rings on his hand assured that every punch would wound—or leave behind distinct bruises.

"Now that you've made your point"—Irial licked the blood from his lips—"tell me: have you found her father? Or the wretch?"

Gabriel shook his head. "Niall didn't want you knowing about that."

"Niall doesn't always get what he wants, though, does he?" Irial watched a pair of coeds sizing Gabriel up. He spared them a smile that had them changing their path to approach—until Gabriel snarled at them.

The moment evoked a longing for simpler days, when he'd first met Niall and the three of them had traveled together. Various Hounds and Dark Court fey joined them here or there, but Gabriel was always with them to keep Irial safe. Niall was an innocent of sorts: he'd had no idea that he traveled with the Dark King, no idea that he himself was a Gancanagh. He was young and foolish, trusting and forgiving.

*Until he met me.*

Gabriel shrugged. His loyalty was to his Hounds first and then to the Dark King. A former Dark King, friend or not, fell somewhere after that. "I'm not disobeying my king, Iri, not even for you. If he wants to tell you, he will. Come on. Let's go back to Huntsdale before he—"

"No." Irial wasn't in the mood to argue, at least not with Gabriel. The Hound was obstinate on his best days. "I'm not with Leslie, so you don't need to intercede for the king. Unless he sent you after me?"

Gabriel held out his bare arms, where Irial's commands had once been written out, where Niall's would now appear. "There are no orders here."

"So go."

Gabriel shook his head. "I thought *he* was an ass

when he was with the Summer Court and trying to stay away from you, but you're both a pain these days. Either work your shit out or walk away from the court, Iri, because this isn't how you obey your king *or* work anything out with the one you claim to love."

Irial didn't answer. There wasn't anything to say. His feelings for Niall and his feelings for Leslie were tangled together. He wanted Leslie to live surrounded by the protection of the Dark Court, indulged and cosseted while she lived out her mortal life. He wanted Niall to woo her and bring her home. He couldn't truly have a relationship with either of them, but he'd done what he could to make them safe to have one with each other. If they were together, he'd have both of his beloveds in one house. It was the closest to a relationship with them that he thought possible. It was also what would make them happiest. They were just too damn difficult to take the obvious path.

*Which is part of why I love them.*

Leslie let herself into the building, wishing for a moment that Irial had walked her home or followed her. She knew she was safe, knew that her building was secure, knew the logical things that should make her feel okay. She still had panic attacks, though. Her

therapist assured her that she was making great progress, but the hypervigilance was worse at night. *And
in close spaces. And in strange spaces. And in the dark
when I am alone.* Sometimes, she thought about inviting her faery guardians in so she wasn't alone. *My very
own monsters to chase away the fears.*

Now that she felt her own emotions, she wished
she could give him the ones that left her shaking in
cold sweats from nightmares she barely remembered.
She wished she could give him the edge of the bad
emotions—to nourish him and to let her sleep.

It didn't work like that, though. Since she'd severed her connection to Irial, she was left with mere
mortal solutions. She went into her apartment, turned
the door lock, but not the bolt. *Not yet.* She flicked
on a light and then another. Then she checked each
window. She opened the closets, peered under the
bed, and pushed the shower curtain aside. It was obvious that no one would fit under the bed: there was
no room. It was impossible to hide behind the shower
curtain: it was gathered. Still, if she didn't check, she'd
be unable to rest. Once she was confident that she was
alone, she turned the bolt.

Her pepper spray stayed within reach, though.
*Always.* Her phone was in reach too. The therapist, the

girls in group, they talked about the difference between being cautious and being unwell. They claimed that she was being rational, that caution wasn't bad, but she didn't feel very rational.

"I'm afraid," she whispered. "But it's okay to be afraid. It's normal. I'm normal."

Silently she fixed a salad and took it into the living room. She slipped a DVD into the machine, so the silence wasn't as weighty. The opening of *Buffy the Vampire Slayer,* a show that she'd found on DVD and loved, made her smile. It was a strange security blanket, but it never failed to remind her that she could be strong. *That I am strong.*

The phone rang. She picked it up. No one was there. She laid it down. It rang again.

"Hello?"

Again, no one was there.

Twice more it rang. *Unknown Caller,* her readout showed. Every time, the caller didn't speak. It wasn't the first time she'd had weird calls. It had happened a few times the past month. Logic said it was nothing, but caution meant she was feeling twitchy.

Resolutely, she ignored the next few calls. Her door buzzer went off twice. She paced as the calls continued for almost thirty more minutes.

So when the phone rang again after ten minutes of silence, she was frazzled. "What? Who do you think you are?"

"Leslie? Are you okay?" Niall was on the other end of the line. "I don't . . . are you all right?"

"I'm sorry." She put her hand over her mouth, trying not to let her hysterical burst of laughter out, and walked to the door again. It was secure. She was safe in her apartment.

"What's going on?"

For a moment, she didn't want to tell him. Whoever was harassing her wasn't a faery. Very few of them even used phones, and none of them would have her number. *Or reason to call.* This was a human problem. *Not a faery issue. Not Niall's issue.*

"Talk to me?" he asked. "Please?"

So she did.

When she was done, Niall was silent for so long that she wondered if they'd been disconnected. Her heart beat too loudly as she clutched her phone. "Niall?"

"Let me come stay there or send someone. Just until we—"

"I can't. We've talked about this." Leslie sank down onto her sofa. "If there were a faery threat, it would be different."

"*Any* threat is unacceptable, Leslie," he interrupted, with a new darkness in his voice. It was the unflinching power of the Dark King, and she liked it. "You don't need to deal with this. Let me—"

"No." She closed her eyes. "I'll change the number. It's probably just some drunk misdialing."

"And if it's not?"

"I'll go to the police." She pulled a blanket over her as if it would stop the shivering that had started. "It's not a Dark Court concern."

"*You* are a Dark Court concern, and that's not going to change," Niall reminded her gently. "Your safety and your happiness will always be our concern. Irial and I both—"

"If doing so negates my happiness, will you still interfere, Niall?"

Niall was silent for several moments. Only his measured breathing made clear that he was still listening. Finally he said, "You are a difficult person to reason with sometimes."

"I know." Her grip on the phone loosened a little. For all of the passions that drove him, Niall would do his best to let her have her distance. On that, he and Irial seemed to agree. Of course, if she so much as hinted that she wanted them to intervene, people could die at a word. The reality of that power wasn't something she liked to ponder overmuch. Instead, she asked, "Talk to me about something else?"

Niall, however, wasn't eager to let the topic drop, not entirely. "You know I want to respect your need to be away from us, but Gabe is in the area. He had to see someone. If you needed anyone . . ."

"What I need is a friend who talks to me so I can think about something good." Leslie stretched out on the sofa, pepper spray in reach on the coffee table, Buffy staking monsters on the television, and Niall's voice in her ear. "Be my friend? Please? Talk to me?"

He sighed. "There was a new exhibit at the gallery I was telling you about last month."

Niall wouldn't ignore the issue, but he would cooperate to a degree. And knowing he was out there protecting her made Leslie feel a little safer too. *They both are.* She felt guilty sometimes for the way they both continued to try to take care of her, but she also knew that having the protection of the Dark Kings was all that kept her safe from being drawn back into faery politics or becoming a victim of the strong solitary faeries. There were those who would happily destroy her if they learned that she was beloved of both the current Dark King and the last Dark King.

For a breath she hoped that whoever called, if they were trying to upset her, was a faery. If it was a faery, Irial or Niall would find out. They would fix it.

The reality of how easily she could sanction violence made her pause. *That,* she thought, *is exactly why I can't come back to either of you.* She forced the thought aside. Friendship was all she could have with them, and even that was tenuous. She kept barriers in place: no speaking to Irial, no seeing Niall, and no touching either one of them. At first, she'd thought she could put them in her past and that they would forget about her, and maybe someday they would reach that point.

"Did you buy anything this time?" she asked.

"What? You think I can't go to a gallery without buying something?" His voice was teasing, sweet, calming.

"I do."

"Three prints," he said.

She laughed, letting herself enjoy the comfort he offered. "*Someone* has a problem."

"Oh, but you should see them," he began, and then he told her about each print in loving detail, and then about others he saw but didn't buy, and by the time he was done, she was smiling and yawning and able to sleep.

Irial saw the boy, Michael, lurking outside the building. He stayed to the shadows, making it obvious that he was trying to be stealthy. He stood in a spot where the streetlights didn't eliminate the cover of darkness, yet still had a clear line of sight to the entrance to the building. The mortal had a large cup of coffee, a jacket, and dark clothes. The combination made Irial aware that the boy intended to stay there for some time.

*Why?* He'd seemed tense earlier, and Irial hadn't missed the glares aimed at him. The glares were not unwarranted; jealousy was a mortal trait. Setting up watch outside Leslie's building seemed overreactive. *Usually.* Irial spared himself a wry smile. *Watching over her is overreactive unless it's me doing it or ordering it.* The difference was that Irial knew the horrors that existed in the world around them—had, in fact, ordered horrors committed—so his cautious streak where Leslie was concerned was logical.

"Why are you here?" he asked.

Michael startled.

He wasn't fey, nor did he have the Sight, so Irial made himself visible. At this hour, Leslie wouldn't be coming outside. *And if she did . . .* Irial smiled. She wouldn't expect him to act any differently. Leslie saw him for who he was, for what he was, and loved him still. Despite being what nightmares are made of, Irial wasn't frightening to her.

It wasn't Leslie who saw him, though. Between one step and the next, he made himself seen to another mortal. If Michael had been a threat, Irial wouldn't do so.

The boy swallowed nervously, took a step backward, and blinked several times. To his credit, he didn't run or scream or do anything awkward. It spoke well of Leslie's character judgment that she'd selected the mortal as a friend.

"What are you doing here?" Irial asked as gently as he could. "Why are you at this place? At this hour? Hiding in the dark?"

"Checking on her." The mortal straightened his shoulders, stood still enough to almost hide his trembling. "What *are* you? You just *appeared*. Right? You did."

"I did." Irial repressed a smile at the boy's bravery. Many mortals did not handle the shock of seeing the impossible become manifest. Leslie had chosen well when she'd made friends with this one.

"It doesn't matter. I won't let you hurt her," Michael said.

Irial waited. Silence often proved to be more incentive than questions.

"I saw you earlier. Everyone did. You're the one stalking her," Michael accused.

Irial let the shadows around him shift visibly, let his wings become seen. "No, I'm *visiting* her, watching out for her. She knows where I am. She expects me to be here. Does she know you're here?"

"No." The boy's gaze flickered nervously to the ground, back to Irial, and then to the building. "I worry, though. She's so . . . fragile."

"No one will hurt her. *Ever.*" Irial shook his head. "Once, I was the King of Nightmares. Now, I'm something else. No matter what I am, I'll be here keeping her safe as long as we both live."

Michael narrowed his gaze. "You're not human."

"She is," Irial said. "And she needs human friends . . . like you."

"Michael." The boy held out his hand. "I'm Michael."

"Irial." Irial shook the mortal's hand. "I know. I watch when you can't see me too. You care for her."

Michael didn't reply, but he didn't need to. Irial

had watched the mortal talk to her, escort her to her building, say things that made her smile. He was a good human. Unfortunately for him, he was also half in love with Leslie, ready to protect her from threats. Irial had seen that clearly several weeks ago when he'd watched them walking at night. If Irial cared over-much for humans, he'd feel sympathy for the boy; as it was, Irial was practical: Michael's emotions made him useful.

"Tell me why you are here," Irial encouraged.

"Someone's been calling her at weird hours," Michael blurted. "After the way you were watching her, I thought maybe it was you. She says not to worry, but she . . . I just . . ."

"I understand." Irial smiled and dropped an arm around the boy's shoulders. "These are the sorts of things I'd like you to tell me, Michael. Come sit with me."

Michael glanced at her building. "Shouldn't we . . . you at least . . . stay *here?*"

"I have a flat across the street for when I'm in town." Irial led the boy to a nondescript building. "That way I'm close if she needs me. If not me, there are others near enough to hear her should she call for us."

"Oh." Michael looked at him for a moment. His gaze was assessing, albeit far too trusting.

In another era, in another life, walking off blindly with a Gancanagh was foolish. *Perhaps it still is.* Irial meant the boy no harm. He was merely a tool, a useful resource. Leslie was what mattered. But for one other in all the world, everyone else was fair game for whatever he needed in order to assure her happiness and safety.

When Leslie woke the next morning, she was still holding the phone. She didn't hear a dial tone, so she asked, "Hello?"

"Good morning," Niall said.

"You stayed on the phone while I *slept*?" She sat up.

Niall laughed. "You don't talk in your sleep."

"I snore."

"A little," he admitted. "But I liked being there to hear it."

"Weirdo." She felt safe, though. Having him there—even only on the phone—made her feel protected. "I'm glad you were . . . here."

"I wish I was really *there*."

"I . . . I know." She never knew the right words to reply to such things. They all fell short, partly because they weren't the whole truth. She wanted to be with him—*and Irial*—but doing so would mean being in the Dark Court.

They stayed silent. She heard him breathing, heard him waiting for something she couldn't give him.

"We should stop talking." She clutched the phone. "I can't . . . I'm not . . . I need time to live, and your court . . ."

"I know." His voice was gentle. "You're too good to live here with us."

"I didn't say that!" She felt the tears threaten. She missed them, missed Niall, Irial, Gabriel, Ani, Tish, Rabbit . . . her court, her *family*.

"I said it," Niall murmured. "I love you."

"You too," she whispered.

"Be safe. If you need anything—"

"I know." She disconnected then. What she needed was to let go; what she wanted was to hold on tighter. Irial was addictive to touch, and Niall had to stay with his court. Being with Irial would kill her. Being with Niall would mean living in the Dark Court. She couldn't have a normal mortal life in the middle of the Dark Court; she couldn't let herself become the person she would be if she lived there. She wasn't ever going to be anything other than human, and humans didn't thrive in their world. They died.

*Self-pity doesn't fix a thing,* she lectured.

So she got up and got ready for class, and she knew that somewhere out there in the streets faeries watched to guard her, that Irial waited somewhere to protect her, that farther away Niall waited to listen and help her believe in herself. She was not alone, but she was still lonely.

Irial followed Leslie without her knowing. It felt wrong to hide himself from her, but he was quick enough to slip out of sight when she turned to glance over her shoulder.

"I'm sorry, love," he whispered each time. It felt too near to a lie, but if she saw him following her so closely she would be alarmed. They'd never spoken any agreement, but he kept himself out of sight except for their once-a-week silent meetings. If she saw him so near, she'd know that he'd learned of her disquieting calls, or she'd suspect that something else was amiss. He'd rather not upset her if he could avoid doing so.

When she went into the red brick building, he waited and watched the courtyard. Mortals fascinated him far more now that he was a Gancanagh again. Their flirty laughs and knowing smiles, their defiant gazes and inviting postures—it was not an easy thing to resist so much potential. He didn't remember being so easily intrigued by them, but it had been a lifetime since he was a Gancanagh. Being Dark King had nullified that for him, just as it now did for Niall.

*Niall . . . who would beat me half to death if I indulged.*

Irial grinned at the thought. It had been too long since Niall had been willing to fight with him. Perhaps when this matter was resolved, he'd tell the Dark King that he'd been pondering enjoying some sport with mortals.

*Business before fun.*

So Irial waited until Leslie was safely in the building and then he went to find Gabriel. Her class lasted for not quite an hour, but he'd be back well before that. It wouldn't take long to find someone who could locate Gabriel. Then, they'd need to decide if Niall should be involved in locating whoever was upsetting Leslie or if the matter could be handled with more discretion.

Class had only just begun when Leslie felt the vibrations from her phone. The professor had a strict "no phones in class" policy, so she tried to ignore the phone, but after the fourth time, she began to worry.

It rang silently in her pocket. Text messages came in, making it vibrate again.

Carefully, she slid it out of her pocket and glanced at the message.

"Time's up," the first message read.

She didn't know the number it came from.

The second one read, "If you want Them exposed, ignore me. If not, come down NOW."

*Them?* There weren't a lot of threats that would make her panic, but danger to Irial or Niall was near the top of the list. The threats were vague. There was no reason to assume that the *Them* meant Irial and Niall. She shivered.

The third text added, "I know WHAT they are."

Her hand tightened on the phone for a moment, and then she shoved it into her pocket, got up, and walked out of class. There was no way she was going to keep her regular routine if someone was out there threatening her. Her hands were shaking as she accessed her voice mail. *Faeries don't leave creepy messages. Faeries don't text threats.* She knew it wasn't a faery.

She stepped into the sunlight outside the building and saw him—her mystery harasser.

Cherub-pretty and too familiar, her brother sat on one of the tables in the small courtyard outside

Davis Hall. His feet were on the bench, and he had one arm across his middle. His unzipped jacket covered his hand; the other hand rested on his knee. He didn't stand when he saw her approaching, but there was little likelihood that she'd be offering him a sisterly embrace. Despite the irritation of seeing him, it was almost a relief. She might not like him, might not have anything but loathing left for him, but he was her brother.

"What the hell, Ren?" She folded her arms over her chest to hide the shaking. "You think you're funny calling and—"

"No." Ren grinned. "I think I'm smart. You get spooked, and your little friends will show up. Do you know how much I can get paid once I prove that there are *monsters* living around us?"

He stood, his arm still against his chest.

Leslie forced a laugh. "Monsters? Really?" She gestured around her. "The only monster I see is *you*."

For an odd moment, she realized that it was true: no Dark Court faeries were in sight. *Because I'm supposed to be in class.* She thought about screaming. One of them was surely in hearing range. *He's my brother.* If they came, if they saw him near her, they'd hurt him. Despite everything, that wasn't her first choice.

"Your boyfriend wasn't human, Les." Ren stepped forward, grabbed her arm, and pulled her closer. When they were near enough that it looked like they should embrace, he let go and pulled his jacket open. Inside, he held a gun, hidden from view by both the jacket and her proximity. "Scream or fight, and I'll shoot you, Sis."

Leslie stared at the gun for a long moment. She knew nothing about guns, nothing about make or model, nothing about their effect on faeries. When she pulled her gaze away, she looked at her brother's face. "Why?"

"Nothing personal." Ren smiled, and it wasn't a reassuring look. "You think I *like* working with low-end dealers? I can make a pretty sum if I collect a freak. Business is business."

"I don't know what you think they are—"

"Don't care. Smile, now." Ren dropped his arm over her shoulders and started walking. She felt the gun muzzle pressing against her side.

"This is a mistake." Leslie didn't look around. *He's my brother. He won't actually shoot me.* Ren was a lot of things, had done horrific things, but he'd never had the stomach to dirty his hands directly. Like everything in his life, he half-assed this, too.

"Let's go home, Les." Ren kissed her cheek and reminded her, "Smile. I'm not intending to shoot you if I don't have to. You're just bait."

She smiled, trying her best to look convincing. "Why?"

"Met a guy. He had a business offer." Ren lifted one shoulder in a shrug. "I saw the pictures. You were living like a freaking celebrity. Looked like you were having a killer time. . . ." He paused and laughed at his own weak joke. "The man who pays more gets the prize. Your old man wants to ante up, I don't shoot him or take him in. He doesn't want to pay, I go with the original plan."

*Blackmail Irial?* The thought of it was ludicrous: Irial would kill Ren. Maybe Niall would find a solution, but Niall wasn't nearby. For all she knew, Irial wasn't either. She saw him once a week. *Last night.* Today, he was who knew where. *This isn't their fault, not their problem.* If they got hurt because of her, she wouldn't be able to recover from that.

Leslie stumbled.

Ren pulled her tighter to him and shoved the gun tighter into her side. "Don't be stupid. You're not strong enough to escape *or* fast enough to outrun a bullet."

"I'm . . . not. I *tripped*, Ren." She tried to keep the waver from her voice.

*What do I do?*

Letting him into her home seemed stupid. Calling out for help seemed dangerous. Her brother had been behind the horrors she couldn't forget. *If I call for them, they'll kill him.* Once, she had wanted to believe he was sick, that he could get well if he got help. *Addiction is a disease*, that's what she'd reminded herself. It didn't mean the things he'd done, the thing he was currently doing, were okay, though. *Not every addict wants to get well.*

"We'll go to your place, and you can call them," Ren said. "He can pay me more, or I can take him to them. His choice."

Leslie felt numb as she walked with her brother. If she called Niall, help would come. Irial would know too. Gabriel would know. *And my brother will die.* If she didn't call, she wasn't sure what would happen. Niall would call her sooner or later; Irial would notice when she wasn't at the coffee shop; and the guards would notice. Neither Dark King would invade her privacy—unless she was in danger. She knew that. *What would happen if Ren shot them? If he knows what they are, what sort of bullets does he have?* She thought about seeing Niall when he was sick from steel exposure. If the bullets were iron or steel, if that entered a faery's body—any other than a regent—it would be horrific. Leslie wasn't ready to make the decisions she felt like she had to make, nor was she able to ignore them. Ren was here.

The tangles of panic and fear and guilt hit Irial like an unwelcome banquet. If they were anyone else's fears, it would be a welcomed treat, but the emotions that assailed him were hers. They'd come flooding toward him over his mostly severed connection with Leslie.

*No.* He hadn't figured her pursuer would enter her classroom. Most mortals didn't escalate from a few calls to a dangerous public scene that quickly.

"Leslie needs help. Get Niall," Irial snarled. "Now."

Mortals paused and shuddered, but they didn't hear. Only faeries heard his order—and he knew that Dark Court faeries would obey as quickly as they had when he was still a king.

He ran to Leslie's classroom; she wasn't there.

*Leslie,* he called, hoping that the thread that bound them was still alive enough to let her hear him. Once in a while a fleeting moment of connection flared in it. He'd felt her panic. Now he needed to feel *her*, to know where she was. He called louder, *LESLIE*.

The thread that once bound them lay silent.

Irial felt a surge of terror. In the centuries he'd led the Dark Court, Irial had only felt true terror one other time. Then, it had been Niall in danger; then, he had been useless. Now, he felt much the same: she was in danger, and he hadn't been there to stop it.

Abject terror filled him as he ran through the streets seeking her, listening for her voice.

Then he heard her: "Ren, this is a mistake."

Irial moved through the streets toward her voice, and just outside her door, he stopped. Leslie's brother stood with a gun barrel shoved into her side. Irial could smell it, the bitter tang of cold steel. Steel wouldn't kill him, nor would the copper and lead of the bullets inside the weapon. They would *hurt*, but faeries—especially strong ones—healed from such things. Mortals didn't. Leslie wouldn't.

If she were fey, he could safely pull her out of reach. If she were fey, she'd likely heal from a gunshot. She wasn't.

*Should've killed the boy then.* He had watched over her, had guards at the ready, yet Ren had escorted her away. *If I'd have killed him then . . .* Irial winced at the thought of Niall's pain—*at our pain*—if Leslie was hurt by his prior decision to let Ren live.

"I'll remedy that mistake," Irial murmured.

Leslie's hand shook so much that she dropped the key.

Ren smacked her with one hand while keeping the gun steadily pressed into her side. "Pick it up. Don't try anything, Les. Really."

"I don't know how you think this is going to work." She snatched up her keys. "You think my ex is going to just show up?"

Ren gave her an unreadable look. "No. I think you're going to find a way to reach him or one of them—I don't care which of them—and until one of them comes through your door, we'll sit in your dive of an apartment and wait."

She shoved the key in the lock and glared at him. "Then prepare to wait, because *unlike you* I don't sacrifice other people to protect myself."

A look of what seemed like regret crossed his face, but it passed in a breath. "We all do what we have to."

Leslie opened the door, and for a brief moment as she stepped inside the building, the gun wasn't against her. It didn't last long enough to be of use.

She jumped as Ren closed the building door.

He gestured with the gun. "Up."

"If I had said the word, he would've killed you," Leslie said.

Ren followed her up the stairs. "Why didn't you?"

"I'm not sure, Ren." She paused on the last stair and glanced back at him. "Because real family protects each other?"

*Could I push him down the stairs? Am I fast enough to get away while he falls?* Letting him inside her apartment seemed like a sure way to be trapped. *He'll sleep, though.* She thought about it, escaping while he slept, but then just as quickly thought about him jacked up and paranoid. He was terrible when he was strung out.

She shoved as hard as she could with both hands, and then she ran.

"Bitch!" Ren cursed and stumbled.

"Pleasepleaseplease." She jammed the key into her apartment door and slammed it behind her. She threw the bolt with a shaking hand, and then retreated farther into the apartment.

She couldn't leave. She couldn't be sure whether he'd shoot through the door. She couldn't think beyond the fear wrapped around her.

*Irial.* She started to speak as they once had, but their metaphysical bond was gone—burned away by her own choice.

*This isn't a faery matter.*

But it was. If Ren was looking for Irial, if he was looking for Niall, for Gabriel, for her Dark Court family, it did concern them. She pulled out her phone and pressed the button she'd programmed but never dialed, closed her eyes, and waited.

"Leslie." Relief laced Irial's voice. "Are you . . . safe?"

"Did you see him?" she started, and then quickly added, "Don't come here!"

"Where are you?"

"My apartment," she said.

"Alone?"

"I am the only one inside my apartment." She shivered. His voice made her want to cry, even now. *Especially now.* He was every monstrous thing she shouldn't miss, every nightmare she shouldn't crave.

"Are you hurt?"

She shook her head, as if he could see. Memories of the way he'd held her when she wept came flooding back. "No," she whispered.

"Stay inside. I'll fix this."

Tears slipped down her cheeks. Hearing his kindness and his darkness made her miss him as intensely as she had those first days after their bond was severed. "Don't come. He wants to hurt you. Someone told him about you, about faeries. He's here to . . . he says he'd let you pay more for his silence, but you can't trust him. You *can't* . . . and I can't . . . If you were hurt, if Niall . . ."

Irial sighed. "My beautiful Shadow Girl . . . no mortal will hurt me *or* our Niall. I promise."

A sob escaped her lips. "Ren's in my building. He has a gun. I should call the police. I couldn't . . . if you were hurt . . . I just . . . I don't want him to ever hurt you, either of you. Neither of you can come in here. Someone else . . . I can't ask anyone else to either. I just—"

"Hush, now," Irial soothed. "I'll stay exactly where I am. This will be fixed, and neither I nor Niall will be injured."

"Promise?"

"We will not be injured by Ren, and I won't move a step. I promise." Irial's voice was the same comforting croon that had kept her steady when she felt the horrible emotions that he had once funneled through her body.

She whispered, "I wish I was with you instead of here."

Irial didn't hesitate, didn't make her regret her admission. He said, "Talk to me, love. Just talk to me while we wait."

Irial wanted to rip the door from its frame, but to do so would mean that the building would be vulnerable. He stepped away from the doorway to her apartment building as Gabriel and Niall approached.

"Push the button to open the door, Leslie," he said. She gasped.

"Open the door," he repeated.

"You said you wouldn't move." She pushed the button even as she said it.

"I didn't. I said I wouldn't take a step, and I didn't." Irial put one hand to the window in front of him, wishing he could move, wishing he could be the one to enter her building. He'd promised. He'd assured her that he wouldn't move. He didn't intend to twist his words with either Leslie or Niall if he could help it. If Niall were going in there alone, Irial wouldn't be waiting so calmly, but Niall had Gabriel at his side, and the Hound would keep their king safe.

A weak laugh from Leslie made him smile. "You

said 'a step,' didn't you? A lot of steps doesn't break the vow."

"Indeed," he murmured. "My clever girl."

"I couldn't stand playing word games all the time," she said, "but I'll try again. Promise me Ren won't hurt you. Promise me you are safe right now."

Irial watched the Dark King in all of his furious majesty drag Ren into the street. Mortal and faery were invisible as long as Niall had his hands on Ren— and he did. One of Niall's hands was on Ren's throat.

"I am safe, love," Irial promised. "So are you now."

"You always keep me safe, don't you?" Leslie whispered. "Even when I'm not aware of it, you're here. I want to tell you that you don't have to, but—"

"Shush. I needed a hobby now that I have all this free time." He felt a burst of love in the tattered remains of their connection. "I'm lousy at knitting."

She sighed. "You need to let go."

"Never. I'm yours as long as I live. You knew that when you left me."

In the street between the buildings, Gabriel waited. Oghams appeared on his forearms as the Dark King's orders became manifest.

For a moment, Leslie was silent. Then, she whispered so low that it was more breath than words,

"I'm glad you were here today."

Gabriel spoke softly enough that Leslie wouldn't hear him through the phone line: "Is she uninjured?"

"I'll be here." Irial walked into the doorway of the building where he had his no-longer-secret apartment and stared up at her window. "But you didn't need me, did you? You'd already got yourself to safety."

"If I call the police now . . ."

Gently, Irial told her, "There's no one for them to collect, love."

"Sometimes, I sleep better knowing you . . . and Niall . . ." She faltered.

"Love you from a safe distance," he finished.

"Yes."

"And we always will. Whatever distance—however far or near you want us—that's where we will both be as long as we live." Irial paused, knowing the time was wrong, but not knowing if she'd ever call him again. "Niall will be here tonight. Let him comfort you. Let yourself comfort him."

Gabriel stood scowling.

Irial held up a hand for silence. "I need to go deal with things. Think about seeing Niall?"

He glanced up at the window where Leslie now stood watching him. When her emotions were this raw, she drew upon their residual connection like a starving thing. He shivered at the feelings roiling inside of her. He couldn't drink them, not now that she'd cut apart their bond, but he could still feel them.

"I . . ." Leslie started, but she couldn't say the words. She put her hand on the window as if to touch him through the glass and distance.

"I know." Irial disconnected and then silently added, *I love you too, Shadow Girl.*

Then he slid the phone into his pocket and stepped up to Gabriel. "Well?"

Extending his arm so Irial could only see part of the orders, Gabriel gestured to the street in front of them. "Walk."

Once they reached the sidewalk café, Irial waited until Gabriel left before taking a seat across the table from his king. When it was just the two of them, he asked, "Shall we try to enjoy lunch? Or do you want to try to reprimand me for the error of my ways?"

The look Niall gave him was assessing. "I'm not sure which of those would please you more."

Irial shrugged. "Both are tempting."

"I asked you to stay away from her." Niall's

possessiveness beat against Irial's skin like moth wings.

"I have trouble with authority," Irial said. "She's safe, though, isn't she?"

Niall smiled, reluctantly. "She is. From *him*. . . ."

"Good."

The waitress had already delivered a drink. Niall's allure to mortals did result in superb service. Irial glanced up and a waitress appeared. "Another of these." He pointed at Niall's glass. "Fresh bread. Cheese tray. No menus just now."

Once she was gone, he sat back and waited.

Niall stared at him for several breaths before getting to the inevitable issue. "You gave me your vow of *fealty.*"

"True." Irial reached out and took Niall's glass.

When Niall didn't react, Irial drank from it.

The Dark King still didn't respond. So, Irial leaned forward, flipped open the front of Niall's jacket, and retrieved the cigarette case from the inside pocket. To his credit, Niall didn't flinch when Irial's fingers grazed Niall's chest.

Silently, Irial extracted a cigarette, packed it, and held it to his lips.

Niall scowled, but he extended a lighter nonetheless.

Irial took a long drag from the now lit cigarette

before speaking. "I'm better at this game, Niall. You can be the intimidating, bad-tempered king to everyone but me. We *both* know that I wouldn't raise a hand to stop you if you wanted to take all of your tempers out on me. There's only one person I'd protect at your expense . . . and her life span is but a blink of ours."

"You're addictive to mortals now."

"I know," Irial agreed. "That's why I won't touch her. Not ever again."

"You still love her."

Irial took another drag on his cigarette. "Yet I did the one thing that would assure that I can't be with her. I am quite capable of continuing to love someone"—he caught Niall's gaze—"without touching them. You, of everyone in this world, know that."

As always, Niall was the first to look away. *That* subject was forbidden. Niall might understand now why Irial had not stepped in when Niall offered himself over to the court's abuse centuries ago, but he didn't forgive—not completely.

*Maybe in another twelve centuries.*

"She is sad," Irial said, drawing Niall's gaze back, "as you are."

"She doesn't want . . ." The words died before Niall

could complete the lie. "She *says* she doesn't want a relationship with either of us."

Irial flicked his ash onto the sidewalk. "Sometimes you need to accept what a person—or faery—can offer. Do you think I'd come see her if she didn't want me to?"

Niall stilled.

"Every week she is at the same place at the same time." Irial offered back Niall's half-empty glass.

Once Niall took it and drank, Irial continued, "If she wanted to not see me, she'd have only to change one detail. I didn't come one week, and a faery—one whose name I will not share—came in my stead to watch her response. She looked for me. She couldn't focus—and the next week? She was relieved when she saw me. I tasted it."

Niall startled. "I thought that you were . . . the ink exchange was severed."

"It was severed enough that we are unbound," Irial assured him. "I don't weaken her." He didn't add that Leslie weakened him, that he came to watch her each week so she could do just that. It wasn't conscious on her part, but she drew strength from him. Irial also suspected that his own longevity decreased as hers increased. That wasn't something Niall needed to know.

"You are hiding things." Niall took the cigarette from Irial's hand and crushed it in the ashtray. He slid forward one of the full glasses that a waitress had wordlessly delivered.

"Nothing that harms Leslie." Irial accepted the glass. "That's the only answer you'll get."

"Because you don't want to know how I'll feel about what you've done." Niall lifted not the untouched glass but the one from which Irial had drunk. "If your actions harm *you*, I would be upset. I hate that it's true, but it is."

"I'm glad." Irial reached out so his hand hovered over Niall's. He avoided touching the Dark King during such conversations if possible. *Because I am a coward.* "Go see her. I cannot give you what you'd like in this life, but I can promise that I mean her—and you—only happiness."

"Life was easier before."

"For you, perhaps. I could taste all of your emotions then," Irial reminded him. It wasn't a lie; he *had* been able to taste them. He just didn't mention that he still could. "You never hated me."

"It was easier when I thought you didn't know that." Niall watched mortals walking along the street. "I still don't like that you see her."

"You are my king. You could command me to stop seeing her."

Niall turned his gaze to Irial. "What would you do?"

"Blind myself, if you were foolish enough to use *those* words." Irial stood, pulled out a few bills, and tucked them under the ashtray. "If not? Break my oath to you."

"What good is fealty if I can't command you?"

"I would follow any order you gave me, Niall, as long as it didn't endanger Leslie . . . or you." Irial emptied the glass. "Ask me to carve out my heart. Tell me to betray our court, the court I've lived to serve and protect for longer than you've existed, and I would obey you. You are my king."

The intensity of Niall's earlier anger was equaled now by hope and fear in even measures.

"You both need me, and"—Irial set the glass down, pushed in his chair, and let the moment stretch out just a bit longer as Niall's hope overwhelmed his fear—"I will not fail either of you ever again."

The Dark King didn't speak, but he didn't have to: Irial could taste the relief, the confusion, and the growing sliver of contentment.

"Go see her. Be her friend if nothing else. *You* are safe for her to touch now. I made sure of it." Irial paused. "And Niall? Let her believe it was me who solved her problem."

Niall's expression was unwavering; he admitted nothing in look or word.

Irial crouched down in front of him and caught his gaze. "She won't think less of me for it. It's you she still sees as tamer than we are. Let her keep that."

"Why?"

"Because you both need the illusion"—Irial put a hand on Niall's knee as he stood, testing the ever-changing boundaries—"and because you need each other."

Niall looked away. "And you."

Irial lifted one shoulder in a dismissive shrug. "Love works like that."

For a moment, they simply stared at each other. Then Niall stood, intentionally invading Irial's space. "It does."

Irial froze. *An admission?* He stayed as motionless as he could, waiting. "Niall?"

Niall shook his head. "I can't forget. I wish I could. . . ."

"Me too," Irial whispered. "I'd give you anything I have to undo the past. I couldn't protect you. Not from yourself, not from my—"

"*Our*," Niall interjected.

"*Our* court." Irial leaned his forehead against Niall's. "I would, though. Not for a touch. Not for a forgetting. I just want to take away the scars."

Niall froze, then.

Irial smiled. He reached up to touch the scar on Niall's face. "Not that you are any *less* for them, but because they mean you were hurt."

"Regrets are foolish." Niall smiled, tentatively. "We had other . . . things I remember too."

"We did." Irial hadn't ever felt as careful, as hopeful, as he'd been these past few months.

"You taste so afraid right now," Niall whispered. "You gave me all the power. The court, your fealty . . ."

"You could sentence me to death on a whim."

"Why?" Niall sounded, in that moment, as young as he'd been when they first met.

"If that's what would make you finally forgive me—"

"Not *that* . . . You stood by. You let me offer myself to the court. *You* didn't hurt me." Niall shuddered.

"I didn't stop it, either."

"I forgive you." Niall's words were shaky. "I know you don't understand why I made that bargain. I didn't understand why you didn't step in—"

"They'd have killed you," Irial interrupted. "If I tried to unmake your offer, they'd have killed you, the mortals you were trying to save. . . . The court wasn't as orderly then as they are now. They're not an easy people to rule. If I could've talked to you without them knowing, if I could've stopped you, if I had told you what you were, if I wasn't *me* . . . There are a lot of ifs, love, but the fact is that it was twelve centuries ago. I've been doing penance as best I could."

"And then a few grand gestures since I wasn't noticing?" Niall laughed. "Give me a court. Give me away to be with Leslie. . . ."

Irial shrugged. "Some people like grand gestures."

"I noticed the smaller ones too," Niall admitted.

Without letting himself think on it too much, Irial leaned in and brushed his lips over Niall's. It was no more than a feather touch, but he felt both of their hearts race. He stepped away. "Go see her."

Niall reached out as if he'd touch Irial, but he didn't close the distance. "Move back into the house?"

Irial stilled. "Into . . . ?"

"Your old room. Not mine." Niall did reach out then. He put his hand on Irial's arm. "I can't offer more, but . . ."

The hope and fear inside the Dark King were dizzying. It was enough that Irial wasn't sure which answer Niall really wanted. *Neither is he.*

"Come home?" Niall added.

Irial pressed another kiss, no longer than the last, to Niall's lips. Then, he pushed him gently away. "Go to her. She needs to be reminded that she is loved."

Niall didn't move, so Irial started walking back toward Leslie's building. He made it several yards before Niall joined him. They walked in silence until they were almost at the door.

"You could take the court back," Niall said. "I'd give it to you."

"Then neither of you would be able to have what you need." Irial frowned. "And it's not best for the court."

"If you weren't addictive—"

"I'd still be unhealthy for her." Irial shoved him gently toward the building.

Niall didn't press the button. He lifted his hand, stopped, and lowered it. "Will you be at the house?"

"Yes." Then Irial walked away.

Leslie paced in her apartment. Some tendril of the vine that connected her to Irial still lived. It wasn't the thing that stole her emotions; it was almost an extra sense that allowed her to taste others' emotions—and to get glimpses of Irial's feelings sometimes.

She knew that he was with Niall: his feelings for Niall were always amplified.

*Like mine.*

She looked out her front window again. If Irial was with Niall, that meant Niall was near. If he was near . . . She pushed the thought away. Him, she could speak to. *Not that I should.* With Irial, she had difficulty not simply throwing herself into his arms and letting go. She let herself be near him, but they didn't speak. Talking to Irial would be the first step in not-talking, and mortals who lay down with Gancanaghs became addicted. Unfortunately, knowing that didn't remove the temptation. Knowing didn't help her forget how much pleasure she'd felt when he held her. Her relationship with Niall, on the other hand, had never reached that place, so . . .

*Who am I kidding?* She snorted at the rationalization she was indulging in: she shouldn't be alone with either of them. It was why she didn't talk to Irial. It was why she didn't accept five out of six of Niall's calls.

The buzzer for the downstairs door rang. She pushed the speaker on, knowing full well who was there.

"Leslie?"

For a moment, she couldn't speak, but then she asked, "Are you alone?"

"Right now, I am. . . . Can I come up?"

"You shouldn't."

"Can you come down?"

"I shouldn't either." She'd already had her shoes on, though, and she grabbed her keys from the hook by the door.

She saw him watching her through the front door of the building as she came down the stairs. It wasn't like seeing Irial, not now, not ever. With Irial, she was sure; they knew each other intimately. With Niall, she was still nervous; they'd never moved beyond kisses and what-ifs.

She opened the door—and paused. The awkwardness, the urge to touch and not-touch, the where-does-one-go-now wasn't something they'd figured out. They both froze, and the moment of greeting passed. Then, it was too late to touch without being *more* awkward.

He stepped to the side, but reflexively offered

her his elbow. It was basic civility for him, but he caught himself as soon as he did it. She could see his doubts, his fear that he'd crossed a line already.

Leslie slid her hand into the crook of his arm. "Should I pretend to be surprised?"

He smiled, and all of the tension fled. "Harbingers of my visit or just the fact that I was in town?"

"Did Gabe send for you?" She didn't look around them. "Someone . . . else?"

"Why didn't you tell me he visits?" Niall's tone was more curious than hurt as he asked.

"Because I want you two to get along," she admitted. "I want . . . I don't know . . . I just like the idea that you are at peace with one another. That you can be there for each other."

Niall gave her a curious look.

"What?"

He shook his head. "I'd move the court here if it made you come back to . . . *either* of us."

"I know." She leaned her head on his shoulder. "And if he thought it would work, he'd be trying to manipulate you to do so. Sometimes I think he wants me in your life more than in his."

Niall paused. "You'd be in both of our lives if—"

"I can't." Leslie's voice wavered embarrassingly.

"So . . ."

She leaned in and kissed him. "So we take tonight for what it is, and then you return to our court, to him. You need him in your life. I can't live my life in the Dark Court. That's not where I belong."

"Maybe there will be someone else who can be king." He stroked her hair.

"How long was Iri the Dark King?" Leslie kissed his throat. "You know better."

"I want to tell you to be with him," Niall whispered. "He could keep you safe and you'd be away from the court . . . and maybe someday . . ."

"You need him with you, and I don't want to be addicted to *anyone*." Leslie wrapped her arms around him, leaned closer into his embrace. "Sometimes things simply aren't meant to be. I'm not able to live in the Dark Court. I'd lose myself if I lived there. You might not see that, but I know myself."

He pulled back and stared into her eyes. "What if—"

"If I thought I could live there, I would," she interrupted. "Being there with both of you . . . it's tempting. More so than I want to admit. I want to ignore the things that happen in the court, not be changed by what I remember. People die. Mortals were killed for sport. Violence is play. Excess is normalcy. I can't live in that without changing in ways I don't want to."

Leslie felt relief at having this conversation finally. She'd expected that she'd be embarrassed by the admission that it wasn't simple horror that stopped her. *That* she knew Niall would accept, expect, even, but her real reason was less honorable. She could accept the cruelty and excess of the Dark Court, and that terrified her.

Niall frowned. "I wish I could lie to you. I want to tell you that none of the horrible things happen anymore."

"They do. If you aren't doing the worst of them, he is. Don't think that he's changed. He'd do anything to protect you . . . including protecting you from yourself." Leslie kept her voice gentle. She knew that there was one time when Irial hadn't been able to protect Niall, but it wasn't something any of them discussed. "He will do whatever it takes to keep you happy, so if you aren't able to do . . ." Her words faded as Niall looked away.

"I know that there are parts of being the Dark King that he still handles." Niall's expression clouded. "I hate being this . . . almost as much as I enjoy it. Some of the ugly things, though, deals and cruelties . . . I can't."

"So he does."

Niall nodded. "There are things I don't see. If we could make it so you didn't see . . ."

She ignored that suggestion. "You know what happened with Ren?"

Niall didn't answer for a moment. Then he nodded. "I do."

"I want to be sorry. I want to be the sweet girl you think I am. I want to say I'm sorry that Irial"— she paused, trying to find delicate words for what she knew had to have happened—"got rid of Ren."

For a moment, Niall stared at her. He didn't speak.

"I'm not that girl," Leslie admitted. "Any more than you're Summer Court. You belong in the Dark Court. With Irial."

"And you."

"No." She sighed the word. "The person I would become in the court isn't who I want to be. I could be. I could be crueler than you are right now. There are reasons that Irial chose me, that I chose his tattoo, and even if you don't see them, *I do*. If I stay away from the court, I can be something else too."

"I'll love you either way," Niall promised. "He would too."

"I wouldn't." She laced her fingers through his,

and they stood there quietly for several moments.

He didn't look away. Cars passed on the street. People walked by. The world kept moving, but they alone were still.

Finally, he asked, "So should I go?"

"Not tonight. Can we pretend tonight? That you're not the Dark King? That I'm not afraid of the things I learned about myself in your court? For tonight, can we just be two people who don't know that tomorrow isn't ours?" She felt tears on her cheeks. She wasn't well yet, but she was sure that she couldn't go back to the world of faeries without destroying all the progress she was making. Maybe if the two faeries she loved were of any other court, she could.

*They aren't. They never will be. And we would've never been together if they were.*

"What are you saying?" Niall asked.

"I can't return to the court, but I can't pretend that you aren't in my life. I *see* you. All of you." Leslie didn't move any closer to him, but she didn't back away either. "I need my life to be out here—away from the courts— but I look forward to your calls, to his visits. I want to talk to him, and I want to . . ."

"What?" Niall prompted.

At the end of the block, Irial stood watching. She'd known he was there, known that he'd be closer if he could, and known that he had made this night possible. She was safe from Ren because of Irial. She was in Niall's arms because of Irial.

She concentrated on the tendril of connection she had to him, trying to let it open enough to feel him—and for him to feel her emotions. She wasn't sure if it worked, but he blew her a kiss.

"Leslie?" Niall looked as tentative as he had when they'd first met. "What do you want?"

"I want you to come upstairs with me. Tonight."

Irial smiled.

Niall stepped back, but he took her hand in his. "Are you sure?"

"Yes. Give us tonight. Tomorrow"—she looked past him to let her gaze rest on Irial—"tomorrow, you go back to your court, and I continue my life. Tonight, though . . ."

"I can love without touching." Niall looked behind him, as if he'd known where Irial was all along, and added, "I learned that lesson centuries ago."

"Tomorrow you can love me from a safe distance." Leslie opened the door; then, she looked back at the faery standing in the shadows watching the two of them. "But it's okay to stop time every so often to be with someone you love."

Niall paused. "You make it sound so easy."

"No." She led him inside. "It's not easy. Letting you go in the morning will hurt, but I don't mind hurting a little if it's for something beautiful."

A shadow passed through Niall's eyes.

"He wouldn't ask you to change who you are, anything between you, if you stopped time *there*, either." Leslie started up the stairs, holding on to Niall's hand as she did so. "But not tonight."

"No, not tonight." Niall kissed her until she was breathless.

And then they let time—and worries and fears and the rest of the things that meant they couldn't have forever—stop for the night.

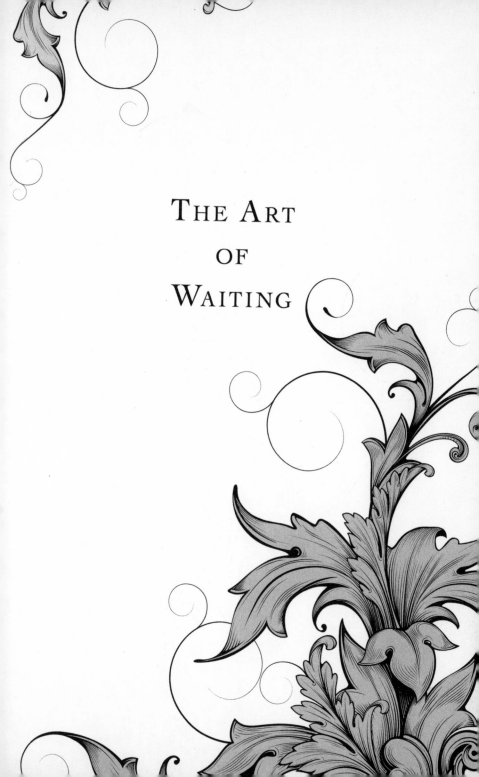

# THE ART
## OF
## WAITING

ONCE THERE WAS A TOWN TUCKED IN the hollow between two mountains. In the winter, the snows fell so heavily that the passes out of the town became sealed by layer upon layer of dense white snow.

When winter would come, the townsfolk spent long months sealed in their hollow, away from outsiders. Sometimes, it was well past winter before the walls of snow and ice melted enough to make travel safe again. And in these melting times the natural springs overflowed, and the hills grew verdant once more. Wildflowers pushed through the last remnants of snow, and trees burst with new life. Every year, the wait was long, but spring reminded them why they stayed in their tiny hollow. No place in all of creation was as lovely to the townsfolk as their own town.

The townsfolk—often sequestered by nature's moods—were quite satisfied with their place in life.

They had learned the wisdom of waiting.

They grumbled about the difficulties to passing strangers, lamenting the inconveniences of long winters cut off from the outside world, but should a stranger suggest the unthinkable—"Why not move?"—they'd smile and shake their heads, knowing well that one cannot teach the inexplicable.

And it was to this town that the man and his young daughter came to live. Once, the man had lived among the priests, learning dead languages and archaic literature. Once, he had traveled, seeing strange sights and mysteries. But when his child began to walk, he chose this small hamlet as their home. He chose to tend the soil. He chose to bury the remains of last year's crop— to carefully carve seedling potatoes, leaving at least one eye on each, and set them into well-watered soil.

Those who had been in the town their whole lives murmured to one another—grizzled heads slowly bobbing as they spoke in hushed undertones—and waited.

They did not ask the man in the planting time; they did not ask during the harvest. Nature would answer in due time.

When the frosts came, the townspeople waited still.

Thick snows fell. *Then*, they began to watch the man.

He stayed that first year, the man with his daughter. He weathered the snows without wavering. And in the melting time, when the springs flowed freely, he smiled alongside those who had always been there.

Nature had answered: the man with his daughter belonged between the two mountains; they fit in the hollow.

More than a decade passed. Snows fell, and springs gushed. The crops flourished as often as not. Strangers paused in the late spring to ask foolhardy questions. The world was as it must be.

But then, one year, a young stranger stopped beside the man and his daughter.

The stranger asked the man's daughter, "Why do you stay here, trapped in this tiny hollow?"

She looked at him, this stranger with his running-so-fast words and his pretty-as-spring smile.

And he asked, "Why don't you leave?"

Her eyes were the green of lush fields as, instead of the answer townsfolk always gave to strangers, she asked, "What's out there?"

Gazing into the distance, the stranger offered, "There are sights, unbelievable mysteries I could show you. I'll be back this way before winter. Come with me; we could travel. . . ."

She smiled. "Maybe."

Late that night, the man listened to the gurgles of the spring. It bubbled, forcing water over the edge, spilling it onto the soil. The water, cold and pure, soaked into fallow fields.

As he stared into the distance—seeing the pass, that narrow fissure that wouldn't again fill with snow for many months—he listened to the spring and waited.

Come morning, he began his day—waiting. Each morning that followed, he began his day—waiting. In the years he'd spent in the hollow, he'd learned the art of waiting, understood it in a way he'd not understood the other long-ago mysteries he'd studied.

He waited as his daughter spent all of her time with the stranger.

He waited as his beloved child rushed about, seeing imaginary flaws in the peace of the hollow.

The stranger spoke much, his mouth brimming with fanciful tales of the world's wonders, things found beyond the two mountains, lessons learned away from the hollow.

By autumn, the stranger became restless.

When the frosts came, they all three gazed toward the pass.

And the stranger announced that he would leave, that she should leave. He told her foolish tales, and the man's daughter laughed—a sound rushing and out of season, a sound not of winter's coming but of flowing springs.

The man gazed at his daughter, hearing that awful sound, that rushing-racing sound. And he told her, "Step inside now."

Softly, she whispered, "Yes, Father."

Then the man turned to the stranger and offered, "You could stay. . . . It's peaceful here."

The stranger snorted.

Once more the man invited, "New faces are welcome in the hollow."

The stranger started to step around the man, calling to the man's daughter.

The man blocked his way. "I've been to the places you spin your tales of. There's no peace there. You don't mention the ugly parts."

The stranger shrugged.

The man held the stranger's gaze and offered, "My daughter has no need of what's out there, but you could stay. Bide with us awhile."

The stranger shook his head. "She'll be fine. We'll have great adventures."

Sadly, the man watched the stranger's darting gaze, watched him look everywhere and see nothing. He didn't pause to contemplate the beauty that filled the hollow; he sought only to take a creature of beauty from the hollow, to destroy the peace that the man had found for his daughter, to capture and remove rather than stay and wonder.

"I want to show you something." The man led the stranger to a well fed by the spring. The water was low now, barely a whisper deep in the earth.

The stranger started, "I don't unders—"

The man shoved him into the hole, that deep earthen hollow between damp walls.

The stranger bellowed, spewing curses and demands, clutching at slick walls.

And the man turned away from the well to face the townsmen who were approaching them.

They nodded their heads at him, silent as was their way.

"I waited, you know." The man spoke in no particular direction. "I waited, but still I had to act."

One townsman answered, "Wait until the snows

fall; then, you can decide if he is able to learn."

The man glanced back at the spring. "He's staying in the hollow. Whether he stays in the well . . ."

"No need to decide tonight," they murmured. "Dinner is liable to be cold if you try to decide now."

"You're right: I should wait. Thank you." The man smiled. "I thought I understood more."

The eldest man quirked his mouth. "Waiting's not so easy as that."

Then the others turned and strolled down the road, and the man and the elder listened to the stranger hollering from inside the well.

When the noise finally ceased, the elder smiled and ambled off in the direction the others had gone.

The man squatted at the mouth of the spring. "You can wait here awhile; we have time."

As the man looked down at him, the stranger had begun to curse again.

The man shook his head and turned away: they both had much to learn.

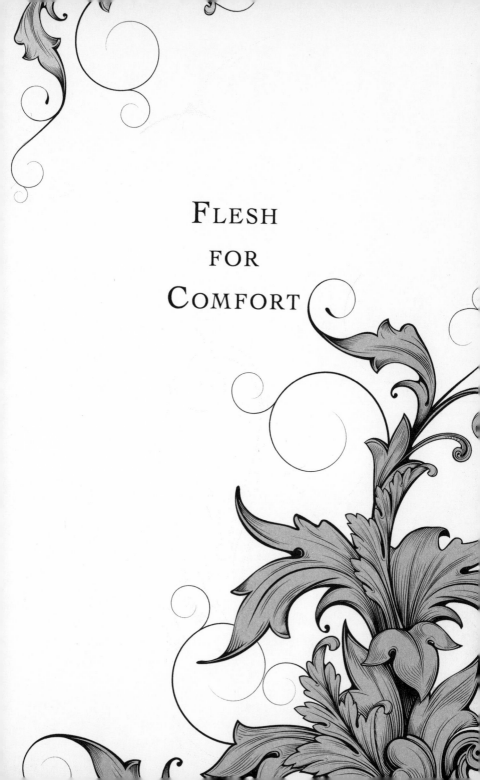

# FLESH
## FOR
## COMFORT

"YOU COULD HAVE ALL, GO ANYWHERE." A little yellow-skinned creature popped from behind the undergrowth and stepped out in front of Tanya's feet. His tufted ears brushed her shin as he tilted his head and widened his eyes. The first time she'd seen him out here in the woods, she'd screamed. No one came, of course, and she'd hightailed it out of the thick tangle of trees.

Today, Tanya stepped over him without slowing her pace. "Go away."

The creature scampered alongside her, darting in an erratic path between her feet. "You thought about let us fix?"

"No."

"You have!" His buttercup skin scrunched in deep wrinkles; his lips puffed out like fresh red currants. "Plenty reasons."

Tanya stopped at a clutch of blackberries. The thorny branches bowed over rotten planks that hid an old well. A couple generations ago, she'd have had to draw water out of there. Thankfully, these days her family had running water. They might be poor, but they weren't mountain-poor.

The creature collided with her, wrapping his spindly arms around her legs. He wasn't skittish like most of the wildlife out here, and she wondered how much of that came from being able to speak to her. He was small enough that she could kick him away, but being small didn't make a thing harmless. Raccoons, possums, and copperheads weren't that big, but a sensible girl knew better than to strike out at them.

She glanced down at the creature clinging to her and said, "Go away."

He stepped back, jammed a bony finger in his ear, and after a little growl, pulled the finger out and began licking it.

Uncharitably, she thought he looked a bit like her Uncle Mickey just then—and Mickey was thought a "good catch." Tanya sighed. She hitched her bucket to her belt and began picking berries.

"Make you more pretty if you let . . . take away squishy parts and make you glow." The creature's slick fingers caressed her calf. "So pretty."

Fat, rounded berries plunked into the bucket.

He laid sallow hands over the curve of her stomach. "Make you glow. Then they want you like animals want water in much-sun."

Tanya stared at his skeletal hands, his fingers like dying branches. She'd tried all the diets in the magazines; she'd tried the tips for better skin. She wasn't the heaviest girl in town, but she wasn't as thin or as pretty as some. If she had money, maybe it wouldn't matter so much, but money wasn't going to happen. That left looking good. Unfortunately, her body wasn't good *enough*. She needed it to be, needed to get away from this smudge of a town. Living and dying in this backwater, growing up to be a baby factory to someone who thought *here* was enough, it just wasn't an option—except it was her only option unless she did something drastic.

She looked into his eyes—brilliant blue pupils surrounded by a sea of black. "Does it hurt?"

He tilted his head until his angular ear almost rested on his shoulder. "Not so-so-bad."

For several heartbeats, the only sound was his fingernails scratching on the rough denim of her pants. She lifted her hand and grasped the largest berry she saw. Gently, she plucked the plump fruit and held it, sliding her thumb over it in silence.

He rested his cheek against her hip. "Make all better. You see."

Tanya popped the blackberry into her mouth and sucked, squeezing every drop of juice from it before she swallowed. If she were prettier, she'd find someone willing to trade flesh for comfort. Then she could get to a city and have beautiful things and sexy clothes.

"I want more than this life." She nodded her head.

His little eyes glinted in the sun; his plump lips curved in a wicked smile. "You can have."

Tanya pulled her gaze from him and resumed filling the bucket, pausing to slip berries between her lips. This wasn't going to be her forever.

"I'll do it," she said. "Tonight."

"Openopenopen." Tiny fingers dragged over the metal screen.

Trembling just a bit, Tanya went to the window and shoved the screen out.

Puckered yellow hands snatched the falling screen from the air and set it aside. "Ready?"

Tanya nodded.

Six of the creatures came in through the open

window. Two were as big as the one in the meadow. The other four were tinier—their wraithlike limbs and loose skin made them seem fragile. They huddled around her, pressing their damp fingers against her skin.

One of the little ones giggled, "Mmmm, lots squishy."

Tanya backed up until she bumped into her mattress. As she tried to go around the edge of it, she tumbled back. "It won't hurt, right?"

The others jumped at the giggling one, flicking their hands at him until he backed away; then they turned to her, stroking her arms and face reassuringly as they leaned over her on the mattress. "So pretty . . ."

The creature from the meadow trailed his long fingers over her face and murmured, "Want to stay here? Or want more pretty?"

"I want out of here."

"Want to glow? Be strong?" His fingernails scraped along her collarbone and danced down her sternum.

"Yes."

As one, they smiled, flashing their jagged teeth. Then they fell upon her, tearing bites of skin and meat from her hips and belly, ripping away pounds of fat. If this was not so-so-much hurt, she wasn't sure she'd

survive what the creature thought was truly pain-
ful. They were literally eating her alive. The sounds
of tearing and slurping added horror to the pain, and
Tanya opened her mouth to scream. The nearest one
sealed his lips to hers, sucking the scream from her
throat, swallowing it down.

It was only minutes before her vision was gone,
and she wasn't sure if she was dying or blacking out
from the pain. Either way, she gave herself over to the
blessed escape from the sound and feeling of being
consumed.

The next thing she knew was the creepily soothing
sensation of rhythmic scraping. She opened her eyes
to see them licking her bloody flesh with sandpaper
tongues. Her skin began to glow golden in the dark
room as the jagged rips sealed shut.

She whimpered, trying to sit upright as they licked
her face with those awful tongues, but her body hurt
too much. The pain receded until it became ache rather
than agony. They continued to lick.

"Less squishy."

"Squishiness'll grow back. All return. We help."

"We keep pretty."

Then, all but the first creature were jumping out
her window, smacking their lips like salivating dogs.

He stood waiting. With a self-satisfied smile, he pointed to the cracked mirror over her bureau. "Pretty."

Slowly, Tanya got off the bed and walked to the mirror. Her skin was flawless, cheekbones outlined by soft shadows. She looked down at her body, hips rounded but not thick. She slid her hands over her skin: nerves tingled like she'd never felt before.

Mouth hanging open, Tanya gazed at the last creature. She fisted her hands and swallowed loudly. "I want to stay like this."

He grinned. "No worry. Just let us fix when not pretty."

Tanya turned back to the mirror, gazing at the sort of face that would attract the attention she needed. She glanced down at a body she hadn't been able to have until now. She pushed down the memories of the screams she hadn't been able to stop and the blood they'd licked away. The pain was horrible, but it was worth it.

She looked at the creature. "Yes," she agreed. "I want you to come back."

# THE
# SLEEPING GIRL
## AND THE
# SUMMER KING

WHEN THE SUMMONS CAME THAT YEAR, Aisling did not resist. In silence, she went to the door.

But Donnchadh, the Summer King, appeared. He clutched her hand. "Stay inside."

"I can't." Aisling glanced out the frost-etched window. Outside, clouds of snow swirled like ethereal dervishes. It was time for Winter to reign, time for Summer to fade.

"You could try . . . just a few moments more." He cupped her face, his touch like midsummer sun. "Your sisters fair did not go so eagerly. Bide with me awhile longer."

Aisling glanced toward the door. The pressure to heed the summons grew like a weight in her lungs, making it difficult to focus on anything else. "It's time. I need to go."

"So you'll abandon me?" He trailed a finger across

her cheek. In his eyes were lush forests where they'd wandered along hidden paths.

"I will see you when I wake, Donnchadh." She opened the door, feeling the release of the tension as she did so. It was harder every year to deny him.

For the first time, Donnchadh stepped in front of her. He leaned down and gently kissed her closed lips.

"Donnchadh?"

He sighed, his breath warm as the last rays of summer drifting over her, and stepped away. "Until you wake then, my foolish girl . . ."

Aisling stepped outside; frigid white spirals wrapped around her as she called out the same words she had spoken every year: "Have you come to fetch me, Cailleach?"

An old woman stepped from the maze of the ice-laden trees and parted pale lips in a smile. Her face was the clear blue of still skies; her eyes were the blinding white of untouched snow. Though she moved no closer, cold breath brushed Aisling's cheek. "It is time for Winter, daughter."

With her face tilted to the sky, Cailleach spun in the wildly blowing snow; her long white hair streamed out like mist. From her pale lips, the weight of winter escaped—sending the thick snows to blanket the earth, releasing the deep cold of true winter.

Then she paused in the storm she had set forth. Clutching her tall wooden staff, Cailleach whispered the dreaded words, "Sleep now."

And as she had done since childhood, Aisling tumbled to the snow-covered ground to become the Sleeping Girl. For a moment, she resisted Sleep, clinging to the pleasure of winter's beauty for a breath longer. Aisling turned her face to the ground, sighing at the rare joy of new-fallen snow against her skin.

Too soon, Cailleach was there, sweeping Aisling into her arms, carrying her to the door, where her sisters, those chosen once-mortal girls who had been Sleeping Girls, waited to watch over her during the sleeping months.

She felt herself being handed into strong arms, and then Sleep took her.

Blossoms would not unfold as long as she rested; life would still while Cailleach roamed with her icy breath. So, Aisling slept with the earth, as silent as the creatures hibernating in their dens, as changeless as the buds waiting to wake in the spring.

Months of storm and ice passed while Aisling slumbered.

Finally, in her sleeping world, she heard Donnchadh's sibilant voice whispering her name; she felt his warm breath slide over her. "Aisling, dream the Spring for us. Awaken."

So Aisling began to dream slender roots sinking into the soil and furred creatures stretching in their dens. She dreamt fish racing the currents, field mice weaving through the grasses, and serpents basking on the rocks. Then her dreaming body smiled at the new life she called to wake with her.

Thus Aisling woke, looking for him, for Summer.

He was not there.

She opened her door and stepped onto the porch. Sun-soaked wooden planks warmed her bare feet. The white willow beside the pond rustled in the breeze. With each breath, she drew in the fragile scent of spring flowers.

She turned her gaze to the budding trees, seeking Donnchadh in the wood where they would run with the creatures of the forest and seek out the fresh waters of hidden springs. With Donnchadh beside her, they would look on the waking world and rejoice. They would dance on the edge of the overflowing river in celebration. Sometimes her sisters would join them; more and more, though, she was alone with Donnchadh.

But for the first time, he was not there.

Instead, in a shadowed patch of snow—a last breath of winter—Cailleach waited. "Walk with me, daughter."

As they followed the twisting path to Cailleach's cabin, Aisling wondered if her sisters had felt relief or despair when they had become too old to be the Sleeping Girl. Did they lament the years of dreaming the world awake or did they rejoice that they were no longer children?

When she'd asked Donnchadh, he would only say, "It's not for me to speak of."

Aisling knew she must choose soon. Every Sleeping Girl had to make the choice between replacing the last Cailleach or joining Donnchadh as one of the many girls who frolicked in the sunlight. To be young with him forever or to be apart from him and age—neither answer made her happy. She thought of the beautiful things she would leave behind if she chose the Winter Path, and she thought of the beauty she might finally know if she carried winter's kiss. And she knew not which answer to give.

Cailleach paused on a flagstone path leading up to a rough-hewn cabin. "We're home."

A dark wood porch curled around the small building; a single weathered rocker sat on the splintered planks. Hand on the heavy black door handle, Cailleach glanced at Aisling. "Are you ready?"

Mouth too dry to speak, Aisling nodded.

Cailleach pushed open the thick wooden door; its swollen wood creaked in objection. In silence, they crossed the threshold, and Cailleach went toward the single source of heat in the room, the cooking fire.

Although tiny, the main room was well-kept. Worn furs were folded in a corner; colorful rag rugs covered smooth floorboards. Across the back wall, a shelf overflowed with leather-bound books.

Aisling turned to follow Cailleach, but a massive gray wolf blocked her path—ears back, tail wagging.

"Faolan," Aisling murmured. Though she'd seen him watch her from the distance over the years, this was the closest she'd ever been to Cailleach's companion. She held out her hand, palm up. "Will you let me sit with your mistress?"

Faolan pressed his nose into her palm, breath warm on her skin. He opened his mouth wider, exposing the rest of his strong white teeth, and licked her hand.

Humming softly, Cailleach stirred the contents of

an iron kettle over the fire. Pausing, she lifted the ladle to taste the spice-scented stew. "Not much longer."

Aisling thought of the sweet berries she'd expected to have this day and said nothing.

Cailleach stepped closer. Steadying herself on the scarred wooden table that took up the bulk of the area, she looked over at the wolf. "I told you it would be today, Faolan."

The wolf tilted his muzzle and yipped.

"Hmph!" Cailleach snorted. She set out a plate of bread and a crock of honey, pausing to wipe her hands before continuing, "Maybe she'll realize how well your hide would line a new cloak, hmm?"

Faolan huffed, licked Aisling's hand again, and turned away. After much scuffling on the worn floor, he settled with his tail end facing Cailleach.

"Big beast forgets his place. You'll need to remind him who's master here." Cailleach settled into her chair and nudged the wolf with her foot, tucking her bare toes under his side and smiling at him. "He's a good listener, our Faolan. And he'll keep you safe in the bright season, when the air is too warm for you to leave the cabin."

"I haven't decided," Aisling murmured.

Cailleach smiled. "I know, but I am hopeful."

With a steadier hand than she'd expected, Aisling lifted a piece of still-warm bread. "How long do we have?"

Cailleach glanced out the window, squinting as she faced the spring sun. "A few more days."

Over the next days, Aisling's doubts and desires flourished.

Each evening, when Cailleach slept, Aisling explored with Faolan, settled on the wolf's strong back when the terrain was unsteady.

Each night, Donnchadh called to her, "Aisling, I miss you. . . . Come with me."

And she went. She spent her nights lost in dance with him, barefoot on the soft mosses of the forest, tempted by his constant whispered flattery. Refusing the lure of Summer himself was not easy—nor what she wanted.

Each dawn, she sat with Cailleach, listening as the old woman shared her knowledge.

And all the while, Donnchadh beckoned from the wood. "Aisling, the daffodils are blooming. Come."

Finally, one morn when Aisling returned from her nocturnal wandering, Cailleach stood in the clearing beside the cabin. She leaned heavily on her staff and gazed into the wood as sunrise broke.

"Cailleach?" Aisling ran to her. Cailleach could not face the full warmth of the sun without feeling ill, not for long.

"Once, long ago, my name was Glynnis." Cailleach stooped by the not-yet-blooming hawthorn bush and laid the staff under the shrub. "I now ask to again be only Glynnis."

Faolan moved to stand beside Glynnis. She placed a pale hand on the wolf's head for support as she stood in the center of the clearing.

Aisling felt the pull, the insistence that she pick up the staff. She stepped forward.

Donnchadh's voice whispered through the trees, "Deny her. Deny the cold." He eased from the shadows; still-wet mud caked his bare feet. "Would you give up our dances beside the river?"

Like a hare in an open meadow, Aisling froze— going neither toward the shrub nor toward the trees.

Donnchadh edged closer. "Did you enjoy feasting on dew and berries under the warm sun?"

Aisling nodded.

"There's much I can show you now that you're too old to Sleep; there are pleasures in the sunlight that you've yet to know." Donnchadh, the Summer King, knelt in front of her and held out his fawn-colored hand. "Stay with me, my Aisling."

Her sisters drifted into the clearing behind Donnchadh. "Listen to the Summer King: come with us."

"Each Sleeping Girl since Glynnis has chosen to stay with me in the sunlight." Donnchadh glanced briefly at Glynnis, his eyes wistful. "Glynnis chose to take the staff; she carries the cold. You do not have to."

Glynnis said nothing, but her whitening fingers tightened on Faolan's pelt.

In a voice like sunbeams Donnchadh asked, "Is this what you would choose, to carry winter's chill? To vanquish me every year?"

Aisling wavered, looking at the face that had greeted her each previous waking for as long as she could remember. She'd thought about the things she would know if she stayed with him, the laughter and the dance, the kisses she'd seen him bestow on her sisters. She wanted that. She lifted a hand, her fingertips almost brushing Donnchadh's face. To wait inside the warm cabin with her sisters guarding the next Sleeping Girl through the winter, watching the snow fall; to spend the warm seasons with Donnchadh for eternity—these were fancies she'd pondered in silence for many years.

He held her gaze. "Stay with me in the sunlight."

Behind her, Cailleach Glynnis was silent. She did not remind Aisling that a new Sleeping Girl would not yet be old enough for several seasons. She did not whisper the weighty truth: that winter's snows could not drift deeply unless the Cailleach carried the cold. She did not admit that she was weary.

Glynnis did not say a word.

The beauty of Winter would be forever lost to Aisling if she chose to go with Donnchadh. Those brief moments when snow cloaked her would be forgotten in time. The freedom to walk where she chose, the privacy she'd known: these would be gone. She would only walk where Donnchadh chose; she would be as one with her sisters, but not her own person.

In that instant Aisling knew she'd made her choice. As a girl, she woke the earth; as a woman, she would drape the earth in her cold blankets. "I will feel the kiss of Winter, not wait and watch from inside the cabin."

Quickly, Aisling leaned down and wrapped her arms around Donnchadh, embracing him one last time.

Then she walked over to the hawthorn and grasped

the staff. "I am Cailleach. As those before me, I will carry the wind and ice."

Ripe with sorrow, Donnchadh's voice carried on a warm breeze, "Fare thee well, Aisling. I shall think of you and what could have been."

Black clouds gathered and ripped open, drenching them.

Aisling lifted Glynnis in her arms, cradling her.

The old woman rested her head on Aisling's shoulder and closed her eyes. "Thank you, daughter."

Aisling lowered Glynnis to the ground as the earth opened, accepting Glynnis into the soil she'd tended for so long. "Be at peace, Glynnis."

Then—eager to be out of the growing brightness of the sun—Aisling wrapped her blue fingers around the staff and walked away from the Summer King.

Clutching the silk-smooth wood of her staff, Cailleach Aisling walks among the trees. She taps it, sending freezing fingers into the soil, the first taste of the winter that will soon follow. Beside her, Faolan lopes, waiting to carry her on his great back when they cross the river.

Aisling pauses and murmurs, "The snows shall fall heavy this winter."

Faolan nudges her with his massive head, keeping her on the path. Silently, Aisling crosses the growing carpet of white, peering into windows, her cold breath leaving frozen snow flowers on the glass.

Finally, she reaches a house outlined by the moon's silvered light. Inside, a girl waits, restless in her bed.

Tilting her face to the gray sky, Aisling opens her mouth. Winds shriek, chilling those slumbering under warm quilts. She spins in the swiftly spiraling snow, and icicles gather on the branches above her.

Frozen tears of joy clatter to the ground as Aisling looks on the winter beauty. The trees shimmer under starlight. White puffs drift in the crisp air as Faolan huffs beside her. And the earth—the waiting soil—is covered by downy snow, unmarred by track or furrow. There is beauty here that she'd once only imagined.

The girl steps onto the porch. She is but a child, hair in braids, but she comes as the Sleeping Girl must. She whispers, "Do you summon me, Cailleach?"

Aisling answers, "Not yet, little one. Sleep now."

The girl tumbles to the soft snow, and Aisling gathers the child in her arms.

She carries the girl to the cabin, where the Sleeping Girl's sisters wait. They accept the Sleeping Girl from her and carry her farther into the house.

As he has every year since she became Cailleach, Donnchadh stands at the threshold. He brushes his warm fingers over Aisling's cheek. "I thought of you these long months. It is strange pleasure to look forward to the snows."

She holds her breath as he brushes his lips across hers. The moment before vanquishing him is still new, will always be new—but it must come. Winter must end Summer, just as the Sleeping Girl must call him back in a few short months.

Gently, Aisling whispers, "Donnchadh . . ."

And at the touch of her icy breath, he vanishes.

"Until spring," she whispers into the empty air.

So Cailleach Aisling turns back to the frozen night; she has much to do before the new Sleeping Girl wakes the earth and Donnchadh reigns again.

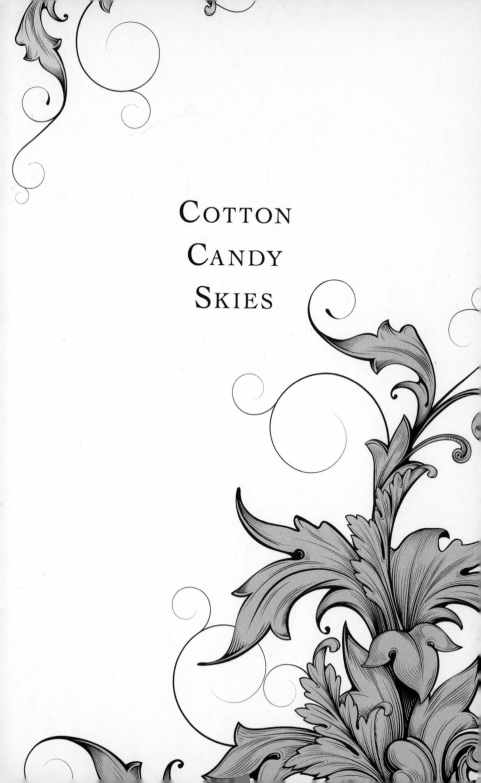

# COTTON
# CANDY
# SKIES

*T*HE SKY WAS THE COLOR OF COTTON candy. *Tish would like that.* Rabbit hadn't made it through a day yet without thinking about his sister. She'd been dead for two months now—two months during which he'd watched his other sister become one of the rulers of Faerie. Ani and Tish had been the children he never expected to have; they'd been his to raise since Ani was a toddler, chin jutting out, Hunt-green eyes narrowed, clutching seven-year-old Tish's hand.

The paintbrush in his hand hung limp. Some days he was able to paint, but this morning didn't feel like it was going to be one of them. He stared at the sky. The clouds were thin wisps, stretched-out bands of darker pink woven into a pale pink background. Trees, some familiar and others peculiar, popped up in the landscape, not always where they'd been the day before—or perhaps the moment before. Few things were predictable in Faerie. That part he liked. Feeling useless, however, was a lot less appealing. In the mortal world, he had a function—he'd raised his two half sisters, been in the employ of the Dark King, and had a thriving tattoo studio. Here, he had no responsibilities at all.

"It's hers." One of the other artists, a faery woman with stars always slipping in and out of her eyes, leaned against a low wall outside his cottage. "The sky. She colored it today."

Rabbit looked away from the artist. If he stared too long at her, he had trouble remembering to breathe. He watched falling stars, comets that whipped past, entire nebulae all glinting in her night-sky eyes. Every time he looked at her, he had to force himself to pull away. Something about her intensity made him fear that he'd get trapped in her gaze. He wasn't sure if such a thing was truly possible, but he was living in Faerie, a land where the impossible was more likely than the expected.

"Not *your* her," she said.

"My her?" Rabbit asked.

"The Shadow Queens. The girl that is two girls." The artist walked toward him.

Talking to the artist was one of the few joys Rabbit

could count on. She was unexpected in the way that not even the fluid world around him was, but she had a sense of calm about her that he craved. Before, when he was the person he'd been for all but these past two months, he'd have asked her to grab a drink or dance, but the idea of doing something so free *now* made him fill with guilt. Logically, he knew he wasn't at fault for surviving, but if he could trade his life in for Tish's, he'd do so in an instant. With conscious effort, Rabbit stopped pondering that.

"Will you tell me your name today?" he asked.

She smiled. "You could ask the queens."

"I could," he agreed. "It's *your* name, though. I told you mine."

"No." She took his brush, touched the tip of it to her lips, and started painting in the air. Glimmering bits of light hovered in the empty space in front of him. "You told me a name that is not what *I* should call you."

Silently, he watched as she created a flower in the open air and beside it a small rabbit that lifted its head and watched them. The rabbit she'd drawn seemed to be rolling in the grass in front of a cluster of yew trees. The illusory rabbit startled, and then ran under the lowest branches where it peered up at the sky sadly.

She handed him his brush. "You are not a small animal."

"My father called me 'Rabbit,' and my sisters did, and . . . it's who I am," Rabbit explained to her again.

She sighed. "It is not *all* of who you are."

"They were my life," he whispered. "Before my sisters . . . I wasn't worth anything, and if they don't need me . . . I am nothing."

Gently, the artist covered his hand, and he felt cold flow from her skin into his.

"Starlight," she murmured. "Close your eyes so you can see."

The words made no sense, but the feel of her body against his was one of the few things that made him feel anything other than hollow. She filled his emptiness with something pure, and even as he felt that light slide into his skin, he tried to escape her touch.

"Paint," she urged. "Keep your eyes closed and *paint*."

He felt tears slip from his closed eyes as he moved his brush. There was no canvas, nothing that would contain the images that he saw in his mind, and he wasn't sure if he'd see them hovering in the air if he opened his eyes. Unlike tattoos, these images were temporary.

Her hand rested atop his as he painted in the air. He wasn't sure how long they stood there.

Today, when Rabbit watched her go, he felt like he kept some of that peace she gave him by her presence.


As he watched them, Devlin considered intervening: Olivia was a perplexing creature on her most lucid days. She turned to stare directly at him, and then held a finger to her lips.

He startled. While he was hidden in the shadows cast by the side of the cottage, she shouldn't see him. It was a trick that he found useful for observing the working of Faerie without the fey or mortals noticing him.

Olivia continued walking toward her own home, and after ascertaining that Rabbit was as fine as he seemed to be on most days, Devlin followed Olivia.

Once they were inside, she sat on the floor. The main room had no furniture at all. It was a bare space with pillows scattered over a woven-mat floor.

"The shadows hurt my eyes today." She waved her hand at him. "Make them go."

At a loss, Devlin did so, letting the darkness he wore to hide himself sink back under his skin. No longer hidden, he motioned at the floor. "May I?"

"For a moment." Olivia kicked a few pillows toward him.

"You can see me."

"I have eyes." She gave him a puzzled look. "Do you not see you?"

"I do, but I was hidden. The others—"

"Are not me." Olivia sighed, and then reached out and patted his knee. "I'm glad you have the girl who is two. When one gets confused, it is good to have help. Maybe you should not go out alone?"

"Maybe . . ."

"The girl used to stay in your skin when you visited me," Olivia said. "It is why you weren't willing to share my cot?"

"I . . . you . . ."

Gently, Olivia squeezed his hand. "Do you need me to take you to her? It can be confusing to walk alone when you are not meant to be alone."

"You are kind, Livvy." Devlin pulled his hand free of her grasp. "Do others see me when I wear shadows?"

Her brow furrowed as she stared at him. "Why would they? They are not me."

"True." Devlin smiled then. "Will you tell me if Rabbit needs me?"

"That's not his name," she murmured.

"Right. Well, him . . . Will you tell me if he needs me?"

She nodded. "He needs *me,* but he's not sure of it yet. Soon, though."

For a moment, Devlin watched her. Years ago, he'd learned that waiting was useful when dealing with Olivia. Her sense of time was unique, as was her sense of order.

Hours passed. Of that, Rabbit was fairly sure. What he didn't know was how many hours passed. The sky didn't shift as it had in the mortal world, and between the irregular landscape and the numbing grief, he wasn't ever entirely sure of the time.

"Are you feeling any better?" Ani stood in a band of shadows that seemed to flex and pulse like water.

Idly, Rabbit wondered if she noticed the shadowed air.

"Rab?"

His sister walked up to him and took something from his hand. He realized that he was still holding the paintbrush he'd picked up when he'd started the day. With effort, he uncurled his hands.

"You need to . . . I don't know." Ani wrapped her

arms around his waist and leaned her face against his chest. "I need you well, Rab."

"I'm trying." He stroked her hair. "I don't know how to be something *here*, though. The world I knew was over there. My family, my girls, my father . . . my art. My court."

His baby sister looked up at him. "You have family and court and art here too."

"I do." He forced a smile to his lips. "I'm sorry."

Tears filled her eyes. "You don't need to be sorry. I just need you to be well again. I want you to snarl at me. I want you to laugh."

"I will," he promised. With his thumb, he caught a tear on her cheek and wiped it away. "Come inside. Tell me about your day."

Ani snuggled against his side and together they went into the little house that was his. She'd invited him to live with her, offered him a replica of their old home, even offered him the right to design whatever he wanted. Instead, he stayed in the artists' area.

*Because I can be alone here.*

He wasn't trying to be maudlin, but he'd lost his sister, seen Irial stabbed, and had no word from Gabriel. In truth, he wasn't sure if he *would*, either. The gate between Faerie and the mortal world was sealed, open only for Seth unless both the High Court and Shadow Court cooperated.

It wasn't that Rabbit wanted to go to that world. He just wasn't sure what he was to do here in Faerie. It had been over a decade since he was without a responsibility.

*You do have a responsibility.*

He looked at the Shadow Queen, his baby sister, and smiled. She still needed him. That much was clear.

*So stop this,* he reminded himself.

"I was thinking about building a few tattoo machines." Rabbit stepped away from his sister and opened an old-fashioned squat, dingy white refrigerator that was covered with stickers for old-school punk bands. He pulled out a pitcher of iced tea.

Ani sat at the garish lime-green kitchen table and watched him as he dropped ice cubes into two jelly jars that served as drinking glasses. The ice popped as he poured the tea in, and he paused. The tea was warm.

He opened the fridge; it was working.

"Did you make the tea?" he asked.

His sister shook her head and started to stand, but Rabbit raised a hand. "Don't drink it."

After taking the glass from her, Rabbit walked out of the kitchen and into the tiny living room. It was empty. He checked the bedroom, bathroom, studio, and even the patio. No one else was here.

The side door, however, was wide open.

Cautiously, he stepped outside and heard Her voice. "You're late."

"Late?" he asked.

"Possibly early." The artist gave him a once-over, and then she frowned. "I find your timeliness troubling tonight."

"Oh." Rabbit looked around. Although he saw no one else, he still asked, "Did you put tea in my house?"

The artist laughed. "I knew it was somewhere." She took his hand in hers as she walked past him and into his house.

Bemused, he let her lead him to his kitchen.

Once there, she nodded to Ani and took a seat at the table. She poured two glasses of tea. The first she slid to sit in front of her, the second she handed to Ani. "Queen."

Ani accepted the tea with a smile. "Olivia."

"Olivia," Rabbit repeated.

"Yes?"

"You're Olivia." He went to the cupboard to get another glass, but as he grabbed it, the faery—*Olivia*—said, "No."

He turned.

She held her glass out to him. "You will share my glass."

Neither Olivia's gaze nor her hand wavered as he stepped toward her.

"Okay." He took the glass and drank. As he did so, he felt a strange peace slide through him. He took another tentative sip. "This is . . . what *is* this?"

"Tea and starlight." She motioned with one hand, lifting it as if she were able to direct the glass from her seat.

Obediently, he drank the rest of the glass. "Why?"

Olivia shook her head. "If I am to stay, you must get used to starlight."

"Stay?" he repeated.

"You require me." She turned to look at the doorway. "I will need the house grown larger and my studio brought here."

Rabbit looked to the empty doorway as Ani started, "I can—"

Devlin walked in, interrupting Ani's words.

"What . . ." Devlin took in the small group. "Livvy?" In a blink, he took the glass from Ani. "Don't drink that."

"Why?"

"It's not for us." Devlin upended the glass, pouring the contents back into the pitcher.

For a moment, the four of them were silent, and then Olivia smiled at Devlin and Ani. "My studio should be here now." She looked at Devlin, and when he nodded, she bowed her head to the Shadow King and Queen. "Give the other queen my greetings."

"You may come to my studio," Olivia told Rabbit, and then she walked toward a door that hadn't been there before. It opened as she approached it, lengthening into a hallway.

For a moment, he hesitated, but it was only a moment. "Did Olivia just move in with me?"

"It appears so." Devlin motioned. "You might want to ask her about the starlight."

After Rabbit was gone, Devlin turned to Ani and gently suggested, "We ought to leave them."

"What if she hurts—"

"Ani?" Devlin took her hand in his and pulled her toward the door. "Olivia wouldn't hurt Rabbit."

"She might not mean to, but—"

"No," he interrupted. "She wouldn't hurt him. I'm not sure she *could* now." Devlin leaned in close to Ani. "She fed him starlight, and it didn't injure him."

"I don't understand."

"She gave him some of her energy, her peace, *herself*." Devlin trailed his fingertips over Ani's jawline and onto her throat. "They are both being nourished by the starlight that is her essence. She will heal your brother."

"Why?" Ani's gaze darted to the doorway that now led to Olivia's studio. "I'm glad she's trying to heal him, but *why*?"

Devlin traced the edge of Ani's collarbone. "Why do you nourish me? Why do I feed you?"

At that, Ani stared up at him. "So they . . ."

"Are together," Devlin finished.

"Together," Ani echoed. "Is that what we are?"

"No." He brought his fingertips back up the path they'd traced, along her collarbone and to her throat. He paused there. "We are much *much* more than merely together. You"—he felt her pulse speed under his fingers—"are the faery who gives me strength, who gives me reason to wake in the mornings, who infuriates me, who enrages me, who enthralls me."

"Oh."

He leaned down and kissed her throat. "You are my passion, my fury, and my soul."

"Ooooh," she breathed.

"Shall I explain further?" He leaned away so he could look directly at her.

And his beautiful Hound gave him a dangerous smile. "And to think you used to try to be a creature of reason." She drew his lips to hers and kissed him with the sort of consuming intensity that was uniquely Ani.

Rabbit stood for a moment, not sure of how to proceed. He understood that something had happened, that it was peculiar to drink starlight, that having a faery decide to move into his home was . . . unusual. At the same time, he'd become caretaker to his sisters the same way: one day he was alone, and the next he was a big brother, acting as father to two tiny hellions. He was a Hound—not completely, but not mortal. Olivia was not a Hound, but she was very much not mortal.

Silently, Rabbit walked into the studio that was now a part of his house.

*My* home. *Our home now.*

She glanced at him, and for a moment, he saw the flash of fear in her eyes.

"Can you tell me your name?" she asked.

*What name does she seek?*

He looked at her, the faery who had apparently decided to move into his home, and wondered what he *should* feel. She sang quietly to herself as she began painting on the wall in front of her. He wasn't entirely sure what to do.

"You are living here now?"

"Yes. With you." She didn't look back at him, but her hand stilled momentarily. "Do you know your name yet?"

"My name . . ."

Olivia made a noise that sounded very close to a growl. "I've waited for you for six centuries, but you weren't born, and then you weren't here, and now you are." She sounded breathless now, out of sorts for the first time since they'd met. "I waited. I've been patient. I've drawn so very many things, but they were not enough."

Rabbit walked over to stand behind her. Tentatively, he slid his arms around her. "Olivia?"

"I should have another name. I have *waited*." She leaned back against him, and he saw the starlight trails of tears that slid down her cheeks. "I knew you would be sad, but I would be here. I would make you whole." She turned in his arms. "I will be whole now. Finally."

"With me."

"Yes," she breathed. Her eyes glimmered with bursts of light, and for the first time, he didn't try to look away.

"You will be with me, have waited, and we are together now," he mused.

She tilted her head up, waiting for the kiss that he carefully bestowed. Whatever peace he'd sought, that he'd only that morning despaired of finding, slid from her lips into his body. It wasn't a forever peace—*not yet*—but it was the most *right* he'd felt since everything had gone so horribly wrong.

*Possibly before that.*

He wasn't fully Hound, but he was Hound enough to understand what Olivia had been waiting for him to figure out.

"What name is yours?" she asked softly. "You know now, don't you?"

"Husband," he confirmed. "Mate. *Yours.*"

And his mate began to glow; her skin shimmered with the same celestial light that was always in her eyes, as she stared up at him. "Yes. Husband. Mate. Mine." She laughed, looking even more beautiful than he'd thought possible, and added, "You are finally home."

Tears were in his eyes, even as happiness filled him. He'd lost one of his sisters, feared for the loss of one faery who'd been friend and family since his childhood, but he'd found the partner he'd never thought to have.

*A mate.*

*A home.*

Olivia stood and gently led him to the middle of the floor. His hand firmly held in hers, she said, "Now, we can finally talk."

And for the first time since he'd entered Faerie, he had no sense of time not because of sorrow, and not because of strange cotton candy skies, but because he was lost in discovering the faery who was to be his mate.

# Unexpected Family

"YOU HAVE GOT TO BE KIDDING." SETH tossed the letter onto the table and paced the confines of his tiny train-house. He'd been so caught up in faery politics, his ever-changing role in the faery world, trips to Faerie, and his recently *much* improved relationship with Aislinn that he hadn't thought about the stack of mail that had accumulated at his postbox.

He snatched the letter up and skimmed it again. Words jumped out at him, words he would much rather ignore: *campground . . . no mail service . . . wait here for you.* He crumpled it and wished that the calm he felt in Faerie was within reach right now.

"Why?" He closed his eyes and took several calming breaths.

*One . . . two . . . three . . . How in the hell am I to get there?* He tossed the letter onto the table with the less frustrating envelopes and back issues of magazines that had accumulated in his box the past few months.

In the last year, he hadn't often had to think much on his mortal life's limitations—like the lack of a car. He had money saved, so he *could* fly: his weird fey status meant that he wasn't sickened by iron like most faeries. He'd never really liked the idea of planes, though. He snorted at the lie he tried to tell himself. *Not liked them?* He was terrified of flying. It seemed unnatural to strap himself into a giant—*heavy*—metal tube and assume it wouldn't fall out of the sky.

When he'd been fourteen, he discovered that flight was a lot less stressful if he got mellow, but he'd stopped smoking awhile ago. He'd made a point to get rid of his bong and every rolling paper in the train; he wasn't going to go back.

*Flying is out.*

That left a bus trip, a train, or a car. None of those options seemed immediately appealing. Seth shook his head. Even from a distance, his parents rarely made anything easy.

He caught sight of the clock and realized that he was already running late.

*Late and bearing bad news.*

"Fabulous," he muttered to himself as he went down the short hallway to the bathroom to grab a shower.

Thirty minutes later, Seth snatched the crumpled letter, shoved it into his jeans pocket, and headed across Huntsdale toward the first of two places he'd need to go before he could leave town. As he walked, he realized that he wasn't sure which of the stops would be more stressful. For someone who'd spent the past few years learning to keep his impulses in check, he'd certainly not given his loyalty to faeries who shared that trait. The Summer Queen was volatile, more so now that she was carrying the full of Summer inside of her. It had only been a week since Aislinn had become the sole monarch of the Summer Court and only a couple of weeks since Winter, Dark, and Summer had worked together to defeat Bananach, but already, Aislinn seemed to be more truly fit to her sole regency than he expected. She was still trying to get a grip on having her court's full strength, but their relationship was everything he'd hoped it could be.

*Perfect.*

*The other faery I need to see . . .* Seth shook his head. *That* was far less resolved. The Dark King was steadfastly avoiding him.

*One mercurial regent at a time.*

Seth walked up the stairs to the Summer Queen's

loft. Just inside the door, he stopped for a moment, watching her as she laughed with her advisors. Aislinn's every movement seemed to send little bits of sunlight into the air around her. Looking at her when she was happy made Seth think of photographs of the solar system: she was the sun, and the rest of her court thrived now because she was so vibrant. Looking at her made him want to do anything in his power to make that sunlight turn to him, but he understood the difference between love and enthrallment. *Being her subject would've destroyed us.* Being equals made relationships possible.

Of course, that didn't mean that he was immune to her. As she laughed at something one of the faeries near her said, the sunlight flared in the room, rippling out with her mood, and Seth drew in a sharp breath.

She turned.

In the space of that one breath, Aislinn was across the room and in his arms. Instead of speaking, she greeted him with a kiss that would've injured him if he weren't fey. Sunlight flared around them, rolled over his skin in a wash of pleasure, and made him grateful that he wasn't shy in public. Aislinn wasn't an exhibitionist, but hers was a court based on pleasure. Any sense of restraint she'd once had was discarded.

*As was my shirt,* he realized as he felt her hands slide over his bare chest.

"Whoa," Seth whispered as he pulled back.

"Sorry." She smiled a little sheepishly. "I'm still trying to get used to the full Summer, and it's spring and—"

He kissed her and then stepped away, keeping one arm around her. "I get it." He reached down and grabbed his singed and steaming shirt from the floor. *The benefits of wearing black T-shirts.* He pulled his shirt back on. "Can we talk for a minute?"

Aislinn's panic made the heat in the room flare uncomfortably. Faeries around her stopped dancing; couples paused in their kissing; and even the rustling of the almost rain forest–thick plants stilled. Her mood made her faeries react; she was their center. It was like that with all regents.

Hurriedly, Seth said, "Everything is fine with us. I just wanted to talk to you without everyone around."

"Oh," she breathed. Her smile returned, and at her joy, the activities throughout the loft, and presumably throughout the whole Summer Court, resumed.

The Summer Queen took his hand and led him through the increasingly plant-filled loft and past a stream—*when did* that *appear?*—that now trickled down a hallway. It seemed as if the division between the outside and inside had vanished in the past week.

He looked at the stream in wonder and then at her with the same swell of awe. Sometimes, it seemed hard to remember what life before Aislinn had been like. He'd fallen in love with her months before she even realized he had stopped hooking up with girls. Instead of going on to art school, he'd stayed here—and ended up going to Faerie and being remade. They were all choices he was sure were right, and not quite a week ago, exactly *how* right had become clear.

*Now I just need my mortal life in order.*

He wasn't truly a mortal anymore. When he was in Faerie, he became mortal, but in the mortal world he was fey. Since his trip to Faerie, he'd spent less and less time around the mortals in his life. He could slip in and out of a glamour with the same ease as breathing, so his new state hadn't meant giving up the Crow's Nest, but on the other hand, he only went to the bar with faeries, so he hadn't been tasked with trying to have a whole lot of normal conversations, either.

Seeing his parents meant facing things he wasn't sure he was ready to face.

Just inside Aislinn's room, Seth stopped and looked up. The bed was gone. In its place was a flowering vine that wrapped around what looked look a vat of flower petals atop a tree. "Ash?"

She bit her lip and blushed.

"I was dreaming, and when I woke"—she shrugged—"it was like this. I can't quite figure out how to get rid of all of the petals."

"Where's your bed? Your mattress?"

"That *is* my bed. It was wood, and I guess I sort of made it start growing. My mattress"— Aislinn floated upward, seemingly mindless of the fact that she now treated the air the same as most faeries treated the ground—"is right here. It just has petals all over it." She sent a small breeze toward the bed, and as flower petals rained around him, she patted the mattress. "See?"

"I do." He smiled. *This* was the world he lived in, had fought for, and wanted to stay in. There were things he still needed to sort out—chiefly the whole balancing the Dark King and being the faery willing to stand for the rights of any solitary faery thing. Those he would need to figure out, but he'd already been thinking about them. His mortal life, on the other hand, he'd pretty much set aside. He'd like to continue doing that, to ignore the letter that he'd shoved into his pocket, but he couldn't.

"I need to go away for a few days, Ash. Not"—he held up a hand as she opened her mouth to interrupt— "to see my mother . . . not *Sorcha*. My human parents sent a letter. They're in trouble and need me to come to help."

Aislinn frowned. "How? Where?"

"I have lat and long coordinates. They're at a campsite in the mountains . . . which means I need to get to California, hike out to where they are, and . . . I don't know. They said it was urgent that I come, and the letter was written at least two weeks ago. I need to go *now*." Seth couldn't entirely keep the bitterness out of his voice, but he tried.

Unlike Aislinn, he had no real desire to stay a part of the mortal world. The one big exception was his parents. They were flaky sometimes, but they were *his*. Since they'd left two years ago, they'd kept in touch with sporadic calls and letters, and on one unexpected Tuesday, a visit. They'd called it a "mission" when they left, but whatever church or cult they'd been with had been another passing interest for his mother. Instead of coming back to Huntsdale, they'd followed one random impulse after another, and Seth wasn't sure if he envied them or admired them.

Aislinn sat on her bed, still frowning. "I can't go

with you. I'm not sure I'm ready to be out in the world without my court yet. I just need a little time to adjust to having all of Summer inside me."

"I know." Seth climbed the vine to sit beside her. "I didn't expect you to."

"I want to," she started.

"Ash?" Seth pulled her closer. "You just used sunlight to get up here. You turned your bed into a tree or shrub or whatever this is while you slept." He threaded his fingers through her hair, and she leaned into him just as the plants throughout the loft leaned toward her as she passed them.

"I could send Tavish or a few of the Summer Girls to protect you." Her words faded. "I mean, some of them are guards now."

A soft rain fell in the room as she became nervous. She didn't bring up his recent conflict with Niall or her fear that the Dark King would decide that he didn't want to be kind to the faery who now balanced him. Seth had no option but to bring it up.

Seth caught her chin in his hand and made her look at him. "I'll be fine. Promise." He paused before admitting, "I'm going to ask Niall to come with me."

Aislinn scooted backward. "I don't trust him."

Seth took advantage of the speed and strength that

being fey gave him. He caught her and rolled her under him. "He is my friend. I trust him."

"You shouldn't. He's the *Dark* King, Seth. He can't be trusted, especially now that Discord lives in his house with him. If I asked you not to spend so much time w—"

"No. Niall is my friend, my *brother,* and Irial is . . . well, not necessarily good, but right now he's so caught up in making sure Niall is happy, I doubt that he even has time to start trouble."

"I still don't like it," she said petulantly. "At least take some of my guards."

"No." Braced on his arms, he looked down at her. "Don't start trying to leash me, Ash. I love you, but I am not your subject. I'm not a part of the Summer Court."

"You're not a part of his court, either. It was different when you trained there. I didn't like it, but now . . ." She stared up at him, tiny oceans glimmering in her eyes. "You're to be his opposition now, the faery that keeps Niall in line, you know. I'm afraid."

Seth kissed her words away.

Several minutes later, he pulled back and whispered, "You're being overprotective, Ash." He kissed her throat. "You're worried and looking for problems."

His breathed his words against her ear. "I'm not a fragile mortal anymore. I've changed."

"Me too." The Summer Queen looked up at him. "Sometimes, I guess that means I'm a little crazy."

"I know." He grinned. "I'm not, though. It works out."

Evening had only just fallen, and the Dark King was in a foul mood. He tossed the phone at the wall, where it shattered into a satisfying number of pieces.

"Bad news?" The voice was unmistakable even in the darkness. Until a couple of weeks ago, Seth's presence would've been a welcome distraction, but the whole  Niall-almost-killing-him-and-scarring-his-face thing put a bit of awkwardness between them.

"No," Niall said. "No news whatsoever. She hasn't called us."

"Since?"

"Yesterday," Niall admitted. "She's going to spend weekends with us and the weekdays at college, but I thought she'd call more often."

The laugh that escaped Seth's lips was quickly turned into a cough as Niall glared at him, but the humor in Seth's expression was unaltered. In that brief moment, it almost felt like *before*, when things weren't tense between them.

"You could call her and tell her you're going out of town for a couple of days," Seth suggested. "I need to take a trip. I thought you might keep me company."

"Why?"

Seth shrugged. "I hate flying. I don't have a car." He stepped out of the shadows. "And I thought you'd be less able to avoid me if we were trapped in a car together. We need to talk."

Warily, Niall watched Seth as he walked across the recently bleached floor of the warehouse. He didn't try to say he hadn't been avoiding Seth.

"Being your opposition doesn't mean I'm going to stop being your brother. If that *is* what it means, maybe I should pass it on," Seth said quietly as he stood in front of Niall's throne.

When Niall didn't reply, Seth added, "You can sit here and miss Leslie, go raise a little hell, or come with me."

"But Irial—"

"Thinks it's a *grand* idea," the former Dark King interrupted as he parted the curtains behind Niall's throne and stepped onto the dais. "I'll mind the children while you are away. You've had a rough few weeks, love. Go take a holiday with"—he waved casually at Seth—"Order Junior."

Seth made a crude gesture.

"My plate's pretty full, boy, but I'll keep it in mind if I need a way to stir a little trouble with your beloved Summer Queen." Irial leaned down and put a possessive hand on Niall's shoulder.

Niall looked up at him.

"Your anger and your gloom are perfectly fine for the court, but the court isn't my top priority." Irial grinned. "The court *will* be my only priority while you're away because it'll serve my goals."

"Which are?" Niall knew the answer, maybe he always had, but he still liked hearing it.

The laugh that spilled from Irial's lips was pure Dark Court. "I have all sorts of goals, but in this case, it's your happiness. Go with the boy. I'll take care of the court as if I were their king because that is what you *and* Leslie would want."

"Wait outside," Niall told Seth, and without tearing his gaze from Irial to see if Seth obeyed or not, Niall grabbed Irial's wrist.

Irial acted as if he didn't notice that he was being held in place. "I know everything you're feeling, all of the time. You're afraid he's going to be your enemy now that he balances you, but things don't have to be antagonistic between you. You're afraid that he'll get surly over that scar on his face, but"—Irial reached up and traced the scar on Niall's face—"most sensible faeries find scars appealing."

Love and lust tangled into a delicious cocktail, and Niall closed his eyes as Irial's emotions filled him. He didn't keep them closed as Irial gave him a kiss that made Niall feel like an idiot for wasting the past hour alone in the dark.

*Seth will wait.*

Minutes passed, and eventually, footsteps interrupted them. Neither Niall nor Irial paid any mind until Seth laughingly asked, "Did you find a cure for your mood, Brother?"

Irial looked over his shoulder at Seth. "Voyeur."

"Not really possible to avoid in Ash's court . . . or this one." Seth looked straight at Niall as he spoke. "And there's nothing wrong with it, so why would I care? I want Niall to be happy."

At that, Irial laughed. "If I didn't know better, boy, I'd think you said the right things just to curry favor." He kissed Niall again and then shoved him away. "Go on or send the boy away for a few hours."

"Sorry, but I need to try to catch a bus if you're not joining me." Seth's emotions were a web of worry and frustration and sorrow, but Niall had no idea which of those were a result of the present conversation and which were ones Seth had felt because of whatever trip he needed to take.

"Go on," Irial suggested. He sat on the Dark King's throne. "Maybe we'll have a party while you're away."

"Good." After a lingering look at the faery who shared his home again after too many centuries apart, Niall turned to Seth. "Where are we going?"

"To see my parents . . . the mortal ones." Seth's worry and anger flared again. "Can you scare up a car or something?"

Niall nodded. "Let's go."

The steed they had belonged to one of the Hounds who was killed during the recent war. It took the form of a Mustang and acted as if it were truly a car—aside from the fact that it required no fuel and steadfastly refused to allow them to play any music it disliked. Radio stations changed randomly, and an attempt to play a disallowed song caused one of Niall's CDs to be spat out in pieces. *Who still uses CDs?* Seth wisely kept that question to himself—and opted not to try plugging his MP3 player in. *Just in case.*

At first, Niall was silent in the driver's seat. He had no comment on the music, the shattered CD, or the traffic, but Seth had been friends with the Dark King long enough that the quiet wasn't unpleasant. In truth, it was comforting in its familiarity.

*Who would've thought that faeries would become familiar?*

They were an hour outside Huntsdale when Niall finally said, "So about the eye thing . . ."

"You mean the 'eye thing' where you were going to shove a hot poker into my eye? Or something else?" Seth asked. This, more than anything, was why he'd asked Niall to come: they needed to talk.

*No more secrets.*

"The poker." Niall released the wheel, apparently confident that the steed would drive steadily on its own. He reached into his inside jacket pocket, pulled out his cigarettes, and extracted one. "I'm glad I didn't."

Seth half laughed. "Me too."

"The scar . . . I'm sorry." Niall glanced at him. "If I could change it, I like to think I would."

For the space of several heartbeats, Seth said

nothing. Conversations about wrongs done and apologies needed would be a lot easier if they could lie, even a little. The faery inability to lie made for a bluntness that was sometimes uncomfortable.

Niall had lit his cigarette and sat silently smoking. He had one hand back on the wheel, but Seth was pretty sure the steed still controlled their destination. Traveling this way was easier and faster than taking a true car, but it was hard sometimes to remember that the vehicle was a living creature. Maybe in a few centuries that would change, but being fey was still new enough that Seth had the urge to remind Niall to watch the road.

Their friendship was too important to both of them for Seth to let their recent conflicts fester and eat away at their bond. He had become fey primarily because of Aislinn, but Niall had still been a factor. He'd also knowingly gone to Niall when the Dark King was unwell—despite the probability that it could result in his death and the reality that it *had* resulted in injury. Likewise, Niall had stood against the former Summer King for Seth, offering his protection when Seth was still a mortal. All of which meant that they had too valuable a bond to let it be destroyed.

"You remember telling me you could taste emotions?" Seth asked.

Niall nodded.

"Do I forgive you?"

"Don't know." Niall took a drag off the cigarette. "You're conflicted about something. For the King of Order—"

"Not a king." Seth winced. He didn't want to be in charge of anyone, and he didn't want to be the one who'd have to stand against Niall ever again either. He'd agreed to it so as to help Niall in the middle of a war, but the past week, the reality of what it could mean weighed on him.

Niall turned and looked at him. "Whatever you call it, Seth. The faery who *balances* me . . . you're not too orderly. Anger, worry, doubt, fear, and"—Niall inhaled—"hope."

"Seems about right." Seth bit his lip ring, weighing his words.

"Can you keep us invisible?" Niall asked the Mustang. When the steed made a growling noise that echoed through the car, Niall pushed the seat back and gave up the pretense of driving. "Peace between the courts would be better. My court is stronger now that I have a balance . . . and now that I have the embodiment of Discord living in the house."

"Leslie's refusals help too," Seth pointed out. "You are all three better by being together but sometimes at a distance."

Niall scowled. "Is that opinion or future seeing?"

"Yes," Seth said.

After that, they drove in silence, broken only by the music that the steed allowed and the sounds of the world outside rushing by. They stopped for fuel or other necessities. At the first stop they switched spots, more for variety than anything, and on the second stop, they switched back because—as Niall put it—Seth didn't relax well in the driver's seat. The illusion of the steed as a car made Seth uneasy.

They had resumed invisibility and were darting in and out of traffic at a pace that was dizzying when Seth finally said, "So to be clear, if I found a way to pass off this whole balancing-the-Dark-King bit—"

"Are you thinking about it?" Niall asked.

"I don't want to be your enemy."

The steed shifted to an SUV with extra-wide seats as they spoke. Seth climbed into the backseat, figuring that the steed was offering a makeshift bed and a little sleep wouldn't be a bad idea.

"Opposites aren't enemies," Niall said after another

quiet moment. "I don't want to have anger between us either."

"No more trying to burn my eyes out or anything else," Seth cautioned. "Your word, Niall. Whether I stay this or I find a way to get rid of it, I want your word that you won't imprison me or attack me again. I don't care how angry you get or how the Dark Court does things traditionally: families aren't to torture each other. Got it?"

"My word." Niall cleared his throat before adding, "And if you see Leslie's or Irial's death, you'll tell me. Promise me that."

"Promise."

At that, Niall reached back and clasped Seth's hand. "Then we shall have a faery bargain, brother. Breaking it will mean the oathbreaker suffers that which he caused—the death of the loved one or the torture."

"Lovely," Seth muttered. "I see where the optimistic streak comes from."

The Dark King laughed then, and Seth smiled at the sound.

Daylight arrived, and the conversations of the past night were not revisited. Niall hadn't expected the discussion to go so gracefully, and he was forced to admit to himself that while Seth was his balance, the former mortal didn't seem to share the faery aversion to truthful discourse. *If I'd been able to have such conversations with Irial or Keenan, would we have had so much conflict?* Maybe it was as simple as the fact that Seth was a fit balance for Niall. *Or his mortality is recent enough that he's not yet learned to play games.*

They didn't revisit the question of Seth's willingness to remain the balance to the Dark Court, but short of tearing down the barrier to Faerie, Niall didn't see any way it *could* change. Of course, there were a lot of things he didn't see about the future, whereas Seth had the ability to look at future threads. *Maybe he sees something.* Most likely, though, it was fear that influenced Seth. He'd had a lot of major changes in such a short time. It was a wonder he hadn't run screaming away from the courts. Many mortals had over the centuries, yet Seth fought to stay in their world. It was part of why Niall admired him. *None of which is going to be the sort of topic that will ease our tensions.* Niall concentrated on things they had first discussed: music, books, stories of past adventures.

The next few days passed uneventfully, so when they arrived at the end of the drivable road to the campground, they were laughing and talking. Niall figured they had time enough to deal with faery matters after they saw to whatever trouble Seth's mortal parents had found.

The steed stopped. Niall and Seth got their gear.

Seth looked at the trail in front of them. "Race?"

They spent the next two hours running up the trail in the sort of unbridled speed that faeries were capable of. They leaped over fallen trees and startled a few deer, who decided to run crosswise to them. As they ran, more and more faeries seemed to be watching from tree boughs and from the ground. *A lot of them.* It wasn't troubling yet, and Niall had no doubt that he and Seth could handle any conflicts that might arise. *Perhaps the summons from Seth's parents isn't because of a mortal matter.*

As they neared the campsite, Seth felt the jumble of excitement at seeing his parents and anxiety over what they needed. They didn't look much different. Despite their surroundings, his father still had hair so short that it was almost regulation. The alert posture at their approach bespoke years of caution, and the assessing gaze Master Gunnery Sergeant James Morgan leveled at Niall would intimidate most people. With an unexpected flare of pride, Seth realized that his father wouldn't be daunted by the Dark Court—and that he should never be exposed to them. Confidence was all well and good, but even in their prime, the strongest, best-trained mortals were no match for faeries.

"Baby!" Linda jumped up and hugged Seth with the sort of exuberance that had made it hard to stay upset with her for most of his life. She wasn't traditionally maternal, but she was so alive and so passionate that being around her made it difficult to do anything but get swept up in her energy.

She pulled back, studied him, and then squeezed him again. "Jamie! Look!"

"I see him, Linda." He stood. "Seth."

"Dad." Seth kept an arm around his mother and extended the other to clasp his father's hand. "Good to see you."

James nodded, and Linda seemed to finally notice that there was another person present. She tensed.

"So, Linda, Dad, this is Niall." Seth gestured at the Dark King. "He's a friend from home. Niall, James and Linda, my parents."

"Nice to meet you," Niall said evenly. His attention, however, was on the faeries who were edging closer to the campsite.

James Morgan stepped forward and extended his hand.

Niall lifted both arms; one hand held a cigarette and the other a packed tent. He couldn't say that he wanted to keep his hand free in case the nearby faeries approached, but Seth saw the tense way that Niall kept surveying the woods.

Linda arched her brow at Niall's refusal; James was less circumspect. "You could drop the tent."

"Good idea." Niall shot Seth a warning look. "I'll pitch the tent, Seth. Why don't you all talk while I do that?"

Without waiting for a reply, Niall walked toward a level bit of ground and began assembling a tent with the sort of precision that comes from having done the task regularly. Seth considered going after him, but figured that this wasn't something to discuss in front of his parents.

*One problem at a time.*

"Your letter said there was trouble," Seth started.

His parents exchanged a look, but neither of them said anything.

Seth sat down on a log that was off to the side of the fire pit. "What sort of trouble?"

"Well, you see . . . there was a protest." Linda smiled. "I was *very* reasonable at first. It wasn't quite a sit-in, like we used to have, but we were peaceful. A few placards, some mild yelling, and walking."

The supportive look on his father's face didn't waver, but he didn't speak, either.

"And then?"

"Well, I may have lost my temper a bit." Linda reached out and tucked his hair back as she had when he was a child. "You know how it goes. I chained myself to some of their machinery. Very calmly, though!"

"And?"

"Well, there's a fine." Linda smiled. "We don't really *have* the funds since everything went to you."

"You had me come all the way out because you needed money?" Seth rubbed his forehead. "Seriously?"

"No . . . you see . . . afterward, there was a bit of a problem with a few locals too."

Seth looked from his mother to his father. "What *kind* of problem?"

Linda folded her arms. "I don't think they're bad, and I'm not . . . I'm not sure why we thought you should come. It just suddenly seemed urgent. It doesn't make sense."

His parents exchanged an odd look, and Seth felt his unease grow. Calmly, he started, "Okay. Tell me everything without me dragging it out of you. I've spent—*days* . . . getting here, and I've had a bit of a rough few . . . weeks."

"Doing what?" his father asked. "You're unemployed, not in school, and have no dependents. What could possibly be so *rough* about that?"

Seth closed his eyes, counting silently to ten, and then smiled. "Mom just admitted she got arrested, so I'm not sure this is the best time to lecture."

"Don't take that tone," Linda snapped.

At that, Niall gave Seth a questioning look; Seth shook his head—which his father saw.

"What *kind* of friend is Niall?"

"One willing to drive your son to see you," Niall said loudly enough to carry across the distance.

The warning look Seth shot Niall was greeted with a grin. The Dark King looked around. "I think I'll check out the perimeter."

"The perimeter?" James repeated.

"Of the camp." Niall gestured. "If you're having trouble . . ."

At that, Linda blurted, "They didn't seem to think we should, um, *leave* the campsite. Every time we try, we get escorted back here. They haven't hurt us, but they've been very firm. Do you really think that's a good idea to disobey?"

"Oh, I definitely do," Niall murmured as his gaze drifted around the woods surrounding the campsite.

"You will stay here," Niall ordered.

Seth winced again. The Dark King wasn't used to being around mortals. "Broth—" Seth stopped himself, flushed guiltily, and walked over to Niall. Seth clasped Niall's arm and said in a low whisper, "I could go. They're my parents, not your responsibility."

The look Niall gave him was a shade away from incredulous. "*You* are still my responsibility."

"I'm not—"

"Stay. I'll be right back," Niall ordered.

And even though Seth didn't *need* to obey, he wasn't an idiot. A few months of training with the Hunt was nothing compared to the centuries of experience Niall had with conflict—and with faeries. *Are they why we're here?* The faeries were now watching them attentively, albeit from farther away now that the Dark King had looked their way. *Is it normal for there to be so many faeries in the woods?* They weren't fey Seth could identify, and the reality of how much Seth didn't know about the world outside the courts struck him. *Are they friendly? Dangerous?* He assumed they were solitary faeries, those who existed outside of any regent's influence, but beyond that he had no idea. All he truly knew was that he was very grateful to have Niall by his side.

"Stay here," Niall repeated.

"Right," Seth acquiesced. "Maybe I'll wait here with my parents while you go for a walk."

Niall grinned. "Brilliant idea, brother."

Expectantly, Niall rolled his shoulders as he walked into the shadows of the woods. Seth was right: this was far more satisfying than sitting in the dark sulking. Once, centuries ago, Niall had enjoyed roaming. The mortal world was filled with solitary faeries, willing mortals, and amazing sights. *Who wouldn't want to roam?* He stalked toward a clustered group of solitary fey who watched him.

One, a faery with distinctly ursine traits, stepped forward. "Don't have any business with the Dark."

"You glamoured yourself and caused trouble for those mortals?" Niall asked.

Faeries spread out in a semicircle, leaving him the option of retreating. One bird-thin faery started to walk behind him.

"I don't think that's a very good idea." Niall glanced over his shoulder. "Striking the Dark King isn't usually a choice that ends well for anyone."

"Says you."

Another faery darted out and grabbed the bird-like one's arm. Stumbling over each other, they moved back to the clutch of faeries who stayed together. The ursine fey watched all of it with an unreadable expression.

Niall frowned. He couldn't taste any strong emotion—no anger, no fear, nothing.

"What did you hope to gain by trapping them?" Niall asked.

A halfling stepped up beside the ursine faery. She was feral in a way that made Niall suspect that her lineage was his court. Shocking violet eyes were even more arresting because of their total lack of lashes. "We want to talk to *him*." She nodded toward the campsite. "Their cub."

"Son," Niall corrected.

"Whatever," the girl said.

"He's mine to protect. The Dark Court would not look kindly on any who harmed Seth." Niall shook his head. "Actually, he's under the care of a lot of regents: the Summer Queen, the High Queen, and the Shadow King are all fond enough of him that troubling him would be unwise."

Another faery laughed. "Don't want to *hurt* him. We hear he's made himself our champion. Thought we'd meet him."

"You can't harm his parents." Niall shook his head. "You ought to *protect* them. If he's your champion . . ."

The faeries shifted and exchanged looks. The ursine nodded once, and they all started donning mortal glamours. One after another they became as mortal-looking as they could. In a few moments, they all looked a lot like the mortals who camped in these mountains, clad in sturdy hiking boots, layered shirts, and worn trousers.

The ursine faery gestured toward the campsite. "We will meet him now. We . . . influenced them to summon him. Now we will greet him."

"I'm not sure—"

"Gave you the courtesy of conversation first because we don't want trouble with the Dark. *Now*, we will meet him, unless you think yourself able to stand against all of us," the ursine continued.

The Dark King grinned. "You think I can't?"

For a moment, no one moved, and then the woods seemed to come to life. Several hundred faeries had waited in the shadows. They dropped from trees, stood from within shrubs, and seemingly rose up from the pine needles on the ground.

The ursine smiled. "I think you are one faery, king or not, and you are not so foolish to take on this throng alone—especially as we mean no ill."

Niall's eyes widened as he took in the still-growing number of solitaries who came forward. "I'm not sure this many fey should go to—"

"You are not our champion, Dark King," the feral halfling interrupted.

En masse they started to walk toward the campsite, and Niall had the unusual sensation of being surrounded by alien beings. These were not the sort of fey he'd spent much time with in many centuries, and even forever ago when he was solitary too, he hadn't known any packs to be this vast.

"This is going to be interesting," he muttered. Then he turned and strode through the crowd toward the campsite.

"I don't understand. Why did you feel like you had to contact me? Did someone *say* something? Or did someone threa—" Seth broke off as he suddenly felt like innumerable threads were weaving themselves to him.

"Seth?" His mother reached out and touched his cheek. "What's . . ." Her words faded as she noticed what he was looking at.

Seth stared at the horde of faeries, wearing mortal guises, swarming toward them.

"Jamie!" Linda yelled.

His father poked his head out of the tent, vanished, and came back out with two guns. He held one out between Seth and Linda. "Don't know which of you—"

"I'm good," Seth murmured. He pulled out a short bone knife he'd had strapped to his ankle. "Stay behind me."

He stepped in front of his parents, despite his mother grabbing his sleeve and trying to pull him behind her. Without faery strength, he would've swayed. Linda wasn't going to win any best mother awards, but he was still her son, and her reaction was straight-up mother-bear instinct.

*Not that it would help against the actual* bear *approaching us.*

Seth swallowed the fear that started to rise. Freaking out wasn't going to help matters.

"That's the guy who was here before," Linda whispered.

"He has a lot more friends this time," Seth's father said in a rough voice. "I don't know what they want . . . or how three of us—"

"Four," Seth corrected as he saw Niall in the crowd. "There are four of us."

"Still lousy odds, son."

Without looking at his parents, Seth said, "Let me handle this if I can, okay?"

"But what—"

"Dad!" Seth glanced back. "Seriously. Trust me enough to let me try first. You wanted me here. I'm here. Now, give me a minute."

Tersely, James nodded.

"Stay right here," Seth told them. "Do not follow me over there."

At that moment, Niall walked up to stand beside him. "I'll stay with your parents." He motioned at an ATV that sat alongside the trail. The steed had obviously wandered up to join them.

"You get them out of here if you need to," Seth demanded.

When Niall nodded, Seth walked toward the faeries, who were watching him with the sort of fixed attention that made him briefly wish that he had the same sort of skills here that his faery mother had in her world. He looked over his shoulder at his loved ones.

*A fence would be nice right about now.*

As he thought it, the fence he'd imagined shimmered into existence. Rusted iron spikes surrounded his parents and Niall.

"Seth?" both of his parents said. Their eyes were wide and their expressions confused.

"Door, please, brother." Niall's voice was dry, but the glint in his eyes was assessing.

"Right." Seth pictured a door in the tall fence.

Linda grabbed the bars, testing them to see if they were illusory.

Niall opened the gate, stepped outside the iron enclosure, and closed the gate. With a casual mien that hid his surprise, the Dark King strolled over to stand beside Seth. "I suppose your parents are safe enough that I can join you."

Absently, Seth nodded.

*How did that happen?*

The faeries waited attentively, and Seth looked back at them. "Why are you hassling my parents?"

"We wanted to meet you," a violet-eyed half-fey girl said.

Another faery tilted his head in an unmistakable posture of challenge. "Didn't think you'd want us to come to *that place*. Were we wrong?"

Softly, Niall told Seth, "There *are* several courts in our city."

Seth nodded. "Right. Well, I live there, and where I am, you are welcome. If any of the regents"—he looked at Niall briefly—"have an issue with it, they can take it up with me." Seth paused and let his gaze drift over the ragtag horde in front of him. "Unless you start trouble with them or theirs," he added sternly. "I stand as balance to the . . ."

For a moment, Seth couldn't say the words. There were a lot of times he'd thought about telling his parents about his *change* the past few months, but he hadn't been sure. He envisioned a sofa behind them, so they could sit.

His mother sank onto the sofa and stared at him, and his father eyed the group with suspicion.

Seth dropped his mortal glamour and watched his parents. He still looked like their child, but his skin radiated light now and his eyes were silvered. His alteration in appearance wasn't as drastic as with many faeries, but it was enough to make clear that he had changed. James stepped back, and Linda reached out for James' hand. Their attention was fixed solely on Seth.

"Seth?" Linda whispered.

"As the balance to the Dark King, I am his equal." Seth took a deep breath and added, "Those faeries who are *mine* to protect are free to enter Huntsdale, but not to start trouble of any sort with the fey of the courts . . . or with mortals."

The horde of faeries shuffled for a tense moment, and then the bearlike faery spoke up. "And if *they* start trouble?"

"You finish it," Seth assured them. "I don't ask you to be weak, or to be subjects, but if you want *my* protection, you don't start shit that complicates my life. You also don't take any bullshit."

The solitaries smiled. A majority of them bowed, curtsied, or knelt. Awkwardly, Seth nodded his head at them.

*What is the right move here?*

Niall reached out and clasped Seth's arm. "Well done, little brother. You're turning into a decent king."

"Not a king," Seth muttered.

"Right . . ." Niall laughed. "So tell your subjects to stay or go."

Heart hammering loudly enough that he suspected most every faery there heard it, he walked over to his parents, who were sitting on a purple and white faux-cowhide-covered sofa his mother had once liked.

*I made an ugly sofa.*

His mother and father sat close together, staring silently at him, hands clasped tightly.

"So . . . those rough weeks? Well . . . I've changed a bit." Seth touched the fence, and it vanished. "I can explain all of it."

His father released his mother's hand and stood. His eyes were wide, but his spine was straight. "You made a sofa and fence appear out of thin air."

"I did."

His mother motioned toward the faeries. "They're not"—Linda's voice dropped—"*human*, are they?"

"They aren't."

"And you?" his father asked in an emotionless voice.

"No, not now," Seth said evenly.

"Well." Linda stood. She laughed uneasily. "That's . . . new. They're . . . new."

"Actually, they've always been around," Seth said cautiously, "but most mortals can't see them. I can make it so you always can see them . . . if you want."

His father wrapped an arm around his mother. After a tense moment, he nodded. "That seems like a good idea."

The fears Seth had when he'd considered telling them came rushing back to him. *This was exactly what I didn't want.* They were awkward, staring at him and unmoving.

His mother stepped away from his father. She took both of Seth's hands in hers. "Are you happy?"

"I am."

"Safe?" his father asked in a rough voice.

"Yes." Seth glanced at the faeries. "Very."

His parents exchanged a look, and then his father nodded. "Okay then . . . are they staying or going . . . wherever they go?"

Startled, Seth looked at his father. "Staying?"

"I only have a few beers, but maybe you can do that thing you just did"—James gestured at the sofa—"and magic up some more refreshments."

At that, Seth laughed. *That* sounded like the father he remembered, understated and adaptable.

"Can we see what they really look like? Like you did when you looked different?" Linda asked quietly. Her eyes were wide, not in fear but in the same childlike excitement that sent her off on hobby after hobby, fancy after fancy.

"Only if they want," Seth told her. Then he turned to the assembled faeries and said, "Glamours are optional around my parents."

They started dropping their glamours, and Seth watched the awe on his parents' faces as they saw the strange wonder of the less human-looking faeries for the first time. Tears slid down Linda's cheeks. "They're beautiful"—she glanced at one very inhuman faery with feline features—"and, well, a little terrifying."

"Yes." Seth pulled his mother into a hug and whispered, "Just remember that they are my, um, *subjects*. From here on, they'll be around, keeping an eye on you, making sure you're safe."

Somewhere in the crowd, faeries had started singing, and a few drums were produced. The campfire was joined by several other fires. Seth envisioned drinks and snacks, and his solitary brethren rejoiced together.

His parents danced and laughed, and Seth shook his head. It hadn't taken them long to get past the initial shock.

"Not bad," Niall said from behind him.

Seth turned. "What?"

"Your first revelry." Niall gestured at the faeries

who were cavorting in the woods all around them. "Later, though, we probably ought to talk about that little surprise trick of yours. No faery can create reality from nothing . . . at least none who live outside of Faerie."

"I didn't know I could do that," Seth protested. "Honest."

The Dark King shook his head, and they stood silently for a few moments. "You're not going to try to give the role of Dark Court balance to someone else."

A squeal of laughter made Seth look at the horde. *My horde.* He looked at his parents and then at Niall. *My family.* Seth had more family than he knew what to do with now.

"No," Seth promised. "This is who I am, what I am. They're mine to protect." He looked at the faery who had injured him last week, who'd protected him last year, who was everything Seth was to keep in check. "I don't abandon those who are mine. You, of all people, ought to know that."

"Just making sure you remembered it too." Niall pulled shadows into a chair behind him. "Go celebrate, brother."

"You could—"

"It's their first revel with their king-protector,"

Niall pointed out gently. "I am not to be out there. Not now." He pulled out a cigarette, lit it, took a long drag, and then grinned. "Anyhow, with this much emotion, I think I'll just sit here and enjoy."

"Son?" His mother waved. "The bear over by the fire says you ought to call for more music."

Smiling, Seth joined his faeries and his mortal parents in the crush. "Another song!"

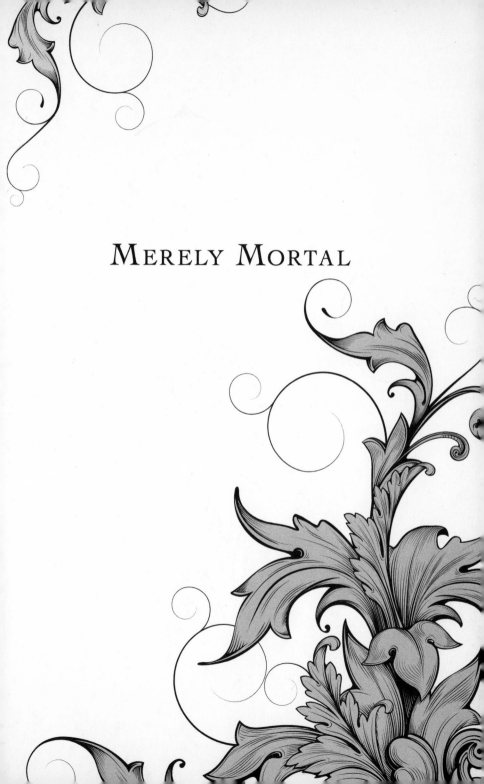

# MERELY MORTAL

"*I* WANT *THIS*." KEENAN STARED OUT AT THE expanse of snow that coated the lawn of the Winter Queen's house. *Our house. Our* home. Outside of her domain, it was still autumn, but within her immediate area, it was always winter. For most of his nine hundred years, that would have been debilitating to him. Now—because of Donia—he had rediscovered how perfect snow and ice could be.

The Winter Queen came to stand beside him. Without any of the doubts—*maybe a twinge*—that he'd felt with her for decades, he wrapped an arm around her waist. She was the reason for everything he had that was good in his life. During the past few months with her, he'd known a peace and happiness he hadn't ever experienced. Even if he lived the rest of his life as a human, he was happier than he'd ever been in all of his years as a faery. *All because of Donia.* Unfortunately, the faery who had given him such bliss wasn't as happy as he was.

"We could stay home," Donia offered again.

"No. You asked what I wanted." He turned to face her, studying her expression for some clue as to her mood, as he had been the past few weeks. Her worry over his new humanity had created an unpleasant tension in her, and all Keenan wanted was to erase her worries and fears, and prove to her that they would be happy whether or not he remained merely mortal. "I want to go away with you. Just us."

"But—"

"Don, it'll be fine." He caught her hand and pulled her into his arms. "We've never taken a vacation. *Ever.* We'll go away, spend some time together, talk, relax."

She exhaled softly, her sigh of cold air muffled by his scarf, and then whispered, "It's so near winter starting, though."

"And last month it was too warm. I'm *not* objecting to being here at the house or on the grounds with you, but we have a few days between summer ending and winter beginning. It's a perfect time to steal away. Let's take time for *us*." He leaned back and stared directly into her frost-laden eyes. "The world was nearly frozen for years, and even if things do stay warm a little longer, the mortals won't object."

Donia turned away, staring past him as if doing so would hide her worry.

Carefully, even though he couldn't hurt her with his touch now, Keenan threaded his fingers through her hair until she looked at him again. "Come away with me. Please?"

"Maybe we should take a few guards. Cwenhild says—"

"Cwenhild worries because she saw you when you were . . . when you almost . . ." Keenan's voice faltered at the memory of Donia's recent brush with death. Nothing had ever terrified him as that injury had.

He kissed her with all of the intensity that the thought of *that* day brought to him. He'd almost lost her.

She was his reason for living; everything that he'd ever dreamed of, perfect in ways that he'd long believed made their relationship impossible. All he had to do now was convince her that whether he remained mortal or tried the admittedly risky routes to regain his faery nature, they *would* be happy.

He felt snow fall around them as she relaxed into the kiss. Big fluffy flakes formed in the air; the brush of each flake was a welcome sensation, proof that she was happy.

Then she leaned away.

"You shouldn't do that," he whispered.

"What?"

"Stop kissing me to worry." He trailed his finger-tips along her face and down her throat. "We'll be fine, and even if we did need the guards, they are only a blink away. You know she'll send guards trailing after us." He paused and hid his fear under teasing. "Or is it that have I lost your attention already?"

Donia smiled, as he'd hoped she would, and said, "No. I'm just not as . . . ridiculously *optimistic* as you are about everything, but that doesn't mean I'm unin-terested."

He widened his eyes and shook his head, hoping that his flashes of insecurity weren't as obvious to her as they were to him. Whenever she pulled away, he had the irrational fear that she'd decide his mortal state was reason to give up on the years they could have, that his loss of faery strength and longevity was grounds for sending him away, that his change was going to lead to her rejection. Lightly, he said, "I don't know. You may have to prove it. There was definite wandering of attention."

"You're incorrigible."

"Yes," he agreed, "very much so."

Smiling, she took his hand and led him to their room.

Two hours later, Donia was smiling to herself. She watched as he tossed their bags into the trunk and opened the door to let her wolf, Sasha, into the back-seat of the Thunderbird. She gave Keenan another kiss and then climbed into the car. With the sort of laughter she'd enjoyed more and more since he'd moved into her house, he spun the car in a circle in the icy drive and zipped into traffic.

As they left Huntsdale behind them, her fears of all the things that could go wrong—the enemies that could break the now-mortal boy beside her, the fear that her own Winter would slip out and injure him—seemed more manageable. They were together; they were taking a vacation; and they were very obviously being trailed by the Winter Court guards.

*I could tell him that I asked Cwenhild to send guards. I could tell him that his mortal fragility terrifies me . . . but that would lead to talking about his foolish plan to risk taking Winter inside his skin.* He hadn't brought it up in the past few days, but he would do so again. He had latched on to the idea that he could lift the Winter Queen's staff, much as she had all of those years ago, and that in doing so, Winter would fill him. He'd even reasoned that it might be painless because he was fey until recently. He discounted the risks: that it would hurt him, kill him. He wasn't any more willing to bow under impossible odds than he had been when he was a bound faery king. *Or when I was dying.*

Donia had tears in her eyes as she looked over at Keenan. He didn't take his attention from the road but still unerringly reached out and twined their fingers together.

*If he knew how much becoming fey could hurt, would he still want to try?*

*If he knew what it felt like to take ice inside a human body, would he want to try?*

*Would I have decided to risk it if I had known?*

"Don?" He squeezed her hand. "It'll be fine. Whatever it is, it'll be fine."

"You're . . ." She let her words drift away with a cloud of frosty air.

"Relax, please." He glanced over at her. "Next week we can deal with whatever you're worried about. Right now, I just want to be together, have a holiday with the faery I love." He smiled before chiding her,

"Remember: you already agreed. Faeries don't lie."

"I did agree." She smiled even as the reminder of faery rules—of the fact that *she* was fey while he was not—made her want to weep. *Faeries* might not lie, but he wasn't a faery now. He'd given that up to save her life.

She angled her body so that she was staring at him. "And I *am* enjoying the scenery."

Keenan laughed, but he kept his gaze on the road as she continued pointedly looking at him. Once she'd thought she took pleasure in looking at him because she couldn't touch him, but now, she realized that it was simply the sight of him that pleased her. His sunlit skin hadn't entirely faded when he'd become mortal. Unlike the mostly snow-pale faeries of her court, Keenan retained the sun-darkened skin he'd had as Summer King. His eyes were an icy blue now, but they were still beautiful enough to remind her why she'd stumbled over her own name when he'd first approached her almost a century ago—back when *she* was the mortal one.

He was relaxed, and even though he'd shed some of the volatility of the Summer Court, he was still impetuous. He'd been born of both Summer and Winter, so even after surrendering his sunlight and his faery nature, his nature was mixed in a way that hers wasn't. Although, as he reminded her regularly, Winter wasn't *only* calm either. Together, they'd found a peace, but it hadn't dampened their passion at all. If anything, their passion had increased because they understood each other more fully.

*Even if I'm not able to be impulsive.*

*Even if I must worry that I'll injure him.*

As a queen, not merely a faery burdened with the ice, she had control of herself. It was difficult, though, and she understood why Keenan had never lain with mortals. Every time they touched, she worried that she would lose control too much, but then he smiled at her, and she couldn't say no.

For years, Keenan had made her believe in the impossible; he had made her strong enough to believe she could defeat monsters, to risk everything for his smile, to laugh even when they were facing daunting trials. *Because he is beside me.* She wanted to believe in the impossible now, but it was different when the risk was that she would lose him. Now that he was truly hers, she wasn't sure she was strong enough to risk anything that could take him away. *Is it better to have him for a few years, knowing he will die, or to take the risk that could either give us eternity—or end the years we do have?*

"Are you with me?"

"I am," she whispered. "I love you."

He did glance at her this time. "You too. Always." He paused, looked back at the road, and asked, "Okay, I give. What's up? I know you, Don. You have that far-away look again."

"I was thinking about us and . . . things." She squeezed his hand. "I'm glad you suggested this trip."

"And?"

Donia gave him a reassuring smile. "You make me happy, and I want *you* to be happy. So . . . no more worrying. We're out here on a normal 'human' holi-day." She swept her arm out, gesturing at the traffic on the freeway, the roadside advertisements, and the lights of buildings she could see along the exit. "You're *new* to being human, and it's been almost a century since I was human. Back then . . ." She laughed at the sudden memory of her father's scowling face. "Do you remember when you asked Papa to let you walk me home?"

Keenan switched lanes and directed the car onto the freeway exit. "He thought I had impure inten-tions."

"You did," she teased.

"I wanted your heart more, Don." He said nothing else until he pulled into a parking spot. He turned off the engine and grinned at her before adding, "Of course, I wanted your body too. I still do. I *always* have."

She laughed. "Likewise."

Keenan felt tension he hadn't even realized he was carrying slip away as he opened Donia's door and took her hand. Traveling with Donia was new. In all of the years they'd known each other, they'd never simply traveled for fun. *Or alone.* In truth, vacation itself was a peculiar experience for Keenan. He'd only ever been away from his court for a few short months in his centuries of living, and even then, he hadn't been able to step away from the thoughts of the conflict he'd be returning to confront. Now, however, he was determined to enjoy an utterly peaceful trip with his beloved.

"Rest stops," Keenan said. "I'm not sure about these."

"You wanted a 'human experience.'" Donia smothered a smile. "'Road trips,' you said. 'Perfectly ordinary nonroyal travel,' you said."

Keenan looked at the litter-strewn ground, tables

fastened down, and overtired families who all seemed to have dogs in their cars. With Sasha in the backseat, they almost looked like they fit in.

*Nonroyal. Just us.*

"You're right." He zipped his jacket. "I believe these sorts of trips include nonscheduled diversions too."

The look Donia gave him was more suspicious than he expected. "Keenan . . ."

"Be right back. You can . . . walk our dog." He grinned at Sasha, who bared his teeth in reply. Keenan laughed.

Donia and Sasha both watched him with expressions somewhere between bemused and irritated as he went into the building advertising itself as a "Welcome Center."

Inside, he started gathering pamphlets on everything from wine tasting to caving to antique malls to a "miniature-golf extravaganza." He pulled out one for a hiking trail, another for an indoor racetrack, and several for bed-and-breakfasts.

"Can I help you?" an older woman offered.

"I'm on a vacation," he said. "With my . . . girlfriend." He looked over his shoulder as the door to the small building opened and a gust of cold air blew in. *Because Winter herself stepped inside.* He stared at her, his forever love. Quietly, he told the human woman, "I'm going to marry her. She's perfect."

The woman looked at Donia. "Is that a *wolf*?" she asked. "You can't bring animals in here. . . . Actually, you can't bring *wolves* in anywhere. What—"

"Sasha, wait for us at the car." Donia opened the door, and the wolf padded outside and to the car.

As Keenan watched through the window, Sasha leaped onto the roof of the car and stretched out. His gaze didn't waver from Donia.

"Apparently I'm not protection enough in my . . . condition." Keenan looked back at the rack of pamphlets.

Donia walked over to stand beside him. She pulled out a pamphlet and flipped it over. "What's a zip line?"

The pamphlet she held out showed a girl hanging from a wire in a contraption that looked like a cross between a trapeze and a saddle of sorts. The girl wore a helmet and gloves, and she looked like she was mid-laugh as she was suspended over a chasm. Keenan skimmed the pamphlet and read *Evergreen Hills . . . four seasons resort . . . trails . . . zip line . . . ski slopes.* He looked at Donia. "Our destination."

Several hours later, they pulled into the parking lot of a roadside motel. It wasn't their final destination, but Keenan saw no need to drive all day. *Stops to rest and enjoy ourselves.* He walked inside, feeling relaxed and exceedingly pleased with how well their trip was going.

The motel was everything that their home wasn't: it was plain and impersonal and somehow oddly charming.

"Do you need me to do this?" Donia asked in a deceptively innocent voice.

"I can do it." Keenan stepped up to the counter. "We need a room."

The woman at the counter looked at him from the tips of his boots to the jeans to gray leather jacket to the loosely wound scarf around his neck. "I'll need ID."

"ID?" he echoed.

"You need to be old enough to rent a room, pay up front, and—"

"Why?" He didn't know if he'd ever rented a room. As he stood there at the faux wood front desk, he realized that his guards or advisors had handled this sort of thing. He glanced over his shoulder at Donia. She turned her back, but not quickly enough that he missed her smothered laugh.

The receptionist said, "You need ID and a deposit in order to rent a room here."

"Identification cards and deposits in case we"—he forced himself to look away from Donia and turned to the receptionist again—"do what?"

"Break things. Steal them." She rolled her eyes.

"What do you think?" he asked Donia as she walked up behind him.

She wrapped her arms around his waist, and whispered, "I think you are used to having someone else do this."

"True." He read the name badge of the woman at the desk—Cinnamon—smiled at her, and asked, "Cinnamon, do you suppose—"

"No." She scowled. "No ID, no deposit, no *room*. Your sort all think that works. Smile pretty, and we'll roll over. Not going to happen."

Donia was laughing out loud. Between giggles, she said, "Just like old times, isn't it? You think turning on your charm will work, and I get to watch you fail."

Shocked, Keenan turned to look at his beloved, and for a moment he was speechless. Donia was *laughing* over the curse, the competitions they'd waged over the mortal girls he'd tried to convince to take the test to be his queen.

As he turned, Donia kept her arms around him. She looked up at him. "If the girls who weren't charmed had known what I know, they'd have been a lot easier to convince."

"What's that?"

She released him from her embrace and put her hands flat on his chest. "The . . . person behind the smile." She stretched up and kissed him, twining her arms around his neck as she did so.

Without stopping kissing her, he swept her up into his arms. They stood in the motel lobby kissing until someone called, "Get a room."

Donia pulled back and laughed. "That was the plan. They said no."

At that, Keenan smiled. *This* was what he wanted: Donia happy. That was what he wanted every day now. The Winter Court mattered to him as much as the Summer Court had, but there was no struggle, no worrying over *how* to take care of the court. Donia's court was healthy and, quite simply, the strongest of the courts. Whether Donia agreed to let him test his theory to become fey again or not, Keenan's primary responsibility would still be one he undertook gladly: making sure Donia was happy. The difference, unfortunately, was that unless Donia agreed to let him try to become fey again, he'd only be able to do so for a blink. Mortal life spans were so brief as to be a heartbeat in the eternity that they *could* have if he became fey again.

He carried her out of the lobby and to the car, where Sasha waited. Beside the car, he lowered her feet to the ground. "So, navigating this human world seems a bit more complicated than I thought."

Donia slid a hand into his inside jacket pocket and pulled out his wallet. She opened it, and extracted two cards. "Not really. Hand her these." She held one up. "Identification." Then she held up the other one. "Credit card."

"Oh." He frowned. "Are those new?"

"No. Cwenhild had them procured for you last month." Donia slipped them back into the wallet, returned it to his pocket, and kissed him again. A few moments later she pulled back and opened her car door. "Come on."

"But if I had them . . ."

She shrugged. "I figured if you couldn't charm her, she has bad taste. Why stay in a motel where they have bad taste?"

"You're a peculiar faery, Donia." He walked around the side of the car and got in.

"We'll find a nicer place. There's a bed-and-breakfast I saw that looked pretty," she suggested as she sorted through the pamphlets they'd collected.

And Keenan figured it didn't much matter why she wanted to stay elsewhere. He'd walk in and out of every hotel and motel along the road if it made her smile and relax.

A short while later, they were settled into an admittedly nicer hotel. Sasha was out wandering now that they were stopped for the night, and Keenan and Donia were alone in their "honey-moon suite." He had opened the doors to the balcony, and snowflakes were fluttering into the room. Donia still marveled at seeing her once-sunlit faery not flinch from the snow. *From me.* She'd thought she was done being surprised when she became Winter Queen. She hadn't expected that—or becoming a faery or that the boy she'd fallen in love with so many years ago was anything other than human.

*Or that he'd ever become a human.*

He'd sacrificed immortality and strength for her. In part, he'd sacrificed his court for her. Now, he wanted to risk the brief human life he still had. *For me.* She knew there were plenty of dangers if he remained human: he was vulnerable to threats from any faery that crossed their path—and Keenan had nine centuries of living during which he had made enemies; he was susceptible to human diseases, aging, and any number of threats; and he was in danger from her. The Winter that she carried in her skin could easily kill him if she lost her temper or lost control in a moment of joy.

*But he's alive.*

Trying to become fey could take away the few human years he had.

*Or give us eternity.*

"You're awfully far away," he said.

She realized she'd been staring, but she wasn't embarrassed as she had been for most of the years she'd known him: he was *hers* now. She could stare all she wanted, so she did. "I was thinking about how beautiful you are."

He smiled. "Can you think that *nearer* to me?"

"Not if I want to have dinner." She walked toward him even as she said it.

"Do you?"

"Not now," she murmured as she slipped into his arms.

Later, when Keenan came out of the shower, he was greeted by the sight of the Winter Queen standing on

the balcony looking out over the not-yet-snowy moun-
tainside. She could've been carved of the ice that was
her domain.

*Beautiful.*

He walked over to stand beside her. Unlike her, he
was not as comfortable with the chill. To the Winter
Queen, it was *more* comfortable to be cold, but he was
mortal now. He shivered.

Silently, Donia drew the cold into herself, pulling
the bite from the air with only a moment's effort.

"No." He went to the bed and pulled the heavy
quilt from it. After wrapping it snugly around himself,
he returned to her side. "I'm fine."

When she didn't release the cold back into the air,
he repeated, "I'm *fine*, Donia. In fact . . ." He bent
to the floor, opened his bag, pulled out thick socks,
boots, several warming layers, a heavy coat, mittens, a
scarf, and a hat. As she watched, he dressed, and once
he was completely bundled up, he caught her gaze.
"I'm going for a walk."

"But . . . I don't have all of that." She pointed at
his winter-weather clothing. "I didn't know *you* had
all of that."

"You're a faery," he said gently. "Unless you choose
otherwise, the only one here who will see you walking

with me is *me*. You don't need all of these layers."

He held out his hand.

She looked down at the thin nightdress she wore.

His hand stayed outstretched to her. "Walk with me. The cold is pressuring you, so we'll walk a little ways."

"We're in higher elevations, and I didn't think about the temperature here and—"

"Walk with me," he interrupted. "I'm already dressed, so you might as well give in before I overheat."

She winced at his words; her reaction to his loss of Summer and his loss of immortality was still as sharp as it had been the day he woke up human. Keenan stepped closer to her and took her hand.

"Donia?" He waited until she met his gaze. "I'm happy. If I'm human or if we find a way to return me to being fey, I'm happier *now* than I've ever been in nine centuries. The only sadness in my life is that you worry over things you don't need to . . . so stop."

Donia half hid a small sob. "I thought about going out later while you slept, but I didn't want you to worry so I thought about telling you I was going but—"

He kissed her, swallowing her frosty breath, pulling her ice-cold body against his heavily clothed one, and silently cursing those layers. He'd happily freeze to death rather than be separated from her skin.

*Which is exactly why she worries.*

With that sobering thought, he pulled back. "I can be careful." He cupped her face in his hands and stared into her eyes. "I grew up in a home of ice with Summer inside of me. That's not so different from living with Winter as a human. I've been trained for this. I can *do* this."

Then he stepped back, held his hand out, and asked in an even voice, "Would you like to take a walk with me?"

Donia could feel the weight of Winter inside her skin; the blissful pressure tangled with worry over the now-very-human love of her life.

"Trust yourself. Trust me. Trust *us*." He spoke quietly as they walked through the lobby, and she realized with a smile that there was something oddly freeing in being invisible to the humans they passed, but not to Keenan.

She'd never shared the joy of the first snow with anyone. It was a heady feeling, this first. She leaned in and whispered in his ear, "No one but you can see me, but they can *all* see you."

He couldn't answer just then, as they were passing the front desk.

The Winter Queen flashed him a wicked smile before nipping his earlobe.

Keenan startled visibly enough that the desk attendant gave him a puzzled look.

"They can't hear me either," she said in a level voice, and then she told him how she wanted to celebrate the first snowfall.

Keenan laughed and said, "There are days I feel like the luckiest person alive."

"That's nice," the desk clerk said tiredly. "Have a nice night."

"I will," Keenan answered with a look at Donia, who understood now the sort of joy that made Summer faeries dance and spin.

She blew him a kiss and raced outside.

By the time Keenan caught up with her, she was standing at the edge of the parking lot. He took her hand and led her farther from the light. Once they were hidden from any passing humans, he kissed her soundly.

When he pulled away to catch his breath, snowflakes were falling like a thick curtain all around them.

"Where to?"

She pointed at the ski slopes in the far distance. "There."

"That's miles away. Let me get the keys," he started.

"No." Donia shook her head. "No cars. I am the Winter Queen, Keenan. I'm not going to start my season with a *car*. We go on foot. Anyhow, the slopes aren't open yet, so we'd attract attention." She paused and frowned. "You'd attract attention with the whole *visibility* problem."

Keenan thought yet again that he'd be too much of an encumbrance to her if he didn't shake his mortality. He didn't bring it up, not tonight. He wasn't going to risk the change back to fey without her agreement. They'd spent too many years at odds for him to want to start his second stretch of eternity with discord between them.

"If you hold my hand, I can be invisible with you."

"Exactly . . . and we can still *run* as if you were fey. Hold on to me," she invited him.

"Always."

Without another word, they ran.

It felt but a few moments until they reached the very top of the mountain, despite their having gone miles. Donia closed her eyes and exhaled. Keenan stayed

beside her, but he released her hand—becoming visible as he did so.

Reflexively, Donia became visible as well. He had faery sight, but they were alone on the mountain. She wanted to be as he was; she wanted him to watch her with his mortal eyes. Never had she scattered snow on the earth when she was visible to any other than faeries. Here, in front of her newly mortal beloved, she would be truly visible. She knew that faeries had seen her create snowfalls, but she'd never noticed their presence. With Keenan, she was as aware of him as she was of the snow and ice.

Neither spoke as she cloaked the world in white. It could have been moments or hours as she walked through the night and covered the earth; all that Donia knew was that everything in her world was perfect.

*With Keenan.*

*In the cold.*

*Where we both belong.*

Finally, she stopped walking and turned to look at him. He lowered himself to the ground as they stared at each other. She stood barefoot and barely clad in the snowy air; he sat in his bulky layers of warm clothing, a mortal in the midst of a thick fall of snow. Her eyes were frost filled, and her skin glistened with the

same icy rime that coated the trees. His eyes were damp from the sting of wind, and his exposed skin was red from the cold.

*He couldn't have been here when he was the Summer King.*

*I couldn't be here if he hadn't surrendered his immortality to save me.*

*He is mortal, but he is here with me.*

"If you're never fey again, I'll still be happy because we are together now." She walked toward him, her bare feet leaving the first marks on the freshly fallen snow.

"Let me try to be fey," Keenan pleaded. "Let me be a *true* part of Winter. Let us have forever."

The wind swirled faster and whiter all around them as Donia lowered herself to the snowy ground in front of him. "What if I lose you?"

"If I stay mortal, you *will* lose me. Mortality means I'll die." He came to his knees so that they were kneeling, facing each other. "We *can* have eternity, Don."

"You don't know how it hurts, Keenan. How do I agree, knowing what that pain feels like? How do I agree, knowing it could *kill you?*"

"I won't do it if you say no, but I believe it'll work." He leaned his forehead against hers. "I don't want you to have to hold yourself back from me. I don't want to be a weakness, but someone who can be fully in your life. I want you, all of you, forever."

Instead of answering, she drew a wall of snow toward them and shaped it into an igloo. Outside, she let the storm rage. She felt it: snow spiraling wildly in the air, the icy wind she'd released continuing to shriek, and ice coating the trees. Inside the snowy shelter she'd built, she had no need to release any more cold. She'd let it loose outside, and now she was able to free Keenan of those layers of clothes and celebrate their first winter together.

Late that night, Sasha crept inside the igloo, plopped down beside them, and nudged them with his head. The wolf didn't speak—as far as Keenan knew, he'd never spoken—but the nudge was message enough.

Donia stood and stretched. "Time to go back."

After Keenan dressed, Donia exhaled and scattered their shelter; the snow that had only a breath ago been a building now joined the rest of the snow spread over the ground. She smiled as she looked around them. The moon was high in the sky, and the perfect snowfall all around them gleamed in the clear white light.

"Beautiful."

"It is," she agreed.

Keenan laughed. "I meant *you*, but the snow is lovely too."

Beside them, Sasha butted Donia with his head again, and a prickle of alarm went through Keenan. He looked to the open expanse of the snow-covered ski slope, but no tracks marred the white ground. He attempted to see farther into the woods, but his human vision revealed nothing.

*She is the Winter Queen. In her element. At her strength.*

The mental reminders didn't allay his fears. Sasha wouldn't hurry them on without reason.

Absently, Keenan lowered one hand to the wolf's head—and was rewarded with a gentle nip. He looked down as Sasha tugged on his hand.

"Don?"

"I don't see any threat." Donia answered the question without his needing to voice it. She understood Sasha more than anyone else ever had. He'd been her companion for years, and he'd chosen to stay with her when she became Winter Queen.

Sasha growled.

"We're coming," Donia assured him as she took

Keenan's hand in hers, and they began to run back to the hotel.

Nothing pursued them, and no danger greeted them when they arrived. Keenan told himself that he was simply too used to there being threats, that he was worrying about his mortal strength being insufficient to protect her, that he was being foolish. None of that eased his mind, but he had no way to ask the wolf what had prompted his behavior.

The following morning, they checked out and were walking across the hotel parking lot when they were stopped by Cwenhild.

The head of the Winter Guard bowed her head to Donia. "My Queen." Then, she frowned at him. "Keenan."

He nodded in reply, but said nothing yet. The cadaverous Scrimshaw Sister still reminded him of other Scrimshaw Sisters who'd drifted through his long-ago childhood home protecting him from the world even as their mien terrified him. An angry Scrimshaw Sister was a gorgeous terror, and like the rest of the Scrimshaw Sisters in the Winter Court, Cwenhild was one of Donia's guards. Seeing her waiting was not comforting. However, she looked irritated rather than alarmed. After a lifetime of needing to assess situations quickly, he relegated this to the "not life threatening" category—which meant the interruption was unwelcome. Moreover, the stern look on her face pricked Keenan's temper. He might not be a king, or even a faery, anymore, but centuries of ruling didn't predispose him to responding well to censure.

"Is anyone dead?" Donia asked.

"No," Cwenhild said.

Keenan put an arm around Donia. "Then why are you here interrupting our *first ever holiday*?"

"Because there were witnesses to your . . . to . . . Human video exists of you looking very inhuman." The way Cwenhild glared at him made Keenan want to either apologize or send her away. His having had Scrimshaw Sisters as nursemaids in his childhood had the unsettling effect of his now feeling guilt when any one of them scowled at him.

"You've certainly left me a mess to fix," she said. "This business of your being *human* is not ideal for our queen. If you were fey, none of this—"

"Excuse me?" Keenan snarled at her. He was grateful then that his temper was easier to restrain than it had been when he was a faery regent, but even so, he had to remind himself that Scrimshaw Sisters rarely wasted time with politeness. He forced himself to say almost calmly, "I am human because our queen was—"

"Explain what happened," Donia interrupted.

"There was a *camera* on the ski slope last night," Cwenhild announced. "You, my Queen, were recorded creating a building in an instant after standing barefoot in a nightdress in a snowstorm a moment prior. The same video shows that building vanishing. It shows you with him"—Cwenhild nodded at Keenan—"embracing in the snow as an igloo *forms around you.*"

"Oh," Donia murmured.

Cwenhild continued, "We had to hire *mortals* with technical skills. There is some sort of video page on the computer-net."

"The internet," Keenan corrected. "There are *numerous* video sites."

Cwenhild waved her hand. "The technician said there were many 'hits.' This is troubling. I propose killing the video maker, but as it's a human, I require your consent."

"You can't kill someone for sharing a video," Donia said resolutely. Her cheeks were tinged pink.

"I apologize for causing you trouble. It's the first of Winter and—"

"My Queen!" Cwenhild interrupted. "*You* don't need to apologize. I'm sure you had good reason to be visible." She glanced at Keenan and, after a moment, sighed and said grudgingly, "And I suppose you aren't *truly* at fault. You are human because you saved my queen's life, and she loves you, and . . . I'll find a solution to this exposure before any of the other courts learn of it."

"Without killing any humans," Donia reminded her guard.

"As you wish." Cwenhild paused and shot a hopeful look at them. "I don't suppose we could destroy this internet thing?"

The laugh that slipped from Keenan's lips was quickly turned into a cough as Donia elbowed him sharply.

"No," Donia said.

Cwenhild sighed. "You might want to return home. Many, *many* people are seeing this video."

Behind Donia, a small group of humans were clustered. One of them pointed at Donia, and a boy who looked of an age with Keenan's mortal appearance stepped away from the group and began to walk their way. Keenan started to move so that he was between Donia and the approaching boy, but Cwenhild snagged his arm. "No."

"No?"

"You are *finite,* and you are valuable to my queen." Cwenhild bodily moved him behind her, and Keenan cursed the scant human strength that made it so easy for her to do so.

*She'd do so if I were fey too,* he reminded himself. As an average faery, he'd be weaker than the Winter Court's strongest fighters. He *knew* that, but logic did little to assuage his pride.

"Get in your car," Cwenhild instructed. "Sasha!"

The wolf bounded toward her. He looked every bit the feral creature he could be, and Cwenhild—despite her human glamour—didn't look much more civilized. She towered over the humans, a fierce young woman with corded muscles and an unwelcoming expression.

At the sight of her, the human boy faltered. He looked over his shoulder, and his friends came to join him.

Keenan opened Donia's door as if there was no alarm, and in reality, there wasn't *true* danger. Humans—like him—were no match for either of the faery women. The true danger was in gaining too much human attention. He'd lived among them for most of his life and had only the barest brushes of exposure. Now that he himself was human, he'd unwittingly contributed to the largest exposure he'd ever known of. *Video of us.* The wrongness of it all made him feel helpless.

Silently, he slid into the driver's seat and turned the key. Without any further attention to the words Cwenhild was exchanging with the group of humans, he eased the car around them and onto the road.

"Turn left."

"Left?"

"Left," Donia repeated. "I am not going home because of one stupid video."

"Don—"

"I am on vacation." She gave him a look, daring him to quarrel, but he wasn't going to refuse the opportunity to enjoy at least one more day with her.

He turned left.

As they drove, Donia sat quietly at his side. They were almost at the resort when she reached out and took his hand. "I'm sorry."

"Me too," he said tentatively. After a moment, he

added, "What are we sorry for this time?"

She laughed, and a small cloud of frosty air brushed his cheek. "For letting my fear keep us from trying to change what you are. I don't want to make your choices any more than I'd want you to make mine. If I were mortal, I'd risk anything to be with you. I *did*." She took a deep breath. "I can tell myself that I might not have done so if I'd known how it hurt or knew that it could kill me, but I walked into what I thought was certain death twice out of love for you. I shouldn't try to stop you, and I shouldn't expect that you'll be happy being mortal. I can't pretend to be mortal. You can't tell me it's enough for you . . . and I don't want to try to keep my Winter leashed. Last night . . . I wanted you to be breathing the snow into the world *with me*. At the very least, I want you to be able to be safe from it."

He steered the car into the resort and waited until he pulled into a parking spot before asking, "Does this mean we can try to make me fey again?"

No stillness in the world could compete with the still of Winter, but he had learned centuries ago that sometimes patience was the best choice. He waited as the car filled with frosty air. He waited as Donia exited the car. He waited as they registered and checked into their room.

Then, she turned to him. "We can look at all of the possibilities before we decide *what* to try, but between the centuries you've lived and the centuries some of our friends have lived . . . I am willing to believe that there is an answer. We can find a way."

Several icy tears slipped down her cheeks, but when he tried to embrace her, she held up a hand. "Your word that we will only try it if we are reasonably certain you won't . . . die."

"You have my word." He knew that the things she wasn't saying were as important as the one she did say: the compromise he'd sought was what she'd accepted. Her other objections—to his servitude, to his pain— were no longer given voice. It was only his death that she was unable to accept.

He stepped forward until the hand she'd held up in a halting gesture was resting against his chest. "Now, what do we do about this video? And more importantly"—he caught her gaze—"can we watch it before it's gone?"

For a moment, she didn't say anything, but then her serious expression gave way to a mock chastising one and then to laughter. "Did I mention that you are incorrigible?"

"Not for hours."

CRXEO

## TWO WEEKS LATER . . .

Donia and Keenan watched the "making of the new ad for Evergreen Hills Resort." In it, they were joined by various faeries pretending to film them, apply makeup, discuss costume difficulties, and one particularly entertaining segment when Cwenhild talked about the fact that their "technical team" and "effects team" refused to be seen on film because of their paranoia that they would be pressured to take on more work than they could handle.

"We thought it was all going to be ruined when someone uploaded the raw footage," Cwenhild said on the screen. "Luckily, the client thought the viral video was an asset, so it all worked out."

The video cut to a resort representative who smilingly added, "Everyone who's been to Evergreen Hills knows it's an escape from the busy lives we all lead, so we thought we'd use a campaign to show that a visit to our resort is filled with magic."

Off camera, Cwenhild snorted. "Magic."

The resort representative sighed. "If you've been on the slopes for one of our moonlight specials, it's easy to believe in magic." Pointedly, he glanced at

Cwenhild. The camera followed his gaze as he challenged her. "Come see us. We can enchant even the skeptical."

As the video ended, Keenan laughed. "Your plan was genius."

"I decided what to do with the money from the ad," Donia said in a casual way. She stepped between Keenan and the monitor. "I bought several houses for the court's use."

"With *one check?*"

"Well, no," she admitted. "I added a bit more. . . . I thought maybe if we wanted another vacation, I could send *them* away for the week, and we'll stay home alone this time."

Keenan laughed again.

"And then, we could go back there on our own. . . ." The Winter Queen nestled closer to him.

He wrapped his arms around her. "Oh?"

"Since everyone keeps assuring me your plan will work, I figure we ought to start planning regular vacations." She looked up at him. "And you promised me a honeymoon too."

The joy that filled Keenan was larger than he thought he could contain. "I think we ought to have two of them, one before I become fey again and one after. Everything I—"

But the rest of the words he would say were lost as Donia pulled him to her.

*Everything I could want in eternity is possible because of you,* he thought, and then he stopped thinking and simply enjoyed being in the arms of the one person in all of forever who made his life complete.